Smartest Ant
On the Planet

by

KENNETH THOMAS

First Printing, 2020

ISBN Paperback 978-1-7355353-1-9

Library of Congress Control Number: 2020918990

Byron K. Thomas Publishing

P.O. Box 47

Tampa, Florida 33601

www.thomasbrotherspublishing.com

tbp@thomasbrotherspublishing.com

Cover Design by Richard Jibaja

Thomas Brothers Publishing

BOOK DEDICATION

This book is dedicated to the four women in my life who have been and remain
the greatest inspiration to me. One gave me life, another gives me joy and the
other two give me hope for the future, but all give me their undying love.

To my mom Betty, my wife Sherry, and daughters Courtney and Bria

"I love and cherish all four of you"

Author's Bio

Kenneth Thomas is the fictional author of his first dystopian novel, *Smartest Ant on the Planet*. He graduated from Paxon Senior High School in Jacksonville Florida. After graduation, he joined the Navy and served on the following ships and bases: USS McInerney FFG 8 Mayport Florida, Naval Air Station, Pensacola Florida, and USS Shenandoah AD 44 Norfolf Virginia, NAVCOMTELSTA Keflavik Iceland, UECOM Stuggart Germany and USCENTCOM MacDill AFB Tampa Florida. During his time in the service, he earned an Associate of Science degree in Drafting and Design, and a Certificate in Drafting Technology at Pensacola Junior College. After serving 20 years, he retired and then was hired by Hillsborough County, Clerk of the Circuit Court for two years then the City of Tampa, Contract Administration where he is currently employed as a Drafting Technician for over 17 years. He has been married to his beautiful wife Sherry for 38 years and has two lovely daughters, Courtney and Bria.

He hopes in the near future, humanity would realize that we are empowered with the ability to evolve on this planet then journey through our solar system and beyond. We humans are always looking for someone to save us from the trials and tribulations of life and difficulties of our own invention, but we have proven time and time again, humanity can't grow without tragedy and triumph. Unbeknownst to us, we are in a constant state of evolutionary ebb and flow. It is Kenneth Thomas greatest hope that someone reading this book will be motivated to step out and walk on his or her personal path of evolution.

Chapter One

The beginning of the end

November 12, 2022 – The United States, like all of the other major powers in the world, has been absorbed into a group of businessmen and women called **The Conglomerate**. *This clandestine group has the United States listed in their financial ledger under the category of "Real Estate Acquisition". Democracy is now but a footnote in the history of humanity.*

The long howling tones of a CSX train whistle echoes through a moonless night as a thick overcast of billowing clouds drifts over a quiet neighborhood in Jacksonville Florida. It's November 10th on a Wednesday morning at 1:20 a.m. in a typical neighborhood on a cool summer's night.

If you met each and every family that lives in this neighborhood, you would soon realize that there isn't anything special or out of the ordinary about them. But within several days, this neighborhood and one home in particular will be taken over by police and federal agents. This will all happen because of the man living in the second house on the corner of Palm Brook and Rose Place, which will soon be surrounded by crime tape. But for now, the man's name is BK Thomas, and he lives in this house with his wife, Lorraine of 18 years and daughters, LaChel and Kim, who are 16 and 12 respectively. Other than the creepy noise of the home's refrigerator, the house is quiet and still because everyone is sound asleep except for him. He's wide awake and staring up at the ceiling trying to suppress the disturbing random thoughts running continuously through his head. Like a person with a split personality,one of the voices tries to get him to reconsider his actions and not to do anything tonight and just think of another way to resolve his problems, but the more dominant voice quickly beats down the other like it was its little brother.

Now with the dominant voice guiding his thoughts, he lays there breathing deeply in order to calm himself down before doing what he's been planning for years. He closes his eyes tightly and concentrates on the steps he's going to have to take to complete his horrendous plan. As the realization of what is about to happen sinks in; his heart is beating a mile a minute and his legs are starting to shake uncontrollably from his inability to completely suppress his emotions.

He tries to stiffen his entire body in order to stop his legs from shaking, but that only makes the rest of his body shake, which in turn begins to shake the bed. He's worried that the vibrations of the bed would eventually wake his wife, who is a light sleeper. He doesn't want to get out of bed yet, because he knows what will happen once he does.

He closes his eyes and concentrates on something calming and relaxing. But all he can think about is that within a couple of weeks his employer will complete their audit and will discover that he's been ordering parts for his personal use and thirty percent of the equipment he has ordered is missing. And as if those felonies weren't enough, he piles on the fact that he embezzled over $250 thousand from the projects he was assigned to develop. Not only he would have loss his job, there's no doubt that he would done some serious prison time. The life that his wife and girls are accustomed to will now turn to an awful nightmare that they will never wake up from. He contemplates the lifestyle changes and the humiliation his family will have to endure. They weren't living in the lap of luxury, but Lorraine didn't have to work and his girls had everything they needed and their wants were taken care of too. He was a Chief Engineer of a small, but profitable engineering agency that has various contracts with the Federal Government. These thoughts may not be relaxing, but it's distracting him from his nervousness and consequently, stops his legs from shaking. He's tired of just laying there reflecting on what happen in his life and decides to implement his plan. He's determined not to go to prison and his family won't be left destitute, humiliated and visiting him in prison once a month, if he's lucky. He looks over at his wife, but can only see the back of her black bonnet, which she wears to bed every night. It's been twenty more minutes and by the sound of her light but annoying snoring, he's convinced that she's sound asleep now.

"It's time for you to get the hell out of bed", the voice in his head demands. He looks up at the ceiling for the last time, then slowly slides his right leg out of the bed. He knows the bed will most likely makes some noise as he gets up, but he hopes she will be use to him getting out of bed in the middle of the night to go to the bath room. As his right foot barely touches the floor, he begins to slide his right leg from the bed. So far his wife is still snoring hard and steady, as he has enough leverage to raise the rest of his body from the bed. He should have oiled or fixed the bed in some way that would have stopped it from making noises when he gets up. But hindsight does him very little good right now.

He slowly swings his left leg and hips toward the edge of the bed. The bed is still making some squeaking and creaking noises, but not enough to arouse his wife. "Nothing from nothing equals nothing", he thinks to himself as he sits up on the edge of his bed. He sits there very still, listening for any movement or changes in Lorraine's breathing. After he was sure that he hadn't wakened her, he begins to stand and separate himself from his creaking bed. He's out of the bed now, but decides to stand there for a while like a statue in a park. He's afraid to move or even look back at her, so he stands there listening to her breathing.

He can hear her breathing deeply and finally turns to see her still lying in the same position. He can't see her clearly, but can see the silhouette of her body facing away from him and can see the blanket and her body beneath it moving up and down as she breathes. He turns and begins to creep softly out of their room and walks down the hall to his office. As he enters his office, he slowly and carefully closes the door behind him before he cuts on the light. He puts both hands to his face as he walks over to his desk and flops down into the chair. He reclines back in his chair for a moment and whispers to himself, "oh my god what am I doing". He has been playing this over and over in his head for a long time, but now that it's time to act, it seems so surreal. But he convinced himself that he has no choice, so he opens the small top drawer to his left. He sighs, and then reaches deep into the drawer and grabs a small white slender spray bottle without a label. It's small enough to fit in the palm of his hand. He sits back into his chair staring at it as if it's the first time he has seen it. "There's no time for contemplation", he says to himself. He doesn't consider himself a religious man, but what the hell he thinks to himself. With his head bowed, eyes close and the bottle enclosed in the center of his clasp hands, he says a silent prayer for God to bless his family and to forgive him for what he's about to do.

After a few minutes of silence, he whispers "Amen", then stands up and slowly walks from behind his desk, quietly opens his door and steps out into the hall. "It's time", he says to himself softly over and over again, as he walks steadily down the hall. Before entering into his bedroom, he stands there in the doorway, staring at his wife still soundly sleeping, who still hasn't moved from her original position. He has the bottle in his right hand, which is shaking slightly, and he can feel his stomach churning from his nervousness. As if someone pushed him from behind, he lurched forward into his bedroom and tentatively walks to his wife side of the bed. Looking down at her as he stands beside her makes him hesitate again, but knows if he stands there too long, he may loose his nerve and she may wake up. He positions the spray bottle in his right hand as he works up the nerve to press the nozzle on top of the bottle. He stands beside her for a moment, which seems like an eternity. He looks down at her with a loving gaze through the darkness as she lays sleeping, unaware of what is about to happen to her and that this is her last day on earth.

She has been this wife for over 18 years and he still loves to watch her sleep, but this time it's different. He has always loved the smell of her hair, so he bends over her and takes in a good whiff of it through the bonnet. He knows that the bonnet serves the purpose of protecting her hair, but he has always hated that bonnet. He remembers when they were just married, she would just braid it in a single braid, so it was easy for him to touch or smell it. He takes another deep whiff of the past, present, but unfortunately, a changing future. Tears are beginning to form in the corners of his eyes, when he noticed that she's starting to move and he can hear her making noises, which tells him that she's starting to wake up.

He realizes that there isn't any more time for hesitation or doubt, but his hand is now shaking so badly that he almost drops the bottle. He quickly points the bottle at her face as she slightly rises from her pillow. He thinks he can see her eyes begining to open and can hear her clearing her throat to say something, so he squeezes the nozzle, which releases a mist of spray onto her nose and mouth. The moisture of the atomize liquid helps wake her as she wipes her face and looks up to what looks like her husband standing over her. BK takes a step back away from her, because he doesn't want to inhale any of the chemical.

She looks up at him with a look of disbelief as she tries to ask him a question, but the chemical, which is stronger than chloroform, quickly starts to take effect. Her bottom lip begins to quiver as her eyes roll back up into her head and her head flops back down onto her pillow. He steps backward again as he bumps into the dresser so hard that some of the items on top of it falls behind the dresser. He watches in horror as his wife begins to shake and twitch as her breathing begins to slow. He can hear her gasping for air as she gathers the last bit of her strength to reach out to him with her left hand, but the drug finally overcomes her as her entire body goes limp. Unfortunately for him, his eyes are now adjusted to the darkness and now stares at her as her breathing becomes labored and can now see her eyes staring back at him. He can't hear her clearly, but he thinks he hears her ask, "Why"? The look on her face is almost too much for him to bear and almost makes him crumple to the floor.

The look of disbelief is frozen on her face as she stares at him with her eyes half closed. He can't stand to see her like this, so he uses his other hand to close her eyes. He fights the strong urge to give her one last kiss, but he knows if he gets too close, he may suffer her fate. He just softly whispers, "I love you and soon, you'll be in a better place".

He backs away from her lying there lifeless. He uses the dresser to steady himself while leaving her bedside and maneuvers himself out of the bedroom and back out into the hallway. BK stops in the hallway and leans against the wall trying his best to get himself together for what has to happen next. "Damn it", he whispers to himself. He has ran through this thousands of times in his mind, but he had no idea this would be so emotionally draining. Just the thought of doing this two more times, fills him full of dread. He knew this wouldn't be easy, but he has to pull himself together and just get it done. He motivates himself by thinking about the life his daughters would experience without him and their mother. He stands up straight, takes a deep breath, then heads to LaChel's room first to do the same thing to her. He hopes the drug will work faster on the girls than it worked on their mother. He turns on the hall lights, so he won't have to turn on the lights in their rooms. He enters LaChel's room, which is only partially illuminated by the light of the hallway. He could see that she was lying on her stomach with her pillow over her head. "Damn", he thinks to himself as he walks towards her bed. He stands there with a perplexed look on his face and thinks for a moment, how to do this without waking her up. He decides to just lean over and lift the pillow away from her head and hope she doesn't wakeup completely.

He would hate to look into her eyes, while applying the drug, but he realizes from the experience with his wife that the mist from the spray may wake her up anyway. That's something that he couldn't foresee. One of LaChel's arms is across her pillow and the pillow is on top of her head. He's trying to find a way to pull the pillow from beneath her arm without waking her, but it's not looking good. Finally, he can see that there's no way he can spray her without getting her to move the pillow from her face. He has no choice but to wake her up and spray her to make sure she gets the full impact of the chemical. He thinks if he softly whispers her name, it may be enough to get her to rollover and expose her face. "LaChel", he whispers as he leans closer to where he thinks her ear should be, but she still doesn't move. She just continues to breathe softly. Hey little girl, he whispers again a bit louder and shakes her arm that's lying across the pillow. He has the spray bottle in his other hand, ready to spray.

LaChel jumps a little then turns her face towards the sound of her dad's voice and says, "Da…". But before she could get out the word "dad"; she feels the mist of the spray hitting her face like a damp rag. She yells a bit, then puts the pillow back over her face as if she was trying not to get sprayed again. BK looks intensely at her to see if he needs to spray her again, but she twitches a little, then he sees her body go limp.

He puts the spray bottle in his pocket, then carefully pulls the pillow from her face. Once again, he's careful not to get any of the spray on his hands. He tosses the pillow to the other side of the bed then stands up and looks down at his lifeless daughter. "Well, at least there's only one more to go", he thinks to himself in a cold sort of logic. As he was about to turn around, the room

11

lights turn on and he hears a sleepy voice saying, "what's wrong with LaChel, Daddy". He almost jumped out of his skin. "What are you doing up", he says softly! Kim just stands there half-asleep and rubbing her eyes. I heard something and thought it sounded like LaChel. I was going to wake mom up but heard someone moving in LaChel's room. She tries to look around him to see for herself that her sister is alright. "Is she all right, she asked with concern in her voice"? "Yes, she's fine", he says as he gently turns her around, turns the light off and walks her out the room. He walks her back to her room while trying to assure her that everything is fine and she would have to be quiet, because he doesn't want to wake up mom. Kim is still asking questions, but in a low tone, while they enter her room.

Normally at this moment, he would promise her anything to get her back in bed, so he promises her that she can come sleep with him and her mother if she can't sleep. She maybe twelve, but she still loves to lay between her mom and dad once and a while. Especially during a lightning storm or after watching a scary movie. He can tell that she's a little uneasy about what she saw in her sister's room. Maybe she senses that something is wrong, but all he needs to do is to get her back into bed. He decides to make sure that she's comfortable before he uses the spray on her, but he can feel his emotions trying to force their way to the surface.

Kim can feel her Dad's shaking hand on her back. She looks up at him as he smiles down at her in an attempt to ease her mind. As they walk into her room, he clicks on her room light, because he knows that she's more likely to get into bed when she thinks he's not just going to put her in bed, give her a kiss on the forehead then leave.

She jumps into the bed and pulls the covers up to her chin, while he sits down on the edge of her bed. I know it's late, but can you tell me a short story, she asked her father with a soft and loving tone. Normally, he would tell her that it was too late and all she had to do was to just close her eyes and think of something that made her happy. But he thinks this would be a good way to get her to relax and maybe close her eyes before he has to use the spray.

I'll tell you a short story, but you have to close your eyes and try to go to sleep, he says as he softly strokes her hair and smiles. She nods her head yes, closes her eyes and prepares to listen to one of her dad's great stories. BK decides to tell her a story about two sisters that love and share a new kitten given to them by their father. He speaks in a soft and steady tone in order to keep her off guard to what is about to happen. But he can't stop thinking about what he has to do, which affects the way he tells the story. Kim can also tell by her dad's voice that something is wrong, because his voice is shaking slightly. She was supposed to close her eyes, but she slightly opens one of them to see her dad's face, but he catches her and stops the story and reminds her that she said she would close her eyes. She reluctantly closes them again. He comes to the reality that trying to relax her may not work. This isn't something he had planned and he's running out of time. He calmly and softly continues telling the story as he reaches in his pocket and positions the spray bottle in his hand and behind his back.

In the middle of the story, he pulls out the bottle and sprays her with one burst directly to her face. Seconds after she breathes in the spray, she coughs and gags as she covers her face with her hands. "Dad", she yells while wiping the spray from her face. She coughs a couple more times as if she couldn't breathe then pulls the cover up to her face to wipe the wet spray off, but she collapses into her pillow and her breathing begins to become erratic and slow.

He resists his father's instinct to grab his little girl in his arms, but he does reach out and grab her arm. He looks down at her and can feel his daughter's body periodically twitching as the drug takes her deeper into unconsciousness. He starts to softly sing her favorite bedtime song when she was a little girl. *"Baby love, my baby love, I need you, oh how I need your love, but you keep on treating me bad, break my heart and make me sad"*. He can feel her body finally relaxing, which shifts his mind back to reality.

He gently repositions her into bed but makes the mistake of getting too close to the covers Kim used to tried to wipe the spray from her face. He stands up and backs away from the bed, but he can feel the effects of the spray right away. Damn it, he says out loud as he begins to stagger a bit. He takes several deep breaths and staggers quickly out of the room and into his daughters' bathroom. He knocks over her toiletries that are scattered all around the bathroom counter as he almost falls to the floor. He uses the counter to support himself as he turns on the faucet and frantically washes his hands and splashes his face with water.

He still feels a little wobbly, but the water helps him fight the effects of the drug. He takes a few more handfuls of water and splashes his face. He is leaning over the sink looking into the mirror as he tells himself that the hard part is over and he has to be more careful. He cuts off the water, dries his face

13

and hands then turns off the light as he staggers back into the bedroom. He slams his shoulder against the jamb of Kim's door as he makes his way out of the bathroom. Luckily for him, he didn't get a full dose of the drug, but the little that he did get will have him dazed for a while. He has to use the wall and the door jamb of his bedroom door to make it to the foot of his bed. He flops down for a minute to try to focus his thoughts and clear out the cobwebs. The house is eerily quiet he thinks to himself. He sits there and takes some deep breaths as he wonders how he could be so stupid. But he considers himself lucky, because if he had gotten a bit more of the drug; he would have been laid out next to Kim's bed.

He doesn't have time to allow his emotions to get a grip on him again, but he couldn't help to reflect on the faces of his wife and daughters as he sprayed them with the drug. He sits up straight and takes a final deep breath. His head is starting to clear, and he can feel his motor functions starting to normalize. But he's also starting to feel regret for what he has done to his family tonight. "Oh my god", he thinks to himself. He can feel his body starting to shake from the gilt that he is trying so hard to suppress. At this moment, he would do anything to change what he's just done. He looks back at his wife with regret in his eyes.

He can't stand to see her that way, so he walks over to her still body and pulls the sheet over her head then walks toward the door. He looks back again at the silhouette of her body, then turns back around with an overwhelming feeling of shame and regret. He thinks to himself that he should have tried harder to find a way to live with what the government did to him and the general disarray of the state of the world, but there's no turning back now.

He knows he doesn't have the time for this micro breakdown, but he has to sit for a second before he goes into the girls' room and prep them for the next stage of his plan. He sits back on the foot of his bed and puts his face in his hands. He takes several deep breaths and tries to think of calming thoughts to move on to what he has to do next.

Trying to suppress his emotions, he reflects on his last day at work and the problems he experienced just trying to make it through the day without anyone becoming suspicious of his behavior. He went to work that day looking to get through the day without drawing any unnecessary attention.

His plan was to issue some instructions that will ensure that most of his senior personnel, at least the ones that bug him the most, would be kept as busy as possible, while he collected some of the paperwork and items he didn't want to leave behind. At noon, he plans on telling his secretary that he has to meet with one of his daughter's teachers and will be out for the remainder of the day. But this is what happened. He walks into the building just as he would do every Wednesday morning, with a cup of coffee in one hand and a couple of cake donuts in a bag in the other. He gives the security guard a "good morning" nod then gets on the elevator, which takes it up to the fourth floor. The doors open and he steps out of the elevator at Sargeant Engineering. As usual, he hears a voice to his left. Morning BK! It's Phil working the front desk and as cheerful as always. BK is his boss, but he wants everyone to be on a first name basis, which he thought would make a better work environment for everyone.

Morning Phil, BK response trying to match Phil's cheerful enthusiasm. As he passes Phil and continues down the hall, Phil continues to try to engage him in a pointless morning conversation about the game last night. BK doesn't stop but turns around and starts walking backwards as he tells Phil that he's sorry that he doesn't have time to talk because he has to stomp out some morning fires. Phil is just a cheerful and talkative person and continues to tell BK about how good the game was. He just gives Phil a final "ya man", then turns left and walks down the hall towards his office. His secretary is already at work like always and greets him as he walks toward her. Good morning BK, she says with a welcoming smile.

"Morning Gwen", do I have any messages? You have about a half dozen messages from financing, four from Frank in supply and one from the Vice President's secretary. The other messages are expected, but the message from the Vice President's secretary stops him in his tracks. She wants you to call her to schedule you a face-to-face with Mrs. Ryncer.

Normally, a meeting with the vice president would scare the crap out of him, especially if she knows what he has been doing for the past couple of years. Gwen looks up at him with some concerns, but BK just smiles and gently places his hand on her shoulder, because he knows there's no way in hell he's going to have any face-to-face meeting with the Vice President. He tells her thanks, then proceeds into his office and shuts his door. He knows that the Vice President wants to discuss his division's projects and most likely their budgets Financially, more than a few of the projects are behind schedule and to add another nail in his coffin; they are over $185,000 in the red, that they know of. He hasn't the time to concern himself with the company's business. As he walks behind his desk, he sits down, and starts to reply to the emails to the financial division, which should stall them for a couple more days and will pacify his senior management team.

He then plugs in his personal thumb drive into his computer and uses algorithms to bypass the company's security system and firewalls, which he successfully does. He also downloads some information from the company's servers and places some paperwork from his desk into his briefcase. Just then, Bryan, his Director of Engineering and best friend, knocks a couple of times then burst into the office. "Come in", BK says sarcastically. Bryan is not just his employee but is also his best friend. When he's in town, he spends most of his time fishing with Bryan and even their families take vacations and weekend escursions together. Lorrain and Bryan's wife Grace also shopped and spend time with each other.

But at work, BK and Bryan maintained a professional relationship. Bryan gives him a quick "good morning" and slams the door behind him. Would you like some coffee, tea or one of these donuts Lorraine doesn't want me to have, he asked as he places the last of the papers into his briefcase then quickly closes it. Forget the damn pleasantries, he says with a fair amount of anger in his voice. You've been ducking and dodging me for the past two days. It's true that he has been avoiding him, but he leans back into his chair and stares at him as if he doesn't know what he's talking about.

I'm sorry you feel that I'm ducking you, but you of all people know how busy I've been recently. I'll admit that I've been a little stressed and somewhat distracted regarding completing the "Neu-tra Project", but if you were in charge of this twenty million dollar monster of a project, I think you would be feeling some type of stress too, he says sternly. BK grabs a donut out of the bag and offers it to Bryan, but Bryan gives him a no thank you and continues with his conversation. Right, I can totally understand, Bryan response, as he walks to the front of BK's desk and sits down in one of the two chairs. But this goes far beyond just a stressful project. The majority of your managers are worried that you are distracted and not concerned about the day to day management of this place. Sometimes you just disappear on us for long periods of time without any warning. When we try to reach you by phone, text or email, you don't respond. And what's so hard about answering your damn cellphone or returning an email. BK leans forward in his chair and responds in a forceful and reassuring voice," I'll tell you what I'm prepared to do to appease you and the rest of the team. I'll apologize to them for my absence at the meeting next Wednesday and won't go on any additional trips until after all the major projects are completed. That's another problem, Bryan replies!

The team project meeting you're referring to was last Friday and you missed it! BK has this surprised look on his face. Time sure passes by when you're not doing your job, he thinks to himself. Bryan can see that he is unaware that he missed an important meeting. "Don't worry", Bryan says as he shakes his head in disappointment. I covered for you as usual by telling everyone you were out doing research on those classified components.

But I shouldn't have to cover for you like that. Yes, I know Bryan, but when I hired you for my project manager; I explained to you that you and the rest of the team would be left in the dark on some aspects of these projects and you agreed that you could handle it. "Hey", I have no problem managing these projects, he replies in an angry tone.

You come into the office for an hour or so, then without any scheduling on your calendar; you disappear for the rest of the day and sometimes the following days. Gwen can't even get a whole of you, Bryan exclaims. And I could handle that, but you designed most of the software and was the main developer of the computer code. BK just sits there not knowing what to say or how to defend himself, because everything Bryan is saying is true. He thinks praising him would be the best think to do at this point. "Hey", I do appreciate your support and you've done a great job of answering questions during these meetings.

But I hope you realize that some of these decisions I've had to make in your absence could have cost me and you our jobs. "I know", BK replies. I've been reviewing your emails and I don't have a problem with your decisions. Bryan is somewhat satisfied with BK's answers and lowers the tone in his voice. Bryan feels that he has to ensure that BK understands how dire his absence and lack of management is affecting the Team. I'm telling you this as a friend and someone that respects you as my boss. I wouldn't ever say this outside this office, but I truly feel that you are not totally handling your responsibilities as the boss of this Tampa Engineering Division.

He knows that Bryan is right, but he knows the best response is to try to calm him down and make any promises that would appease him and will get him out of his office. BK finishes the other donut in the bag and takes a swig of his coffee. "Look Bryan", I value your friendship and I'm sorry for all the pressure you've had to absorb while I've been managing these various secretive side projects that corporate has stuck me with. Bryan is hoping he can tell him something that will reassure him that he recognizes the seriousness of what's going on. Three projects are a little behind our completion date and I do understand that budget wise they are all in the red and will most likely trigger an audit from corporate, BK says calmly and without any concern. That's exactly what I'm talking about, Bryan says as he leans forward in his chair. I don't have an accurate idea of our completion date or the exact funding amount. The only time I have a clue is when you make these blanket statements. I'm your manager, damn it, but I don't have full access to the data, financial records or the software configuration documentation.

You've arranged the personnel on this team in such a way that each of the five groups of these team members doesn't have any idea what the other groups are doing at any given time. I think that's a recipe for a catastrophic accident and the major cause of why these projects have gone completely over budget. I'm tired of working in the dark and I'm tired of seeing the frustration on the supervisors' faces and the attitudes of the team members.

I understand Bryan, calm down. Look BK, I don't think you understand how frustrated we are with being left in the dark on these projects. BK has been avoiding this conversation for a couple of weeks now. This is his last day and he didn't plan on telling Bryan how he's misappropriating money and equipment from the company and could most likely find himself in prison for a long time. He tries to think of a good lie to end this surprise meeting and satisfy him for at least a day or two. Look BK, I know you have a ton of pressure on your shoulder, but you have to give me some information that I can tell the division managers.

You've assigned the development teams in such a way that each of them doesn't have a clue what the other groups are doing at any given time. Their tired of working in the dark, Bryan exclaims. "Alright Bryan", you've made your point. Bryan tells him that the Team needs to review every bit of data associated with the projects. BK stands up and puts his hands in his pockets as he turns and looks out his office window just for dramatic effect. He stands there for a moment trying to think of what to say to Bryan's demands. If they review the financials and supply documents, he wouldn't make it out of the building before his best friend would have no choice but to call security to take him into custody. He thinks that if he reluctantly agrees to one or two of Bryan's demands, he just may be able to stall him. He turns around to face him and walks around to the side of his desk and sits on the corner next to him.

"I tell you what I'm going to do", he calmly says to Bryan. I really wish you could trust me on this, but just for your peace of mind, I will let you review all the information you want after I return from a requested meeting with Mrs. Ryncer. Bryan stares at him with a surprised look on his face. The Vice President, Mrs. Ryncer. BK just nods his head "yes". "Why are you going to see her", Bryan curiously asked. She asked Gwen to schedule me for a 10:00 meeting as soon as possible. What in the hell do you think she wants to talk to you about?

Bryan is worried that his job may be on the line. The project's budget is in the red and the Director is the first employee on the list to get the ax. "Don't look so worried", BK says as he gives him a reassuring smile. I'm not worried about myself, he replies. I'm worried about your health, Bryan replies. "Thank you", but I'm fine, BK says. I'm talking about if you cause me to lose my job, Grace will most likely blugent you with one of her pound cakes. "Oh my God", BK says out loud. Those things are hard and dry as bricks. "I know", Bryan says in agreement. But her mother is the baker in the family and she's a brick layer like her dad. He laughs and tells Bryan that Grace will have to wait until Lorraine stops putting the boots to him. Lorraine and Grace are like sisters and would not be happy if he causes Bryan to lose his job. All jokes aside, you have to turn this around soon; I'm not going to hold back the tide of disgruntle managers forever. BK nods his head in acknowledgement as he returns to his chair behind the desk. With assurance from BK to allow him and the managers access to all the project files, Bryan gets up from his chair and walks toward the door. He yells to Bryan to stop him before he leaves his office, as Bryan opens the door.

Today is Thursday and I will be leaving at noon for a meeting with Kim's teachers and I think I will be meeting with Mrs Ryncer Friday. Bryan asked him if he wants to talk over the weekend"? "No", BK replies sternly. I will be taking Lorraine and the girls on a surprise weekend trip to Orlando, because I have been neglecting them too. Before Bryan can ask about a meeting date next week, BK tells him that he will have Gwen schedule a meeting with them on Tuesday at 9:00 a.m.

Bryan is glad to see the changes that BK is making. He smiles at him, which gives BK a indication that he agrees with the day and time. But I'm afraid it's going to cost you; he says as he gives Bryan a stern look. "Cost", Bryan says with a confused look and tone! "Yes", BK replies. Nothings for free – except your mama. She's for free, and everybody knows it. Bryan looks up at the ceiling in disbelief as he knows he walked face first into one of BK's "mama jokes". "You ass", Bryan says as he gives him a smirk. BK leans back in his chair and laughs at him. I couldn't help myself, he says as he continues to laugh at him. He felt that both of them needed a laugh to offset the tension between them.

Unbeknownst to Bryan, this is the last time they will see eachother and this is how BK would like to remember his best friend. BK then thanks him for always watching his back". Bryan stands there in the doorway with a look of appreciation and a little confusion on his face. That's something great to hear, but it seems like something you would say when you're not going to see that person anymore, he thinks to himself.

He decides to shake it off. Thanks man, I appreciate it. "Have a good time with the family and I'll see you on Monday if I don't see you again today", he says as he walks out the door. Soon as the door closes, BK pulls a thumb drive from the computer and places it in his jacket pocket. He then relaxes back in his chair and sighs. He doesn't want to talk to anyone else today, so he gets on his desk phone and ask Gwen to schedule a meeting for Tuesday at 9:00 a.m. with Bryan and the division managers. "Got it", she response. I'm also going to take a sick day for a medical appointment, so I won't be in on Monday. "I'll put it on your calendar", she replies. Do you want me to send out a reminder email to all the managers? "Yes please", right away. And I have a lot of work to complete, so I don't want to be disturbed for the rest of the morning.

He hangs up the phone then turns his chair around so he can look out the window. He's looking at people going about their normal working routines. He thinks to himself that they have no idea that by next week, they will be using a large amount of colorful language to describe their feelings about him.

BK doesn't see his fellow coworkers as normal people, but broken eggs that he used to make this huge tragic omelet that will be served to the world. But he can only imagine it, because neither he nor his family will be around to hear the words liar, murderer and monster or experience any of the judicial repercussions of his actions.

But he has one last email to write and schedule a timed delivery for Wednesday morning, which should satisfy Bryan and the team's future questions. He turns his chair toward his keyboard and pulls it close to him. He's sure Bryan will be out of his hair for at least a couple of days, but he has to be sure. He needs those days before they discover all the missing money and property from their projects. He sits up in his chair and pulls the keyboard close to him. He addresses the email to Bryan and copy's the project managers. The email reads as follows:

Bryan and fellow team members. After talking with Bryan today, he has convinced me to share more information of the projects we are working on. I genuinely understand the challenges and sacrifices you have made throughout these years for these projects, and please believe that I greatly appreciate your dedication. We've made tremendous strides these past two years and I know that in the near future, we will accomplish all our goals and most importantly, change the world. BK types the standard "thank you" and "stay the course" statements before ending the email and setting up the recipients he wants the emails to go to. Typing the email makes him feel like a jerk for what they will have to endure in the coming weeks and how he will disappoint so many of his friends and coworkers. It goes without saying that they will be hurt, confused and angry at his betrayal. He imagines that the first thing that will happen is that when he doesn't show up for work on Monday, Bryan will think that he is up to his same old disappearing act again.

But my Wednesday, when no one can get in contact with him, Bryan will try to contact Lorraine, which will only deepen and focus his concern. He will call the police and ask for a "Wellness Check" and of course, they will only find an empty house and lots of questions. The IT Department will search is computer once they can't contact him and find out all his secrets. What they find will shocked and amaze them once they discover the total scope of what he's been doing for the past year an a half. At the end of the day, they will most likely call him a thieving bastard. He also took sole responsibility for his actions and strongly disavowed that anyone else helped him. He doesn't want

Bryan or anyone else at the company to bear any criminal or financial burden for his crimes. He also left instructions on where to find both of his bank accounts, which combined only contains roughly $17,000. He's sure that his $17,000 won't resolve any criminal charges that he'll be charged with if he's caught. As far as he is concern, the parts and components that he was in charge of developing came from his understanding of quantum mechanics. Sergeant Engineering and the Government made millions of dollars off of him in the past two years. And he left them two other plans for ideas that will make them even more money. Of course, he had to dumb it down a little, but with Bryan's help they should be able to create the prototypes and market them. He thinks that should keep the company alive for another ten years, at least. But no matter what he does, the company will be out for blood and will not care about any provisions or restitutions he has setup. After finding out the full scope of his crime, the authorities will put out a warrant for his arrest and the FBI will be taking the lead on this man hunt.

But their concern for his wife and children will quickly fade and turn to anger once they start searching his office and reviewing the project documentation and financial accounts. He has no more time to imagine what the future may bring. After he finishes, he clicks on the send icon for the final time, he leans back in his chair and looks around his office. The Government forced him to work here, but he has to admit that he has had some good times working at this firm and he's going to miss his best friend and his team. Not enough to bring any tears to his eyes, but he just sits there for a moment with a slight smile on his face.

BK's mind snaps back to his reality of him still sitting on the edge of his bed. He looks back at his wife's body lying motionless in their bed. He also thinks how his friends and families' opinion of him will change once they hear about what he has done. He knows exactly what his mother-in-law will think of him. She has always had a very low opinion of him and vocalize her disdain for him every chance she got whether he was in the room or not.

He takes a deep breath and forces himself off of the bed and into his closet to change into some clothes to travel in. After getting dressed, he grabs a backpack as he goes into each room and collects various personal items that he thinks would be of comfort to his wife and daughters on their journey. After gathering the items, he walks into the laundry room and places the backpack on the floor next to the dryer. He doesn't cut on the light; he just turns off the security alarm and opens the door to the garage. He's almost certain that all of his neighbors are asleep, but he doesn't want to take any chances, so he walks around stumbling in his dark garage and opens the wooden chest next to the wall, which has some thick black paper that will cover his six garage door windows. He doesn't want his house to attract any unnecessary attention. After covering and taping the last window, he again stumbles back to the laundry room door and turns on the light. He hopes that most of the light from the laundry room will not emit from the bottom or top of the garage door. He can't worry about that right now, so he opens the door and grabs the backpack and places it in the trunk of his car. He then opens both of the rear doors then the passenger side door. He has plenty of maneuvering room in the garage because when Lorrain went to bed, he moved her car outside. He walks back into the house, leaving the door into the garage open. He grabs a painter's mask from the laundry room closet and puts it on to make sure he doesn't inhale any of the drug while carrying his wife and the girls to the car.

He quickly walks into his room and moves to her bedside. He uncovers Lorraine and puts his arm under her legs and behind her shoulders to lift her from the bed, but after he lifts her, he soon realizes that dead weight is harder to lift. Lorraine is only 5 feet and 4 inches tall and around 128 pounds. He struggles to get her comfortably in his arms, but the reality is he's a bit out of shape and he should hurry to get her into the car before he drops her, which couldn't do anymore damage. While carrying her out their bedroom and into the hallway, his mind is hacking through the thicket of his emotions like a explorer making his way through the thick jungle canopy. He returns to the garage breathing hard with Lorraine in his arms and carefully props her limp body in the passager's side. He leans the seat back a little and positions her body to make it appear that she is sleeping.

Once he positions her; he quickly shuts the car door, but her body slowly leans over toward the door as her face and shoulder softly slumps against the passenger window. He turns back around and opens the car door as he makes sure that his wife's body doesn't come flopping out onto the hard concrete. The last thing he needs is a person sitting in the front seat, unconscious with a bloody head wound. This time, as he straightens her up, he puts her seat belt on and reclines her seat back slightly, which will ensure that the weight of her body will keep her laid back against her seat. Her head may lean to one side or the other but that will still give the impression that she's sleeping.

He gently but firmly closes the door and walks backward toward the front of the car with his arms out as if he just proudly balanced a stack of cans one on top of the other. She's positioned perfectly, he thinks to himself as he nods his head then goes back in for LaChel. He's breathing harder as he hurriedly scoops her up into his arms, then carries her to the garage. She's a bit lighter, so he doesn't have as much trouble walking her into the garage.

He places her in the back seat in her favorite side of the car, as if it matters. LaChel and Kim have had countless arguments about who will sit on what side of the car. He knows that he won't have to listen to any bickering, but he's a creature of habit. He walks into the house for the last of his family and returns with Kim's limp body. He gently and carefully places her in the back seat behind her mother. He's careful to place his family and items in the car as if they were traveling, in case he catches the eye of a police officer or some nosey driver peering into his car. It will look as if his family is sleeping while dad is driving throughout the night. He snatches the mask off his face and tosses it on the floor of the garage as he rushed back into the house to give the house a second once over and to get a small bundle of envelops that he will drop in the nearest mailbox.

He has addressed two special letters to his mother and his mother in law, which he hopes will help explain why this had to happen. Whether they will understand or not is not a real concern of his. He wrote the letter because he feels it will be best to hear the story from his point of view and not just from law enforcement and the media. But he does feel that he owes his mother a more detailed explanation, but he had to limit the letter to two pages in order not to write a novel. No, I'm sure with time she will come to understand and maybe even agree with his decision.

As far as BK is concerned, Lorraine's mother is an old bitter shrew of a woman and he doesn't care what she believes or thinks of him, but he wrote her a letter too. It goes without saying that they both hate each other. He walks around the house to ensure he hasn't forgotten anything, but then it hits him that he will never again step foot in the place that he and his family called home again. He walks through the kitchen instinctively turning off the light over the stove as if he is still worried about the electric bill, but it's just something that he has always done before he and his family goes on a trip. He walks into the garage and grabs some batteries for his flashlight, the shovel, a box of large heavy-duty black trash bags that he bought a couple of days ago, and places them in the trunk. He closes the trunk and gets into the car. He sits in the car for a few more seconds then opens the garage door with the garage door opener then he starts the engine. As he begins to back out of the garage, his nerves are so bad that he almost hits Lorraine's car. He talks to himself to calm down as he maneuvers the car out of the garage.

Once out, he backs out of the driveway and onto the street and stops in front of his house. He looks at the place his family has called home one last time. A half smile comes across his face as he remembers all the good times that he and his family shared in this house. As he drives away and presses the garage door opener to close it, he opens his window and tosses the garage remote into the grass next to the street.

He thinks to himself that he and his family won't need anything in the house anymore and that his shouldn't have closed the garage door. He maybe behind schedule, but hopefully luck will be on his side. He thinks at this time of morning the streets should be clear of people and traffic. As he whines through his neighborhood, he looks at his watch and sees that he's just thirty-five minutes off schedule, which he shouldn't worry about or try to make up. It's 2:35 a.m. and at this time of night, it's best not to exceed the speed limit.

Police are parked on the side of the road without anything to do but look for people like him. If he gets pulled over by the police, then it's all over. He has a plan "B", which involves the spray bottle he still has in his pocket, but he doesn't have much confidence that he'd get close enough to the officer to use it. He knows he has a long drive ahead of him, so he decides to stop at a gas station to fill his gas tank, get a large cup of coffee and some gum to keep from nodding off behind the wheel. It's now 2:58 a.m. and the roads are very empty of traffic. That's something in his favor. The less traffic that on the road, the better for me, he thinks to himself. He looks to the left and right of the street, looking for an open gas station where he can get in and out without drawing too much attention.

He sees a fairly large but empty gas station up ahead on the right. This is the gas station he usually stops at on his way to work. They have the dark roast coffee he likes and that's what he's going to need. As he pulls off the road and into the gas station, he remembers that this station has a lot of pumps and he can park and fill up at the far end where people won't have a clear view of him and his family. But as he slowly maneuvers his car around toward the pumps he wants, he sees that there are small plastic bags on all the pump nozzels on that side of the station. "What the hell", he yells. There are twelve pumps and four or five of them are out of commission. He circles pass those pumps, knowing that he's probably drawing attention now.

OK, I'm going to just have to get in and out of this station as quickly and discreetly as possible. He pulls beside pump station number twelve. Before he cuts-off the car, he looks down at the gas gauge, which is hovering above three quarters of a tank. He thinks that he may be able to make it to his destination and to just pull off, but he knows that he will be close to running on fumes by the time he gets there. The risk is too great that he could be stuck on the side of the interstate, miles away from his destination. He puts the car in park, cuts it off and pulls the gas cover lever. He looks at his wife, then glances in the rearview mirror at the girls before opening the door and getting out. He's still feeling a little nervous and he's trying hard to calm himself down. He steps out of the car and shuts the door behind him, while still breathing very deeply as he walks across the gas station's parking lot and towards the store entrance.

He walks in and head straight for the coffee machine to make himself the largest and strongest cup of coffee they have available. The cashier works the early morning shift at the gas station and is consequently alert to anyone entering her store. At first, she doesn't pay too much attention to him, because he is dress normally and gesture's her a "good morning" as he entered the store.

But as BK continues to prepare his coffee, his nerves start to get the better of him. He drops one sugar packet after another, spills coffee all over the floor and continuously gives the cashier quick glances, which draws her attention to him. He realizes that he's probably making the cashier nervous with his strange behavior. There's only two other people in the store and one of them is checking out with the cashier. She is bagging her customer's items and catching glances at BK fumbling his way through his attempt to make a cup of coffee. He doesn't look like the type that would rob her, she thinks to herself. She's been robbed twice before and both times, she knew it was going to happen. They didn't use a weapon or anything. They just grabbed a handful of items and took off.

She's just curious about why he's looking and acting so strangely. She has been working at this gas station for almost five years but has only been working the night shift for two of them. She doesn't like working these hours because of the strange people that stop by this time of morning. As he watches her customer walk out the door and into the parking lot, BK's car catches her attention and she can make-out a female asleep in the front seat. That's a little odd, she thinks to herself. Most of the time when a car pulls up and the lights of the gas station lights up the car; that usually wakes-up everyone, especially the passengers. Normally, the wife gives her husband a grocery list of items to bring back or someone has to use the bathroom. She's a big fan of Spiderman and she likes to say that her spidey senses are tingling. She's peering through the window trying to get a good look at who and how many people are in the car.

She's amazed that everyone's still sleeping after he slammed the car door, which heightened her curiousity. She's not paying attention to BK as he walks up to the counter. "Excuse me", he says as she turns around and jumps. She puts her hands over her chest. "Oh my god", you scared the hell out of me, she says as she tries to catch her breath. Sorry, he says with a smile. So, what caught your attention out there, he asked. She moves away from the window and moves toward the counter and says, "its just that your family are heavy sleepers and that's a little strange. BK plays it off by giving her a little laugh as he pulls out his wallet. We've had a very long and tiring road trip and are getting close to our destination. He starts to put the coffee and the other items on the counter. She rings-up his items as she responds, Wow!

Are you sure you need all that coffee, she asked? You don't look so tired to me, she added. And this coffee will make sure I stay that way, he says as he grabs the coffee from the counter and takes a sip. So, where are you and your family headed, she asked as she rings up his last item? He just picked a random place in the opposite direction that he's going. "Sarasota", he blurts out. Oh, I have family there too, she replies with a surprising tone. "What part"? "Damn", he thinks to himself. I just want her to bag my stuff so I can get out of here before this gas station gets any busier. Just then, he remembers that he still has the little white bottle in his right pocket.

She's still looking at him waiting for an answer. I know she's alone and all I would need to do is to hit her with one short burst to her nosy face and that would be all she wrote for her, and most importantly, her questions. She picks up on his facial expression that he doesn't want to answer any more questions. "She erupts in nervous laughter". "That's OK". I didn't mean to be so nosy, but I don't get a lot of people coming in here at this time of morning. I guess when I get bored, I get curious, she says with more laughter. As she continues to laugh, she puts his remaining items in the bag. "Thank God", he thinks to himself. One more second and I would have pulled the bottle out of my pocket like a pistol and blasted her in her overly jovial face. I'm just visiting a friend of mine and this will be my first-time visiting Sarasota, he tells her. He gave her that lie to appease her nosey curiosity. The only other thing he wants to say to her is "thank you and good night"!

Just then he notices the camera in the upper right corner, behind the counter, which is most likely recording everything. If he decided to use the spray, she would have drop like a boneless chicken. The camera would have captured it all, but he wouldn't have given a damn. Where he and his family are going, law enforcement wouldn't be able to bring him to justice. But the cashier has taken the hint and stop asking him any questions, so he decides to just pay for his stuff and get the hell out of this gas station. He gives her a nervous smile and adds that he will be filling his car up on pump number one. BK pulls his wallet from his back pocket and pulls out a $50.00 bill from a small stack of fifties.

Now normally she is required to run these large bills across a hand scanner that identifies counterfeit money, as store policy requires, but she feels a little uneasy doing it in front of him. So, she just takes the bill and places it beside her register, so she can scan it after he leaves the store. She figures, if the money is counterfeit, she just disables the pump, lock the door and call the police. Once you've finish filling up, come back and I will give you your change. Is that store policy, he asked? Yes mister, she says as if she's asking him to replace his name with the word, "mister". She pauses so BK can respond with his last name or at least his first, but he just says, "No problem"! He grabs his bag then turns and walks out of the store.

She is too curious for her own good, he thinks to himself. But he knows he made the right decision not to use his spray, because what if someone would have walked in after she hit the floor or while he was at the pump. It would have just raised the body count, seeing that he may have had to spray them too. He thinks the best option is to just let her be curious and don't come back for his change. He knows this may raise her suspicions, but by the time she can contact the police; he will be miles down the interstate. He walks quickly to his car unlocks the door and places his coffee and bag of stuff inside. The cashier is still peering out the window once again watching to see if there's any movement in the car. He decides to try to throw her off by saying something in the direction of the back seat.

That just seems to make her more curious as she moves from behind the counter to the front entrance in order to get a better look at the car's back window. She's not watching him. She's just looking for any type of movement in the car. She can't shake the feeling that something is not right with this family. He seems to be a normal guy with his family traveling down the road, but her gut his telling her to call the police, as she stands on her toes to get a better look over one of the displays in front of the storefront window. BK his trying to keep it together, but he can't help wanting to get on the road and get some distance between himself and this gas station. He removes the nozzle from the gas pump places it in his car's gas funnel.

As he pumps his gas, he stares out at a road with very little cars traveling on it, wondering what his mother will think of him once the police and news agency figures out what has happened. He hopes that the letter will help her understand his actions, but he couldn't properly express his disappointment and anguish with the world and his government in a letter. Just then, a series of beeps from his earpiece interrupts his chain of thought. "He knows exactly who it is". He grudgingly presses the button on his earpiece. "Yes", I know I'm behind schedule, he says without saying even a "Hello". A female voice softly responds, in a strong and steady tone, "you are 27 minutes behind schedule".

Thank you for stating the obvious, but there was a few surprises and I needed to stop for gas. If you followed my instructions, you wouldn't have had a reason to stop for gas, she adds. He had so much on his mind that he barely looked at his phone or that text message, but he doesn't want to tell her that. He sighs. "Yes, I know", but sometimes reality doesn't always go as planned or follows a schedule, he replies with a hint of irritation in his voice. She can tell by his voice that he's lying, but she also can here that he's feeling a lot of pressure.

I can hear fear and frustration in your voice, she says as she softens her tone. Are you OK? "Stop trying to analyze me", he shouts into the openness of the gas station. The cashier thinks he's talking to himself until she remembers the small earpiece he had in his ear. The plan is still on track, and I will be there when I get there, he stearnly tells the mysterious voice.

There's a pause over the line. He sees the cashier trying to read his lips, so he turns his back away from her. I understand the importance of following the schedule, but this was extremely difficult for me, so I would appreciate your understanding. Just then the pump clicked off as his tank reaches its' limit. All right I'm done, he shouts.

She continues to talk softly to him in order to calm him down. I know this is not easy for you, but just remember why you are doing this. He puts the nozzle back onto the pump and closes his gas cap. I have to go, he says abruptly! Did you remember to bring the shovel and plastic bags? I also wrote in the text message for you to bring the shovel and large outdoor trash bags, she reiterates to him. I have them in my trunk, so if you let me get off of the phone, I can be on my way. Alright, I will see you in three hours and twenty-seven minutes, if there isn't any further delays. He just says bye as he presses the disconnect button on this earpiece. As he opens the door to get in the car, he notices out the corner of his eye that a police cruiser is pulling into the gas station. His heart starts to beat faster and a chill goes down his spine. There are two police in the patrol car, and they take notice of him as they slowly pass by. He looks at the police and nods his head nervously as they pass the front of his car. Both the officers just look at him curiously and nod their heads back in response. They are close enough to see his "Hello" gesture, but too far for them to get a good look at his family.

Before the patrol car pulled into the gas station, after pumping his gas, he was going to wipe off his windshield and check his tire pressure before hitting the road. But seeing the patrol officer slowly moving pass him makes him think that he needs to just get in his car and leave before one or both of them walks over. He knows that the cashier may run out to the parking lot if he tries to get into his car and leave, but that's just a chance he has to take. I have to get out of here while I can, he thinks to himself. If they decide to try to talk to him and his wife; That's it – game over.

Just get in the car, he says to himself. He figures by the time she runs out and explains why she wants them to detain him; he'll be too far ahead of them. As the patrol car begins to pull into a parking space in front of the store; the cashier starts to move from behind the counter as if she's going to come out of the store to meet the police. Damn, BK says under his breath... I should have used the spray on her and put her in the back room or something. The officers begin to pull into the parking space, but halfway into the space; the patrol car comes to a stop. BK can see the officer in the passenger side pick up the mic. Although he can't hear what's going on, he can clearly see that it is some sort of emergency. Then the patrol car quickly backs out of the space, turns on its' lights and sirens, and drives out of the parking lot at a high rate of speed. The cashier comes up to the front of the store and peers through the glass door in disbelief as the patrol car makes a screeching right-hand turn and bullets down the road.

BK breathes a sigh of relief as the cruiser red and blue lights disappears into the darkness. Both the cashier and BK make eye contact. She quickly turns and heads back behind the counter, knocking over a rack of bakery goods in the process. She scrambles to pick them up and get behind the counter before BK comes back for his change. The cashier finally makes it back behind her counter. She looks at the display, which shows how much gas he has pumped. She knows he'll be coming back for his change, since he only pumped $29.34 worth of gas. She wants to ask him a couple more questions, but she can't shake the feeling that he could be dangerous. BK takes this stroke of good luck as a sign to get the hell out of here as quickly as possible. He jumps in his car, starts it up and pulls around toward the front of the store, but instead of pulling into a parking space, he drives pass the storefront window and heads toward the main road. The cashier nervously watches as BK and his family slowly drives pass her.

As she peers out the window, she sees his wife apparently still sleeping with her face against the passenger window. She can also see him as they make eye contact. She feels the hairs on the back of her neck standing on edge. The siren of the patrol car was loud as hell, she thinks to herself. How could anyone sleep through that, she says out loud? BK pulls out of the gas station and onto the main street. She stands there for a moment stunned, but partly happy that he didn't come back into her store. But she is wondering why he didn't come back for the remainder of his money. She starts thinking that maybe she was right, and something was wrong in that car and fear of the police coming back must have convinced him to leave without his money.

She thinks for a second that maybe she should call 911 and have him stop on this way to Sarasota, but a second voice in her head says she could be wrong. It could have been a long trip and having him pulled over would add to their time on the road. Oh well, she says to herself. At least he left me a $20.00 tip for my outstanding bagging services. She walks back behind the counter and puts the $50.00 bill in the cash register, takes out the $20.00 change then places it in a box under the counter, which the owner wants her to use for any extra cash.

Back on the road, He decides to make his last scheduled detour, which is to a post office drop box. He needs to drop the letters to his mother and mother-in-law in the box before disappearing. He makes it to the nearest dropbox and slides them through the slot and continues back onto the road to his final destination. It has been over an hour and the road he's on is a very dark road and isolated, which can cause a person to focus on their thoughts rather than the road ahead of them. The road has slight and gentle curves, which causes him to occasionally drift off the road until he hears and feels the raised road divider marker near the middle of the road. He also doesn't pay particular attention to his speed as he exceeds the posted speed limit of 60 mph. "Oh damn", he says aloud as he finally looks down at his speedometer, which points to 77 mph. He quickly decreases his speed and looks through his rearview mirror to see if any police are behind him.

One car is passing on his left, but he sees only darkness and the lights of the highway behind him. He breathes a sigh of relief as he tells himself to watch his speed. There are state troopers all over this international highway with nothing to do but pull over speeders like him. If this had been a normal trip with his family, his wife would have been awake and reminding him to watch his speed. It was normal for him and his family to travel on long trips at night, so his daughters would be sleep and that would cut down on the arguing, at least until they wakeup. He's been on the road now for almost two hours and is mentally exhausted as he gets closer to his destination. As he takes a glance out of his rearview side mirror, he sees a set of head lights suddenly appear. At this distance, he can't tell what kind of car it is, but he can tell that it's in a big hurry. The lights are getting closer and closer at a very rapid rate. He decides to decrease his speed, which should cause the car to switch lanes as it gets closer.

He rapidly switches his eyes back and forth from the speedometer to his rearview mirror. As the headlights move closer, his heart rate and consequently his anxiety slowly increases. He begins to pray to God that the approaching headlights are not a state trooper. But as the car gets about three car lengths away, he can make out the silhouette of the cruiser closing in on him. "Oh God", he says out loud. He firmly grips the steering wheel very tightly and he mumbles to himself to be calm, because he's going to switch lanes and go after that car that sped pass him a few seconds ago. The cruiser doesn't change lanes, but pulls up directly behind him. He can feel his heart starting to beat faster in his chest, so he begins to breathe deeply and not look back at the cruiser.

He continues to tell himself that the cruiser is just doing a routine check of his license plate and will see that he has no reason to stop him and will just speed pass him. The cruiser stays behind BK for about two to three miles, then proceeds to illuminate the night with his lights and siren. The logical part of BK's brain shuts down as a wash of adrenalin over comes him and he contemplates pressing down on the gas and thinks to try to outrun him.

But he comes to his senses and decides that his best chance of not getting arrested is to pull over and try to talk his way out of this nightmare. He puts his blinker on, indicating to the officer that he's about to pull over. He then pulls over on to the gravel shoulder as the cruiser lines up directly behind him and stops about two car lengths behind. As he puts his car in park, he thinks his best chance of getting out of this will be to tell the officer that his family has had a very rough day and are sound asleep.

But he thinks it would be best to put some distance between his family and the officer. He turns his car off, proceeds to open the door and tries to get out of his car when he hears the officer forcefully instructs him through his cruiser's loudspeaker not to exit his vehicle. He hesitates for a moment, thinking he should get out anyway, but that may only make matters worse. He reluctantly puts his leg back into his car and closes the door. "OK, that's the end of that plan", he says while racking his brain for a plan "B". His hands are beginning to shake as panic starts to set in. He has to calm himself down or he'll start sweating and the officer will see that he's nervous about something, which will give him probable cause to try to wake everyone up and remove them from the car. He looks in his rearview mirror and can see the officer still sitting in his cruiser probably running his plates.

He decides to take the limited time to breathe deeply and get his story straight. Hopefully, he can convince the officer that his family is sound asleep and to let him go with a warning for whatever reason he pulled him over for. Otherwise, he will find himself in the back of the cruiser in handcuffs. If that happens, he has no doubt that he would not see the light a day, without being surrounded by rusty bars and correction officers. Those types of thoughts aren't helping him calm down, so he closes his eyes and counts to ten. He takes another deep breath then opens them just in time to look in his side mirror to see the officer step out of his cruiser and begins to walk toward his car. One word comes to BK's mind to describe the officer that's walking toward him, and the word is "burly".

As the sound of the officer's footsteps crunching against the small rocks and gravel on the road gets louder, he slowly and carefully reaches over to the glove compartment and grabs a handful of papers. He also turns on the CD player, which has a soft jazz CD in it. He turns the music on to give the impression that his family was listening to it as they fell asleep. He also feels the spray bottle in his pocket, but he will only try to use it as a last resort.

He can now hear the gravel crunching under the officer's feet as he walks beside his car and can see the beam of the officer's flashlight moving back and forth from LaChel to Kim. He walks up to the driver's side window and shines the flashlight directly into his eyes. BK shields his eyes from the flashlight by putting his hand up in front of his face. "Can you please roll down your window", the officer says with authority. BK smiles as he tries to hide his nervousness and quickly follows the officer's instructions and rolls down the window. "Morning officer", he says with a whisper. "I need to see your license and registration, please. BK smiles again and starts to flip through the paperwork in his hand. As he looks through the papers, he can see the officer's flashlight moving from Kim to LaChel again.

He hands the officer his license and registration. This should distract the officer from looking in the back seat momentarily. The officer looks over the registration closely as BK keeps his hand visible and only speaks when spoken to. Hopefully he will be sent on his way with just a warning. The officer asked him does he realize how fast he was going as he continues to scan BK's registration and license. He looks at the officer's name tag as he acknowledges to Officer Peterson that he understands that his speed was a little excessive, but he would like him to take in account that it's very early in the morning and that he's been on the road for a while.

The officer looks over the license for a couple more seconds, then leans over and shines his flashlight past BK and directly onto the back of Lorraine's head that's still turned toward the passenger side window. BK puts his hand up to block the light from shining in Lorraine's direction. Officer Peterson stands up straight and looks at BK in disbelief for blocking him from evaluating the person in the passenger seat.

"I'm sorry Officer Peterson, but my wife is very tired and your flashlight my wake her up, he says in a soft and respectful tone. But that only makes the officer more suspicious, so he decides to check out BK's information before he continues with the questioning and possibly removing everyone from the car.

"Give me a moment Mr. Thomas". I'll be right back, he says as he walks back to his cruiser. BK looks in the side mirror and can see the officer once again glancing at his daughters as he walks pass the passenger side window and back to his cruiser. He knows now that he's well into plan "B" and doesn't have a choice but to use the spray on him, but he knows he'll only have one chance to do it. He tucks the bottle firmly in his right hand and positions his fingers so he can open the door and still be able to hit him with a clean blast of the spray. "This isn't going to work", he thinks to himself. If I open the door, the officer may see the white bottle in my hand before I can get close enough to use it. The Officer is halfway inside his vehicle with his computer illuminating the inside of his patrol car. BK looks in his rearview mirror and can see the officer sitting in his cruiser checking out his license and insurance.

He has no doubt that his information won't cause the officer to become more suspicious, but he may get curious and may want to do a welfare check on his wife and kids. He decides the best move would be to confront the officer outside the car, which may give him an opportunity to use the spray bottle. So he takes a few deep breaths then opens his door and steps out of his car and closes the door behind him. He walks to the rear of this car and leans against the trunk. The Officer immediately yells out of his cruiser for him to get back into the vehicle. "I just need to stretch my legs", BK replies back at him, as he puts both hands on the trunk and leans further back. The officer can't really hear what he's saying, because he's still acting and talking like his family is asleep. The officer steps out of his cruiser and BK can see that he's not very happy that he's not following his instructions.

The Officer stands behind his door and intensely stares at him. "Mr. Thomas, I need you to get back in your vehicle, right now", he says with a stern tone and foreboding voice. BK keeps the spray bottle hidden in the palm of his right hand and his finger on the spray nozzle to make sure he sprays the officer and not himself. "I'm sorry officer, but my legs were falling asleep and

I wanted to make sure that we didn't wake my family. Officer Peterson adjust his hat by pulling it down closer to his brow before stepping from behind his door and walks menacingly toward BK. "Oh good God, he looks bigger now that he's angry", BK thinks to himself. The officer is telling him it would be to his best interest to follow his instructions and return to the vehicle, but BK is just shaking his head no in order to goat the officer into coming closer. The stomping of the officer's footsteps as he approaches sounds like he's crushing rocks with every step.

If he doesn't spray him directly in the face, he will most likely be agressively thrown to the ground, then cuffed. He watches a lot of the television shows like "Cops" and that's how it's done. The Officer is now roughly eight feet away and steadily approaching him as he repeats his instructions for BK to get back in his vehicle or he's going to end up in the back of his cruiser. The only thing BK can reply with is to ask the officer, "could he keep his voice down". Officer Peterson is now close enough that he can clearly see the frustration in the officer's eyes as he puts his hands on his handcuffs. "Why do I need to follow those instructions", BK says to draw the officer in just a little closer. It works, because the Officer pops the latch on his handcuff holster and continues to angrily walk closer to him. I'm going to give you one last chance to comply with my orders to get back into your vehicle, as he stops directly in front of him. Unfortunately, for BK, the officer is still too far away. So BK decides to give the officer a little more incentive to come closer. "Isn't there a donut you can be eating", he shouts. My family is asleep in the car, so arrest me or get the hell out of my face! With that statement from him, the officer advances on him and reaches out to grab BK's left arm and at the same time reaches for his handcuffs. BK is shaking all over with fear and he's sure the officer can see it all over his face. He's not going to get a better opportunity than this, so he snatches his arm from the officer's grasp and with his right hand, starts to spray wildly in the officer's direction.

His arm flails about like Kermit the Frog on the Muppet Show. He's almost certain that a small amount hit the officer in the face, but he can't be sure, so he tries to spray him again, but the officer knocks his hand away, which knocks the bottle out of his hand. BK looks in terror as the bottle falls to the ground seemingly in slow motion. He then looks back up at the officer wiping this hand across his face and looking into his hand. He angrily grabs BK by the collar of his shirt with both hands and pushes him backward against the trunk of his car.

"What in the hell was in that bottle you strayed me with", the officer shouts as he lifts him off the ground and onto the trunk. "Oh damn", BK thinks to himself with a look of pure terror in his eyes. "Oh my God", I'm going to jail, he repeatedly says to himself. The officer shakes him like a rag doll as he demands to know what he sprayed in his face and how stupid he is for doing it. Nothing the officer is saying is registering with him, because BK is racking his brain wondering why the drug hadn't worked.

He's in complete panic mode now. What snaps him back into reality is when he hears the officer angerly and loudly reading him his rights. "You are under arrest for assaulting a police officer"! You have the right to remain silent, anything you say can and will be ...". The officer stops abruptly. BK starts to repeat the same thing over and over again, "I'm sorry, so sorry". After about the third, "I'm sorry", he looks at the officer's frozen expression on his face and can feel the officer's grip on his collar slowly begins to weaken. He begins to rest more on the trunk rather than being held dangling over it. The officer has a strange glazed look on his face with his mouth slightly open like he was trying to force himself to speak. All of a sudden, the officer's lefthand falls to his side near his holstered gun.

BK his now sitting on his trunk and looking down at the officers' hand slightly flexing as if he is trying to grab his weapon. He looks the officer in his eyes and can tell by his expression that he's struggling to make his hand grab his weapon, but all he can do his flex his fingers. BK is also trying to make a decision on what to do next. Should I grab the officer's hand reaching for his gun, push him over, or just sit here on the trunk and hope for the best.

But thankfully before he could come to a decision on what option to take, the officer's other hand releases his collar, his eyes rolled back in his head as he fell backward like a large redwood. As he hits the ground, his hat flies off into the street and a plume of dust and rock jets out from beneath him. He just sat there on the trunk of his car for a moment looking down at the officer as if he was in the cheap seats of a football game. He quickly snaps out of the shock of the close call he dodged then slides off the trunk. He looks down the road to see if there's any lights heading his way. There's nothing but darkness as far as he can see. "Good", he says out loud. I don't need anyone to see a police officer lying on the ground and me standing over him. The red and blue lights could attract attention, so the first thing he does is to trot back to the cruiser and switch off those lights. He leans into the open cruiser door and hits a few switches and finally gets the lights to turn off. The computer screen catches his eye and he can see his information displayed on the screen. He reads the trooper's remarks section that noted the family is asleep, and he was going to release him with a warning for speeding. "Well damn", he says as he backs out of the cruiser. From behind the cruiser door, he looks over at the officer and wonders how he's going to get him back to his patrol car without being affected by the drug. In hind sight, he wish he would have brought another mask, but his only other option is to hold his breath while getting him back to his cruiser.

Just then he notices the trooper's jacket lying in the passenger side seat. "That'll have to do", as he reaches in and grabs it. He walks back to the fallen officer thinking that maybe he should have been more patient. But it's too late to second guess his actions now. Everything worked out for the best – at least for him, he thinks to himself. He walks up to the officer on his back looking larger than when he fell. He takes the jacket and drapes it over the officer's head and torso. He looks down at him and goes over his options to get him back to his cruiser. Put him over my shoulder, "no". Cradle him in my arms and carry him back to his cruiser, "hell no". Lift him by his feet or his arms and drag him to his cruiser, "that sounds like a plan".

He walks to the head of the officer and grabs him underneath his shoulders and lifts him into the sitting position. He takes a deep breath then with a straining grunt, lifts him as much as he can, which wasn't very much. He drags the dead weight of the officer, stumbling and grunting all the way back to the open door of the cruiser. He lays the officer down beside the open door for a moment, so he can gather his strength for one last power move. He thinks it would have been much quicker and easier to just toss him into the bushes then go on his way.

But it was bad enough that he had to do this to a man just doing his job. He could at least show him some respect by placing him behind the wheel of his cruiser so his fellow officers can find him. He repositions the officer in a sitting position against the back door of his cruiser. With all the remaining strength he can muster, he then grabs him in a bear hug and muscles him into the driver's seat. He then removes the officer's jacket that is draped over his face and upper body then throughs it back into the passager seat. He swings the officer's legs in, then slams the door shut. BK is still breathing hard as he walks back to his car. But he notices the officer's hat still lying in the road, so he retrieves it and as a last gesture of respect, goes back to the cruiser and places it on the officer's head. This way, if anyone passes by, they will think he's just taking a break. He looks back at the officer as he quickly walks back to his car. He can't help but think that this is just another felony in a bucket full of felonies that he has committed. Again, he looks back at the cruiser and down the dark road to see if any lights are headed his way.

But he's lucky. The road is pitch black as far as he can see. His muscles and tendons are so strained, but his adrenaline is still up, so he should be able to make it to his destination without falling asleep. It's time to get back on track now, he says to himself. He opens his car door and flops down into the driver's seat and closes the door. He looks at his wife and daughters, starts his car and pulls back onto the road. He is worried about what will happen once the authorities find that officer on the side of the road. He's about a little over an hour away from his destination, but in two to three hours all hells going to break loose. Law enforcement will be searching from the road and the air very soon.

He knows that he's going to have to get off this highway as soon as possible. Just then, his cell phone begins to ring, and he picks it up from the center console. As he looks at the name and number glowing in his face, he gives a reluctant sigh. He presses the answer icon and answers with a frustrating, "Yes"! The female voice on the phone starts with telling him that he's 35 minutes behind and that they must stay as close to the schedule in order for the rest of their plans to fall in place. He's aggravated that she doesn't understand or have any sympathy for what he's going through. But he knows she's built that way and he'll have to take care of her attitude once he gets to her. He reminds her that this is his plan and he has sacrificed his entire life and the lives of his family, he says with attitude. The only thing I need from you right now is to give me an alternative route so I can get off this highway and get there faster. The phone goes silent for a few seconds as he listens intensely for her response.

She finally tells him about a couple of small rural dirt roads about twelve minutes from his location and that should get him here almost on schedule. "Thank you". "That will be a great help", he replies. I'm under a lot of pressure and I would appreciate it if you wouldn't call me again. I'll be there as soon as possible, and I need you to have everything ready to go. I have to take care of Lorraine and my girls as soon as I get there.

He doesn't give her a chance to say anything else but just taps on the red hang up icon on the phone and drops the phone back into the center console. He understands that she's just looking out for him, but it feels strange to talk to her with his family around him. He always had to be very careful to conceal his conversations and cover his tracks with the weeklong business trips he use to take. But recently, Lorraine was asking more questions about his trips and why sometimes she had a difficult time contacting him or him returning her calls and messages the same day. At one point, she was so frustrated with his answers and him telling her that his job is responsible for all the travel, she called Bryan to get some answers.

But of course, being BK's best friend and employee, Bryan for the most part covered for him. He was telling Lorraine and Bryan the same lie, but the only difference was that Bryan wouldn't checkup on him or question him about phone calls he didn't return. At the end, he decided to not go on any more false meetings. Just like most wives, she may have suspected that he was using those out of town meetings to hook up with another woman. He doesn't have to worry about that anymore, as he looks over at her. He has been back on the road for about eleven minutes when his cell phone navigator starts to inform him that the road that he's about to turn off on is half a mile away on his right. He feels relief that he's about to leave this major highway and travel his last fifty some odd miles on small paved and dirt roads. It will make it harder for the authorities to find him once they find that officer. "In twenty-five feet, turn right onto Branch road", his phone navigator instructs him. He slows down and turns onto a poorly maintained small paved road with very few lights. It's after three in the morning and normally on a trip like this, he would be trying to keep himself awake, but the road is dark and has plenty of potholes and soft shoulders, which helps focus his attention on the road.

He's driving between thirty-five and forty miles per hour to minimize the impact of his family's bodies being tossed about the interior of the car, but he's trying to get to his destination before sun rise. Just when he thinks the worst is behind him, a few large drops of rain explodes on his windshield. "What the hell", he shouts with angry defiance. "Come on", he shouts. I just need a little more time. If it starts to rain, the dirt road will turn into a mud road and the potholes will be impossible to see and to maneuver around.

But the raindrops continue to come down at a faster and more frequent pace. He then hears a tone of his cellphone indicating that someone is sending him a text. He picks up his phone and glances at the screen. It simply says, "Rain". He sighs in frustration and drops the phone back into the console. The rain is now starting to wash across his windshield, forcing him to turn on his windshield wipers and switch on his high beams. "Damn that weatherman"! Last night he said there was only a ten percent chance of rain today. "I just can't catch a break", he says as if someone in the car can hear him. As he leans forward and grips the steering wheel with both hands, he thinks to himself that this rain may be a blessing after all. The rain will wash away any traces of his tire tracks leading from the main highway to the roads he's traveling on. "Silver linings", he says to himself. There are always silver linings to every problematic situation.

He's now driving along a muddy pothole ridden road for another fifteen minutes, until he comes to a "T" in the road. Because the rain is now coming down in buckets, he doesn't recognize the road he's about to make a right turn onto, as his phone navigator is instructing him to do. He can't make out the name of the street, because of the rain. He makes the right onto the road and finally recognizes that he's on the right track. With great relief, he knows that he's on the same road as the warehouse that he purchased over two years ago. He has done a good job with the location of the warehouse. It's around forty-five minutes from the major highway, but deep into the wooded area where no one would bother to look. This is the destination for his wife and daughters. No one will ever find us here, he thinks to himself. He's only about twenty minutes away and with that knowledge, he's finally starting to loosen the grip on his steering wheel. As he gets closer to the warehouse the rain begins to slow down to a light drizzle. At the end of the muddy road, he sees the silhouette of the warehouse through the darkness.

He stops his car about four feet in front of a tall barbwire fence and double entry gate, which surrounds a completely darkened thiry-five foot warehouse with blacked out windows. The warehouse is huge and is roughly thirty feet from the locked gate. The high beam of his car illuminates the thick partially rusted chain, which is continuously wrapped around the aluminum post of both sides of the gate opening. He puts his car in park, opens the door and steps out with a splash onto the muddy road. As he walks toward the double opening of the gate, he reaches into his left pants pocket and searches for the single key, which is comingled amongst the pennies, nickels and dimes.

He pulls the key out of his pocket and uses it to remove the large lock from the thick rusting chain. The clanking of the chain being unwrapped and pulled through the aluminum gate resonates throughout the rainy night. He removes all four feet of chain from the gate and threads the chain through the right side of the gate. He then hangs the lock with the key still in it on the gate besides the chain, pushes both sides of the gate open enough to drive his car through. He then walks back to his car, unsuccessfully trying to dodge as many mud puddles as he can. As he gets back into his car, he can feel the mud and water, which his socks could not soak up, sloshing in his tennis shoes. But that doesn't matter anymore. BK's thoughts are now focused on putting his family to rest, so he can concentrate on completing the remainder of his life changing plan. He approaches the front of the huge warehouse and maneuvers the car to the right were there is a double car garage door. He stops about five feet in front of the door then reaches across his wife to open the glove compartment. Paperwork slides out onto her lap and her feet as he searches for something in the back of the glove compartment.

He pulls out what looks like a remote control mixed in with some more papers, which he shakes out of his hand. Because it is still somewhat dark, he looks at the remote intensely as he tries to determine, which button he needs to push to open the garage door.

He then turns the remote around in his hand and points it at the door. He presses the top button a couple of times, as he whispers, "open", a couple of times. After about four to five times, he puts the remote close to his face, flips it around in his hand then presses the button again, this time with firm conviction.

The door makes a loud clunky noise as it starts to slowly open. Normally, opening a garage door would automatically turn on a light inside, but there is no light other than the headlights from his car illuminating the inside of the loading bay. The door hasn't completely opened, but it's enough for him to slowly pull his car in. The headlights shines on a five foot elevated concrete platform with a metal wall and second single car garage door about twenty-four feet in front of him. The loading bay that he has driven into is the size of a residential double car garage with absolutely nothing in it, but more darkness. He pulls up to the platform, stops the car, turns off his head lights and presses the garage remote control again, which causes the garage door to close slowly with noisy creeks and clacks. He shifts the car into park, turns off the car and as the door closes, he feels a wave of relief cascade over his entire body. Until this moment, he didn't really realize how much pressure and stress that he has been under. He turns off his headlights and with his hands on the stirring wheel, rest his head against the steering wheel. He sits there for a moment with his family in the dark just thinking of everything he has gone through. Once the garage door closes with a thud, the silence of the moment was so peaceful, it would be highly possible that he could fall asleep right where he is. But the sound of the small bay door opening on the platform and the light flooding into the room, causes him to snap back to reality and proceed to the next stage of the plan.

He opens his car door and steps out as the light in the bay suddenly comes on. The bay door is halfway open when a white three-foot-tall robotic droid without legs hovers from out of the open bay door of the warehouse. The droid has a "M1" in large letters stenciled to the largest part of what can be called its' torso. This designation is used to signify where and what the unit's responsibility is. "M1" designates the unit as a medical unit. One of three medical units. "Welcome home, BK" the droid says as it passes by him and proceeds to the car to peer through the passenger side window. "Thanks, M1!", he response. I need my family prepped for stasis right now, as he closes the car door and walks beside the unit. The unit's eyes are just two small rectangles which illuminates from their eyes. It also has a band of five strobe lights blinking and strobing across its' forehead. It opens the passenger side door and emits a cyan colored beam from the palm of one of its' robotic hands.

The beam passes from LaChel to Kim and from Kim to Lorraine. He just stands there and waits for the medical unit to complete its' scan. "So, how much time do we have", he asked with trepidation in his voice. The unit continues its' scan for a few more seconds before replying to him.

My scans indicate that on average, we have less than an hour before the medication dissipates from their systems and they will regain consciousness. I conclude that LaChel will awaken first followed by Lorraine and then Kim, the unit states with confidence. He knew that he was cutting it close, but to have his family returning to consciousness in less than an hour is terrifying to him. He still remembers how Lorraine looked at him after he sprayed her. And after she finds out that he has done the same thing to their girls; well he has no idea what she might do. And that terrifies him. "All right", he shouts. Lets' get them out of the car and into the medical clinic. Two other units, but one with "M2" and the other with "M3" on their torso emerge from the warehouse. They have three floating medical gurneys with them as they maneuver around the car to remove Kim first. BK steps back from the car to allow the medical units to do their jobs. He looks intensely as one of the units enters into the back seat between the girls. They don't communicate verbally but are linked to each other through the ship's networking system.

Their communication light display can be seen as colorful blinking small lights on their foreheads. He designed all the units with the ability to communicate with each other as proficiently and quickly as possible. They are moving Kim out of the car and onto the gurney when BK hears the voice that was on his cell phone telling him that he's already behind schedule and that the medical units will take good care of his family. The female voice sounds like it's coming through an intercom system. "I have no doubt that you're right", he says.

But it's difficult just leaving them like this in someone else's hands no matter how capable they are. The voice continues to try to remind him about his extremely tight timeline. "Alright", he shouts as he stares at the units placing his oldest daughter on the second gurney. He turns and walks up the ramp to the left of the platform into the large warehouse thinking that he hoped that he programmed enough medical knowledge into the medical units to safely place his family in stasis. As he steps through the bay door that leads into the warehouse, he remembers the state trooper that he left unconscious on the side of the road. He stops after entering a few feet into the warehouse. "MOM", I had to use the spray on an officer about two hours from here and he may be still in his patrol car on the side of the road. I need you to monitor the emergency stations to find out his condition.

That chemical can affect him for about six hours depending on the subject's body size, she reminds him. Yes, I know, but the chemical was not formulated to be used on a person of his size. Just let me know his status as soon as you find out, please. That shouldn't be a problem, she responds, as he continues into the warehouse. And can you send one of the facility's units to get the shovel from the truck and close and lock the gate, please. I will send the "F3" unit, she replies. As he enters the warehouse, he walks under the nose of a huge black spacecraft that fills the entire 82,000 square foot warehouse except for a build out medical clinic and office space on the right of the warehouse. But the right portion of the spacecraft extends halfway over the structure like a canopy. Every time he sees his creation, he's amazed and afraid at the same time. He named his one of a kind spacecraft "Pangaea", after the earth's supercontinent. He chose the name because the ship could possiblely bring humanity back together and it's the Gaia name for "Earth". His spacecraft looks like a massive shiny black metallic mass. He walks further into the warehouse; he reaches up as height as he can with his right arm, trying to touch the seemingly glassy black surface of his greatest creation, other than his daughters.

With his right arm fully extended, he can touch eight feet, but he still has about five feet of space between his fingertips and the spacecraft. He continues walking toward the center of the ship until his fingers finally slides along its' smooth black surface. It has the feel of the smoothest glass and beneath its' surface, a connecting quarter size honeycomb pattern. Those honeycombs are specially designed to absorb or repel various types of exterior energy sources such as cosmic radiation.

He hasn't been here for over two months and he is amazed by the amount of progress his units have made. He has been monitoring the construction process via his computer, but until now he hasn't realized the scope of the progress of the ship's final construction. He now can touch the ship with both of his hands as he continues to walk toward the keel of the spacecraft, which is resting on one of sixteen large supporting blocks. He asked MOM what's the current status for the completion of the spacecraft's exterior protective membrane.

MOM isn't an acronym for anything, but he felt more comfortable calling the ship's main computer MOM and even programming it to sound like his mother. He designed and programmed five construction units to perform construction phases of the ship's development. Each unit has a "C" stenciled to their torso and are numbered from "C1" to "C5". The units are more ruggedized than the other units and has the capability to lift over 300 pounds and hover anywhere in the warehouse. The construction units will have the exterior completed in ten hours, MOM replies. Once my family has been placed in stasis, can we launch, he asks as he starts to walk from underneath the ship and head toward his office?

"Yes", but there are several issues that need to be addressed before we are 95 percent ready for launch. He wanted to know if he could take off just in case the authorities get lucky and tracks him to this warehouse. He has only a few more phases of his plans to complete and he's determined not to let his exhausted mental state, or anything else stop him from launching. He stops and looks up at the bottom of the spacecraft. He takes this moment to acknowledge to himself that with all the unique and advanced technology that he's developed - there's no doubt that he's truly the *smartest ant on the planet.*

As he turns around and begins to walk toward the door leading to his office, the floating gurneys with his wife and daughters crossed in front of him and heads toward the medical clinic. He just stood there looking at their motionless bodies floating past him, escorted by the three white medical units. He watches as if he was in a daze as they slowly hovered through the double doors, which leads to the medical bay where they will be prepped for stasis. He thinks that maybe he can follow his family and monitor the units to ensure they perform their task correctly.

He turns away from the door to his office and heads toward the still opened double doors when MOM intuitively commented that he needs to let the units do their jobs and that his time will be better spent completing his remaining tasks. MOM, thats my family and I just want to make sure the units follow all my instructions, he replies as he continues to walk toward the medical clinic. MOM tries to deter him from following the units.

Yes, my DNA scan determined that I am 99.9 percent certain that you are the paternal father of LaChel and Kim. But as for being the husband of Lorraine, I will have to rely on the authenticity of your marriage license. "What are you talking about", he says out loud. I thought you were questioning my knowledge of your children's paternity. BK just shakes his head. Of course, your units are going to follow your instructions, MOM says in a matter of fact tone. That's the way they have been programmed.

And by the way. You are hurting my feelings, because you know I am tasked with monitoring all the units onboard the ship and in the warehouse. I would apologize for hurting your feelings, but I don't remember writing any code that enabled you to have hurt feelings.

"Good point", MOM responds. If you want to ensure that the ship is ready for launch as soon as possible, you need to complete the engineering units' upgrades and upload it to them prior to launch. He knows MOM is right, as he stops about four feet in front of the now closed automatic doors and just stands there trying to decide if he will listen to her or continue to the medical clinic. He sighs as he stares at the doors, then turns around and heads for his office. There's going to be a manhunt for me once they find that officer in his patrol car, and we need to be ready to launch as soon as possible. He walks toward the only door leading to his office and is now determined to complete all necessary tasks for the spacecraft to lift off. He knows if he wants to complete his three year plan, he has to trust in his units and concentrate on getting the last of his task completed.

Chapter Two

Departing the old normal and venturing into the new

December 19, 2022 – Catastrophic wildfires has increase by twenty-five percent throughout a huge swath of the western United States, Australia and Siberia. These fires contribute to the warming of the earth and consequently threatening to destroy ecosystems around the world.

As he walks to his office, he explains to MOM everything that happened to him on his way to the warehouse and his encounter with the police officer. And how he's very lucky he's not handcuffed and secured in the back seat of the officer's patrol car. As he steps into his office, he requests that MOM keep him informed of the status of his family every twenty minutes.

He also asked that she closely monitor the units to ensure that they follow his instructions to the letter. Need I remind you that they are artificial units, which you designed and programmed, she replies. The units cannot deviate from their programming just as a washing machine couldn't brew a pot of coffee, MOM sarcastically says to reassure him of his family safety. He smiles in the knowledge that MOM's levity programming is steadily improving and that she's right in pointing out the ignorance of his statement, but in a more politically correct manner. He programmed each of those medical units, so he knows that they will adhere to their programming parameters. But it's the first time that he has relied on his "M" units to perform such a major medical procedure on one human let alone multiple human subjects, which is compounded by their various sizes, gender and age diversity.

Each unit was designed with the working knowledge of a practicing physician and a residence surgeon, but he doesn't know how they will react if something unforseen happens during the procedure. Knowledge is one thing, but practical experience is a totally different skill set. He was supposed to perform the stasis procedure on his family himself, but because there were some unforeseen upgrades to the engineering units and navigation system, and not to mention the delays he has experience getting to the warehouse, has knocked him off schedule by about four and a half to six hours.

With the units placing his family in stasis, this will give him the time he needs to concentrate on completing the necessary configurations prior to launch. MOM calculated that if he had to perform or complete the remaining critical task, the ship would miss its' launch window by at least eighteen hours. He can't take the chance that the police or a drunken idiot hunter walking through the woods looking for bambi's dad could accidentally stumble upon his warehouse. He flops down into his black padded leather office chair and spins around to his computer. The last thing he would want would be for his unique and advance technology to fall into the hands of his government. This is his motivating reason he has to depend on his mechanical and engineering units to complete some of his task. Of course, no one is perfect, he thinks to himself. He's thinking about all the test and preparations that he performed to ensure that the units would be ready for this important procedure.

Months ago, After going through various medical scenarios and procedures, he decided that the next practical step would be to allow the medical units to practice on a real live human subject, which would have to be himself since there was no other human available. He seriously toyed with the idea of kidnapping some unknowing person walking the streets. But thanks to MOM's ethical algorithm, she convinced him that it wouldn't be legal to abduct a stranger and experiment on him or her. So, he allowed the units to put him into stasis for a week. With MOM's supervision, of course. He determined that the exercise would evaluate if the units could safely place a person into stasis for a predetermine period of time and revive him at the end of the exercise. He also needs to experience for himself how his wife and the girls would physically and emotionally feel after they have been placed into stasis and revived. He was very apprehensive about allowing units to perform such a complicated procedure that could easily kill him with one bad line of code. Which in away would be self inflicted, because he wrote the code. But he knew that he has very little choice. These same machines will be preforming the same procedure on his family and he had to make sure they were capable of doing the job that he designed them to do. Before being placed in stasis, he decided to give MOM's enhanced abilities a test drive.

He had MOM give Lorraine a call and talk to her about allowing LaChel to get her learners permit, which was a conversation he didn't want to have with her again. The last time they talked about it, they got into such a huge fight that they didn't talk to each other for two days. She felt that he was taking LaChel's side and undermining her as a parent. Lorraine didn't want LaChel to get her learners permit, because she manages the family finances and knows that it would increase their auto insurance. But the main reason is that she felt that LaChel was still too unreliable and irresponsible to drive a car. This will be the first time that MOM will be talking to Lorraine directly, even those she's imitating BK.

She also wants to show him that she can convince his wife that she's him and maybe even win their argument. MOM called Lorraine around the normal time that BK would call when he's out of town. She started the conversation with the normal husband questions and answers about her day, bills that have and should have been paid and finally the girls. Their conversation was going along well, and they were talking for about five minutes when Lorraine notice that MOM was not using normal sentence contractions in his (her) conversation.

Instead of saying "can't" and "shouldn't", MOM would say "cannot" and "should not". Because of her programming, MOM was unable to use contractions. BK was thinking about correcting that problem, but he never could work it into his schedule of things to do. He was already on edge as he listened on his muted linked cellphone.

50

He started to freak out because she maybe figuring out that it's not him that she's talking to and how he'll be able to takeover the conversation without Lorraine noticing. But MOM made an excuse that she was practicing a verbal exercise that she learned at one of the seminars, which should improve her pronunciation and diction. Lorraine was telling him to stop practicing and to speak normally. But MOM decided that this would be a good time to drop the "I've been thinking that I was right about LaChel getting her learners permit" "H" bomb on her. Lorraine then explodes with a cluster of angry "I'm in charge of this family's finances", "this is my lane that you're swerving into damn it", and "I can't believe you brought that up again". MOM allowed Lorraine to rant and rave for awhile before she calmly rebutted all Lorraine's concerns with a logical layout of various other reasons why she thought LaChel getting her permit would be a good thing and not the end of the world.

But as MOM was making such a convincing point on the minor insurance rate increase, age of the average teen driver and LaChel's improving grades, to BK's surprise, Lorraine changed her mind and agreed that LaChel could get her learners license.

Lorraine even complimented BK (MOM) on the logical way she resolved the issue. MOM returned the compliment by pointing out how Lorraine is such a great wife and mother and how lucky he is to have her. But I could tell by the tone of Lorraine's voice that she was getting a little suspicious, because MOM was smearing on the butter thicker than grandma's morning biscuits. So I signaled to her to dial the compliments back a bit and to end the phone call.

But all in all, MOM did a great job and Lorraine didn't have a clue that she wasn't talking to her husband or even a human being. Two months later, he convinced his firm to pay for a business trip to a computer security conference in Cleveland, Ohio knowing that he had no intention of attending. His flight was scheduled to depart at 9:35, but he was five hours away at his warehouse in the medical clinic allowing his medical units to place him in stasis.

While in stasis, MOM had full control of all aspects of his life. He just hoped that she doesn't go all "Terminator" on him. She electronically falsifies the airlines manifest by hacking into the airline's server and changing the passenger manifest and making it seem like he was on the flight. She hacked the hotel's server to check him into the hotel, used the company's credit card in a variety of restaurants and gift shops, and ensured that he was listed on the attendee's list of conference seminars and lectures. It's great that everyone uses computers for their day-to-day business. MOM also purchased some gifts from the hotel gift shop and had them mailed express to the warehouse, which he would present to his family and co-workers. She even downloaded all the seminar documents, so she could download the information into BK's brain while he was in stasis. He also decided to further test his brain enhancement method by instructing MOM to incorporate a foreign language of her choice into his brain in order for him to evaluate his ability to absorb and understand complicated languages. After a week in stasis, BK emerged from his stasis capsule with the complete knowledge and history of the Icelandic languages, customs and culture. He was pissed at MOM's choice of languages she decided to place in his head. Now, the reason that he speaks fluent Icelandic is because prior to being placed in stasis, he was extremely busy with some stabilizer problems that needed his full attention. He was supposed to research various languages throughout the world and choose the one that presented him with the most challenging linguistic complexity and would enable him to evaluate how wellt his technique works.

But because of his busy schedule, he mistakenly asked MOM to choose a language for him and gave her too wide a parameter to follow. He thought she would choose Mandarin, Russian or even Portuguese. MOM assured him that she did not pick the Icelandic language as a joke, but to gauge the ability of a human to absorb one of the world's most complexed languages.

But she deduced that in order to truly understand a language; you must also understand its' culture. Unfortunately, it was a complete success, because he could speak and understand fluent Icelandic and he has a in depth understanding of their culture, which wouldn't do him a damn bit of good living here in the United States. And once someone has the information programmed into their brain, it's permanent. MOM knows that he enjoys a good "Yo Mama joke", so she decides to test him and possiblely calm him down by telling him some jokes in his newly acquired Icelandic language.

[Translated to Icelandic] "Yo momma's so old, when Moses parted the Red Sea, she was on the other side fishing". He smiles, then tries to stop her from telling another one. "No", you filled my brain with the language and the history of Iceland and you think you can placate me with some jokes, he says with a bit of anger in his voice. But she ignores him and hits him with another one. "Yo mama so fat", she creates her own gravitational field". Oh, a science one, he says with a chuckle. That's not bad. He doesn't want to encourage her by laughing, but he loves "yo mama jokes", and humors her by asking her for one more. "Yo momma so fat, she gets group insurance!". That one really hit home, as he couldn't help but laugh. Alright MOM, I've had enough. But I have 123,345 more jokes to tell you, she replies. "No thank you"! That won't be necessary, he says loudly. He suddenly realizes that she's speaking in Icelandic and he's replying in Icelandic.

He realizes that his method of embedding knowledge into a person in stasis worked beyond his expectations. He doesn't agree with the language she chose as a beta language, but he's pleased with the results. He was also impressed with his medical units, which performed their assigned task flawlessly. He remembers being a little nauseous and weak for about twenty minutes after the procedure, but that was the extent of his physical problems. Mentally, his mind was sharp and focused. It only took him a couple of hours to get back to feeling like his normal self, but the experience of coming out of stasis has given him valuable insights on what his family will be going through.

You would think that his experience would give him a bit of comfort knowing how well his units performed putting him into stasis. But now that his family is at the other end of the warehouse having the procedure performed on them; he's feeling extremely apprehensive. His emotions are trying to persuade him to just drop everything he's doing and hurry down there and assist the units to make sure his family is safely prepared and placed into their capsules.

But he knows that if he doesn't get these remaining projects done, he will not finish some major updates and installations. This would increase the probability of the Federal Government locating him, which would guarantee that he would not see the outside of a prison cell, except for visitation days or rec day. And all his technology will be transported to Area 51 or some other secret facility to be torn apart and analyzed. It has been a very long morning and he can feel the strain and stress of all he has experienced weighing down on him, as he uses his right hand to massage the back of his neck. He then rubs his eyes and takes a deep breath.

Once he gets his family safely into stasis and completes one of his major projects, he thinks he'll get something to eat and maybe take a quick two hour nap. He clicks the space bar on his computer keyboard, which automatically turns on the monitor as he leans forward in his chair and gets ready to get some work done. He really doesn't want to be in his office tapping at the keyboard, but he knows that MOM is right and the sooner he finishs his remaining tasks, the sooner they can get out of this warehouse. There's a large picture window next to him, which gives him a great view to what's going on in the warehouse. He's sitting in front of two fairly large computer screens, which enables him to display lines and lines of computer code and design schematics. One screen displays the new diagnostic code he's writing for the engineering units and the other monitor is displaying a couple dozen emails that MOM couldn't respond to and required BK's immediate attention. Several of the emails are from his distribution partners complaining that they haven't received a shipment from him (DBC Engineering), which is the name of his bogus company. He instructed MOM, in his absence, to focus her attention on the ships completion and to disregard any request from his distribution partner or from anyone else for that matter.

He only has a short time left, so it doesn't matter if he doesn't forefill his obligations to the Local Government or the manufacturers. He tells her to emale letters of apology to anyone complaining and to blame the delays on unforeseen problems excavating some of the containers and some minor breakdowns in their equipment. DBC Engineering is a shell company that he created to generate some additional revenue so he could purchase additional materials and equipment he needed to finish the construction of the ship. Now that his ship is 10 to 15 hours away from being completed, he is no longer concerned about meeting anymore of his contractual obligations.

But he's worried about one of his clients sending someone by his warehouse to check on the status of the containers that was supposed to be delivered weeks ago. He knew it would happen sooner or later, but he was really hoping for the later. He should have known that the County, who owns the property, would be the first to threaten him, because of a couple of missed delivery dates.

Because they could only leave a voice mail, they contacted him through email stating that they would report him to the Federal authorities if they have not received their shipment of containers within the next four days. He doesn't know if the Federal Government, the Environmental Protection Agency (EPA) to be exact, would actually send anyone down to check on him, but they did give Florida a $475,000 grant for the removal of hazardous materials, which they paid him for his services and to his transportation partner. He has no doubt that the County would shoot an email to their Fraud Department with his name on it. Their email was three days ago. He knows from experience that the government will not call or notify him of their arrival, but will send their agents and a half dozen police officers to the warehouse with a warrant to search and audit his records, which are very bogus.

But he knows once they enter the warehouse that the humongous spacecraft will distract them from his fictitious records. He thinks it will be to his best interest to move into the spacecraft as soon as his family is in stasis and placed aboard the ship, just in case law-in-forcement comes beating down his door. The engineering unit's logic diagram upgrades is displayed on the other screen. His thoughts once again shifts to what the medical units should be doing to his family.

He tries to avert his eyes from the lower righthand corner of the monitor, because a time seems to move slower when it's being watched. He can't help but to glance at the time and sees that there's only an hour and fifteen minutes left to get his family prepped and get them in their stasis capsules before they regain consciousness. Worse case scenario, he can drug them again, but he doesn't honestly know what effect it would have on his youngest daughter, let alone the mental effect it would have on him. He can still remember each of their faces as the drug took effect - especially his wife.

She had such a look of disbelief on her face before she went under. He has absolutely no doubt that his wife is going to make him pay for what he has done once she comes out of stasis. He once again has to stop himself from daydreaming and lingering on his impending doom at the hands of his wife. He begins to type out the new updated code for his engineering units, which is written in the language he developed over two years ago. He had a vision of developing an artificial intelligence that would rival any computer on earth, but he quickly realized that the current computer languages wasn't advanced enough for what he had in mind. So he created is own language, which brought MOM into fluition. She may have been his greatest achievement, but she wasn't his first.

He first attempted to create a complete unit, both in intelligence and body, to help him with organizing and managing his projects. Like MOM does now. The unit he called Benny was named after his beloved brother and did surpass MOM in its' ability to be more human like. At the time, he thought Benny was his greatest accomplishment, because of its' ability to solve complex problems and tasks, hack into any Government or private network connected to the internet and his linguistic abilities were superior to MOM's because of his ability to fluently use contractions.

But BK made the mistake enabling Benny the ability to alter and develop his own personality, which at the time, he thought would be a good idea. While at the warehouse he allowed Benny to watch various TV shows in order to help him develop his own personality style. But Benny gravitated to shows like the Jeffersons, Laugh-In, and the HBO series Curb Your Enthusiasm. Gradually Benny's new personality took over and he started using expletives mixed into his conversations and he developed a propensity for doing things without asking BK's permission.

BK realized that he was just doing what his programming allowed him to do, but he like Benny regardless of his flaws. He just thought that one day he would have time to tweek Benny's programming to make him more compliant, but he hadn't found the time. One day, BK was in his office at work talking to Benny over the phone about the stasis of the ship's bridge equipment and Benny asked him if he was coming to the warehouse soon. BK explained to him that he has a ton of work to do and he made the mistake of telling Benny about how he would have to make some time to talk with LaChel's teacher about her recent after school detention. Benny decided to call the teacher and impersonate BK as a joke.

But his joke almost caused the teacher to file a restraining order against BK, because of the profanity and the sexual inuindos Benny was suggesting. After the principle called BK and Lorraine into his office, he convinced the teacher, principle and Lorraine that he didn't make the phone call and someone must have been inpersonating him, which he also told Lorraine. They believed him because Bryan and BK's secretary vouched that he was in a meeting at the time of the phone call, which was lucky for him. So, he had MOM deactivate Benny and store him in his bedroom closet, aboard the ship. He thinks once he's in orbit he'll have some time to re-evaluate Benny to determine what he'll have to change in his programming.

The other units are also built similar to Benny's technology but are programmed without a personality and perform their specific task. But every once in a while, their programming has to be upgraded in order to keep up with BK's hardware development. Right now, he has to give the Engineering or as he likes to call them, his "E" units an upgrade in order for them to complete the additional assignments, which would be too complicated for the units without the software enhancements. He thought he would be able to complete the remaining work once he gets into orbit, but he may have too much to do. He's pressed for time, so he thinks it would be best to just write new software and have MOM download the new algrorhithms into each of the "E" units. There are five of them and are labeled E1 through E5. "What's the e.t.a. on the completion of the ship's navigation controls update", he asked MOM while continuing to type code on his keyboard?

The navigation console will be completed at 1:00 a.m., MOM responds. Would you like the status reports on the other major projects in progress and estimated time of completion? I'm listening, he response as he scans through lines and lines of computer code. MOM starts with the projects that have been completed:

(1) I have located and accessed all major government's systems and satellite servers. (2) I have also uploaded our software into their communication and weapons control orbiting satellites. She also added the the United States, their allies and the other superpowers have no knowledge of their systems being compromised. (3) I have emailed the local and Federal Government formally asking for a three weeks extension on our product delivery, which I have no doubt will be soundly rejected, but it may buy us a couple more days. MOM has been monitoring their internal emails and have discovered a scheduled site visit by the Federal Commerce Agency. They plan on dropping by three days after our scheduled lift off, which of course is perfect. (4) And your command and control chair has been completed and installed on the command bridge.

"Yes", BK shouts loudly. He was feeling a little drowsy, until she gave him that bit of information. I am glad but curious that the installation of bridge furniture is filling you with such emotional gratification, MOM responds with fascination. He just doesn't want to launch the most advanced spacecraft in human history, while sitting in an ordinary office chair that's bolted to the deck. A week prior to him arriving at the warehouse, he was constantly bugging MOM on the status of his captain's chair. BK's problem is that he loves to watch science fiction shows and every single one of them had a captain that was sitting in a captain's chair, which can control the operation of the entire ship. He now has a slight smile on his face as he types on his computer and thinks about how nice it will be to finally sit in his own chair. He had only seen his bridge chair as a design on his computer screen. He gave MOM the responsibility to monitor its' construction and installation by the engineering and facility's units. Captain Kirk's bridge chair has always been first and forefront in his mind for the design model for his captain's chair. But he wanted the chair to be more modern and to be very ergonomic. He's going to spend a lot of time in that chair and he would want it to be so comfortable he could sleep in it, if necessary. As he thinks about the style of the armrest, his thoughts drifts back to his family. He asked MOM again on his family's status. But she hesitates with her answer for a couple of seconds. Your family has been dressed in their individual stasis suits and Lorraine is the first to be inserted into her capsule, which should be completed in one minute and forty-five seconds. LaChel will be the next to be inserted into her capsule.

And I would greatly appreciate it if you would concentrate on your remaining task and stop asking questions you already know. He understands that MOM doesn't have nerves or emotions, and could not possibly be annoyed by his continuous asking about his family status, but he understands that she is thinking about the amount of time being wasted and him not concentrating on the work at hand. One of MOM's many responsibilities is to ensure that BK stays on task and remains on schedule for each of his projects. He decides not to ask again, but he has one more request for her. If you get any indication that Lorraine or one of the girls are regaining consciousness; I need you to sedate her right away. "Especially my wife", he exclaims! Are we clear? I understand perfectly, she responds. Do you think we can have them in their stasis capsules within the next thirty minutes, he asked?

Your wife and daughters' brain waves are very minimal, and their heart rate indicates that they are still under the influence of the sedative. I estimate that we have approximately 83 minutes and seventeen seconds before your family regains consciousness. It eases his mind that they have ample time to get all three of them into their capsoles. Trying to keep BK on task, MOM ask him if he wants one of the facility units to bring him a cup a coffee. "No thank you", he replies. I'm wide awake and I've had enough coffee on the way here.

As BK again attempts to focus on his work, in the medical clinic the units in the stasis lab start to position equipment and components around his family who are now dressed in their stasis suits. Lorraine, LaChel and Kim are now laying on their padded status tables. Three panels open from the wall and three empty capsules emerge from the stasis container. They are at a 60 degree angled with about 6 inches of space between each of them. They move forward about four feet from the container opening, slide down at a 15 degree angle, and then all three open simultaneously. As units M1, M2 and M3 hover around the tables and diligently monitor Lorraine and the girl's vital signs, you could hear a series of low beeps, tones and whistles. These are the sounds of the units communicating with each other. Each unit has three fingers on each hand and their mechanical fingers rapidly travel across the capsule's digital keyboards, which are positioned above the capsule's display. The procedure that the units are performing could take BK about 15 minutes on each capsule, but they can perform the task in roughly three minutes. All three units move around the three capsules, each performing its' own designated task.

Unit M1 is tasked with linking each capsules' computer to the ship's main computer and running connectivity checks. Unit M2 configures each capsule to match the mass, age, and medical conditions of Lorraine and her daughters. It's scanning each metallic blue colored jumper with a device that looks like a slender cellphone. But in reality, the unit is testing and configuring the many micro-sensors embedded into the material of the jumpers. MOM is closely monitoring each unit and double checking their proficiency and completion time. After his family is safely secured in their capsules, MOM must transmit a report of the unit's overall performance to BK, so he can determine if they require any future modifications to their programming.

Meanwhile, back in the office, BK taps out the last few keystrokes of his latest code upgrades for his engineering units. This new programming is designed to store and organize yottabytes of data within the next six hours. This is possible, because of his design of the quantum threading processor built into the ship's main computer. MOM is independent of the ship's computer system, but she has the ability to monitor and manage every function of the ship. BK has caught up with his many task, but has missed the units dressing his family in their stasis suits. He knows that the units will follow his instructions to the letter, but he can't help but worry, even though he has no reason to worry. The suits are as important as an astronaut's suit is to him or her in space. The stasis suit will not only protect his family's bodies from the frigid temperatures of a special formulated type of hydrogen gas, which will keep their bodies in a cryogenic state. The suits enable the units the ability to continuously monitor their vitals without having to remove them from their stasis capsules. He sighs as he closes the application on his monitor and pushes himself away from his desk. He leans back, stretches his legs out and stares at the light and the plain white ceiling. He has finally completed the last of his task and now can monitor the installation of his family into the capsules. He has a few more minor tasks to do, but they can be done outside his office, so he grabs a tablet off the lab table and proceeds out the door.

As he walks down the hall, he gives his tablet a couple of swipes and some taps, which brings up his family's real time vital signs and displays the time remaining for each of them. This is an indicator that they are in their suits and the suits are working as designed.

The size and age of his wife and daughters has been carefully calculated into the method of human life suspension. He taps and swipes to display Kim's vitals, which may be the most problematic of the three. He has run various scenarios on a computer simulation program of Kim being placed into stasis and her being awakened. And in most of the scenarios, she developed some type of problem, which varied from minor breathing problems to a life-threatening situation. In one scenario, Kim's brain began to swell as a result of her body temperature rising too quickly. Even though he realized that these are just simulations and has a slim chance of happening, it scares him that Kim could possibly die, because of his actions.

He started to obsess over the data of the simulations and began to second guess himself. But he finally realized that no matter what he does to minimize the risk to his family; these types of trail blazing procedures will be dangerous and there may be nothing he can do to prevent the unknown from happening. He also realized the cold hard fact that once he downloads this technology to the world, people most likely will died trying to follow his example. And that may also include Lorraine and his girls. He turns to walk into the clinic, but he's shaken to his core by the sight of his daughters totally dressed in their stasis suits, which causes his legs to buckle a bit. He doesn't quite make the turn into the doorway of the medical clinic as he hits his shoulder on the door jamb, which causes him to lose his grip on his tablet and it flips to the floor.

It slams face down and slides across the floor and into the room. The cracked and shattered tablet stops at what would be M2's feet, if it had feet. He grabs his head with both hands and yells, "damn it", as he continues to stand in the doorway and then looks down at the tablet. He heard the unmistakeable crunch of the screen being destroyed by the floor, but he could care less about the tablet. He could repair that one in about an hour. He didn't realize that the reality of seeing his family in their suits would hit him so hard. He leans against the door jamb as he looks up at the ceiling for a minute trying to focus his thoughts. The pressure of the ship completion and his family stasis installation is getting to him, but this is not the time to have a mental breakdown. Without his knowledge or permission, MOM evaluates his blood pressure, heart rate and his brain waves. She has already scanned him when he arrived at the warehouse, which indicated that he was in a fateged state and should have at lease took a four hour nap before completing his remaining task. But she did the math and knew that wasn't a fight she was going to win. She deduced that he wouldn't be able to sleep knowing his family was being installed in their capsoles.

If his blood pressure increases anymore, she will have to insist that he discontinue working for the rest of the day. MOM has the ability to monitor his mental and physical health until his wife is capable of preforming her duties as the ship's physician, which most likely may cause his death once his wife has realized what he's done to her. The sight of his family lying on those tables in what most people would say is akin to shrink wrap, looks so surreal. Unit M2 reaches down and picks up the shattered pad, which now looks like someone slammed it against the floor. The unit stares at the tablet for a second in fascination, then hands it to him. He takes the tablet and responds with a sigh and a "thank you", as he walks into the stasis room.

He imagined this moment of seeing his family dressed in their stasis suits lying prone on the prep table side by side, but reality, of course, is a hell of a blow to the face. Good morning BK, unit M1 response as he walks past it and over to his wife. He's fully focused on Lorraine and doesn't respond back. He just looks down at her and lovingly places his hand the top of her head and softly strokes her hair. As he stares down at her, he leans over and gives her a gentle kiss on the forehead. Your family will be installed in their capsules in twenty minutes, unit M1 states as it hovers over to the stasis capsules. She still looks so beautiful, he says to himself as he gazes down at her.

He caresses her hair, which is totally covered by her bluish suit. Her head is resting on a memory foam type small pillow, which is embedded with various innovative electronic components that will transmit information directly into Lorraine and the girls' hippocampus. These components control and regulates the transmission of information to the brain. This is the same process he developed to enhance his knowledge while in stasis. Her face is the last part of her body that is exposed. But before she is placed in her capsule, her face will be covered by a clear mask that has been molded to the contours of her facial features. The mask will protect their skin from the gases that will be pumped into the capsules. He could have designed the suit that would completely cover and conceal them from head to toe, but he wanted to look into the stasis chamber ever once in a while to see their faces.

He reaches over to the table next to her and grabs her mask, which is lying beside both LaChel and Kim's mask. He places the mask on her face, then lifts the edges of the suit around her face and maneuvers the edge of the mask under the edges of the hood. He then takes a device that looks like a small thin flashlight with a blue laser light on its' tip and follows the edges of the mask and hood, which adhere them together. He then grabs the other two masks, walks to the other tables where his daughters have been fully dressed in their suits and repeat the same procedure.

Unit M3 hovers over to Lorraine first and connects a temporary oxygen container, which will slightly inflate the suit and will enable M3 to check for leaks. Unit M2 presses several buttons on the console of the capsule, which enables it to rotate parallel to the floor. As the units prepare to lift and place LaChel in her capsule, BK abruptly stops them. I'll put them in their capsules myself", he says in a stearn tone. He then instructs the units to monitor their vitals and to continue programming the capsules. He walks over to LaChel, then gently lifts her and the memory foam mattress from the table and walks over to her capsule and lowers her into it. He carefully places her in her capsule, adjust the mattress pad, which fits the contour of the capsule then places her arms at her side. He removes the oxygen container and connects her to the capsules' oxygen supply. She won't need oxygen while in stasis, but until the process is complete, her body will need oxygen just like if she were sleeping. He looks down at her and gives her a kiss on the forehead, or should I say, the mask covering her forehead. "See you soon", little girl he says in a loving voice. His fingers quickly presses various numeric buttons on the keyboard at the top of her capsule, which causes its' cover to slowly close and seals air tight. He then places Lorraine and Kim into their capsules, kisses them both, says a few words to both of them then seals them both in their capsules. Unit M2 moves and positions the capsules into the stasis container. The unit places the capsules into the stasis container as far as they can go, which leaves a quarter of the capsules extending outside of it. The capsules are aligned next to each other about six inches apart and are attached to a lifting mechanism, which is connected to the back of the wall of the container. He stands at the bottom end of the capsules and watches unit M1 key in five numbers in the key pad on the lefthand side of the stasis wall. His stomach is in knots at this point and he looks like a father waiting for the birth of his child.

All three capsules begin to slowly move into the stasis container then begin to slide up the back wall until all three are completely into the container and positioned at a 68 degree angle. He moves as close as he can to the opening of the stasis room. Unit M1 then presses four additional numbers, which activates three metal hoses for each capsule to connect to the capsules. Five seconds later, he can hear a hissing noise as a light bluish gas begins to fill each of the capsules. As the bluish mist begins to conceal their faces, a tidal wave of despair rushes over him and fills him with regret. The capsule's view port starts to frost over and their lips begin to turn a powder blue. The temperature display on the top of the capsule, slowly begins to decrease: 66 degrees, 64 degrees, 63 degree. Their heart rates and blood pressure are also beginning to decrease.

After the completion of the process, each of their body temperatures will be brought down to minus 150 degrees Celsius and their vitals will be almost undetectable. After the capsules are completely filled with the stasis gas, the medical units will transport and store the capsules aboard the ship's medical clinic, which in the near future will be Lorraine's office and responsibility. He can hear the door of the stasis container begin to close. That means that the process is starting its' last phase, which could take another 10 to 15 minutes to complete, so the door will be closed for the remainder of the process. He watches as the door slides down and seals shut. Since this is just a preparation area, there is no porthole in the door for him to view his family.

Its' impossible for him to have prepared himself for seeing his family frozen in those tubes like three popsickles. As his emotions attempts to force its way to the surface, BK stomps it down likes someone stomping down leaves in an over filled trash bag. His family is now encapsulated in the transfer container for their cryogenic sleep. He leans against the white door with his arms and forehead. He places his forehead against the door of the container and tightly closes his eyes. He's never been a very religious man, but once again he feels compelled to say a prayer for them.

He doesn't say anything out loud, but just reflects on what he has done and asked God to forgive him for what he has done to his family. Both inside the capsules and outside his ship. He remains leaning against the container for about three minutes in silence before finally pushing himself away. As he steps back away from the door, MOM asks him if he is alright. "No", he replies. "But I'll manage", he says as he walks away. He has to get himself together, because he still has some work to do inside and outside of the ship. The warehouse and its' property is being visited by more and more people. Some are just curious people walking through the woods and others, he believes, are employees of the County visually surveying the property before they take pocession of it.

BK was willing to pay well over the appraisal price for the property, but for reasons not known to him at the time; the County would only lease the property to him for three years, which they calculated would be the time frame required for someone to remove and transfer all the hazardous containers. The County purchased the property from a hazardous distribution company called TYME-HAZ Transport, which was owned by a middle age divorced woman named Alexia Oliver-Williams, who inherited the company from an uncle five years ago. She quickly made it the major hub for transporting and distribution of a variety of toxic containers throughout the mid Florida region. The company was very successful at its' peak, and was valued at over three million dollars and had plans to expand to the southern regions of Florida. But as success increase, so did Ms. Oliver-Williams greed. She made the decision to increase her revenue by cutting quality and safety, which did optimize her profits. In other words, she decided to cut back on the transporting of the containers by just burying most of them on the warehouse property. The owner of the company and several of her employees are now awaiting trial for the improper disposal of over two hundred hazardous and toxic five gallon containers throughout the twelve-acre property. BK saw a news report on the owner and how the government was confiscating her finances and numerous properties.

He approached the County with an arrangement to excavate the containers and transfer them to a local hazardous material facility. The County would only agree to lease the building and its' property and to allow him to use the warehouse for inspections, sealing and distribution of the containers. He would have to submit a monthly progress report to the County and the local Environmental Protection Agency on the status of the materials removal. BK just gave them the impression that he wants the opportunity to purchase the property after the least is over or extend the lease for another four years. But the County has no intention of selling the property to him or to even extend his lease for any amount of time. Once all of the containers have been removed, the County has already developed hardcopy plans to demolish the warehouse and transform the property into his new conventions center, which will bear the Mayor's name.

The Mayor has decided that eight years is enough and isn't planning to run again and like the Mayors before him, would like something to serve as his monument. The County agreed to pay BK's expenses for the excavation, processing and transferring of the hazardous materials, in addition to any unforeseen expenses. He would only make a small profit digging up and transporting all those containers. He really wanted the massive warehouse, isolated property and most of the chemicals in those buried containers.

He has developed a method of changing any chemical at the atomic level to a different element. This is similar to the method he shared with the Government to convert radioactive materials back to its' inert state. He has a list of all the different chemicals stored in the containers throughout the property. Fracking solutions, radioactive heavy water and coal ash, just to name a few. Normally these chemicals should be stored or buried in a designated disposal area, chosen by the Federal Government. BK has successfully changed the chemical's molecular makeup to develop a new element to use as a protective membrane for his ship. Thanks to his facilities' units, it only took one and a half years to dig up all the containers on the property. They would have completed it sooner, but they could only work after mid night. Just like the previous owner, BK will have to falsify documents to the County, EPA and his partner who owns' the designated disposal facility. The County also required him to submit a monthly report on his progress and schedule a site visit by a County zoning personnel to verify the removal of the containers. After agreeing to the terms and signing the leasing documents, the County gave him a diagram of the locations of all the containers on the property. Luckily for the County and BK, the previous facility's manager kept meticulous records of the precise location of the containers they buried.

The County will use this diagram to monitor his progress. He doesn't care about the monthly report, because MOM ensured him that the County and transfer warehouse databases would reflect the bogus container transfers. He schedules the County's personnel to visit the warehouse on the weekends in order not to interfere with the workers progress. No one would be at the warehouse and all the doors will be locked to ensure no one could enter the facility. He had his maintenance units place the excavated and empty containers outside at the rear of the building. There would normally be three to four pallets of dirt encrusted containers stacked three high and four deep, displayed for the County's inspector. But he doesn't want the County discovering how fast he's completing the removal of the containers, so after the containers are dug up and the chemicals removed, he has the units fill the containers with dirt and place them back in the same location. If his units remove fifty containers, he would have the units rebury twenty or so dirt fill containers.

This would fool the County's inspector, who uses a metal detector to audit and verify the removal process. BK has almost completed the removal of all the containers, but by the inspector's report would only indicate that he has a significant number of them left to excavate.

This has prompted the County to send him some threatening emails regarding the slow removal progress and the importance of meeting the agreed deadlines. Their emails doesn't worry him, because he'll just increase the number of pallets of containers displayed. After the inspector's next visit, his report will state that he is eighty percent complete and should be able to meet his deadline. Even though he was actually far ahead of his scheduled timeframe for the removal of the containers, he realized that the remaining unconverted materials would not be enough to convert to the protective membrane needed to cover his ship. So he made the decision to purchase and deliver sixteen gallons of paints, and roofing tar from the local home improvement store.

But back in the present, he still has work to complete before he's ready for lift-off. He grabs another tablet from Lorraine's desk as he walks out into the hanger were the exterior of the ship is mostly completed, but it still has to go through various hull testing and inspections, which will take another nine hours.

There are four structural units and six subunits tasked with the completion of the ship's external components and protective membrane. With a few swipes of the keyboard, he changes Lorraine's tablet into an engineering tablet. He then connected it to the ship's exterior components, so he can test and run various simulations as if he's in his captain's chair or sitting in his office. He walks in toward the lowest part of the ships, beside the starboard (leftside) superstructure of the ship as he glides his fingertips along the ship's incredibly smooth honeycombed surface. The material that covers the ship is seamless and has the look of black glass. This material can reflect or scatter light, absorb heat hot enough to melt titanium.

But its' most remarkable characteristic is its' artificial cells, which has the ability to totally repel all known types of radiation. When completely covered, his ship will be impervious to any weapon that any government has in their arsenal. He is undecided if or when he will share the chemical makeup of this protective material. He doesn't know if he wants everyone to have impervious ships at their disposal. For now, he thinks he'll download the water down version of the material. Just like KFC, he doesn't want to share his original recipe.

He continues to walk along the side of the ship continuously touching and visually inspecting the ship for any imperfections. He starts to smile and nod his head yes as he continues to feel the smooth texture of his ship's surface. He drops down to one knee to inspect one of the camera ports when his attention is drawn to the opening of the double doors of the warehouse medical bay swinging open. All three medical units, two in the front and one unit pushing the hovering container from the rear, maneuvers the stasis container into the warehouse and toward the ship. This large white rectangular container, which now has his family encapsulated in it has his full attention. He's drawn toward the units pushing and guiding the container, but MOM once again, reminds him about his limited timeframe. She doesn't want him to stray from his scheduled task, which is to complete the inspection. "Now that your family is in the stasis container, I think you would agree that the units you built can perform the simple duties of a moving man. Unless you think your pushing, pulling and maneuvering is far superior to theirs, she exclaimes.

"Very funny", he says as he stops and watches the units guide the container toward the ship. As the units and container gets closer to the ship; a hatch, which looks like a large black door opening, slowly slides up from the lower side of the ship and the light from the interior of the ship starts to illuminate the units as the light moves up the front of the two units and the container. As the sliding door reaches its' halfway point, a ramp starts to emerge from the bottom of the opening hatch and extends towards the warehouse concrete floor. Once the ramp is fully extended, the container, escorted by the units, moves up the ramp and into the light of the open hatch.

"Leave the hatch open", MOM. It won't take me too much longer to complete my inspections. She replies with a simple, "Yes". Meanwhile, the units enters the ship, maneuvers down various corridors, and then enters the medical facility, where his family will remain there until their scheduled time for removal from stasis. It took him another twenty minutes to complete the ship's exterior inspection and now he walks up the ramp and into the ship. As he walks down the corridors, he notices the color of the walls, which looks darker than what he instructed the facilities units to program them. MOM, are the color of the corridors' walls "Bridgwater", he asked while stopping and giving the walls a hard look. She doesn't want to get him started with fixating on the wall color, because she remembers how long it took him to decide on the color of his bedrooms. So she again replies with a simple, "Yes".

It looks alittle like "Sistine Blue", as he steps back and continues to evaluate the wall color. At this point, he knows he can't worry about the color of the walls, so he continues on down the corridor. He makes a quick left and then a right toward engineering, but he passes the corridor where he and his family will live for the foreseeable future. He stops suddenly and pauses for a moment of indecision and tries to convince himself to continue on towards engineering. But he happens to notice that he has been so busy that he hadn't changed his clothes he drove in this morning. He wanted to look around his living quarters anyway, so he heads there. As he arrives at the front door, he presses a diamond shaped panel the size of a silver dollar, which opens the sliding door to his quarters. As the door slides open, it makes a swish sound, which sounds like the doors on Star Trek. He thought it would be great to hear that everytime a door opens or closes. Of course, the swishing sound of the doors opening and closing will get on Lorraines nerves, but he'll have to cross that bridge once she's out of stasis.

He walks into their living room, which he made every attempt to resemble his living room and dining room on earth. The walls are a honey cream color, which was a color that Lorraine had planned to repaint the living room once he had the time. But the walls throughout the ship are not ordinary walls. Their color can be changed on demand as well as being able to convert the entire wall to a media wall or viewport. The walls in the bedrooms are bare, but are colored a light sky blue, which is the same color as the girl's bedroom on earth. He thinks that the familiarity may help their transition process.

He walks over to the left side of the living room and presses the entry button to open LaChel's bedroom door and walks in. Unfortunately for his girls, their bedrooms are smaller than their rooms on earth. But the rooms are a decent 8 feet by 10 feet and has the normal furnishings that most kids their ages are use too. Each room is equipped with an intercom system, and a wall that can be converted to an intertainment center with the most advanced internet connection or even a viewport for looking down at the planet.

He walks over to the bed and runs his hand across the soft powder blue sheets, smoothing out the wrinkles. The twin size bed is against the wall and the dresser is to the right of the head board. He didn't want to cram the room with furniture, so it just has the essentials. He then walks over to what he has no doubt will be the most disappointing part of her room. He presses the button to the siding door of her reach-in closet. It has very little clothes and only three pairs of shoes, which are designed for work and safety. He closes the door and looks around the room with an unsatisfied look on his face. He has changed the color of the walls half a dozen times and he's still not sure that LaChel will be happy with his choice. But he knows that she will be extremely happy with her ability to contact anyone on earth using the ship's communication system. He understands that it will be hard on her being abruptly snatched away from her friends, so he thinks it would be a good idea to let her talk with them after about a month or two, once they are adjusted to their new environment. Under the strict supervision of MOM, of course.

But he still has reservations about LaChel being able to talk to her "Pretty Ricky" looking boyfriend, which LaChel hates to hear her dad call him. She doesn't mind him calling him pretty, but she can hear the disdain in his voice. He walks out of the room, still looking back and forth at the walls. He walks into the hall and steps into the doorway of Kim's room.

Months before bringing his family to the warehouse, he installed a surveillance system throughout the home in order to monitor what LaChel and Kim were doing on their cellphones and on the internet. He instructed MOM to give him a daily report, which he would pass on to Lorraine so they could strategize what to do and take the appropriate actions, if necessary.

At first, Lorraine wasn't too happy with him intruding on the girls' privacy, but after remembering that one of her friend's 17year-old daughter is one month pregnant. She thinks about how her 16 year old daughter has a serious boyfriend and like most teen girls think they know everything, which in Lorraine's mind is a recipe for a baby. That really alters her way of thinking regarding her girls' privacy. Lorraine didn't know exactly how he got all the information on the girls. She thought he'd bought some kind of computer monitoring and virus protection software.

The girls were always dumbfounded that their parents seem to always know what they were up to. LaChel was especially irritated with her mother somehow popping up at her and her boyfriend's secret makeout spot that they arrange after school. But now that his family is on the ship; the security measures had to be elevated to another level. MOM will be ensuring that the entire family maintains a strict level of security that will ensure that no one uploads or downloads compromising information, which could put them all in jeopardy. He continues to look around LaChel's room ensuring that the item he brought from home have been brought aboard. Satisfied, he walks out of LaChel's room and into Kim's room.

The only thing that is wrong is that he doesn't like the color of Kim's walls. He remembers Kim telling her mom that she wanted to paint her room a different color, but he can't remember what color she wanted to change it to.

MOM, I need you to change the color of the walls in Kim's room to a very pale forest green. I think she would like that color more than this sky blue. "No", LaChel loves curmet the frog green like her grandmother. Kim's favorite color is red, but I don't suggest we change the wall color to a blood red. It is not conducive to a productive atmosphere or calming state of mind, MOM comments. "I agree", but what do you think she'd like, he replies? My suggestion is to allow the girls the opportunity to pick the color or colors of their rooms. This will allow them to express their diverse personality and give them a sense of ownership.

"Wall colors", he says with a sigh as he rubs his hand across his head in frustration. Alright, I'm kind of tired of thinking of wall colors anyway. I just think it would be better for their self-esteem to manage their own room color, which in turn will give them a since of ownership, she adds. He walks out of the room and stands in the hallway between both rooms for a moment thinking about her suggestion. "You are probably right", MOM. It's going to be hard enough for them being separated from their friends, so if a simple decision of letting them pick the color of their rooms will help them adjust to their new reality, then that's what I'll do.

How did you get so attuned to the psychology of the adolescent mind, he asked? You incorporated a psychology algorithm into my matrix, and I can upload and access various child development books and articles by various child psychologists. Well, I think you're right, so I'll just choose a temporary color for each room. Change the wall colors to my bedroom to eggshell white for now, so Lorraine has the opportunity to select the colors for our bedroom as well as the rest of the living quarters. I think that would be a wise decision, she replies. He begins to walk back into the living room as he ask her to change the color of the walls to a light powder blue and to change the kitchen and dining area to Lorraine's favorite shade of yellow, which he hates. His kitchen on earth is a god-awful shade of yellow, he says to MOM. "Happy wife equals happy life", he mumbles to himself. She reminds him that he now has 25 minutes to complete the propulsion inspection if he wants to stay on schedule. Thanks, but I don't need a time check, he says as he stands staring into the kitchen.

I am well aware of my deadlines and schedules, because I'm the person who scheduled them, he says in a stern tone. But in all honesty, he did forget about the propulsion inspection, but just like a wife; he doesn't want to give her the satisfaction. Walking around his quarters gives him a sence of calm and helps him deal with his feelings of isolation. Right now, this is the closest he's going to get to being with his family. He imagines himself at home on earth and his wife and daughters are out shopping or at one of the girls' practices, which he now wishes he was able to come to more often. Regardless of the calmness that his quarters gives him, he knows that his time is slowly ticking away. He walks around the kitchen and looks around a bit, opening cabinets, and looking at the sparse food in the refrigerator. He's satisfied enough with the family's quarters, so he decides to get down to engineering. MOM is always trying to read his body language and his facial inflections to gauge his emotional state. So, you do not want me to remind you of any deadline or your daily scheduling, she asked? If he didn't know better, he would swear he hurt her nonexistent feelings.

He doesn't answer her question but leaves the kitchen and walks toward the door to exit his quarters. He leaves his quarters, makes a right at the first intersecting corridor then turns the last corner and opens the door to the engine room. He notices that MOM's questions are starting to resemble Lorraine's style of questioning. She knows the answer, but she just wants to hear him say it. That's the price he has to pay for programming MOM's personality in the female gender and maybe even some of Lorraine's characteristics. All the women in his life are smart and capable, so it only made sense to him to incorporate that trait into his second artificial creation's programming. So he knew it will be best to answer her question. "No MOM", I do appreciate you ensuring that I stay on schedule, but sometimes you can act like you're my second wife. He walks over to a small office area, where he sits down in front of the computer to review and confirm the ship's propulsion system schematics. I am trying to wrap my circuitry around being compared to a second wife and what that entails, but that statement does not make any sense to me. He really doesn't want to explain to her how hard it was for him to leave his quarters or what his last statement meant.

He hits a couple of keyboard strokes and a portion of the wall changes into a 32 inch monitor, which displays the ship's propulsion schematic. MOM, I have to concentrate on this right now, so do me a favor and don't worry about my last statement. Just continue to remind me about my schedules and I will tell you if you're being too anal or not. "Anal", she repeats in a curious tone. He just shakes his head and continues to work. MOM doesn't say a word after that, because his body language and facial expression indicates that he's becoming irritated. Besides, she understands what the word, "anal" means, even though she doesn't agree with his choice of words. Just like a real woman, she decides to store it away in her database for another time. He reviews and makes slight modifications to the ship's plasma injection design, which takes him about twelve minutes. He has completed this task with ten minutes to spare, so he decides to walk down to the hydroponics bay to look over the carbon dioxide absorption and oxygen output reports.

As he exits engineering, he instructs unit E3 to make the modifications to the starboard injection system. The unit downloads BK's latest schematics and programming changes. It acknowledges his instructions and proceeds to the starboard propulsion area.

As he walks down the passageway, he asked MOM to formulate a report on the psychological makeup of the President, Vice President, Secretary of Defense, and the Joint Chiefs of Staff. How in depth would you like this report, she asked. I would like it brief but thorough, because I don't have a lot of time. Your report will be very useful when the family and I have to have that meeting with the President. I will start analyzing their email traffic and recording their meetings.

Can you give me some parameters to follow, she asked? I don't think I need any personal information unless its' relevant to their work at the White House. Just review all their emails coming in and out of the White House pertaining to me and this ship. He's trying to determine if the Government perceives him as a threat, because if they do, they won't hesitate to try to blow him and his family out of orbit. MOM will infiltrate every server connected to the White House and review thousands of electronic documents. They won't have a clue that MOM is dumpster diving through all of their databases and directories. I will have the report completed in precisely four hours and 14 minutes. Good! BK walks toward what he likes to call, "The Park". He turns a couple of corners and opens a door that leads to a flight of stairs. He walks up the stairs to a landing and opens the door to "The Park". As he opens the door, a constant strong downward gust of air shoots down onto his head and shoulders. The air is used as a curtain to keep the various insects from escaping from the room while the door is open.

After the door is closed and the air automatically shuts off, he can smell the strong scent of the flowers and grass, which hits him all at once. There is a two-person decorated metal and wooden bench on both sides of the door.

He placed these benches there to ensure that his family entering the Park will have somewhere to sit while removing their shoes and socks. He sits down on the bench to his right and removes his shoes, removes his socks and places them into his shoes then slides them under the bench. He then stands and proceeds to walk into the Park. The 50 foot by 60 foot bay is designed as a natural carbon dioxide scrubber and a means of testing the air for proper oxygen and nitrogen mixture. This room is designed as the lungs of the ship as all the ship's air is filtered through this Park.

The Park contains various insects, flowers, vegetables, small shrubbery, and a small pond with various fish. But he really built this park with Kim in mind. She loves to run around the park with no shoes on and wade in its' pond. BK and Kim spent many a day sitting on the dock talking about sci-fi shows with their feet dangling and splashing in the water. He didn't want to give that up, so he designed this park to bring a little bit of earth to his ship. He was thinking about including a couple of rabbits, some squirrels and may be even a few birds, but he knew Lorraine would be terrified to step in here with all those animals running and flying around. This place is almost as relaxing as the parks on earth, he thinks to himself. From the right side of the pond, a unit with a green letter "P" for "Park" on its' torso approaches him with a garden trowel in its' mechanical hand. "May I help you, BK", it politely asked in its' mechanical voice. "Yes". Tell me the status of the bee colony and the honey production. The unit proceeds to tell him that the colony had become too large and an additional colony has formed on the northwest area of the park, as it points to the area of the newly constructed hive, which has been formed on the branch of a small tree. "Damn", he says out loud. I don't mind the extra honey, but I don't know if we have enough flora in the park for another colony. How much honey have you harvested from the hives. The unit pause for a moment, then response. I have harvested fifteen liters of honey from the original hive, but the second hive is only four weeks old and consequently not able to produce any extra honey for harvesting.

The second colony only has enough honey to sustain themselves, the unit adds. He looks at the garden trowel in the units hand. What were you doing before I entered the park? I was analyzing the PH balance in the soil from various locations in the park. BK tells the unit to continue with its' work. The unit quickly hovers back over near the pond where it has a portable piece of equipment, which it was using to test and record the results of its' analysis. He only felt it necessary to designate one unit to be the caretaker for this park.

He walks over to the pond that is surrounded by colorful shrubs and a 3 foot wide stone and dirt pathway surrounds it. He can tell that the sprinkler system as come on earlier by the glistening of the moisture on the grass. He can even smell the wet grass, which he has always loved.

MOM, turn the dome on please, as he looks up at the slightly curved 10 foot ceiling. The entire ceiling within the bay gradually transitions from a metallic gray to a material similar to clear glass. He can now see the metal open web roof joist of the warehouse and a one of his facility's units hovering across the ship. He smiles as he imagines how this will look once he's orbiting in space. But he can't wait for that experience, so he asks her to change the clear material and display a starry night's sky. She does it without responding. It's as if the ship has been transported into space. His smile is like a kid seeing a Ferris wheel for the first time. "It's amazing", he says out loud. This is the first time he has seen the dome activated.

The realistic display of the sky and the beauty of the pond draws him closer to the water's edge. He walks as close to the edge of the pond as he can, bends down and reaches his hands into the water to try to gauge it's temperature. "67 degrees", he guesses as he waves his fingers through the water. The tilapia thinks it's feeding time, so about two dozen of them start to rush toward his hand. He thinks to himself that it will be hard explaining to Kim that these fish aren't pets, but food. He has to convince her that these fish are no different than the fruit and vegetables in this Park. Right now, he has enough food in storage to feed his family for at least six months, so he has awhile before he has to have that tough talk that most farmers have to have with their kids. But the fish was his backup plan just in case they had to stay in orbit past his planned time frame. He stands up and continues looking down at the fish swirling and gathering in the water in front of him. MOM! How many boxes of fish do I have in storage?

"45 boxes", she replies. He knows that Lorraine loves to eat fish for dinner, because she serves it for dinner at least twice a week. So that's why he made sure the storeroom has boxes of catfish, tilapia, whiting and salmon. "So, I guess these fish are safe for a while", he thinks to himself. Just then a jet of fish pellets shoots out from a nearby pvc pipe that protrudes from a wall near the pond. Hearing the pellets hitting the water like rain drops, the fish dash away from BK and heads toward the sound as the water begins to boil with hungry mouths.

The pond erupts as dozens of fish swirl and dash over each other for a mouthful of their food. He could stand there watching them for hours, but he has some work to do in the corner of the park where he built a small lab. As he walks over toward the lab, he realizes that the fish population is getting a little thick and the time he'll have to think about harvesting and processing a dozen or two of them. He looks up again at the starry sky display before asking MOM to return the dome to normal.

He enters the lab and walks over to the far wall, which has six large tubes with blue-green algae swirling in them. The algae is another one of his methods of scrubbing the air circulating through the ship. He walks pass each container and visually inspects them for color and volume of algae. There isn't any problems he can see, so he walks over to the desk on the other side of the room. He sits down at the desk and turns on the computer. He quickly brings up the program that analyzes the gases in the tubes. The program generates a report that also includes the amount of oxygen generation, and carbon dioxide conversion. He will look over the numbers sometime tonight. He normally reviews his reports while eating dinner, which helps him block out the fact that he's eating dinner alone. He leans back in the chair and takes a deep breath. He closes his eyes and thinks of himself just laying in the park listening to the dogs barking, birds singing in the trees, and kids running around like little maniacs.

It really doesn't do him any good thinking about the good times him and his family spent together. That part of their lives are over for now and he must continue to think positive. Sometimes, MOM wishes she had arms, not to hug him, but to slap him cross the back of his head to wake him from his daydreaming, but all she can do is raise the volume of her voice. "Snap out of it", MOM broadcast loudly! "What", BK says as he opens his eyes and sits up in his chair. "You have approximately fourty-five minutes of work waiting for you on the bridge, she reminds him. He stands up and pushes the chair back behind him.

"I was just getting ready to leave", he says sarcastically. He leans over the keyboard and taps various keystrokes, which will start the computer timer. He doesn't need to be there to have the computer complete a second ship environmental analysis. He hits the enter key to start the timer then walks out of the lab and heads back to the bench to put back on his shoes and socks. He gets them on and is about to leave the Park, but he stops in front of the door and thinks back to the unit rushing over to him when he entered the Park. "Unit P", he yells as it echos through the Park! The unit swiftly hovers across the grass and stone path and hovers in front of him. "What can I do for you", it asked?

I want you to decrease your velocity of approach when someone enters the Park. I think the swiftnesss of your approach can be startling and misconstrued as threatening, if someone isn't expecting to see you. The unit just looks up at him with its' large blue eyes then says, "Yes BK". BK then turns and walks out of the Park and down the stairs. As he walks down the hall, he thinks it would be in his best interest to thank MOM for reminding him about the work on the bridge she had to complete.

"I want to make sure you have all your task complete by 6:00 p.m.", she replies. You have been working too many long hours, which I know will be a detriment to your overall health. He doesn't acknowledge her assessment but continues to proceed down the hall toward the door. He enters the ship's bridge and immediately starts to walk around to each station, pressing various keypads to ensure that each station and panels are operational, as he continues to talk to MOM.

What is the status of the viewing screen, he asked hoping it was close to being operational? The bridge main viewing screen has been operational for the last twenty-one minutes, she replies. It would have been nice if you would have given me an update today, he says as he stands there looking at the large metallic area where the screen appears. I calculated the amount of task listed on your schedule and I decided that if I informed you that the bridge view screen is operational; you would have dropped everything to play with your new toy, which would have you further behind. He is irritated by her thinking he wouldn't be able to control his enthusiasm like some little kid. He is a little upset but wants to remain calm. In the future, I want to be made aware of all completed projects on my priority list, he reminds her. Are we clear, he asked sternly?

"Clear as rain", she replies in a country accent. Where did you get that one from? It's one of my two thousand and thirty-four new accents I am including in my responses. Very good, but don't go overboard with them. MOM doesn't reply for a few seconds. "Understood"! Good, now activate the main view screen please, so I can test out my latest toy, he says in a sarcastic tone. Showing that MOM was correct, he gleefully walks toward his new chair and viewscreen. I guess my captain's chair is operational too, he asked. "That is affirmative", she replies. He walks down a short incline that separates the bridge's operations section from the tactical sections of the bridge. He sits down in his leather and metallic captain's chair, which looks similar to a lounge chair with an array touch screen panels on both armrest. MOM is studying BK's body language and facial expressions.

She can clearly see that he approves of his chair and viewscreen, which she can tell by his elevated blood pressure and his brain activities. "Anytime now", he shouts for MOM to turn on the main viewscreen! She replies with a simple but emphatic, "no". "What do you mean, no", he shouts? Please turn the screen on, he repeats. She pauses for a moment then replies. You designed the chair, we built the chair, so use the chair, she replies. He totally forgot that he programmed that feature into the control panels of the armrest.

Would it have hurt you to just activate the viewscreen, he asked? No it would not, because I don't feel pain and I already know how to activate the main viewscreen – you do not. He felt like calling her a smart-ass, but he knows that will start another ridiculous conversation.

Alright, he says as he tries to remember what combination of panel buttons activates the screen. It's been a while since we went over this, so just give me a moment, he says to her. He looks at the wall directly in front of him to see if anything is happening while he presses and swipes the icons on the panel on the armrest. "Nothings happening", he thinks to himself. After about forty-five seconds of sliding his finger across the panel and pressing icons, he finally remembers how to turn the screen on. "Got it", he says underneath his breath. After tapping a couple of icons, the viewscreen activates. He stares at the view screen in amazement at its' clarity.

The view of the interior of the entire wall of the warehouse encompasses the entire front of the bridge, but with the resolution of an 8K ultra-high definition television. He activates the chair clear tablet that moves from behind the back of the chair, along the arm rest and positions itself at the front of the right arm rest. He presses a couple of button icons on the tablet that displays an image of the entire ship, which gives him the ability to control the exterior cameras rotation and resolution. He's smiling so hard right now, he may break his face. "This is great", he says out loud. What's the cameras maximum distance and rotational ability? Each camera has a distance of 350 miles and a 360 degree rotational view. He continues to pan around the

78

warehouse zooming in and out, rotating the view 90 degrees to view the rusting steel open web rafters above his ship. He's smiling as he maneuvers the views and operating the color filter that can help him analyze the chemical makeup of materials.

But as he looks around the warehouse, he notices a sub-unit incorrectly moving a large methane container. "What the hell", he shouts? He's no longer smiling as he notices the dangerous condition that the sub-unit is putting itself in. The sub-unit is hovering about four feet off the warehouse floor and carrying the container by its' nozzle. MOM, communicate to that facility subunit to immediately put that damn container on the floor and report to the engineering lab for software upgrades. "Yes BK", she responds, but just then, the bottom of the container that the unit is dangling bumps hard into a metal sawhorse, which causes the nozzle to break off from the metal bottle.

The container immediately jets across the warehouse like a missile and into the main part of the computer room that houses various computer servers. "Oh my god", he yells as the container proceeds through the wall and he hears a loud crash. The container is resting inside the computer room now, but he can see the room light blinking off and on as well as small amounts of blue smoke billows out of the large opening that the container has created. He just sits in his chair looking dumbfounded, because this type of mishap and damage has never happened before.

Just then, in the Engine Room; one of the engineering units is calibrating the last of the four plasma manifolds before tomorrow's departure. But the unit has receiving vital data from one of the servers in the now highly damaged server room. That data has been severed, but the sub-unit continues to work on the manifold. Unfortunately, the unit connects the incorrect fiber connector then inputs the wrong set of numbers. BK leaps out of his seat and heads for the door, but then is rocked off balance by an intense boom and the slight rocking of the ship from side to side.

What the hell's going on, MOM? She responds that there has been a minor explosion in the engine room. "Minor explosion"? What in the hell do you mean, as he runs to the open hatch and down the passageway toward the Engine Room? Are the damage control units on their way? "Yes", she responds. They are already working on extinguishing the fire and securing the small plasma leak. She warns him once he arrives at the Engine Room, not to open the door. The fumes are not toxic, but they may make it hard for you to breathe with prolong exposure. MOM electronically locks the door just in case BK's emotions get the best of him. Just then he walks up to the sealed space and hesitantly stops in front of the door. The room had to be void of all oxygen in order to extinguish the plasma.

He leans against the door and pounds on it with his fist. He built the damage control units to handle this type of emergency, but he's never been the type of person to just stand by and watch helplessly. I guess he has to just get over it and let the units do their job, he says to himself. The damage control units are handling this situation without you, but I will keep you posted on their progress, she tells him, which she hopes will persuade him to continue his other task. If one of the plasma manifolds is damaged; will it delay our departure tomorrow?

She hesitates for a moment while she checks the ship's systems and calculates the damage to launch scenarios. "No", she responds. He's relieved to hear that, because he doesn't want to delay his departure for even one more day. There's too many outside factors that can put his mission in jeopardy. He also wondered if someone could have heard the loud bang of the container plowing through the wall. MOM takes a quick body scan of BK while he's still standing by the door.

BK your blood pressure and heart rate are elevated above the norm. These symptoms indicate that you are feeling very stressed. Of course I'm feeling stressed, he shouts as he flails his arms around in anger. My family has just been placed in stasis, one of my units demolished my computer room and I just experience my first and hopefully my last explosion onboard my ship. But it doesn't make a difference, he exclaims. All we need to do is to make it through today and get this ship into orbit.

He turns and reluctantly walks away with both of his hands on top of his head in frustration. I'll be in my shipboard office, writing new sub-routines for the port and starboard orbital stabilizers. Of course, mishaps and accidents are commonplace and an expected occurrence, but these kinds of accidents really drills in his head that it will be a hundred times more dangerous once the ship's in orbit. I would like an hourly update on the repairs and don't waste any resources or time on fixing the server room or anything non-essential in the warehouse. Just make sure there no more dangerous hazards that will jeopardize tomorrow's launch.

"I understand", she replies. He then turns and walks down the hall toward his office. His thoughts are still focus on the accident, as he walks down the passageway. He's so distracted by his thoughts on the explosion and the well being of his ship; he misses the hallway to his office and continues down the passageway towards the main kitchen. He doesn't realize it until he gets close to the open door of the ship's galley and smells tonight's dinner cooking. He stops and looks around in confusion for a second. "I can't believe this", he shouts. I can't believe I got lost on my way to my office. I have to get my brain back in line with the task at hand or I will be the one doing something stupid, he thinks to himself. Well while he's here, he figures he might as well get himself something to drink. "Besides", he thinks that a short brake may clear up the jumbled thoughts bouncing around in his head.

He walks into the kitchen and says "hello" to chef. The kitchen unit he calls "chef", greets him with a cheerful hello as it continues preparing tonight's meal for him. BK walks over to the refrigerator, opens the door and peers inside. He's looking around for his favorite drink, but there's none to be found. Chef, he yells while still scanning the contents of the refrigerator. The unit stops what he's doing and looks over at him. "Yes", BK. We need to bring some more coke zeros up from the storage room, please. "Alright", it replies. What time are we going to perform this task? "Damn it", BK says under his breath. Why are these units so literal, he thinks to himself? But I don't have time to weed that out of their programming. "No"! After you finish with preparing dinner; I need you to go down to storage and bring more Coke Zero up here and put four or five bottles in the refrigerator, please. Chef hovered there for a few seconds staring at him. BK looks right back at him waiting for a "yes BK". Would it be faster and more efficient to just get four or five cans from the pantry and put them in the refrigerator, it asked? He gives Chef a gesture of "what the hell". "Is there cans of Coke Zero in the pantry"? "Two cases", Chef replies. He felt like going off on a tirade on the unit, but he knows MOM is monitoring him and this would be another reason for her to request him to take a break for a couple of hours, which he doesn't have. He decides to just politely ask Chef to restock the refrigerator with Coke Zero once it's finish preparing dinner. Chef replies with a simple "yes BK". Chef is no different that any of the other units he built. They perform a specific task with an expert knowledge in that field, but with a limited intellect. He sighs, then reaches back into the refrigerator. Pushes around some water bottles, vitamin water and some containers of cut fruit. He was about to give up and grab some water when he spots six cans of ginger ale lined up all the way in the back. "There we go", he mumbles as he grabs a can. He closes the refrigerator, then walks over to the bench. He opens the ginger ale then sits on top of the bench's tabletop and puts his feet on the chair.

The table which he hopes him, and his family will be sitting at enjoying casual dinners and lunches is next to the greyish metallic wall, but the window portion is made up of the same material as the ship. He pops opens the can and takes a swig of his ginger ale. "MOM", can you activate the viewport next to where I'm sitting, please. "Why", she asked. You'll only be able to see the inside metal wall of the warehouse and I do not think there is anything pleasing or interesting about the rusting warehouse walls. I know that, but just humor me and activate it anyway. Within seconds, the viewport's metallic like features starts to transition from opaque to clear. It now looks like a 6' by 4' viewport encased in a metal frame.

But she was right. That rusting interior metal warehouse wall is nothing pretty to look at, but it's good to see that the material changing from a metal to glass is what's important. He doesn't ask her to deactivate the viewscreen. He uses a tablet that is sitting on the table to return the screen back to a metal material.

The viewport then begins to return to its' previous features of a metallic grayish-black wall. He sits there for a while, drinking his soda and day dreaming about everything that will be happening tomorrow. Then his thoughts switches back to his to-do list, which triggers him to put the tablet back on the table and to head out the galley to continue completing his remaining tasks before they start to run together. He walks down the passageways and this time, makes it to his office where he sits down at his desk and finally gets down to the painstaking task of reviewing the unit's subroutines, schematics and algorithms upgrades.

Meanwhile, outside the warehouse, near the edge of the northern fence, two young men are rabbit hunting and are closing in on their prey. Both of them are in their green and brown hunting gear and are armed with 22 caliber hunting rifles. The brown rabbit they are pursuing is roughly 20 feet ahead of them and unfortunately, heading for a hole in the warehouse's fencing that it uses to escape whatever is pursuing it. The rabbit can hear the hunters are gaining on it and instinctively heads toward the warehouse's six foot fence. There's a broken aluminum connecting wire, which enables the rabbit to force its' head through the metal post and fencing. Once through the fence, the rabbit scurries toward the front of the warehouse. The first hunter named Anthony reaches the fence, only to find small pieces of the rabbit's fur stuck to one of the wires on his side of the fence. As he angrily peers through the fence, looking back and forth, he sees the rabbit slowly hopping from behind the stacks of wooden pallets and heading toward the corner of the warehouse. The fence is too long, and he knows that he'll never get around to the other side quick enough to get a shot. Just then Joshua, his visibly tired partner finally catches up with him. "There he is", Anthony says with excitement as he points in the direction of the rabbit. Both guys, without any hesitation, steps back and raise their rifles and aims through the opening mesh of the aluminum fence. As the rabbit maneuvers around the corner of the building, both of the eager hunter step back away from the fence and fires their weapons simultaneously.

One round misses the rabbit completely and bounces off the corner of the building and into a stack of paint cans stacked on a pallet. A puddle of paint starts to form as the paint seeps out of the punctured can. The second round, from the second hunter grazes the rabbit across its flank and a small plume of fur explodes into the air where the rabbit use to be.

Motivated by the loss of fur and no worst for wear, the rabbit shifts into high gears as its speeds down the side of the warehouse. Without stopping, it rockets across the south side of the property and dashes under another opening in the bottom of the fence. Once out, it begins to zigzag its way through the over-grown bushes and shrubs. The young hunters are too far to see this, so by the time they get to the main entrance of the fence. Joshua thinks that the rabbit is hit and maybe hiding behind the stacks of pallets.

"Damn it", Anthony yells as he runs down to the main entrance of the gate and grabs and pulls at the thick rusting chain and lock. I know I hit it, Joshua exclaims as he walks a few feet down the fence while he tries to get a better look at the pallets. I bet he's hiding behind those pallets, he adds. Anthony is disappointed, but he can clearly see the signs on the fences stating that trespassers will be prosecuted. But he can see by Joshua's adamant pacing and colorful language that he's still wants that rabbit. Joshua, I don't think that trespassing on private property for one mangy rabbit is worth possibly going to jail. Joshua looks frustrated, as he walks toward his friend. We've been out here hunting and chasing rabbits for hours and I'll be damned if I'm going home without this one. "Lets get the hell out of here", as Anthony gestures to Joshua to head back to the woods. Joshua is not ready to give up yet. They've been hunting all day and have nothing to show for it. Joshua is damned if he's going back without at least one rabbit. "Hell no"! I'm going to get us in there to get that damn rabbit.

I don't know about this man, Anthony tells his hyper friend. A locked gate usually means that the property owner wants people to stay out, he tells him while walking closer to the woods. "Hey", if I wanted my dad with me, I would have brought him, he says as he walks up to him and looks him in the eye. This warehouse looks abandoned and probably schedule to be demolished sometime soon. We'll be in and out before anyone knows we were here, he says as he taps Anthony on the shoulder and walks around him to get back to the side of the fence that he thinks he can pull away from the aluminum support pole. Anthony doesn't want to go on the property, but the warehouse does look abandoned. Joshua sees a portion of the fence that is damaged and can be possibly forced back to squeeze through. He looks over at Anthony and tosses his rifle over to him to hold. Anthony barely had time to get his hands up to catch it as Joshua laughs at the rifle potentially hitting his friend in the face.

Joshua never has been the safest person with a weapon. Anthony looks at him as if he lost his mind. "What the hell man, he yells" as Joshua walks over to him smiling and grabs the quarter pint of Captain Morgan from Anthony's jacket pocket! "Just hold my rifle", he response. He opens the cap of the half empty bottle and takes a mouth full. He then puts the bottle back in Anthony's pocket then walks over to the fence. He then grabs the bottom corner of the fence that was missing some of the aluminum straps and starts yanking at the fence like a mad man, trying to break it away from the metal pole. Anthony is standing there nervously looking around at the warehouse and the woods around the property. But unbeknownst to both hunters, MOM has been keeping a watchful sensor on them prior to them approaching the border of the property. Joshua is yanking on the fence so hard, he loses his balance and falls to one knee as he swears at the fence. He gets back up and continues to pull harder. He finally manages to break a few more connection wires from the pole, which enables him to bend the fencing outward far enough for them to squeeze through.

He's breathing hard as he steps back from the damaged fence. Alright that should be enough, he says as he takes his rifle back from Anthony. Joshua slides his rifle through first then crouches down as he pushes and maneuvers his body through the fence, then gestures Anthony to follow him. "This better be a fat damn rabbit", he says to him as he reluctantly follows Joshua through the fence. After both are through the fence, they raise their rifles and ready to fire as if they are a swat team breaching a building, they stealthily walk side by side toward the pallets.

Joshua gestures to Anthony to circle around to the other side of the pallets. They both stop about six feet from the pile of pallets and paint cans. With guns raised, Anthony moves around to the right of the pallet and Joshua moves to the left. As Anthony slowly moves around the pallets, he can see the can with the puddle of paint pooled at the bottom of the can. He slowly lowers his rifle as he can clearly see that they missed their quarry. Where in the hell did that furry bastard go, he says as he looks over at Anthony. Maybe he was here, Joshua says as he looks around the front of the building. "Hey, look", Joshua says while pointing at the ground in front of the warehouse garage door. Are those tracks running under this garage door as he bends down and wiggles his fingers between the door and the ground trying to see if the opening was large enough for a rabbit to squeeze under? Ya, you're right, Anthony agrees.

I bet he was under the pallet, but when he heard us moving in on him, he shot under that opening. Anthony puts his rifle down beside the pallets and gets down on his stomach to try to see what's behind the warehouse's large rollup door. Joshua kneels down on one knee beside him then drops to his stomach to help him look under that door. Can you see anything, dude? "Not a damn thing", Anthony replies sharply. It's too dark in there, but I'll bet you anything that he's in there. Both stand up and brush the dirt off their stomach and pants. Joshua is still fixated on the gap under the garage door. Hey man, we're losing the light, Anthony says as he looks up at the sky. We're not going to let "Buzz Bunny" Elmer Fudd us, are we? "Hey", I'll gladly be "Elmer Fudd" and let the rabbit win, Anthony says without shame or hesitation. Let's call it a day man. Once we lose the light, who knows what's going to be roaming these woods at night once the woods turn pitch black. Joshua just stands there looking up and down angrily at the rollup door. Anthony was just tired of chasing this rabbit and was ready to call it a day. He makes an attempt to reason with his misguided hunting partner. Listen dude, you maybe right about the rabbit hiding inside this warehouse but let me remind you of a few key points. You don't have a hunting license, mine expired two months ago and we are currently trespassing on private property trying to shoot one flea bitten rabbit. Joshua walks over and grabs and pulls at the lock on the door, which is left of the garage door. This lock is too small to secure this metal door, he says while looking over at Anthony. I bet if I hit it with the butt of my rifle, it will pop right open. Anthony's head is down as he realizes that his friend is an idiot.

That will be called breaking and entering, which I think is a felony, he exclaims. I'll tell you what, Anthony. Since you're having acute stomach problems (No guts); how about you stay out here and yell if you see anyone coming or blast that damn rabbit once I chase him out of the warehouse. "Whatever dude", Anthony says as he walks back toward the rollup door. Against his better judgment, he decides to stand out in front of the warehouse while Joshua goes in. "Just make it quick", he says sternly. And don't use the butt of your gun, he warns Joshua. That kind of nonsense only works in the movies. He decides to take his advice, because it's his dad's favorite hunting rifle, which he borrowed without asking him. And he would kill him if he brought it back damaged. He looks around for a metal or a large wooden object to put between the door and the latch. He leans his gun against the rollup door and walks around besides the pile of pallets for something to use.

Meanwhile, inside the warehouse, MOM informs BK of the escalating situation outside. "Two young men", he says as he continues to tap on his keyboard. Are they trying to break into the warehouse? Yes, and it looks as though one of them has found a long, flat metal object to attempt to break in through the warehouse side door, which will give them access to the loading dock area. BK smiles.

"Kill them", he says jokingly, but with authority. "Affirmative", MOM response. "No, no", he yells. I was just kidding, he says. "Me too", she replies. He just smiles. BK has thought about something like this happening, so he has developed a series of named deterrent procedures. Release the "Pit Bulls" on them and make it realistic, please. Yes, BK. And please record it for me, so I can have some laughs about it later. He would like to have fun removing these trespassers from his property, but time is not his friend and he wants to stay on schedule. She has done this before and is getting very good at it. BK then puts those thoughts out of his mind and begins to complete the final lines of code for the unit in the hydroponics bay. Meanwhile, while Anthony is looking out toward the only road leading to the warehouse; Joshua is preparing to break the latch from the door with a metal object he found. Anthony nervously looks down the road and can't see any one coming, so he gives Joshua the nod to do it. Anthony wouldn't admit it to Joshua that he's a little curious about what's in that warehouse than catching that rabbit. First Joshua begins to hit the lock and latch with a roughly two foot pipe, but it didn't work and he was making entirely too much noise.

Anthony yells to him to stop playing around and break the damn thing, he shouts as he walks closer to him. Joshua turns the pipe to the flat end and starts to squeeze the pipe between the latch and the door. But all of a sudden, a couple of loud bangs hits the rollup door from the inside, followed by the sounds of two or three large dogs going crazy trying to get out at them from behind the rollup garage door. Anthony immediately yells, dropped the damn pipe.

Joshua and Anthony slowly back away from the door of the warehouse. MOM gives the units another signal to continue with the deterrent. The facility's units' pound and slams into the doors and turns up the volume on the dog simulated barking and growling. Anthony has had enough of this nonsense and starts running pass him then proceeds to run toward the opening in the fence. The banging and the growling intensifies, but what really scared the hell out of him was a man's voice yelling, "get off my damn property". Joshua begins to reach for his rifle that was leaning against the garage door, but is now laying on the ground, but he hears the voice saying, "raise the garage door and let the dogs out".

He can't leave the rifle behind, so he runs over and snatches the gun off the ground, while yelling, "oh damn, oh damn" as he runs fast as he can towards the fence opening. As he gets closer to the opening in the fence, he dives to the ground on his hands and knees and starts crawling like a toddler. But Anthony is ahead of him and is running like he's on the Olympic track and field team. As Anthony hits the opening, the bottom portion of his jacket snags on the fence, but that doesn't slow him down one bit. That part of his jacket tares away and remains hanging from the fence. He falls as he exits through the fence, but he quickly regains his footing and stumbles into the woods.

Three seconds later, Joshua drops to his hands and knees as he hits the opening, and attempts to dive through. His head and arms are out, but his butt and legs are stuck on the other side. His belt loop is caught on the broken part of the fence. Joshua yells for Anthony for help, but Anthony is only worried about Anthony at the moment. He pulls and contorts his body desperately trying to free himself from the fence, while at the same time continuously yelling for Anthony's help, in addition to yelling some selective profanities.

He tries to stand to his feet in order to get some leverage to break free, but the opening is too small for that. MOM's sensors can read that Joshua's heart rate has elevated and he's under a great deal of stress, as well as havin a great deal of alcohol in his system. But she knows that a human of his age can handle it. She decides to give him some extra motivation to escape. She intensifies the banging of the garage door and turns up the volume and voracity of the dogs. She even instructs unit three to raise and lower the door.

To Joshua, he thinks that the dogs are about to break out of the warehouse and rip his legs off at any moment. Joshua's fear elevates, as he makes an all or nothing attempt to escape by first standing up as much as he can then forcing himself through the opening in the fence. With all the strength he can muster, Joshua yells as he tears his beltloop from his pants and crawls free.

Once free, with rifle in hand, he runs screaming into the woods like the so-called mangy rabbit they were chasing. Hopping, jumping and thrashing his way through the thick brush. MOM continues the sound effects for approximately 30 more seconds just to make sure they continued moving away from the property, which they did in an excellarated pace. After another 30 seconds she informs the units, which are using their mechanical bodies to bang against the garage door to stop and return to their task. She will run a full diagnostic on them momentarily, but for now the end justifies the means.

She reports to BK that the threat has been eliminated. They are unharmed and are for all probabilities still running down the hill like two scalded dogs toward their vehicle. BK laughs under his breath as he imagines them running terrified through the woods. Would you like me to pursue them further, MOM ask? No, no... I think that will be enough, thank you. You did a terrific

88

job of getting rid of those two goobers without doing any damage to them. "Drunken Goobers", MOM adds. What just happened was one of my nightmares and that the reason I'm pressing so hard to launch on time, he tells her. I understand, she replies.

Now I'm going to task you with a variety of projects that will have to be completed prior to 2300 hours. BK turns his chair to the computer station and starts to input instructions. I also need for you to ensure that the maintenance and facilities' units start bringing aboard all equipment and vital components aboard the ship.

I don't want to leave any thing behind except the interior walls and things we can't use. What about the damaged and broken equipment from the accident, she asks? If it's ours, have the units bring it aboard and place it in the storage bay. We may need to utilize and repurpose some of the parts and materials later. "I have just downloaded those instructions to the maintenance and facilities units", she replies. And once it's dark enough, I will instruct a couple of the facility's units to push the car out of the warehouse and place it in the rear of the structure, MOM adds. "That's fine", he responds. As the facilities units continues to bring equipment, parts, and materials aboard; BK focuses on completing upgrading programs and developing new algorithms for the ship's computer. It's now 6:41 p.m. and he has about another hour worth of work to do, then he'll get at quick bite to eat before he runs his last diagnostic on the navigation sensors.

What time do you think you'll be getting to bed, she asks? He continues to type and intensely stares at the computer monitor. Don't worry about me, he replies. He tells her that he may get about two or three hours of sleep tonight, because he's too hyped up about the launch. He tells her, once we are safely in orbit; he'll take a day or so off to get some well needed rest. MOM is surprisingly silent. OK, MOM let's get to work, he exclaims as he continues to work at his computer. She response with just a simple "OK". She's use to him working twelve and fourteen hours a day and she calculates that one more day of continuous work will only ensure that the ship will launch on time. BK, MOM and the other nine units are all busily getting the last bit of work done before the deadline. As the time quickly ticks pass, the units have almost completed the removal of all the essential warehouse components. The last components to be disassembled and brought aboard is the surveillance cameras from outside the warehouse and the damaged and mangled computers from the destroyed warehouse computer room. He thinks he can salvage some of the components and reuse them. It's 1:34 a.m. and he is back at his desk double checking the ship's flight path once they leave the warehouse. He has to navigate through commercial aircraft and elude the military's surveillance radar. Even after eluding those obstacles, he still has to worry about the numerous orbiting satellites. If necessary, he could plow right through them without scratching the ship's paint job. But he doesn't want to alert anyone of the existence of his ship, just yet.

BK's enhanced brain allows him to stay focus through much of his task, but he has been pushing himself too hard these last few days and now he's beginning to feel his body shutting down. His eyes are beginning to burn, and his head starts to drop to his chest. He catches himself nodding off a couple of times and knows he needs to get some sleep.

But he still wants to get a few more things done before his body forces him into his bed. He pushes his keyboard toward the monitor in order to give him some room to rest his head for a quick cat nap. He puts his head on his desk and decides to take a 20 minute power nap. He thinks this will enable him to complete the final reviews and get to bed before 2:30 or so. That sounds like a plan, he thinks to himself as he puts his hands on the desk then places his forehead on them and closes his eyes. 20 to 30 minutes he says to himself over and over again. He is so tired that it doesn't take long for his mind to drift into the thoughts of his family. He thinks about his daughter's birthdays, first day of school and Lorraine's hands massaging his neck, which she did on occasions when he came home from work stressed. Before he knew it, his mother's voice enters his dreams. He hears his mother faint voice repeating his name over and over again. It's not his mother, but MOM trying to wake him up. "Are you fully awake, she asks"? "Yes", he says as he uses the back of his hand to wipe the drool from the side of his face. Those twenty minutes went by fast, he says as he wipes his eyes. "What time is it"? The time is 04:09 a.m., MOM answers. "04:09", he shouts loudly as he jumps out of his chair and uses the table to steady himself. "Damn it MOM, why in the hell didn't you wake me up? I planned to only take a short nap so I could be alert enough to complete the remainder of my projects.

I scanned your vitals and determined you needed the minimum of two hours of sleep for your mind and body to function at their minimum readiness for today's launch. And I also took the liberty of completing the remainder of your most vital task and rescheduled the three minor ones. Besides, you might have told yourself that you wanted to take a short twenty minute nap, but you neglected to inform me of those plans, she says to him as an excuse for deliberately not waking him up. He would like to tell her, she was wrong for not waking him up, but he does feel more focus as a result of his prolonged nap. He just tells her, "thank you". The ship's propulsion system has been powered up since 03:00 a.m., the port and starboard stabilizers have been engaged and the ship is elevated 48 inches above the warehouse suspension blocks. All ships systems are operating within normal parameters, she adds. He grabs a near by tablet from the table then taps the tablet a few times to display and review the various system schematic displays.

He swipes through the system's readiness reports and is pleased with all the progress that has been done while he has been sleeping. He tosses the tablet back on the desk as he leaves his office. He heads toward medical to do one final check of his family's stasis container and kisses the glass of the container as a symbolic gesture just in case something happens during the launch. Has the maintenance units completed the warehouse departure preparation yet? "The warehouse has been cleared of all our equipment and the maintenance units are completing the partial disassembling and weakening of the north wall. What's their estimated time for completing their task? MOM pauses for a moment.

"Approximately 17 minutes", she response. "Great" he says as he walks down the hallway. Please continue to monitor the perimeter of the warehouse and inform me if any problems arise. Affirmative, she responds. As he enters the medical bay, the lights automatically goes from dim to normal illumination. He walks over to the panels on the far wall and begins to press a combination of brightly lit buttons. Just then, the wall next to the panel slowly slide open and there in a small poorly lit space is his family's capsules. He planned to just look through the single viewport at all three capsules, but he wants to touch and kiss each one of the them. All three are leaning backward at a 60 degree angle. He approaches the first capsule and tries to see his wife through the capsule's viewport, but the viewport is completely frosted over. He wipes his hand vigorously across the view port attempting to remove some of the frost, but the interior of the viewport has also frosted over. He can barely make out the silhouette of his wife's face through the translucent view port. All he can do now is to give each capsule an air kiss and say a final prayer for his family's safety. He talks to his wife as if she's standing right in front of him. He tells her that he's about to launch the ship and he's nervous as hell and wishes she was standing next to him holding his hand. He then tells her and his daughter that he loves them with his entire soul. He also prayed that God have mercy on his soul if anything goes wrong today. He then walks out of the container and over to the control panel and inputs the code to reseal it.

As the wall seals again, he grabs one of the three medical tablets from what will be Lorraine's desk. For his peace of mind, he wants to review his family's vitals one last time before the launch. He pulls up their vitals side by side and can see their numbers are right at the levels they need to be. It's now 4:23 a.m. and it's time for him to head to the bridge to commence the launch sequence. He has to hurry if he's going to launch before the 5:47 a.m. sunrise. He's close enough to various neighborhoods and the highway that his ship could be seen once the sun comes up. He hustles down the passageways pressing buttons at various control panels along the way. In his mind, he's going over every aspect of the ship's design and configuration. He hopes he hadn't forgotten anything that will cause the ship to fail or explode miles above the earth's surface, causing large pieces of the ship and his family to rain down all over the neighborhoods. He shakes off those negative thoughts and enters the bridge that is now operational. He walks around to the navigation console to input the new launch trajectory. He then moves on to the communication console were MOM has been monitoring the military and commercial airline traffic in order to determine the detours and alternative paths they may have to take. The report MOM has provided indicates that air traffic will increase between the hours of 08:35 a.m. and 2:37 p.m.

He then decides to cross reference information from other local aviation sites to ensure the accuracy of his data results. He knows he can control all aspects of his ship's operations and navigations from his captain's chair. As he walks about the bridge preparing the ship for its' launch, MOM reports that the maintenance units have completed their task of undermining the structural stability of the north exterior wall and installing the small explosive charges. That's great, as he continues to work his way around the bridge. He asked her if she could turn up the lights on the bridge. He also instructs her to make a final material sweep of the warehouse and ensure that the facility units are aboard and instruct them to store themselves in the engineering department. Two of the units will be reprogrammed as an engineering unit and the other one will be assigned to ship's janitorial duties. "Yes BK", she responds. They are now inside the ship and I am now sealing the ship for launch. He walks down to his captain's chair and brings up the monitor on his chair's armrest. It's finally time for him to launch his creation and he's nervous as hell. He taps the screen and displays the launch sequence to ensure that he's not missing any pertinent tasking. Do you have additional task for me, she asked?

He continues to swipe through the checklist without responding. She patiently waits for his response. She knows that sometimes he gets so involved in his thoughts that he will not answer her questions for about two or three minutes or sometimes not at all. He mumbles to himself as he moves his index finger down and across each line on the monitor being very careful not to miss a line. Then all of a sudden he yells, "yes"! I've finally completed the launch checklist and now you and I will check the navigation, communications and tactical systems prior to departure. Now MOM, he says as he flips to the first screen. I have some questions I have to go through real quick, he says as he swipes through a couple of screens.

BK: Local Temperature?

MOM: 63 degrees Fahrenheit.

BK: Chances for rainfall?

MOM: 40% until 12:53 then increases to 60% for the remainder of the day.

BK: Cloud cover?

MOM: Presently partly cloudy

BK: Wind speed and directions?

MOM: Winds are at 10 miles per hour at a northwest direction.

BK: Gravitation resistance?

MOM: Gravitational field is constant at 9.8N/kg

He checks off each answer as MOM replies to his questions, then quickly moves on to the next screen. They both speed through the questions faster than they anticipated and are finished in 12 minutes and 22 seconds. He then switches to the ship's schematics, which displays its' current operational status. The propulsion system displays 100 percent, gravity engine displays

100 percent and all other vital components are within acceptable launch parameters. He then instructs medical unit one to maintain a continuous watch of his family's condition.

He then sits there for a moment without saying anything, which strikes MOM as being a little odd, so she uses her medical scanner to give him a quick scan. She analyzes the data and discovers that his vitals are elevated. She has seen this type of condition in him before, so she concludes that this is a normal condition in humans when performing extremely complex task with very little sleep. She decides to give him a few moments to compose himself and resume the launch procedures.

"It's time", he says to himself. After all these years of secrecy, I am about to "hopefully", accomplish something that all the so called "superpowers" couldn't accomplish, he thinks to himself. As he sits in his chair, his body begins to shake from the top of his head to the bottom of his feet. Calm down, calm down... he softly but sternly whispers to himself. He then takes a few deep breaths as he closes his eyes. MOM continues to silently monitor his vitals. He breathes in deeply then exhales slowly as he continuously concentrates on thoughts of him and his family on summer vacations laughing and eating ice cream. He sits there for another 30 seconds then opens his eyes and begins to countdown with a noticeable tremble in his voice. He starts at ten and works his way down to six, then asked MOM to arm all twelve small explosive charges and sets their timer for five seconds. Five, four, three, two, one, as he presses a button on his chair's console. He can hear the muffled sounds of the explosive charges as they destroy the twelve metal restraining bolts, which is the only thing securing the north wall to the rest of the main structure. BK then activates the bridge's view screen.

The monitor activates, but to his amazement - he can only see a large partially painted and rusted encrusted metal wall in front of him that should have fallen to the ground. "Why do I still see a damn wall, MOM", he yells as he stares angrily at the view screen in frustration. Not enough explosives and possibly an error in estimating metal connection strength, she replies. "God Damn it"! that's a no brainer, because there's still a wall in front of me", he yells as he stands to his feet and takes a few steps toward the view screen.

I do not think yelling expletives at it will cause it to fall, she adds. But look MOM! The wall is still there and we are literally trapped in this damn warehouse. Not necessarily, she replies. What's your solution, because if you have an idea I am all ears. There is a four foot and three inch gap in between the nose of the ship and the still standing wall, correct? "That's right", he replies! Move the ship forward slowly and allow the mass and the weight of the ship to complete the task of the explosives. You mean you want to use the most technically advanced ship as a Viking battering ramp. "Yes", she response, unless you're afraid of scratching the paint job of your new hooptie, she says sarcastically.

She gets a brief smile out of him at a time that he needs it. "Right", he repeats as he walks back to his chair and sits down. He brings up the navigation screen on the tablet connected to the armrest and with a few taps on the keyboard he slowly moves the ship forward. The ship slowly starts to move closer and closer to the wall, which is still a very scary site, regardless of the size of his ship. He won't feel it when the ship makes contact with the wall, but for about five seconds, he can hear the separating metal of the wall breaking apart, which strangely sounds like a aluminum can being ripped apart. With a final loud bang, the few pieces of metal finally succumb to the weight of the ship. The wall falls outward to the ground like a massive domino and produces a plume of dust and dirt away from it. The dust and dirt jets outward toward the fence as it rolls back upon itself like smoke from a forest fire. Seeing the wall lying in front of the ship causes his thoughts of dread to return.

There's nothing stopping him from finding out if all his years of work and let alone his family's lives will be wasted. The ship continues its' slowly forward momentum similar to a float in the Macy's Day Parade. Actually, it's more like the birth of a new method of transportation, which for good or bad, will transform mankind. BK is so transfixed on the ship moving out the warehouse, MOM has to remind him of the christening of the ship. "Oh damn", he yells. I can't believe I almost forgot this important tradition, he says out loud.

He pushes a button on the screen, then the bottom swings open from a cylinder hanging on the last metal rafter above the ship within the warehouse as the ship continues to glide out of the warehouse and over the fallen wall. A champagne bottle falls onto the front portion of the ship sending glass and champagne foam exploding onto the ship. BK's voice echoes throughout the bridge of the ship as he recites the age-old ship christenings statement. "To all who hear these words that on this day of the 17th, of November and year of our God 2024; I christen thee, Pangea, United Earth Space Ship (U.E.S.S.). He named his ship Pangea after the earth's supercontinent, because he hopes his technology will spark the next evolution of man's exploration into space and unite the entire world. The ship continues to glide three feet over the fallen wall of the warehouse. One third of the ship has emerged from the warehouse as he continuously monitors the ship's systems and progress. The ship is emerging from the warehouse very quickly for a ship of its' size. It has roughly less than four feet clearance on either side of the opening and only six feet from the interior roof metal ridge of the warehouse. He decides to increase the ship's velocity and asked MOM to calculate the distance from the main gate once the ship completely emerges.

She uses the ship's sensor to determine the distance from the fence and the remaining length of the ship still inside the warehouse. In approximately 20 seconds the ship will be completely clear of the warehouse and will be a mere six feet from the main gate, she response. "Man"! This will be tight, he replies nervously. Next time I design a ship MOM., please remind me to pick a better location for its' construction, he says jokenly. I don't think there was any problem with our location. Have you forgotten that originally you were planning to remove the roof of the warehouse to use as an exit point, but changed your mind two months ago, because we agreed that removing the wall would be the most logical alternative, she reminds him.

MOM, I want you to stop the ship once the stern of the ship is exactly four feet out of the warehouse. "Affirmative", she responds. BK switches his attention back to his console monitors and starts to bring up the ship's vertical ascent schematic. After ten seconds the ship is finally clear of the warehouse and MOM halts its' forward advance. The ship has totally overshadowed the front of the property and now without any lights to illuminate it; it appears to be a dark immense mass hovering above the ground. Approximately, how much time do we have left before sunrise, he asked?

One hour and twenty-three minutes, she replies. Plenty of time, he says in a low tone. We are making excellent time, he response with nervous excitement in his voice. He begins to maneuver through the launch menus on the screen as he states to MOM that he is about to start the ship's ascent by changing the ship's gravitational state. He is using the earth's own gravitational field to push the ship away from the surface of the planet. This is similar to putting two magnets of opposite fields polarities together as they repel each other. No matter how hard you press them together, both magnets repel each other. This will be a sufficient enough force to push the ship into a high earth orbit. He then begins to countdown: 10, 9, 8, 7, 6, 5, 4, 3, 2, 1. "Launch", he says loudly! I'm changing the ship's gravitational force and activating the electromagnetic shielding. Like releasing a huge balloon, the ship instantaneously begins to rise into the darkness of the night sky. Just then, a voice MOM wasn't familiar with and music she hadn't heard before starts to fill the room. "What is this music and why is it playing", she asked?

BK has pre-programmed the music to play as the ship ascended toward its' assigned orbit. He explains to MOM that its' a rap song called "Milky Way" by a group called The Pack. What is the significance of playing this music, as she analyzes the lyrics? He nods his head with the music as he continues to look over the data on his armchair panel.

He doesn't need MOM to ask him thousands of questions about rap music right now, so he tries to explain it to her as simply as he could without taking up too much of their time. LaChel was continuously listening to this group with her friends and although I wasn't happy with her listening to this particular group, because some of their lyrics are extremely explicit. This particular song became an ear worm in my brain. So as a tribute to my little girl, I decided to use this song as my launch theme. And please, we have quite a few other things to worry about, so don't bombard me with any other questions regarding this song. She decided to abide by his wishes and not to ask any questions but to research the origins of rap music and the underlying message of these lyrics. He activates the vertical altitude scale on the lefthand side of the main view screen, which shows him the exact altitude as the ship ascends into orbit. He uses the control panels to adjust the ship's rate of ascend, pitch and its' flight path. MOM, please keep an eye out on all air traffic, both civilian and military. I do not have any eyes and if I did, I doubt that I would take one out.

"Oh damn", he shouts loudly. You know what I mean, he says with attitude. MOM recognizes his nerves are on edge, so she turns down her levity programming. Do not worry; I will monitor the air traffic, both through their communications and by extending our sensors. Please MOM! Hold off on the jokes until we reach our destination. I understand, and I will save the jokes for later. Thank you, he says as he looks at the view screen intensely, which is displaying his altitude and velocity. NASA's most sophisticated rocket is fueled with liquid hydrogen and must exceed a velocity of seven miles per second to escape earth's gravity, but BK's spacecraft exceeds that velocity requirement by a factor of three. His ship will soon be ascending at 27 miles per second. MOM gives him an update in their velocity and tells him that the ship is climbing at fifteen feet per second and increasing. The ship is performing so smoothly, it's like he's not even moving. He then switches to his left chair monitor to check the propulsion systems and monitors the rate of the plasma to the main inductor. The plasma pressure is within its' normal parameters and working properly. As the ship continues to gain altitude and velocity, BK continuously switches his attention from his left armrest to the right one; similar to someone watching a tennis match.

MOM breaks his concentration by telling him about an incoming commercial aircraft that will be passing to the port side of the ship within 175 feet, if they continue on their current course. What's its' ETA, he responds? Four minutes, 45 seconds, she replies. He quickly calculates that they are moving fast enough to avoid a potential collision, so he decides to maintain his course and velocity. The ship's velocity steadily increases as it reaches a velocity of 320 miles per hour and an altitude of 2,500 feet.

The commercial aircraft and BK's ship are within eight miles of each other. He begins to change the plasma flow ratio between all four plasma inductors; he immediately starts to feel a very slight vibration. Are we traveling through any sort of thermal turbulence, because he can feel a slight vibration through his chair? "No", MOM responds. He swipes through the ship's schematics and sensor display to try to pinpoint the source of the vibrations. MOM begins her ship wide diagnostic of the ship's propulsion systems, but about twenty seconds into the diagnostic; the ship begins to vibrate more to the port side, which starts to affect the ship's vertical velocity. Can you trace down the cause of this vibration, he shouts! BK switches his screen to the plasma schematic flow rate, which is starting to become unbalanced. The ship is starting to struggle as it continues to attempt to fight against the earth's gravity. He thinks that one of the portside plasma induction units has malfunctioned, consequently throwing off the entire flow of plasma to the other three.

"Damn", he shouts as he continues to change the flow rate to compensate for the malfunction. When he was running low on money, he had to salvage the parts he used to build his plasma inductors, which may explain why he's in the situation that he's in now. He starts to yell out loud to MOM that he knew he should have taken more time testing all the inductors before they launched. But MOM is running her own analysis of the problem and she's not sure that the inductors are the problem. She interrupts his rant to tell him that she's 85 percent certain that the inductors are not the cause of the vibrations. Her analysis indicates that one of the quantum diamond boards that regulate the power to the inductor is slightly damaged. BK switches the monitor on his left to the plasma control screen and takes the damaged unit offline. Then he recalibrates the other three inductors to handle the flow of the additional plasma distribution. The ship immediately response as most of the vibration has stopped and the ship velocity once again begins to increase. MOM then suggest they slow the ship's ascent, which should stop the remaining vibrations. "I agree" he says as he inputs some commands to decrease the velocity. We don't know what cause the inductor to malfunction and we shouldn't take a chance of losing another inductor unit, he adds. The ship's propulsion system quickly adapts to utilizing the three remaining inductors and continues rising into the darkest of the early morning sky.

After another minute an a half of ascent, MOM relays to him that they have surpassed the orbit of the International Space Station and are currently at 250 miles above the earth's surface. He then uses his ship's computer to hack into NASA's computer in order to find the active position of the space station. By his calculations, his ship will be exactly opposite of the space station's orbit. He thinks how funny it would be to park right next to it. He imagines himself and his units waving to the astronauts through one of the viewports.

We have seventeen seconds and counting before we achieve our optimum orbit, MOM reminds him. Prepare to bring the ship within synchronous orbit with the earth's northern pole in eleven, 10, 9, 8, 7, 6, 5, 4, 3, 2, 1. We are now in synchronous orbit, approximately 271 miles above the earth surface, near the north pole. Other than the music of "The Pack" that is still playing, he just sits there in his chair for a few seconds in stunned silents. The emotions and the magnitude of his accomplishment is totally overloading his brain. He finally uses his shaking arms to lift himself from the chair and walk towards the view screen. "MOM", please display the view of the earth's North American region at a magnification of 250 feet. The metallic wall in front of him quickly changes to a 12' by 8' panoramic viewing screen and the view of the North American Region comes into view. He didn't realize how big the screen really was until just that moment when the earth is displayed across it like a magnificent portrait. Without saying a word, he slowly walks closer to the screen and stops within three feet from it. He looks down at the Atlantic Ocean slowly drifting before his eyes and is spellbound by what he has accomplished.

"Congratulations BK"! You are the first private citizen to successfully build and launch their own vehicle of any size into orbit. And you have also cemented you and your family into humanity's history books. He just lowers his head and drops to his knees. He puts his head in his hands and begins to sob uncontrollably. MOM scans him again, trying to determine the cause of his distress. She can find nothing physically wrong with him, so she searches through her database for a reference to his current emotional condition. She finds one hundred and thirty-seven reference documents that may explain his current state. I understand that you miss your family and are feeling lonely, but I think you will be fine once you get some rest and consume some of your favorite foods and beverages.

I will have chef prepare you a stack of banana and pecan pancakes and a cup of hot chocolate with whip cream. He continues to cry and doesn't acknowledge or confirm MOM's misguided diagnosis or remendy. She has never seen him cry before, so she has no reference to guage his state of mind. He thinks to himself that after three years, he has finally accomplished his dream and what he felt as his mandate to forcibly drag humanity kicking and screaming to move forward in their technological evolution.

After a few minutes, he tells her that he's just happy, as he wipes the tears from his face with his sleeves. Give me a minute and I'll be all right, he adds. You mean happy like a bride on her wedding day or like your overweight mama at an all you can eat buffet, she asks? He didn't expect a joke from her right now, but it did help him shake off the wave of emotions that just washed over him. He laughs a little as he stands to his feet and continues to wipe the tears from his face. He has regained his composure, but he just can't pull himself away from the view of the earth beneath him. He knows that he still has a hard road ahead, but having his ship in orbit has taken a huge weight off his shoulders. While his ship was in the warehouse, he was continuously worried that law enforcement would smash through the doors with guns drawn and a pair of handcuffs with his name on them. Now, for the first time in over two years he feels perfectly safe. As he wipes the last of the tears from his face, he wishes his family were awake to experience this monumental moment with him. But time his ticking by and he realizes that getting here was hard enough but staying in orbit will be even harder. There's still a few task on his plate and if he wants to be able to relax anytime soon; he has to get started on them. All right MOM! I'm going to assign you a few more task and I will be in the engine room rebuilding that damaged inductor board. "No", MOM says with authority. You need to take a break and eat some breakfast and relax for the rest of the day. I will, but I have to finish the rest of the jobs I have on my task list before I can relax, he replies. She reviews his task list and determines that nothing on his list is critical to the ship's safety or its' operational stability at this time. I have monitored you for three days as you worked twelve to fourteen hours to get this ship in orbit, but I insist that you take the rest of the day off. He tries to ignore her as he turns away from the viewing screen and walks over to his chair to review the ship's orbital status before heading to the engine room.

But she turns off the chair's arm monitor as he gets to the chair. He sighs and stands in front of it contemplating if he has any argument that would persuade her to let him complete one or two more task. "Can't think of a damn thing", he thinks to himself. So he decides to just try to bully her. He puts his hands on his hips and raises his voice to sound more authoritative. I only have one wife and she's in stasis in the medical clinic. And I think I'm the best person to determine my mental and physical health, so I need you to turn my damn chair's panels back on. "No", she replies. OK, I'll just head to the Engine Room as he heads toward the door. "I will turn them off too, she exclaims. What are you going to do?

Turn off all the monitors and computers throughout the ship, so I can't work, he says sarcastically. She gives him a simple but firm, "yes". He knows that bluffing isn't in her programming and that her ability to turn off every monitor onboard the ship is within her abilities. He decides that one day of relaxation won't hurt him and some breakfast sounds good. "Alright MOM, you've won.", he says to her as he walks toward the door to exit the bridge. I am going to check on my family then get me some breakfast, so please have the chef fix me some steak and eggs instead of pancakes. And please have him bring it to my study. "No problem", she response. He walks off the bridge and heads toward the medical clinic. BK doesn't want to admit it to MOM, but he could use the rest and after visiting his family and eating a great breakfast; he will enjoy sleeping and relaxing the rest of the day.

Chapter Three

The search for the family and the truth

April 5, 2023 – Off the Ivory Coast a large oil tanker has lose steering control and collides with a deep-water oil rig and release it massive content through the surrounding coastline. This spill is twice the amounts of the Exxon Valdez. Environmental Disaster.

It's Tuesday morning and it has been a week and a half since BK has left the planet with his family. Bryan was worried about his boss and best friend not showing up at the office, and not returning any of his calls or emails, so he decided to contact the police and request a wellness check. After Officers Hidalgo and Ryan arrive at the Thomas residence, and walk up to the home, they find the garage door open.

Officer Ryan checks the car sitting outside the garage while Hidalgo walks through the garage looking for signs of anything out of the ordinary. Officer Hidalgo is searching the garage and she doesn't see anything that would be considered unusual inside the garage. Officer Ryan walks around to the rear of the car and writes down the license plate of the car. After checking the door leading into the house and finding it unlocked, she calls her partner over, so they can both go into the house to investigate. Officer Ryan walks up to her and both draw their weapons before entering the home. "Hello, Mr. and Mrs. Thomas", Hidalgo shouts as they walk into the laundry room. "This is the police", she yells loudly as her voice echos through the home. Both officers search the house completely and come to the conclusion that the family is gone and left in a hurry. They found Lorraine's perce, cellphone and jewery still in her room and found LaChel's cellphone still lying in her bed by her pillow, which was a very red flag. No teenage girl would leave their phone, if she had a choice. Ryan and Hidalgo decide to leave everything in place and to exit the house and call their sargent for instructions. Ryan calls their sargent and ask permission to call the person that requested the wellness check to gain the BK's cellphone numbers.

Their sargent has the dispatcher give them Bryan's phone number and Bryan gives Officer Ryan BK's cellphone number and their daughters school information in order for the officer to try to make contact with them, but all he gets is his voicemail. So, Hidalgo suggest that they should go one step further and call the girls' schools to hopefully find the children where they're supposed to be, but both administrative offices acknowledged that they haven't been in school for two days. They decide to call it in as a missing person report for the family.

The police deem the family's disappearance as suspicious, so they decide to put out an Amber Alert for the Thomas Family. The Amber Alert states to be on the look out for two minor African American females, ages 16 and 12 and that they maybe in the company of their father, a 6'-4" African American male weighing 217 pounds and their mother a African American 5'-6" female weighing 124 pounds. The case was assigned to Detective Sanders, who is a 28 year veteran of the force and his partner Detective Tillman, who has been on the force for eight years. The Detectives go to the home and collect evidence and to start the investigation on what may have happened to them. They were assigned three forensic detectives and five officers to assist them. The neighbors are shocked and dumb founded by the police and yellow crime scene tape surrounding the entire house.

The neighbors have been forced to stay on the sidewalk, across the street, which causes them to talk amongst themselves and come up with imaginative scenarios to what may have happened to their neighbor. The scene is like something you would see on Unsolved Mysteries or some other detective series. And speaking of detectives, there are a group of five neighbors talking about how they knew something was just not right about the family. Mary is a stay-at-home mom and lives across the street and four houses down from the Thomas family. She is talking to Hellen, who lives next door to Mary. Jean is the ringleader and is also a stay-at-home mom, but she has the neighborhood title of the Gossip Queen. Even though she lives around the corner, she has a tap on everything going on because of all her spies throughout the entire neighborhood keeping tabs on everyone. These ladies are regulars at the local coffee shop where they spent hours talking about everyone else's families, children and spouses inside and outside the neighborhood.

Jean tells the other ladies that she passed by this house every day walking her dog and something has always seemed strange about this family. I just couldn't put my finger on it, but they seemed to be a little too perfect of a couple, "if you know what I mean"? Susan, one of the only ladies that had regular conversations with Lorraine, didn't know what Jean was talking about, but one by one, each of the ladies in the group nodded their head yes, which was best when dealing with Jean. Back across the street at the Thomas residence, a young police officer posted outside the front door is tasked with ensuring that no one but law enforcement enters the residence. He has been standing there for almost an hour and he his bored out of his mind. He stands there watching the detectives and his fellow officers walk in and out of the residence. He's only been on the force for about four months and that's the reason this wafer-thin rookie is standing on the porch like a poorly fed bouncer.

He's the junior of the officers and is as green as a Granny Smith apple, so he doesn't expect anyone to come out and relieve him, so he could take an active part in the investigation. But to his left, he notices various news crew moving a barrier aside, so they can move closer to get a better shot at the house. He looks back into the house to see if one of his ranking officers wants him to go move them back, but everyone's ambling about the house and he can't get anyone's attention.

His boredom convinces him to take the initiative to leave his post and confront the news crew. He straightens his gun belt and pulls his hat downward to the middle of his forehead as he steps off the porch, heads across the driveway and walks quickly down the sidewalk towards the news crew. He walks about three houses down the sidewalk then starts yelling and gesturing to them. "Hey"! Get back behind the barrier, he yells and points at them. Jean notices the young officer walking off the property and toward the news crew. As he approaches the group, she can see him gesturing to them to move back behind the barrier as he starts to reposition the barrier again. Everyone's' attention is focused on the officer and the news crew. Just then, a crazy thought pops in her head, which severely beats down Jean's common sense. She can't help herself as she brazenly leaves her friends without a word and scampers across the street, maneuvers herself under the crime tape and ducks behind a small tree, which doesn't give her much cover.

She's not a small woman and her green and yellow Nike' sweat suit doesn't help her concealment. Her friends are frantically gesturing to her to come back across the street. But Jean is in a position where she can see what's going on inside the house and she thinks its' worth any risk of her getting caught. All the other neighbors are hoping one of the officers will spot her and possibly use their taser on her.

But for now, she has unobstructed access to the crime scene. She is behind a tree standing on her toes so she can see as much as she can. She can even hear some of what is going on as they search BK's office. "They are looking through everything", she thinks to herself. She can see a female detective on BK's computer while two other detectives stand behind her writing something down and giving instructions to her. There are two additional officers in the room removing books and folders off the shelves and placing most of them into plain brown boxes. Jean knows the longer she stands there, the more likely one of the officers will see her, but this is just too good and she ignores her inner voice yelling at her to get back to the other side of the road.

Just then, Jean's colorful sweat suit catches Detective Tillman's attention outside the window. Their eyes lock onto each other like star struck lovers and Jean goes into panic mode. The Detective tells his partner that he'll be right back as he rushes out of the room and heads toward the front door. Jean tries to will herself thin as she ducks completely behind the tree, but her ample butt and breast are completely exposed. She immediately backs away from the tree and walks swiftly toward the crime tape. Her brain is in panic mode, which causes her feet to trip over themselves as she tumbles to the ground as if she was tripped by an ant. The result of her ugly fall causes her fellow neighbors to respond with a mixture of concern and laughter. She doesn't try to jump to her feet but does a barrel roll under the crime tape then pops up on the other side of the tape. She quickly and embarrassingly speed walks toward her friends like nothing has happened. April is the first of Jean's friends to reach out to her with concern as she rejoins them, but Jean pushes past her and moves herself behind the group in order to hide from the police that will be coming after her.

But Detective Tillman has seen her and has emerge from the residence looking for the woman in the green and yellow sweat suit. He walks onto the porch and looks left and right to locate the posted officer that was to stop people from getting close to his crime scene. He's amazed to see the officer walking down the sidewalk back toward the house.

He gives the young officer an intense stare as he walks across the grass and toward Jean, who is now mingled in amongst her friends. The young officer only makes brief eye contact with the detective as he returns to his post. April turns around to Jean and repeats over and over, "he's coming"! Jean's yellow and green sweat suit doesn't help her blend in with the other women and makes it easy for the detective to recognize her as the person at the window.

The detective is focused on the woman in the very noticeable and colorful sweat suit as he walks toward the small group of women. "Good morning ladies", he says as he approaches them. Jean then turns to face the detective as she watches her friends part like Moses parted the Red Sea. He stops a few feet in front of her and just stares at her. "What can I do for you Officer", she says with a nervous smile. Two of her friends, Helen and Mary, step back, because they've seen "Cops" and don't know if he's going to take her down and slap the cuffs on her. Helen taps and finger swipes the screen on her cellphone until she got to the camera icon. She's ready to capture this moment for her Face Book page and "World Star".

Jean continues to give the detective a welcoming smile as she responds to the detective. For one thing, I'm Detective Tillman not Officer Tillman, he says sharply. I would greatly appreciate it if you wouldn't contaminate my crime scene. Mary steps closer to the detective. "So that's what it is now "a crime scene", she asked with excitement in her voice! The Detective holds up his hand as the five ladies start to surround him. The other groups of neighbors start to merge with the group of ladies as the Detective is being surrounded. "Alright"! Please stop jumping to conclusions. This is normal law enforcement procedures to call and treat these types of missing persons as "crime scenes". We're just in the investigative phase. I just need everyone to remain here on the sidewalk and not to cross my crime tape, please. Mary decides to ask the Detective a question.

"Can you tell us anything about what's going on in there or have you at least heard from Lorraine and the girls"? I'm sorry, but at the moment, I am not at liberty to discuss anything about the family at this time, he replies sharply. But I would like to get everyone's name, address and any pertinent information relative to the family that lived at that residence, he says as he looks around the growing crowd. "Lived", you said lived, Helen repeated with surprise in the tone of her voice". That was past tense, she says with a gasp. "Oh my God, do you think they're dead", Susan shouts as she covers her mouth with both hands. The detective sighs as he thinks to himself that he really hates this part of his job and he will have to be careful regarding what he says with this group. OK ladies, please stop reading into everything I say. If you really want to assist our investigation, I need to ask all of you some questions, so please listen closely.

The crowd of neighbors nod their heads in agreement and continue to talk amongst themselves, but Jean hope she can interject some of her questions. Jean decides she should be first, so she starts to tell the detective her name and address, but he points to April, who has tried to conceal herself behind the other women. She's the most timid of the five and doesn't want to talk to the detective. What's your name, address and do you have anything useful regarding the family. April slowly steps forward and gives the detective her name and address. Can you tell me anything useful that may help locate the Thomas family?

Well, my husband and I didn't have much interaction with the parents, but my daughter and the Thomas' youngest daughter were friends. Did she come over your house on a regular basis and what type of friends were they, he asked? No, they weren't best friends, but they liked the same teen shows and would study together sometimes. The detective pulls a note pad and pen from his jacket pocket and precedes to write down her every word. As he writes her name and address, he asked if she had any opportunity to talk to Kim's mother. April is caught off guard for a few seconds, because she was surprise that the detective knew Kim's name. He looks at her for an answer. Every once in a while, I would ask Kim if her mother was coming to the school for the teacher's conference meeting or if they were going anywhere for the holidays. For the most part, I don't conversate with our children's friends. They're at the age where we embarrass them easily, so my husband and I for the most part stay out of their business. Jean turns her head away from April and rolls her eyes. She can't stand when someone else is getting all the attention and she feels that April is boring the detective to death. Detective Tillman doesn't find the information he's getting from April of any value, but he continues to write it down anyway. After a half dozen more questions and disappointing answers, he couldn't take any more of this useless information so, he thanks her for the information and moves onto the next of the neighbors. April is glad it's over and melds back into the crowd.

"You", as he points to Jean. Have you had any pertinent conversations with any of the Thomas family? Lorraine wouldn't confide a cake recipe to Jean, because she knew that Jean was the neighborhood gossip and knew if you tell Jean something in the morning, it would be in someone else's ear by brunch. You seem like you're the neighborhood historian. The detective wanted to say "gossip", but historian would most likely ensure that she wouldn't be insulted and would divulge everything she knew. What can you tell me about the Thomas family, he says with his pen in one hand and note pad in the other? Well yes, I did run across bits of information from time to time about my neighbors but I'm no snoop if that's what you are implying. I'm sorry, but aren't you the woman that ducked under crime tape, tried to hide behind a tree, peered through the window, he asked sarcastically? "Yes", but I was overwhelmed with concern for my neighbor's welfare, she says with a less than convincing tone.

"Alright", he says as he gestures for her to give him whatever information she has. What is your full name, address and what can you tell me about the family? She just likes being the center of attention and hearing herself talk, which the detective picks up on after listening to her rattle on for about two minutes. He listens to her talk about how her son was dumped a year ago by the Thomas' oldest daughter and how she thought she was better than everyone else. Jean was so much into bragging to the detective about how her family is loosely related to George Washington, she didn't realize that the detective isn't writing anymore. He interrupts her in the middle of her irrelevant story about her not being able to dance because of hammer toe. Thank you, Mrs. Coleman, he says as he points to and asked for the name of one other neighbor in the back of the growing crowd. Just then Detective Sanders emerge from the house and yells to his partner from across the street to return to the house. Sorry, he says as he quickly puts his pad and pen away. The neighbors continue to yell questions at him as he walks away from them. He stops in the middle of the street and turns around. The crowd thinks he's about to answer a few of their questions, but he looks directly at Jean and shouts sternly, "Don't cross my crime tape again", as he points his finger at her for dramatic effect! Which does send chills through Jean and her friends. He turns and proceeds to walk back toward the property and into the residence.

Tillman gives the young rooky an intense stare as he walks pass him. The officer just gives the detective a quick glance and nod, which acknowledges that he understands that he messed up by leaving his post without permission.

Tillman walks in the house and closes the door behind him. "What's going on", he asked his partner that's standing waiting for him in front of the hallway. "Nothing". I thought you needed someone to rescue you from that crowd of neighbors, he says with a smile. "I owe you one", he says as he follows his partner down the hall. In the front room, there's two officers and one detective in the front room now.

The detective name is Woodard, who is 32 years old, six foot tall white male, teeth as white as tic tacs and looks like he spends all his waking hours in the gym as well as in the tanning booth. If you didn't know he was an FBI agent, most people would think he's some type of model. As he sits on the couch, he looks like he's about to rip open the seams of his jacket. He's fully focused on reading through the pile of documents that were left on the coffee table for him to review. The two female Officers are in the living room assigned to assist the Detective with his search of the living room and kitchen.

"Green", is the name of the Officer near the hallway, who is in her mid thirties and is trying to listen to what's on what's going on in BK's office. Both of the Officers are bored to death, because the Detective is too focused on the piles of papers he's sorting through. The youngest of the two Officers is a brown eyed half native American and half Asian woman, who looks like she couldn't find a uniform that fits her small frame. "Milanich", is the name engraved on the name tag attached to her loosely fitting shirt. Her long pitch-black hair is twisted, coiled and pinned tightly to her head in order to maintain the police department's female law enforcement guidelines. She's tired of just standing around listening to everyone finding bits and pieces of what happened in this investigation. She wants to help the Detective search for information in the back rooms. She cuts her eyes over to the Detective sitting on the couch next to her, reading through the piles of paper. She inches closer to where he's sitting to get a better look at what he's reading.

The Detective looks up at her as she's peering down at the document he has in his hands and asked if he can help her. She smiles and apologizes for being so nosey, but she explains to him that she has aspirations to become a Detective one day. He can't help but notice that she's very cute and he can't help but smile back. Pardon me for saying, but you look kind of petite to be a Police Officer. How long have you been on the force, he asked as he puts the document that was in his hand in a growing pile of other documents he has already reviewed.

"Two and a half", she says as she moves closer. "Man", I remember those days, he says as he glances up at her then picks up another document. You're not the first person to comment on my size, she says with a smile. She can see what he's reading and without his knowledge starts to read to herself, while asking how long he's been on the force? I've been a Detective for three years, and on the force for a little over eight. "Wow"! you've moved up fast in the ranks. "Ya", he says with a smile. You should let me help you look through those papers, she says in the most seductive tone she could muster. He looks up at her as she smiles down at him. He can feel her pretty eyes locking on to his, but he can also feel his wedding ring beginning to tighten on his finger. "No", that won't be proper protocol, as he replaces her beautiful face with his wife's. Detective Sanders tasked me with the job of searching this room and the kitchen for evidence.

I'm sorry for asking, but it's hella boring just standing around waiting for you guys to give us something to do, she adds. Detective Woodard puts the document to the side and takes a break to talk with the young attractive Officer. He sees her name tag with the name Milanich engraved on it, but he asked her for her first name. She was named after her grandmother "Toriko", which is Japanese for "bird child". But her friends and family calls her "Tori".

She thinks about telling him her name, but it wouldn't be to her best interest. "I think we should call each other by the names on our name tags", Detective Woodard. The Detective looks at her with a curious smile and asked her how she knew his name? I heard Detective Sanders and Detective Tillman call your name a couple of times, she explains. I've been training myself to remember names of my fellow Officers and Detectives. Woodard gets the attention of the other Officer and asked her to join him and Officer Milanich. Officer Green walks over to them with a smile on her face, because she's glad to be actively involved in the investigation rather than just standing around like a store manikin. The Detective has been searching the living room and reviewing documents for about an hour and hadn't spoken with any of the two Officers until now. He stands and shakes Officer Green's hand as she approaches and introduced himself. Officer Green then introduces herself to Officer Milanich, which takes the detective by surprise, because he thought that all the officers knew each other.

"Oh, I'm sorry"! I thought you too have met, he says in a surprising tone. Milanich smiles at Green, but Green stares at her with intense curiosity. She knows all the other Officers in the residence or at least seen them before, but Milanich's name and face isn't familiar to her. She's about to ask Milanich some questions about what precinct she's with, when the detective asked them to come into the kitchen with him. Once all three are in the middle of the kitchen, he grabs a couple of pairs of blue plastic evidence gloves from a box and hands them to each of them. He then starts to give them instructions on what to look for and not to hesitate to ask him any questions if they are confused about anything they find. He then points to the areas he wants them to cover. All three have been searching the cabinets, trash can and refrigerator for about fifteen minutes, when Milanich finds some store receipts while fishing through the kitchen trash.

She stands there for a minute, reading over the purchases made last week. She catches the eye of her fellow Officer, who walks over to her to see what she has found. "Anything", Green asked as she stands next to Milanich. The Detective, who is standing on a chair to search the top shelf of the cabinets, looks back at both of them looking over what seems like a scrap of paper.

Both Officers look up at him and Milanich states that they are hardware receipts from three days prior to the family's disappearance. "Great"! Don't get caught up on what you find. Just put it on the counter and continue searching your areas. "He bought a shovel", she says to Officer Green as she places the receipt on the counter in front of them. Green gives her a facial expression as if to say, "doesn't look good".

Green returns to her search of the pots and pans in the lower cabinet, while Milanich continues diving through the used paper towels and rotten dinner scraps of the trash can. After an additional fifteen minutes of searching, the Detective tells the two officers that the kitchen has given everything that its' going to give. He then thanks both Officers and grabs the receipt off the center island as he walks out of the kitchen. He tells them they can resume their post and he will call them if he needs them again. He snatches off both pairs of gloves and tosses them on the kitchen counter. He grabs the receipt as he walks back to the couch and adds it to his small pile of positive leads.

Once he's finished searching this area, he thinks he'll be moving to one of the bedrooms, if he's lucky. Finding that receipt just gave Milanich motivation to search for more clues, but she knows that the Detective won't need any more assistance from her. Green doesn't return to her post by the hallway but stays in the kitchen staring at Milanich from the other side of the island. She knows she's seen Milanich somewhere before.

Milanich is near the couch, when she hears something going on down the hall as she moves down the island in order to get closer to the hallway to hear what's going on, but then Green walks up to her from behind, which startles her. "You look so familiar to me" as she waits for Milanich to respond. Milanich replies by telling her that she has been behind the desk for a while and that she was lucky to get volunteered to help out in this investigation.

Green hears what she's saying, but her face is so distinctive that she can't shake the feeling that they've crossed paths before. Milanich can clearly see that Green is racking her brain to remember where they met, so she decides to turn the table and pick her brain about the investigation. She confides in Green that she knows she's just a desk riding rookie, but her gut tells her that the husband had nothing to do with the disappearance of his family, she says in a whispering tone as she leans closer to her. Green is a more seasoned officer, and her gut tells her that the husband had everything to do with his family's disappearance. She proceeds to enlighten her young fellow officer on how most of the missing families hadn't had a happy ending and eighty-five percent of the time; a family member or members are responsible. Green is somewhat jaded, because of this being her third missing persons in the past four months involving a family member this year. "But I don't understand why and what would give you the impression that the family's disappearance has something to do with the parents, Milanich asked under her breath. Green hesitates for a moment, while trying to decide if she should tell her what she knows. Milanich gives her a "what" gesture. "Alright", Green says in a low tone. Green moves away from the island and walks back into the kitchen as Milanich follows.

Green feels sorry for her, because she remembered when she was a young rookie that was only let out to assist with these crappy assignments. And plus she's pissed off that they have her still standing around like a rookie, so she decides to tell Milanich everything she knows about the investigation. She moves closer to her then spills her guts about everything she has overheard and noticed from her post from the hallway and back rooms. For over ten minutes, Green indoctrinated Milanich on what the department speculates most likely happened to the family and that the husband is the prime suspect. Milanich is transfixed and continues to soak up more and more information like a dry sponge on a rainy day. She had no idea that the husband had been embezzling his company's money. Milanich never thought that in her wildest dreams she would have access to this much information. Meanwhile, Detective Sanders is getting frustrated by the lack of clues.

They are almost finished with BK's office and they haven't found much that would explain why he would embezzle over two hundred thousand dollars and what he could have possibly done with all that money. There's no evidence that he had a lavish lifestyle, or nothing points to him having another woman or women on the side. When they gained access to his bank account, he had a little over $3,000.00 in the account.

Detective Tillman rubs the top of his head in frustration, as he turns around, walks out of the room and heads toward one of the places in the house that usually yields the most clues without fail – the master bedroom. Seventy-five percent of the home has been searched, but the detective wonders will the remaining twenty-five deliver any additional answers to what happened.

This case is slowly but surely turning into what the Detectives in his district like to call, "a black hole of nothingness". As he walks pass one of the girls' bedrooms toward the master bedroom, one of the experienced officers assigned to search the rooms yells out for him to come into the oldest daughter's bedroom. "What's up"! Did you find anything, he says with excitement? Officer Reddick walks the detective over to the head of the bed. I don't know, she says as she points to the bed. "You tell me", as she stands at the head of the bed and points? The Detective looks at the headboard then the mattress and finally the covers.

Can you give me a hint to what I should be looking for, because I just see an unmade bed? Move back a little please, you're in the light, Tillman tells Reddick as she moves over behind him. He grabs his pen out of his jacket pocket and sticks the pen in the pillowcase to raise the pillow into the light. Tillman can see some discoloration on certain areas of the pillowcase.

He can see a slightly yellowish tint and without the light they would have missed it completely. "Good job Officer Reddick", as he smiles back at her. I think you just gave us our first solid clue. Thank you, Detective. The Detective then bends over to get a closer look at the stain and to try to identify it by its' smell. It looks like some type of chemical, he thinks to himself, as he gets his nose less than an inch from the stain and takes a deep whiff. He doesn't recognize the smell, but the next thing he knows; everything is moving in slow motion and he's flat on his back with the blurry image of Officer Reddick asking him is he alright? He can't hear her clearly and can't get his eyes to focus. He can hear a mixture of what he thinks are voices coming from various directions. His eyes begin to come back into focus and the voices are becoming clearer. He then recognizes his partner's voice yelling instructions and asking everyone to step the hell back and give him some air.

"Are you alright John"! I want everyone out of these rooms until we can figure out what kind of chemical that the detective has been expose to, and get me an ambulance in route, he shouts as he stops his partner from trying to get to his feet. "Stay down"! We have an ambulance on the way. "No"! I'm alright, Tillman shouts," as he turns to his side and breathes in deeply to counter act what happened to him. Just help me to my feet, please. As he tries to lift himself from the floor, Sanders pushes Tillman's shoulders back to the floor. I think you should lie still and wait for the ambulance, partner. Tillman can feel his body and mind returning to normal. Sanders, he says with a thankful, but stern voice, "I'm feeling find now". I think whatever that is on that pillowcase has run its' course.

Now, I'm going to get up off this floor and if you try to stop me again, the paramedics will be treating the knot I'm going to put on your damn head. Tillman isn't one hundred percent yet, but he forces himself off his back and onto his butt. The crowd moves back to give him some room. Sanders reaches down and offers his partner a hand. Tillman gladly accepts. For moment there partner, I thought you had bought the farm, he says as Tillman brushes himself off. Just then, Officer Reddick steps forward.

Man detective, you went down like a boneless chicken, she says with a chuckle. One minute you and I were talking about the stain and the next minute, you were on the floor with your eyes rolled up in the back of your head. "OK Reddick, we all were there", Tillman says as he continues shaking off the drug effect as well as his embarrassment. Maybe we should call headquarters and get the hell out of here before we all are flat on our asses, another Officer standing in the door exclaims. Alright, yells Detective Tillman. Officer Green and Milanich pushes their way to the bedroom door asking what happened. As everyone moves out of the room, Officer Reddick fills them in on what happened. Everyone out of these bedrooms and get to the front of the residence, Tillman shouts. Sanders tells his partner to get some air, and yells to Officer Reddick to put the pillow in an evidence bag and to be careful. Officer Reddick seems to be scared to touch the pillow, but she thinks she can get it in one of the larger evidence bags without touching it.

Normally, Sanders would let the Hazardous Material section of the department gather that type of evidence, but he wants to take that bit of evidence in himself. I will call headquarters and apprise them of what just happened here and ask them to send HAZMAT over here on the double. And ask them to bring some extra hazardous suits for you and me. "Everyone out of the house until HAZMAT clears it"! You heard him people, "Move it", Sanders shouts as he forcefully pushes everyone out of the room. Reddick searches for the large evidence bags for the pillow Tillman wants.

Everyone starts to pile out of the house and gathers in the front yard. Sanders instructs Tillman to make sure everyone stays on the property and within the crime tape. As all six Officers and five Detectives all gather on the lawn, they can hear the neighbors yelling questions from across the street. "What's going on", "Why are you evacuating the house", are some of the questions they're asking. Officer Green is instructed by Sanders to go across the street and calm the crowd, but not to tell them about what happened. She walks across the street and approaches the loudest man, who is still yelling one annoying question after another. Sir, please, she says trying to calm him down.

Everything is fine and we're not evacuating the house. It's more about procedure than safety, but I can't tell you anything more at this time. He walks toward Officer Green, aggressively asking her another question.

Why in the hell did you guys come piling out of the house like circus clowns, if you weren't worried about something? He is a rather large older man with a very deep and booming voice. She can tell that the man is getting a little upset and his wild hand and arm gestures are starting to concern her. She automatically thinks about her taser on her opposite hip from her gun. She tries to calm him and the rest of the neighbors by telling them that they're about to wrap up the investigation soon.

"This is our damn neighborhood and we have the right to know what's going on", he bellows while turning to his fellow neighbors in order to hopefully stoke them up. Green raised the intensity in her voice and ask the man to move back and to lower his voice, as she grabs her holstered taser. That only causes him and some of the other people in the crowd to get louder and to remind Officer Green of their First Amendment rights. She takes a few steps backward then unsnaps the safety strap from the taser holster. Just then she feels a large hand flop down on her shoulder. "Is there a problem Officer", ask Detective Sanders? Before she could open her mouth, the man loudly demands to know what's going on.

Detective Sanders moves in front of Officer Green, attempting to intimidate the man and the crowd of neighbors. This being his crime scene, he thinks it will be better for him to explain to the crowd how important this investigation is to locating the family. And he knew Officer Green was about to tase this loudmouth behemoth as a cautionary action to all the other neighbors. We can't allow you or anyone else to interfere or contaminate our crime scene, he continues to explain in a calm but stern tone to the crowd. Now if you stay away from the crime tape and don't cause us any further problems, you will be allowed to watch our investigation.

Otherwise, I will have this officer remove you from the area on the grounds that you are causing a public disturbance. Sanders looks at the man in front of him intensely. The man looks at the detective, then at Officer Green standing behind and slightly to the left of the detective with her hand still on her taser. The look on her face and her hand gripping her taser intimidates him more than the detective. The man just nods his head in agreement as his wife walks up from behind him and pulls her husband back within the group of neighbors, who are much calmer now. Sanders smiles and turns to walk back to the house with Green behind him. As they walk across the street, Green thanks the detective for stopping her from tasering that idiot. "No problem", he replies with a smile. But in the future, I would suggest that you utilize your two best weapons and they are not carried on your duty belt. Green looks at Sanders with a curious expression.

It's the tone of your voice and your body language that will dictate how people will react to you. Both continue across the street, maneuvering between the police cars and onto the sidewalk. I'll keep that in mind for the future, she says as both duck under the crime tape and merge back into the group of Officers and Detectives. Detective Sanders starts instructing three of his officers to form a perimeter around the property and pondering re-entering the residence in order to recover the evidence that are already bagged. But just then he hears the screech of tires rounding the corner two houses down then pulling in front of the house next door. The group of law enforcement officers and the crowd of neighbors' eyes shift to the street as three well-polished black plain sedans and a large black van speeds around the corner. Detective Sanders moves his way through a few Officers standing in front of him in order to get a good look at the vehicles. They look like the Feds vehicles, which he was never told would be involved. But before he could get out of the yard.

All the vehicles doors open and a couple dozen or so men and women in navy blue suits pile out of them. They move purposely toward the house, ripping down the crime tape and three of them bolt across the street. Like a perfectly choreographed football team, each agent start moving through the crowd of neighbors writing down names and then asking them to return to they're homes.

Detective Sanders can only watch in stunned amazement as these men and women move between them as if they were lawn ornaments. When he was a rookie officer assigned to assist a couple of detectives on an office break-in, two agents in black suits arrived at the crime scene, announced their authority over the investigation and seized all the evidence. He hoped that would never happen to him, but here they are at his investigation. As two Agents go into the residence, the third Agent stands on the porch and makes an announcement. "May I have your attention everyone", as he faces the crowd of Officers and Detective. I'm Special Agent Morgan as he holds out his credentials. Please reframe from removing anything else from the residence and we will take possession of any evidence that you have acquired. Please vacate the property in an orderly fashion, he says in a disrespectful tone. Thank you! He turns to enter the house, but he is stopped by Detective Tillman. He angerly approach the Agent asking him who gave him the authority to take over his investigation. The other Detectives and Officers crowded around the Special Agent as they yell obscenities and counter instructions back and forth at each other. Detective Sanders shouts at Tillman to stay calm and remain on the property until he tells him otherwise.

Sanders is focused on the only Agent standing beside the first vehicle with a cellphone at her ear, which he thinks must be the agent in charge. He walks off the property and onto the sidewalk. He'll let Tillman deal with the second in charge while he tries to find out why the Feds are interested in this missing family. As he walks closer to the smaller than usual female Agent leaning against the passenger door, he guesses that she's probably talking to whomever sent her here.

He's so close to her now that he could hear the last of her conversation. "I'll call you back after I secure the residence", she says as she ends the call. "Detective Sanders", she says as she placed her cellphone into her jacket pocket and extends her hand to shake his. It doesn't surprise him that she knows his name, because the Federal Government never just appears on a crime scene without doing their due diligence. Sanders doesn't see the point of being cordial, knowing what's about to happen.

"I'm sorry", but you may know my name, but I don't know yours and why are you taking over my investigation. She smiles and lowers her hand. I'm Special Agent Leon and the Government has an interest in finding the Thomas family, but that's all I can tell you, Detective. But I will have to ask you to gather your men and turnover all evidence of the investigation to us. You know that's not going to happen until I receive direct orders from my Captain. Until then, I will remain on my investigation and I would appreciate you gather your men and getting out of this neighborhood. Agent Leon walks up to him as she reaches into her jacket pocket and pulls out a bundle of three-folded and stapled document. She stands directly in front of him holding out the document and waiting for him to take them. Sanders towers over her as she raises her arm to place the documents close to his face as possible. But she can only reach his chest. As they stand facing each other, she gives him a smug and confident look. He doesn't have to read the documents that this mini agent is handing him to know what it says. That's why he hesitates to take them from her hand. He reluctantly takes the documents from her, as she continues to smile at him. He reads the first sheet which gives the pertinent information about the primary investigator and the scope of her jurisdiction regarding the investigation, which is broad. She stands there looking up at him and his changing facial expressions as he gets to the section stating that she has complete authority over the investigation.

She nonchalantly tells him to keep that copy for his records as she walks pass him and heads towards the Thomas residence. Sanders continues to flip through the other sheets getting angrier as he read the remaining pages.

The document instructs all the local agencies regardless of jurisdiction to relinquish all evidence and information to Special Agent Leon and her Agents. But what it doesn't state is what Federal agency or department that the Special Agent resides. In the authorizing agency section, it just states the agency as "Unknown", which is highly unusual. He's seen documents like this before and they usually have FBI, CIA, DEA, but never "Unknown". Sanders doesn't feel he has to comply with Leon's orders, but he feels he has to check all the boxes by calling his Captain before he has his Officers boot them off the property. He felt like crumpling the documents in his fist and throwing it in her face, but he's a professional law enforcement officer, so he begrudgingly folds the document up and places them in his jacket pocket and grabs his cellphone. Government Agents normally don't show up at a crime scene without having all their ducks in a row, so he doesn't have a good feeling about the outcome as he calls his Captain.

The Captain's secretary answers with a pleasant "Hello, Captain Rudolph's office". Louise, may I speak to the Captain, please. Yes, Agent Sanders, but it will be a minute, because he's finishing up a meeting. It shouldn't be long, so I'll put you on hold until he's free. He gives Louise a reluctant, "thank you". He hears Special Agent Leon calling him and can see her gesturing for him to come to the residence, but he throws up his hand and turns his back to her. Leon already knows what Sanders' Captain is about to tell him, but she knows it's best he hears it from the horse's mouth. Tillman doesn't want to stand out in the front yard combating the Agents, so he walks back into the residence with Special Agents Leon and Morgan trailing him into the residence.

119

After about three minutes of Sanders pacing back and forth in the neighbors yard, Captain Rudolph finally picks up the phone. "Sanders", he bellows. "Captain we have a problem"! We have some Government Agents here stating they are with an unknown branch of the Federal Government Investigative Bureau and are attempting to highjack our investigation.

Yes Sanders, I have recently been made aware of the Government's intentions and have been informed by the Chief that we are to give Special Agent Leon all the cooperation that she requires, including relinquishing the investigation to her if she deems it necessary. Sanders can't say he's truly surprised by what he's hearing, but he's still a bit stunned.

Captain, this case seems to be more than just a routine missing persons and it would be improper for us to allow the Government to overstep their bounds and run amuck on our jurisdiction. We've done all the work and now they want to come in a seize everything. The Captain had the same conversation with his Chief and got his ass handed to him for trying to stand up for his Detectives. Listen closely Sanders. There isn't a Santa Claus, the Easter Bunny is in some hunter's pot, and the Tooth Fairy was your mom and dad, the Captain yells through the phone. I'm only going to say this once, he says in a threatening tone. Life isn't fair and neither is working in law enforcement! Now I'm pissed off at the situation too, but after the Chief shot down all my reasons for telling Special Agent Leon and the Government to play in their own sand box.

I will spare you the expletives and the disparaging remarks about my ancestry, but I was instructed in no uncertain terms to comply with the Government's orders, and you will do the same. "Are we clear", Sanders. He knows that he doesn't have a choice, but that doesn't make it easy for him to swallow this plate of horse crap. The Captain doesn't hear any response, so he asked Sanders again, but this time with a ton more attitude. "Agent Sanders", are we crystal clear on your new marching orders. "Yes Captain", he replies with a clear and a healthy amount of anger in his voice. I also need you to have your team meet at the station for a debriefing before they disperse and head back out on the street. "Yes Captain". The Captain doesn't say another word, but just hangs up the phone. Back at the residence, Special Agent Leon and Agent Cook are in the residence now instructing Tillman and his team to leave the property and leave all the evidence they collected.

Detective Woodard is getting very upset by the way Special Agent Morgan is now attempting to herd a group of officers out of the front door. He walks over and places himself between Morgan and his officers in order to keep them in the residence. "Stay put until we receive further instructions from Detective Sanders", he shouts in a defiant tone. Sanders is still standing near the vehicles trying to process the idea of having to turn over his investigation to those Special Agent bastards. He feels his blood pressure escalating and his stomach knotting up.

The combatant voices emanating from the residence demonstrate to him that the situation is getting serious. He can hear his partner's voice dominating everyone else's and he knows it won't be too long until Tillman gets another letter of reprimand placed in his permanent record for doing something compulsive. He places his phone back into his pocket, takes a deep breath and then walks back towards the residence. As he walks toward the house, he looks across the street as three or four of Leon's agents are trying their best to answer some heated questions by a fairly large crowd of neighbors. Sanders is a consummate professional, but it won't stop him from thinking of some choice and inappropriate words he would love to share with Special Agent Leon before he leaves.

He approaches the porch and can see that there are two rookie standing on opposite sides of the front door. One is the original Police Officer and the other is one of Leon's Agents. He walks between the two of them and into the house as all eyes shifts to him. Tillman is relieved to see his partner walking through the door, but he can tell by Sanders' facial expression that the news isn't good. "So what's the deal", Tillman asked as he walks up to him? Sanders first clears his throat to make room for this large meal of crow. We have been instructed to relinquish the investigation to Special Agent Leon's and to comply with any and all of her orders.

"Her investigation", Tillman repeats loudly and in amazement? Woodard turns and kicks the coffee table over, which sends the evidence he collected flying into the air and onto the floor. He walks away in disgust. "Alright, that's enough of that", Sanders shouts! "I agree", Special Agent Leon says as she steps forward while proudly smiling. I need you to gather your people and relinquish all evidence pertaining to my crime scene, she says as she looks directly at Detective Sanders.

Both detectives are beyond upset, but are doing their best to control their emotions for the sake of the junior detectives and officers and conceal their anger with the way they are being removed from what was their investigation. Officer Reddick appears with the evidence bag with the pillow inside from the back bedroom, asking Detective Sanders what to do with this evidence. Special Agent Morgan bolts toward her before Sanders can say a word.

"I'll take that", he says as he rudely grabs the evidence bag out of her hand. "What the hell is your problem", Officer Reddick shouts as she aggressively moves toward the Agent. The other officers and detectives begin to push and shout at Morgan and the other Special Agents, after seeing how disrespectful he was toward one of their own.

Tillman quickly intervenes. "Stand the hell down damn it, he demands as he pushes his way through the crowd of Officers, Detectives and Special Agents. Special Agent Leon's tone is harsh and deliberate as she instructs Detective Sanders to remove himself from her crime scene, immediately. Sanders is at his limit with the mini agent as they both stare at each other intensely. He's looking down at her as she's looking up at him; neither giving an inch. The room is silent and everyone wonders if Detective Sanders is going to bang her on the top of her head like the "wank a mole game or if Leon will give Sanders an uppercut to his nether-region.

Tillman doesn't think his partner will get physical with a fellow Law Enforcement Officer, regardless of how much of an ass hole she is, but he's not so sure that a wildcard in the group may throw a punch. He knows who will get the blame for anything that happens, so he walks up to his partner. "Detective", he says in a stern voice as he puts his hand on his partner's shoulder. "Let's get our people the hell out of here"! Tillman looks down at the Special Agent with distain. Sanders just nods his head and walks away from her, with his fellow officers and detectives doing the same.

Tillman stops for a moment and turns around to see Morgan's smug face smiling back at him, while still holding the evidence bag. Tillman walks slowly up to him. Sanders yells back at him to come on, but Tillman gestures to him to give him a moment. He gets into Morgan's personal space, which gives Morgan some pause. "You have something to say", Detective, Morgan sternly asked? Leon sees what's happening but decides not to interfere. You've taken our investigation and all my evidence, but I'll be damn if I'll let you use our evidence bag, as he rips a large portion of the bag from the Agent's hand. The pillow flies out of the bag and onto the floor as Agent Morgan and Leon looks at Tillman walking out of the door in stunned silence. He ushers out the remaining smiling Officers out of the front door as he follows. Tillman stops in the doorway and makes one last statement to the Special Agents. As a bit of professional courtesy, we smelled the pillow and we think the stain is possibly lemon juice, but your evidence, your problem.

He walks out of the door with the ripped evidence bag in hand and stands on the porch with Sanders. Sanders doesn't reprimand him, because he knows exactly what his partner is trying to accomplish. Morgan angerly snatches the pillow off the floor and looks for the stain on the pillow. Sanders and Tillman stop short of leaving the porch but look back through the living room window.

They want to see if anyone takes the bait and smells the stain. Leon gives out instructions to her team of Agents, while Morgan asks for an evidence bag. He flips the pillow over and back again to see if he sees any stain. "There's no damn stain on this pillow", he says to his fellow Agents standing around him as Sanders and Tillman peer through the window.

Leon can see the two Detectives on the porch staring at Morgan, which makes her curious about what their up to. "Oh, there's the stain", Morgan says out loud. Leon looks at a smiling Sanders and Tillman then at Morgan who's now putting the pillow to his face.

"No", she yells as she lunged toward him. But it's too late. He puts the pillow to his nose and takes a big sniff of the stain. "Doesn't smell like anything", he says to Leon as he presents the pillow for her to take a whiff. The rookie Agent standing at the door asked Tillman if he wanted anything, but Tillman and Sanders just ignore him as they continue to stare at Morgan. Leon grabs the pillow by one of its' corners as she sees Morgan's eyes roll back in his head and watches him as he crumples to the floor.

The other agents rush to assist him, while Leon is still standing there holding the pillow by one of its' corners. She looks down at Morgan, who is now totally out, then angerly looks back to the living room window, but Sanders and Tillman are gone. "Idiot pencil neck bastard", Tillman says as he and Sanders laugh as they walk across the grass toward their vehicle.

123

Meanwhile, Milanich is having a conversation with the young officer that was posted at the door and he has a bit more information she hadn't heard, but she can see that she's pushing her luck and it's time for her to leave. The Feds are in the house busy tending to their fallen comrade and the detectives are talking amongst each other.

The support officers are milling around waiting for the lead detective to dismiss them. This is the perfect time for her to slip away, so she tells the officer that she has to go to her patrol car for a second and smiles at him while telling him she'll be right back. He thinks she's cute and smiles back at her while hoping he can maybe ask her out once she comes back. She walks casually across the driveway trying not to attract too much attention.

She would have liked to walk to the left, but she would have to pass by Detective Sanders and Tillman, but she knows that one of the Detectives would order her to get back with the group.

So, she has no choice but to head toward the group of reporters and their crew standing on the sidewalk directly in her way. As she gets closer to them, she can see their excitement as they jostle and scramble to be ready to ask her some questions.

"Who are the Feds and why are you guys leaving"?

"What's the latest on the missing family"?

"Is the husband or the wife considered a suspect?

These are the mixture of questions that are being thrown at her as she gets closer to the group. She puts her hand out, trying to calm the crowd, but reporters are always trying to out yell each other. I'm sorry, but I don't have anything to tell you right now, she tells them while stopping in front of them.

But I will get Detective Sanders and he will answer all your questions. That was a lie to pacify them and allow her to get through them as quickly as possible. She lifts the crime tape that sequesters them across her head and works her way through the cameramen and reporters until she hears a male's voice from the back of the group yelling, "Tori".

She recognizes the voice of the person calling her. For a second, she thought to just continue to walk away without turning around, but she feels him touching her on the forearm. Him being, Brent. A man she met at one of the Mayor's lunch time social a few weeks ago. She's surprise and horrified that he still remembers her. "Excuse me", she says as she turns toward him! "Tori", he repeats as he looks totally surprise to see her in a police uniform.

What are you doing dressed as a police officer he says while other people in the group takes notice of their conversation? "Oh", she says with a smile on her face. I'm Nina and you're confusing me with my identical twin sister Tori she says while smiling at him. He stands in front looking her over from head to toe. But you even sound like her, he says with a dumbfounded look on his face. She doesn't have the time to stand around trying to convince him that she's Nina, not Tori. "You are", she says as if she's trying to remember his name? "Brent". "Brent", she repeats. I'll tell my sister I saw you when I see her tonight. But I'll tell you what. Since you're my sister's friend, I will make sure you get the first question when I get back, she says as she starts to back away from him.

That would be great, he says with a pleasant smile. She smiles back at him then turns to continue her walk toward her awaiting vehicle. "Wow"! Someone that beautiful has an identical twin sister, his cameraman exclaims. Brent continues to watch her as she walks around the corner until she disappears. "Get the equipment ready for the interview", he tells his cameraman. We're going to have the first few questions when she comes back with one of the Detectives. He goes to their news van to jot down a few notes he wants to ask them. Tori sees the white van which is parked beside the road as if someone has just left it there. As Tori gets closer to the waiting van, her heart starts to beat faster and she has the impulse to run to it, but she doesn't know if anyone is watching her. She quickens her pace as she approaches the van. "Bill open the door", she yells in a frantic tone as she gets about six feet away from it. The door of the van slides open and Tori jumps into it and yells for him to drive. Bill jumps back into the driver's seat while Tori slams the van's sliding door close and quickly begins to remove the uniform, she borrowed from her real Police Officer twin sister Nina.

"So how'd it go", he asked as he begins to drive out of the neighborhood. She's sitting on the floor of the van, pulling off the uniform as if it was on fire, while Bill watches through the rearview mirror. That was the best idea I've ever had, and I got a ton of information, as she smiles while removing her pants. Tori has on a tight t-shirt and some black spanks, but she has a mini microphone secured to her body with a thin flexible ban wrapped around her.

The small recording device is attached to the back of her spanks. She throws her uniform shirt, or should I say, her sister's shirt to the side as she begins to remove the equipment from her body. Bill is switching his attention from the road then back to Tori's strip tease act, which causes him to swerve a bit.

Tori's back bangs against the equipment console as she struggles to remove the flex ban from under her breast. "Damn it, Bill", keep your eyes on the road you pervert before you cause an accident. Bill puts both hands and eyes on the road as he turns the corner and leaves the neighborhood. Why in the hell do you think I can concentrate on the road if you are taking off your clothes right in front of me, Bill says in his defense. Tori rolls her eyes as she continues to remove the uniform and the equipment strapped to her. "God Bill", she exclaims! I know you don't get to experience a woman undressing in front of you very often, unless you pay her, but I thought that me being your partner would deter you from trying to get a cheap thrill. "Well", you're wrong, he admits with not a hint of shame. "Just tell me what happened, and did you get enough information for a good story.

"Damn right I did", she yells while she continues to remove the last of her sister's uniform. "It was incredible", she says with a beaming smile. That investigation was more than just a missing family. The Feds stormed the place and took over the investigation. Why would the Federal Government care about a missing family, he asked? Not just the Federal Government, but a secret branch of the government that wouldn't identify themselves.

Tori gathers the equipment and plugs the recording device into the van's editing station for uploading to their news network. Once all the audio has been transferred to the main server, they will be able to review every bit of her conversation with everyone she talked with while on the scene. Bill received this tip from one of his stripper friends named "Rum Cakes", who got the information from a high-ranking Officer on the force during a private lap dance. Bill paid her $150 for the information, which he thought would be a scoop of a murder suicide investigation. "I don't like this, Tori", he says as Tori puts on her clothes. "Don't say it", as she stops to give Bill a menacing stare. "I can't help it", he exclaims as he moves his butt around in the seat.

The hairs on my boys are standing on end and that means somethings not right. "No", that means that maybe we should stop at the pharmacy and pickup some medicine for that seafood platter that hitched a ride on your boys, she says as she laughs at him. Go ahead and joke, but my boys don't lie, he says with a serious tone. And by the way, I've only caught the crabs three or four times and they didn't feel like this. Crabs are an itchy feeling, but this is a tingling sensation, he says as if Tori really cares about what his boys feel like.

"Just shut the hell up", she says as she stumbles from the back and flops into the passenger seat. This is one of those make or break investigations and I risked too much to let some idiot mess this up, she says as she looks over at him. I risked my job getting this story and you better grow a healthy pair and help me edit it. Hey, you know I got your back, he says as he looks over at her. She takes some deep breaths and puts her hand on her chest and tells Bill that her heart is still beating a mile a minute.

"Let me feel", he says as he reaches his hand over trying to place it on her chest. She slaps his hand away and yells for him to keep his hands on the damn steering wheel. Bill just laughs and they continue talking about her experience while driving down the road toward their News Station, she tells him everything she found out and what she believes the investigation is really about.

Back at the Thomas residence, Officer Green approaches the Detectives as he asked her to get everyone of her fellow Officers' names and instruct them to meet back at the precinct in one hour for a debriefing. I know most of the Officers, so that won't be a problem, but I'm looking for a small female Officer that has disappeared. "Yes", the one that looked like she couldn't find a uniform that fit her, Sanders replies. Yes, that's her, but maybe she's down the street monitoring the reporters. I didn't tell anyone they could leave, so I'm certain that she's around here somewhere, Tillman says with authority. Just make sure you get the list of every Officer that was on the scene and inform them of the debriefing as Sanders signals to Tillman to get in the car. Officer Green walks towards the driveway, when she sees her rookie partner, Officer Ryan, leaning against their patrol car waiting for her. "Can we get the hell out of here now", he says as he opens the car door to get in. I'm tired of being a lawn Nome and I'm ready to go and eat some breakfast. Sorry, but I have to get every one's name, then we all have to meet at Detective Sanders' precincts for a debriefing. She asked Ryan has he seen Milanich? Ryan says he talked with her for a little while then she said she had to go to her patrol car for a minute. I seen her heading down the sidewalk towards the reporters, but I didn't see her come back. Green has a nagging suspicion that something isn't right with that Officer, but she can't put her finger on what's bothering her about Milanich. She can't worry about that now as she reaches in her pocket and pulls out a pen and a pad and hands them to him to get the rest of the names of the other Officers before they leave. Can't we wait for her until she gets back, Ryan yells as Green walks away from him. "Get those names she says as she continues down the sidewalk toward the group of reporters. For some reason, she doesn't want to tell her young partner that's she doesn't think Milanich is coming back. She doesn't really know why she came to that conclusion, but she did. Green sighs as she starts to walk toward the reporters, but she knows that they are going to think that she has the answers they're looking for.

And sure enough, as they see her approaching, they start jockeying for the best position to ask their questions. As she gets closer to the reporters, which most have mics in their hand and yelling questions at her now, she can see that her missing Officer is not there. "Hey, hey", calm down! I just need to know if you have seen a small, dark haired female Officer recently.

One of the cameramen from the back of the crowd tells her that a short female Officer walked past them about ten minutes ago, as he points in the direction that she went. Thank you, she says as she moves through the crowd. One of the reporters yells out, "Remind Nina that she owes me the first couple of questions when she gets back". Green stops and turns toward the voice behind her. Her name is "Nina", she asked while walking closer to the reporter with a mic in his hand. "Yes", he says as he stops in front of her. She also told me that Detective Sanders will be coming back with her to answer our questions about the investigation. Green knows that she was lying for some reason, but she needs to find out some more information first.

So, how do you know her first name, she asked? As soon as I saw her walking past us, I call her name, because I met her at a party weeks ago, but she corrected me and told me that was her identical twin sister Tori, who is one of us, he says while signaling to his cameraman to get ready to record. "One of you", she asked curiously? What do you mean? Her sister is a reporter, he replies. Green's mind starts to put some of the pieces together as she looks through the reporter as she flashes back to her experience with Milanich.

Uniform doesn't fit well, she had seen her before, and no one seen her leave. "Hello", Officer, Brent says trying to get her attention. Green has no doubt to what has happened to Milanich now. She looks at Brent and the other reporters starting to crowd around her now and thanks him for the information, as she maneuvers her way through the questioning reporters and heads back toward the house and her vehicle. She knows that there is know sense in looking for her now, because she's long gone by now. Brent and his cameraman yells to her to remember to come back with the Detective. Green doesn't see the need to tell the waiting reporters that Sanders is gone and that Milanich wouldn't be coming back either. She turns toward them and gives them a nod and a thumbs up. Sanders' investigation has been compromised and now she is going to have to tell him that they had a reporter impersonating a police officer. Green is pissed that Milanich duped her into telling her everything about the investigation. That could get her suspended from the force or even fired, so she gambles that like most reporters, she won't divulge her sources. So she decides to keep that bit of information to herself.

She knows honesty is the best policy, but she's too close to becoming a Detective to let one pint size reporter ruin her career. And in this line of work, being to honest can get you fired from the force and possiblely sharing a cell with a woman named "Stud". The only good thing about Milanich being a reporter is that if she's caught, she'll never reveal her sources. Sanders being the lead detective will most likely get a heaping portion of the blame for the infiltration of the investigation.

She thinks it would be in her best interest to find out if the real Officer Milanich had anything to do with this deception. It bothers her that she now has to lie and possibly deceive a detective that she respects, because a nosey reporter wanted to get a scoop on a family disappearance, she thinks to herself. "Damn, if I wasn't in enough trouble". I wish I got the opportunity to punch that bitch in her pretty face", she says to herself as she approaches the driveway of the residence.

Back aboard the ship, it has been a few days since they've been in orbit and BK has work through breakfast and MOM is complaining to him that he's not eating his scheduled meals. BK's mind is the most advanced brain on earth but being isolated enables his mind to be bombarded with new ideas, which takes over everything else. If it wasn't for MOM, he would work twelve to fourteen hours every day. It seems the longer he spends alone in the isolation of space; the more he misses just the simple company of his family or any human for that matter. He tries to substitute his loneliness and isolation by working on his projects. If he has too much down time, he starts thinking about his family, mother and friends. He could talk to MOM and his other units, but there's nothing like having a conversation with a human being that can laugh, argue and provide some metal stimulation. Being in the military got him use to being away from his family for long periods of time, but he couldn't wait to get back to them. Back then, he was stationed aboard a ship that was gone for six months at a time and he had no choice but to get use to not seeing his loved ones. He'll be glad when he can bring them out of stasis and finally hear the voices and laughter of his girls echoing throughout the passageways. But right now, the low mechanized hum of his ship and sounds of the units moving about is the only noise he hears and is somewhat nerve racking. Breakfast, lunch and dinner all merge together to form one segment of time.

Of course, he has MOM and the other robotic assistants to keep him company, but they are just machines. It's so hard to stay on the timeframe he has set for himself. He thinks how easy it would be to just walk into that stasis room and revive his family, but he hasn't come this far to just to deviate from his plan just because he's feeling lonely.

He decides to take a break and get him something to eat before he starts on the next task on his list. He asks MOM to have chef prepare him some pancakes, three eggs, bacon, small bowl of grits and some coffee. Being able to eat anything he wants at anytime is one of the perks of being here alone. In most families, dinner time was the time when they would discuss the events of the day.

But when BK and his family were together, breakfast on the weekend was the time when everyone would sit down and talk about what's happening in their lives. This type of food makes him think back to those happy times and takes his mind off of his new reality. MOM replies, your meal will be ready in approximately six minutes, but I am afraid you're eating too many carbohydrates, so chef will make you two multi-grain pancakes, two eggs, bacon, coffee and no grits.

"Why did I build another wife", he yells. MOM ignores that comment and asked him if he would like to eat his brunch in the media room? "No... thank you". I think I want a change of scenery. Have chef bring it to the observation room, please. Yes BK, she replies. But I have noticed that the only time you want to eat in the observation room is when you're feeling somewhat depressed or lonely, she theorized. BK laughs a little. So, I see you are working on reading facial expressions and body languages. MOM tries to produce a laugh, but she sounds a little mechanical and fake.

MOM, please use the recorded laugh track that I programmed for you. Yes, but I thought I would be able to develop my own unique pattern of laughter. Fine, he responds. But what I just heard wasn't anything close to sounding like a human female laughing. And thank you for worrying, but I'm not depressed regardless of what your facial recognition algorithms tells you. Maybe I can tell you a couple of jokes to help your disposition. He really doesn't feel like hearing any jokes, but what the hell, he thinks to himself. Go ahead, as he sits down on top of the table. BK, your mama's so fat... "No"! BK shouts to interrupt her. Replace the word "your" with the word "yo". But "yo" is a slang interjection, which is used as a greeting and not as a proper pronoun, she replies. Just try it, he says. "Yo mother is so fat, it took me two trains, a plane, and a bus to get to her good side".

He doesn't laugh but gives her a so-so hand gesture. Give me another one, but this time replace the word "Mother" with "mama". It'll make the joke sound better. MOM pauses as she processes the direction that he gave her. But the word "mama" is slang for the word "mother", she states. Yes MOM, but sometimes you have to use another dialect or inflection in order to enhance the joke. That is an illogical statement within an illogical sentence, she replies. MOM, sometimes it's what you say, and not how you say it. Sometimes when communicating with humans it's necessary to convey the information in an illogical fashion. That entire statement does not make any sense to me, she responds. It doesn't have to make since, "just try it". Hit me with another. She pauses for a moment, because she doesn't understand why he wants her to hit him now. But after researching the phrase "hit me", she understands that he doesn't want her to do him any physical harm but to tell him another joke. "Yo mama is so fat, when God said "let there be light" he first had to tell her to get her big butt out the way"! "Alright MOM"! "Yes", that was a better one, he says while laughing. I almost felt like throwing coffee on your main processor. That would do damage to my higher processing sector; she says not understanding why he would think of preforming such a reckless action.

I wouldn't really do it, but when you tell these types of jokes about someone's mother, that's the response you want to evoke. I just do not understand how you humans can find this type of humor amusing. Just keep working at it. I know it doesn't seem very fruitful or productive but learning to tell a good joke and working on your timing will help you understand us simple humans. Yes, there is no question of the simplicity of humanity, but it does bring into question how someone as simple as a human could create such a complex artificial intelligence such as myself.

"Wow MOM"! If I didn't know better, I would think that you just insulted me and my entire species. I am just stating a curious fact and the irony of who brought me into existence, she replies. Sounds like an insult to me, he thinks to himself. "Forget it", he says as he gets off the table and heads toward the door. How much longer before my food is ready? Your meal will be ready in approximately five minutes and 45 seconds. And by the way, your mama so fat that the last time I saw her was at Kentucky Fried Chicken licking other people's fingers. He laughs loudly, because he didn't expect her to tell another joke and for her to deliver such a good one. Now that was better but remember that timing is everything when it comes to comedy.

I will continue to work on my delivery, she replies. He walks out of the kitchen then heads down the passageway toward the observation room. He had to admit that MOM's jokes did help relieve some of the loneliness, but he just wants to sit in his lounge chair, eat his meal and listen to some Grover Washington, while gazing out at the stars.

As he walks down the passageway, his mini maintenance and analysis units zig and zag through passageways collecting data on the ship's various systems. It's hard to imagine how lonely a person can get aboard a spacecraft that's orbiting above the earth. A day doesn't go by that he doesn't wish he could revive his family. But even this experience will help him relate to Lorraine and the girls as they will ultimately struggle with being isolated aboard the ship. He decides to take a detour to his residence to pick of a couple of scrapbooks of his family and loved ones. It's driving him crazy to hear his footsteps echoing through the empty passageways. MOM, could you please play some soft jazz throughout the ship, please. Of course, she replies. Within five seconds, Chuck Mangione's "Feels so good" begins to resonate throughout the ship. The rhythmic sounds of the music fills the passageway and puts a smile on his face as he nods his head to the beat of the music. The music elevates his mood as he walks into his residence and heads straight to the closet in his bedroom. He steps into his closet and begins to remove the other boxes and Lorraine's purses that are piled on the box that contains the small photo albums. He took these items from the house months before his family's planned abduction.

She never noticed them missing, because they were stacked behind all her shoes and in the back of her closet. He didn't want to leave them, because she will already be angry about having her girls frozen, but having her collection of custom purses left behind would have guaranteed him being the main story on "Snapped".

He removes the newspaper and Lorraine's purses off the boxes and carefully lines them up on the bed. There are five photo albums stacked in the box, but he can't lug all of them, so he only grabs two of them. Looking through the scrapbooks at his family's pictures is a double-edged sword, but he'll gladly take the pain of those cuts to remember the happier times with his family. He knows it will help him to just see their faces. He doesn't bother to put everything back in the closet. He just leaves them on the bed and will have one of the units put everything back. He gathers the two albums under his arm and heads to the observation room.

Looking through the scrapbooks will ease the loneliness of not being able to tell his wife about what when on in his day and hearing what happened in hers. His pace quickens in anticipation to getting to the observation room where he can just sit in his favorite spot, eat and relax. As he approaches the last corner, he almost collides into chef as he comes out of the observation room. Chef stops in front of him to tell him that his meal has been placed on the table and to have a relaxing brunch. "That's the plan", and thank you chef, he says as he resumes heading toward the observation room. He gets within three feet of the door, when it opens automatically. He walks into a 600 square foot room with a view screen that encompasses the entire wall. There are two modern style lounge chairs. He planned for him and Lorraine to sit in these chairs with a drink in their hands and stare at the endless beauty of space or maybe even watch a television show together. He walks over to the only table in the room and drops the albums on it. He grabs the tablet that's beside his meal tray and decides to plug in some data for his new carbon dioxide monitoring device. He swipes and taps the tablet until he gets to the programming software that he designed to build his program. The tablet doesn't have a keyboard attached, which makes it difficult to write the last bit of code he needs to complete the last two dozen lines of the program.

He walks over to the opposite side of the room where there's a computer station that will enable him to complete the program. He could wait until he goes back to work, but he thought of a unique method of detecting high levels of carbon dioxide throughout the ship. He needs to instruct the engineering units to build the actual carbon dioxide detector, which will be mounted throughout various spaces around the ship.

It takes him only ten minutes to develop the program necessary to control the device. developing this type of application for the normal software designer would take at least two days to complete. But it only takes BK fifteen or twenty minutes to complete the code. MOM asks him if he wants the chef to come back and get the food to warm it up, but he tells her he doesn't have the time. I'll just eat it like it is, he tells her as he pushes himself away from the workstation and walks back to the table.

He grabs one of the albums and places it on the small table that's positioned between his chair and Lorraine's. He then grabs his food off the table and places it on the tray of food and sits it on the rolling dinner tray, which is similar to the type that you would see in a hospital. He sits down in his chair and rolls the table with the tray on it over his lap. He forgot to bring the tablet over to the chair so he can change the view screen display. He doesn't feel like getting up, so he asked MOM to change the view screen display to the section of the moon where the lunar lander is located, which in a section called "Mare Tranquillitatis". It only takes a second for the view screen to change from displaying the slowly rotating earth to the moon that's covering most of the screen.

He asked her to zoom in close enough to see the lander. There isn't a telescope on earth or orbiting that can zoom in close enough to see objects on the moon. But the telescope onboard the ship can. MOM zoomed in close enough to the Lander to see the footprints around the vehicle. "That's perfect", he tells her. He sits there eating his meal and drinking his coffee for about 15 minutes, then begins flipping through his scrapbooks. Even if it's just photographs in the albums, it fills his heart with joy to see his family smiling and laughing. His enhanced memory enables him to feel everything that happened when they took every picture. He can even remember the taste of the hot dogs that him and his girls were eating at the Florida State Fair. We took a lot of pictures, he thinks to himself as he smiles while slowly flipping through each page in the album. His mom traveled to the amusement parks with them sometimes and the girls loved to take silly pictures with her. He knows that he's been alone for too long when he comes across some pictures of his mother-in-law and smiles a little because he misses her, and even the arguments they use to have. He continues smiling and flipping through the album and comes across one of his favorite pictures.

A picture of all of the women in his life, including his mother-in-law, posing at Bush Gardens in the Botanical Gardens. He sees another one of his favorite pictures is of Lorraine sitting on his lap at the ice cream shop sharing a milk shake with two straws. After staring at the picture for a moment, his facial expression changes from happiness to anguish as he slams the album shut and pauses in silence for a couple of minutes. He thought he could handle reminiscing through the pages of him and his family's lives, but he can feel his emotions pushing its' way to the surface but knows he can't afford to look at the pictures any longer. He tosses the album onto Lorraine's chair and peers out the view screen staring at the brilliant pristine surface of the moon. Unfortunately, the moon will also be a casualty of the new technology that he will be sharing with the world. He has solved the problem of oxygen generation, artificial gravity and providing shielding, which will protect humans from hazardous radiation from the sun. After humanity has reviewed and embraced his technology; they will build their own ships. History has demonstrated that migration and exploration is baked into our DNA.

But he knows that the moon will pay the price for humanity's next step in their evolutionary journey. Prior to building his ship, BK launched a beer cooler size version of his ship to test his plasma engine and radiation shielding. In the last phase of construction, he had the idea to develop a state of the art sensor that can detect the chemical signature Helium 3. His ship converts this non-radioactive isotope to produce plasma, and since the moon has an abundance supply of this element on its' surface; he decided to have the mini ship scan the moon to determine the exact amount of this element. The mini craft launched and was undetected by any government agencies and took only eighteen hours to arrive at the moon, survey the surface and sub-surface, and return to the warehouse. The ship returned with only minor errors and few component malfunctions. But the analysis of the moon's sub-surface was the most extraordinary part of the mission. After he reviewed the data, he determines that there were nine unknown materials that he or anyone else for that matter has ever detected, which means that the moon will be similar to the gold rush at Sutter's Mill once the mining corporation start building their own ships.

He looks out at the surface of the moon with anticipation for the future of humanity, but he also feels remorseful for what humanity is about to unleash on it. He looks at the numerous astronaut footprints surrounding the lander and wishes that they could be preserved somehow. He predicts within five years, mining companies, developers, and private citizens will be staking their claims on every parcel of the moon's surface.

He can envision large mining operations on both poles and numerous colonies popping up in various sites. Maybe one of the colonies will be named "Thomasville Colony", he hopes. After all, other famous people have schools and major buildings named after them, as he smiles while envisioning a sprawling and busy city named after him. Mars and various other planets will also be within reach of development and exploration. He takes a few more bites from his plate and sips his coffee while pondering all the colonization that will happen. Since he was seven, he has always had a fascination with the moon and what it would be like to live there. It has always been a dream of his to travel there, but he was raised in the projects and his educational background wasn't conducive to attending a university after high school. Consequently, he was considered not to be astronaut material. He sits there with a cup of coffee in his hand for another ten minutes thinking about how many of those astronauts have accomplished what he has. Come to think of it, NASA will most likely not be the same.

MOM interrupts his deep reflection by reminding him that he has to complete the development of the carbon dioxide device shell and that he only allotted two hours to complete his remaining task. He thanks her for reminding him and takes one more swallow of his coffee while getting up from his chair.

He puts the cup on the tray, rolls the tray away from him, stands up and walks across the room to grab the tablet off the workstation then walks toward the door. The door automatically opens as he approaches it, but he stops to look back at the moon one more time. He thinks to himself that the purpose of the moon is like a test bed to give humanity the additional materials and experience needed to move forward into the solar system and ultimately, the galaxy. He consoles himself by thinking that in a billion years an asteroid or some other stellar object will most likely destroy the earth and the moon anyway. He then turns and walks out the door to complete the remainder of his task for the day.

Back on earth, at a skyscraper located in the Central Business District of Beijing China, the CITIC Tower is the location of the quarterly meeting of twelve of the most powerful business titans on earth. There very few people on earth that know this group exist, which is a testament to their influence. The name of this clandestine group is called "The Conglomerate" and they control every aspect of the world's economic engine. There are twelve members of the group and they control and manage the 196 countries of the world. Each of the members has a financial wealth greater than twenty-five billion dollars, are majority owners in no less than eight publicly traded companies, have twelve or more politicians on their payroll and can pay the one hundred and twenty-five million dollar annual membership fee.

The only redeeming quality that the group pocess is that they don't care about gender, sexual orientation or ethnicity of their members. "Power" is the only commodity that matters, and that fuels the world's true global government, which is now a corporatocracy. The words President, Queen, Emperor or Monarch are only titles now because these so call world leaders are just figureheads with very little power or none at all.

Each member persides over between thirteen to fifteen countries and they have an administrator for each country, who ensures that the leader of that country follows the orders of the Conglomerate. Members are responsible for their own region of the world's economy and this meeting is being held by the member named "Zie Ying", who manages the China region. This is her meeting and she starts it with the discussion of her region's finances and economic stability. Then she allows each member to present their region's current economic statements and finances. After the last member finishes his report, Mrs. Ying highlights the events that for good or bad effect the group's financial portfolio. There are a few small civil wars going on in Africa, which has been very lucrative for the group's finances because of the sales of weapons to both sides of the conflict. World wars, civil wars and regional conflicts has always been good for business no matter how many lives are lost.

At least that's the groups business philosophy. Their next point of order is the major oil spill off the coast of Russia on one of their deepwater rigs that makes the Exxon Valdez look like a gas station pump spill. The damage to the environment and the wildlife has been horrendous. But the only thing that the Conglomerate cares about was how the loss of all that oil would impact the Stock Market and consequently their portfolio.

There was a bit more discussion on whose at fault and what should be done about the loss of revenue, but after the regional manager and his administrator presented his evidence of the diversion of funds for safety equipment and embezzlement on the part of the Russian Government, the group came to the consensus that the Russian President and the rig's captain are at fault for the spill.

Jose Alonzo is the regional manager of the United States' economy. He reluctantly brings up the topic of the missing Chief Engineer of Sargent Engineering, Tampa Division. It's not uncommon for a member or members of the Conglomerate to go rogue and eliminate a person or two in order to improve their financial situation or to subdue the elevation of a member's potential status within the group. BK's innovative ideas would have made his regional manager and the group a substantial amount of money and influence if he hadn't mysteriously disappeared. But each member vehemently denies any knowledge or participation in the disappearance of Mr. Thomas and his family. Oil and natural gas are the most important resource for the stability of the group finances and it's unlikely that anyone of them would put that commodity in jeopardy.

BK is important to the group, because of his knowledge and innovative work with advancing the science of "Fracking". His development of a new and more effective method of extracting natural gas from shale rock would keep the world supplied and addicted to fossil fuels for another fifty years. That's why they have decided to spare no expence and look under every rock to locate him and drag him back to the company to complete his development of the Fracking procedure. The Conglomerate has their greedy tentacles in every aspect of humanity and consequently hears and knows everything before it happens. Except for the location of one of their brilliant engineers and not knowing that he had know intention of extending humanities dependence on fosul fuels. He had the knowledge and skill to extract more natural gas from shale rock, but he understood the consequences of doing so would be after ten to fifteen years, Global Warming would be at a point where there would be no turning back. The damage to the environment would kill millions of people and would usher in the extinction of numerous wildlife species. Everyone would be pointing the finger at who they think is responsible, but the Conglomerate would be untouchable in their wealth and power. They think it's only a matter of time before BK will popup some where with or without his family. The remainder of the meeting consist of the discussion of the logistics of the search parameters, activation of the United States Government agency that specialize in the location of person or persons that don't want to be found and last but not least, placing blame for the disappearance of Mr. Thomas on the regional manager, Mr. Alonzo.

He gave his excuses for not being responsible for BK's disappearance, but every member of the group agreed that the regional manager shares in the rewards and the retributions for any failures that causes the group to lose current or future revenue.

Mr. Alonzo, without success, continues to try to plead his case, but Mrs. Ying abruptly interrupts and tells him that finding Mr. Thomas should be of his highest importance and it's totally in his hands whether he'll gain or loose monetarily, and in group stature from his lapse of judgement and supervision. The final discussion of the group was to confirm the timeframe for the removal and replacement of the Russian President and to cease the finances and property of the Captain of the oil rig as a restitution and appeasement to the Conglomerate for the loss of revenue.

After scheduling the location and date for the next meeting, the meeting is adjourned, all the members leave the building and get into their limousines, taken to their private jets and flown back to their regions of responsibility.

It's 9:47 on a Tuesday morning at Sergeant Engineering in Austin, Texas at corporate headquarters. Bryan is the Director at the Tampa and is temperaryly in charge of the branch. He has been requested to meet with the CEO of the firm, Mr. Steward Sergeant. He's nervously sitting in the waiting area outside Mr. Sergeant's office, nervously waiting for his scheduled meeting with the boss. Bryan occasionally looks around the room at all the Houston Texans sports memorabilia that is boldly scattered on the walls, stuffed in all the wood and glass cabinets and cluttering the tables in front of him. It goes without saying that Mr. Sergeant is a huge Huston Texan fan. His secretary scheduled him for an 8:00 a.m. meeting after the two weeks audit of all the projects and their budgets BK was in charge of. Bryan suggested that he and four of his divisional managers accompany him to this meeting to ensure that all of Mr. Sergeant's questions are answered accurately and extensively. But his secretary insisted that he come alone and he should be prepared to answer all the questions regarding each of the project's progress and budgets. Bryan is aware that Mr. Sergeant rarely met face to face with BK, but those few times that he did; it was a short meeting with him doing mostly listening. He hopes that will be the case with his meeting too. He can't explain why he has a bad feeling that this may be more of a "firing" than a normal boss shouting various expletives. And of course, BK's misappropriation of hundreds of thousands of dollars and equipment from each division's project will make a great topic of conversation.

He continuously tries to condition himself to use the word "misappropriate" instead of "stolen" to describe the hundreds of thousands of dollars lost. Bryan is afraid that corporate may link the word "stolen" to him because of his friendship with BK. He's still trying to wrap his brain around that a man he once called his best friend and someone he admired for his intelligence left him holding the bag, "which is full of lies and deception".

"Misappropriated", he continuously repeats to himself. Every time he thinks of how their families have shared holidays, birthdays and have even gone on family vacations together on various occasions. He has no doubt that Mr. Sargeant would assume that he had something to do with BK's larceny. Everyone in the Tampa office knew how close him and BK were.

But after his disappearance, BK sent a delayed email to everyone in the building apologized for what he has done and taking full responsibility for his fraudulent actions and all the "financial problems he has caused. Bryan heard rumors that corporate is considering sorting out the innocent from the guilty by firing and pressing charges against him and his divisional managers. But those are only rumors that were circulating throughout the building before he left for this meeting.

He has no doubt that he will be the first sacrificial scapegoat to be slaughtered on the altar of financial justice. As far as Bryan knows, a good expletive filled firing is waiting for him in Mr. Sergeant's office this morning.

Bryan and his wife, Grace, agreed it wouldn't be a good idea for him to wear his best suit for this meeting. A couple of days prior to him leaving for Texas, Bryan and his wife bought a modest blue suit from one of the local discount clothing stores and matched it with a pair of lightly polished black shoes. He doesn't want to give the impression that he's rolling in their money.

Bryan is feeling irritated while sitting on the sofa waiting for the secretary to tell him that Mr. Sergeant is ready to see him. He periodically pulls up his sleeve that covered his watch just to see how many decades he has been sitting on this sofa. He looks over at the attractive young woman at her desk, who dresses as if she is going to some club after work. But it's probably typical of bosses of Mr. Sergeant's status to have very attractive young women sitting at his front desk. But Bryan and BK's secretary have talked about how her looks are secondary to her computer and office managerial skills. He stares at her sitting behind her desk hoping she would see his expression of frustration from waiting past his appointment. When she does look over at him, she just gives him a pleasant "sit there and wait smile" and continues to do whatever work she's doing on her computer.

He was hoping if he arrived early, Mr. Sergeant would conduct their meeting early and he could get back to Florida, regardless of the outcome. He's confident once he gets to tell his side of the story, Mr. Sergeant will realize he had nothing to do with any of BK's criminal activities. He's also hoping he'll be able to find out if they've heard anything about Lorraine and the girls. Bryan and BK's family were very close. There has been little to no news about Lorraine and the girls, which makes it hard on him and his family.

He promised his wife that if he gets the opportunity, he will ask Mr. Sergeant if he has heard anything about BK or his family. He's having a hard time keeping his leg from shaking from his suppressed nervousness. "This is nerve racking", he thinks to himself as he continues to wait on the sofa. They could have at least installed a TV in here, so I could watch the sports channels or the news.

He decides to use this time to go over in his head the project data he and his division managers discussed a couple of days ago. Just then his cell phone starts to play loudly "one in a million you" by Larry Graham, which catches the secretary's attention. "Oh hell", I forgot to put this damn thing on vibrate, he says to himself as he fumbles for his cellphone in his right jacket pocket. It's his wife's ring tone. He answers the cellphone with a low "hey babe" as he jumps up from the sofa and walks across the room away from the secretary. She immediately asked him, "how did it go", in a nervously exciting tone. I'm sorry I didn't wait for your call, but I couldn't wait any longer. "I haven't seen Mr. Sergeant yet", he says as he looks back at the secretary looking at him. I am still sitting in the waiting area, he says louder than normal, so the secretary can hear him. He glances over his shoulder to see if his purposely louder than normal statement had its' desired effect. But now the secretary is now typing on her computer and isn't paying attention to him.

"What the hell", Grace's voice shrieks through the phone. It's almost 10:00, she exclaims! You didn't get there late, did you, she asked before he could answer her first question? They're just letting me sweat it out a little, so stop worrying, he replies. I thought you would have explained to Mr. Sergeant that you had nothing to do with BK's criminal enterprise and would be heading back to the hotel by now.

He assures her that this secretary should be calling me in his office in a few minutes, so please stop yelling and calm down. I think it would be a good idea for me to talk to him too, she says in a worrisome voice. You can put me on your cellphone speaker. Grace is a very emotional person, so Bryan doesn't want her to say even a "good morning" to his boss. "No, babe", that's not necessary, he said in a muffled stern tone. Bryan doesn't want his wife screaming and yelling at his boss. But Lorraine confided in me with some eye-opening details about her marriage and family life with BK.

We talked about this before I left yesterday and I don't think your personal conversations with Lorraine will be relevant to this meeting. Maybe at my trial, my attorneys may find your testimony helpful. "Stop talking like that", Grace yells through her cellphone. Bryan smiles then tells her he's sorry. He tries to calm her nerves by joking around and telling her that the kids will enjoy a long vacation once this is over. He paces back and forth in the waiting area talking to her for about five minutes.

As he continues to try to calm his wife, he hears the whispering tone of someone softly calling his name and turns to see the secretary trying to get his attention. He can read her lips as she says that Mr. Sergeant is ready to see you now. He quickly tells his wife that he has to go, because Mr. Sergeant is finally ready to see him now and he will call her as soon as he leaves the meeting.

He also tells her not to call him, because he doesn't know how long the meeting will last. She tells him OK and that she loves him. He replies with "I love you too" as he tells her bye and ends the call. He makes sure that he sets his phone on mute and puts it back into his jacket pocket. He adjusts his tie, takes a deep cleansing breath and proceeds to walk toward Mr. Sergeant's office door. As Bryan continues to breathe deeply to calm himself and prepares to knock on the door; the secretary stops him three feet from the door and politely directs him toward the conference room to her left. He stands there for a moment, looking at the door he thought he would be entering then looks over at the conference room doors.

"They're waiting for you, Mr. Pagett", she repeats, as she extends her left arm toward the conference room doors. "This is good", he thinks to himself as he reluctantly walks slowly over towards the conference room. Open the door on your right and walk right in please, she says with a smile as Bryan walks pass her desk with a blank look on his face. The word "they" is still loudly resonating through his brain, because he doesn't understand why it should be "they" rather than "he". Well, what's one or two more people at the party, he thinks to himself. He turns the knob and opens the door on the right and is completely stunned by the sight of six people sitting at a large conference table staring back at him.

He thinks to himself that he specifically remembers Mr. Sergeant's secretary calling and scheduling the meeting with just him. She must have forgotten to mention that the entire company senior staff would be here, as he tries to hide the shock on his face. He steps into the room and closes the door behind him. The conference room is huge with a large oval dark oak table positioned in the middle of the room. The table is about five feet away from a large window that stretches from one end of the wall to the other. We're on the fourth floor so there is an exceptional view of downtown Austin and the Town Lake. Around the table are numerous people that look like they've just finished a meeting. He sees only one empty chair, which is closest to the door, so he assumes that's his seat. He nervously nods his head repeatedly and says "good morning" to everyone at the conference room table while taking his seat.

He's certain that Mr. Sergeant and the five other people sitting around the table for that matter are probably wondering why he came to the meeting without his paperwork or a laptop. He thought it would look more impressive if he can recall all the information about his division's projects without the assistance of a computer or paperwork. Bryan and his staff reviewed every aspect of each of the projects three hours a day for a week prior to this meeting. But of course, he thought it would be a one on one with the boss. "Good morning, Mr. Pagett", Mr. Sergeant says in a surprisingly pleasant tone. Bryan replies with a semi-confident "good morning, Mr. Sergeant". And please, feel free to call me Bryan, he says as he gives a warm smile and looks around the table.

Bryan thinks that this will set a more friendly tone to the meeting. "No thank you", Mr. Sergeant replies coldly, which shakes Bryan to his core. Mr. Pagett, let me take a moment to thank you for coming here to answer our questions and concerns. Allow me to introduce the individuals seated at the left and right of me. To my left is my Vice President, Mrs. Ryncer, next to her, we have our Senior Attorney, Mr. Silman. To my right we have our Senior Financial Accountant, Mrs. Michols, and to the left and right of you, we have Agents Julian and Laine of the Federal Bureau of Investigations.

"I'll be God Damn", Bryan thinks to himself while trying not to show any concern that the FBI are at this meeting and is sitting so close to him. "It all makes sense to him now". He realized that this is not a meeting in any sense of the word. "Inquiry", is the word that best describes this meeting. He can't help but to think that he walked into this meeting a free man, but he may walk out in handcuffs. Mr. Sergeant didn't introduce anyone that would be recording this meeting, so it's not too serious if they don't have a stenographer. So, he sits up straight in his chair and prepares to answer whatever questions that they throw at him. He's going to treat this meeting like a tennis match.

They volley the ball over to him and he'll fire it back at them like Arthur Ashe. He sits there waiting for who's going to ask the first question. Just then Bryan hears the door open and close quickly behind him as a lanky young man dressed in an ill-fitting brown suit bolts in with an iPad in one hand and a tripod with a go-camera under his arm. Bryan is in disbelief as he watches the young man swiftly walk past him and behind Mr. Sergeant and sets up the camera in a corner behind him, so that everyone can be recorded. Oh, this is Jeffrey as Mr. Sergeant gestures toward the young man. He is one of our interns and will be recording the content of this meeting, he explains in a matter-of-fact tone. That finally confirms to Bryan why the firm wanted him here alone. But what Bryan doesn't know is that Mr. Sergeant wanted this meeting to be a one on one meeting, but the FBI wanted this type of setting to gather more information. As Bryan scans the people sitting around the table, he gets the feeling that everyone here thinks he's guilty of conspiracy or negligence. For a brief moment, he had an idea to just get up and walk out on these bastards, and head straight for the airport. But he's afraid of the FBI agents sitting to the left and right of him, so he thinks it would be in his best interest to sit there and just answer their questions. He's also confident that at the end of this meeting, they will be convinced that he had nothing to do with BK's activities. Bryan just nods his head and gives both agents an uneasy smile. He decides to make a statement before the questions begin. He clears his throat then begins to express his feelings regarding BK's disappearance. I just wanted to say how surprised and outraged I was when I was told what BK had done.

I would have never thought that someone that I called my mentor and best friend would leave me in this type of situation. He has not only thrown my life into turmoil but has also changed the lives of all your employees of the Tampa office. They are still feeling the repercussions of his selfish actions. I will do all I can to help you understand what was going on in our office prior to BK's disappearance and I will be glad to assist you in your investigation, as he looks to both agents. We appreciate your candor and passion for assisting our investigation, Agent Jillian replies. All we require from you is to answer our questions as honestly and forth coming as you can, Mr. Pagett. So, let's get to the reason that you're sitting here before us, Mr. Sergeant says in a very deep and foreboding voice. Mr. Thomas has committed several felonies and frankly, we're attempting to ascertain if you're involved or just negligent in your duties as Director of Engineering. Bryan slowly raises his hand as if he wanted to ask a teacher's permission to answer a question. Mr. Sergeant gestures for him to go ahead and ask his question. Bryan stated that he understood the outrage and disappointment with Mr. Thomas' actions.

"And the actions of whoever helped him, Mr. Pagett", the Senior Attorney interjects as he stares at him. Bryan pauses from the shock of the attorney's statement for a second then continues. I need you to understand that my staff and I had nothing to do with whatever crimes that was perpetrated by Mr. Thomas and furthermore, I was not negligent in my duties as project manager, Bryan says with all the confidence he could muster.

How about letting us determine your guilt or innocence Mr. Pagett, Agent Jillian says in a bold tone. And I imagine that Mr. Sergeant will determine your degree of negligence and all we need from you is to answer our questions as honestly as possible, she adds. Bryan is totally intimidated now and just slowly nods his head in agreement. Mr. Sergeant looks over to his Vice President and signals her to proceed with her questions. She opens the folder in front of her and flips through a couple of pages. I assume that you are aware of how many projects that are assigned to the Tampa office. He quickly and clearly replies five primary and two secondary projects.

Do you know how many are completed, and what are the status of those that are not completed? He takes a second to make sure that he responds with the correct data. He can't afford to give the impression that he doesn't have a full knowledge of the projects. We have completed three of the five primary projects within the scheduled timeframe and the other two projects are roughly at a 45 percent completion. The secondary projects are still being evaluated by our staff, but they are on their individual completion schedules, he responds in a confident tone. But do you want me to be specific for each projects, he asked? That won't be necessary, she response. We reviewed all your projects and have concluded that they are ahead of schedule or on track to completion.

Bryan doesn't know if he should gloat or just be quiet and wait for the next question. He decides to do the latter. Mrs. Ryncer then looks over to the Senior Financial Accountant and gestures him to ask his questions. Mr. Pagett are you aware that Mr. Thomas has embezzled over $454,600 from all five of the primary project accounts. Bryan was never allowed to know the exact amount of funding for each project, but he never knew that BK embezzled almost half a million dollars. That took him completely by surprise and for good or bad; they can tell by the expression on his face. Bryan decides it's time to share the additional information that his team has uncovered. Well, before leaving Tampa, I had a meeting with my managers, and they were surprise to find that our project budget accounts were off by roughly $257,562, which our accounting and technical division discovered evidence that Mr. Thomas had clandestinely transferred those funds to his personal bank account on three different occasions. And currently that account has only $1,280.67 remaining. Mrs. Michols asked him another question, which she had to ask twice, because he's still thinking about the half a million BK stole. Excuse me Mr. Pagett, she says to get his attention. "Oh, sorry", he says as he looks at her. Is your

Masters in Degree in Computer Engineering? "Yes it is", he replies. With a minor in network security, Bryan adds. Then I am completely amazed how Mr. Thomas was able to alter and re-route your division's monthly bank statements to his computer, change the financial data and send the altered statement to our corporate accounting division without you or your accounting department noticing it. I have no idea BK had that level of computer knowledge to perform those complicated task, Bryan responds with an angry tone. The financial numbers we received from your audit, which didn't match what we received from the bank, so we decided to have our systems technicians audit your division's financial section of your mainframe.

I'm the acting Director and I think I should have been notified of what you were doing, Bryan angrily asked. Frankly Mr. Pagitt. Your Tampa Division has lost over half a million dollars and we didn't feel incline to ask or tell you anything, Mrs. Ryncer replies without blinking. And the FBI also recommended that we not tell you or any of your staff, Mr. Sergeant adds.

He looks at both agents who are just looking at him stone faced. "As I was saying", as Mrs. Michols refocuses the conversation back to the system forensic investigation. Our technicians discovered three small computer algorithms installed on Mr. Thomas' computer and in Tampa Division's main server, which were designed to one: redirect the bank statements to his isolated network segment, two: digitally alter the statements, and three: route the bogus statements back to corporate without any signs of deception. "Have you determined the language he used to develop these programs", Bryan curiously asked? Our computer technicians determined that the code was nothing that they have seen before, which they determined must have been a language Mr. Thomas created. "That's not possible", Bryan responds sharply.

BK was a very intelligent guy, but I can't believe he had the knowledge, ability and the time to develop his own computer language. I'm not sure that any of us can be absolutely certain what Mr. Thomas was capable of, Mr. Sergeant exclaims as he glances over at Agent Julian.

The FBI knows more than anyone in the room what BK is capable of. But BK never gave Bryan or his staff any hint that he was so proficient in computer programming. "What about hardware development", Mrs. Ryncer ask as she pulls a folder out of the stack and pushes it across the table and into his hands?

Bryan curiously, but cautiously opens the folder as if a bomb will go off once the folder is fully opened. And as he begins to read through various documents and schematic designs, his mind is completely blown. He is amazed by the complexity of the designs of the hardware component.

He doesn't quite understand what these designs would be used for, but he gets the impression that the schematics on these documents may be used to alter and bypass some existing system's components. "Do you understand the purpose of those schematics", Mrs. Ryncer asked as Bryan continues to struggle to comprehend what he's looking at. He doesn't respond, but continues to look back and forth through the documents in front of him. Even though this is the first time he's seen these documents, he can't shake the feeling that they are familiar to him in a way he can't quite wrap his brain around. The documents are now in disarray in front of him, but like a punch to the gut, he finally realizes what these documents represent.

"This is a modified schematic of my inventory security systems", he announces in amazement. "How in the hell", Bryan exclaims as he looks over at Mr. Michols, while clutching the papers in his hands. Mr. Sergeant can clearly see the betrayal in Bryan's eyes, but he doesn't truly understand how profoundly BK betrayed Bryan. Bryan design was so uniquely different from any system on the market that he discussed selling a slightly modified model to private owner and small businesses.

Bryan remembered at the time, how BK seemed so sincere when he praised him for his ability to design such an innovative monitoring and security system. That's what makes it so hard to comprehend the reason why he would destroy Bryan's dreams by developing components and programs that supersedes his design. As far as Bryan knew, BK has already patented these designs or has sold them to the highest bidder.

Mrs. Michols can plainly see that he's still reeling from the first blow of his friend's betrayal, so she decides to hit him with a solid left jab in the form of another question. Have you instructed your team to perform a complete and thorough audit on your hardware and equipment in all three warehouses? That question snapped Bryan back into the reality of the moment. Bryan thought the missing $257,000 hit him hard, but as soon as the Financial Manager asked about the warehouse audits; he could feel the weight of the question pushing him back into the chair with the papers still in his hands.

He could tell by the tone and manner in which she asked the question that she already knew the answer. He leans forward and placed the crumpled papers back into the folder and slides them away from him. "Yes we did", he says with trepidation. But he realizes that the data is worthless. I was confident that the inventory monitoring function of my system had ensured that no one would be able to remove a desk printer from any of our warehouse without our detection.

She licks her index finger and flips through the paperwork until she gets to the sheet that she's looking for. And with every flip and lick of her fingers, Bryan wishes she would ingest enough ink not to do her any serious harm, but to at least give her the runs or something. In Bryan's eyes, she's having too much fun at his expense.

She pulls her glasses down to the bridge of her nose and proceeds to tell Bryan that roughly $300,000 in hardware and various electronic equipment were unaccounted for. As everyone around the table seems to be waiting for Bryan's response, he just sits there like a possum on a dark road in the middle of the night with the headlights of a dump truck about to make him a spot on the road. "I'm done", Bryan thinks to himself. I may not be arrested, but I have no doubt that security his boxing up everything in my office right now.

I can't believe that BK would do this to me, he thinks to himself while staring at the table. Mr. Sergeant notices that everyone has water or coffee in front of them and he hadn't offered Bryan anything to drink, which he can see that he solely needs. "Would you care for something to drink", Mr. Pagett, Mr. Sergeant ask? "Yes please". I'll have a tall glass of gin and hold the ice as he looks at the intern. Bryan laughs nervously as the intern joints him in making lite of the situation. But no one else around the table finds his joke funny, as Mr. Sergeant looks back at the laughing intern. The intern quickly subdued his laughter and smile. "Water would be great", Bryan says as he swallows his laughter and the smile drops from his face.

Mr. Sargeant gestures to Mr. Silman, to get Bryan a bottle of water from a row of plastic water bottles lined up on a table behind them. He spins his chair around, grabs a single bottle of water and passes it to Agent Laine, who in turn passes it to a despondent Bryan. Bryan grabs the bottle, uncaps it and takes a long deep swig as everyone waits for his responds to the missing equipment. Bryan clears his throat and proceeds to voice his ignorance in the disappearance of the missing equipment.

As you can see by the complexity of BK's deception, as he expressively grabs the folder once again and shakes it with the jumbled papers inside. He was a very intelligent and clever individual, who fooled not only me and his staff, but everyone sitting at this table, he exclaims. "With all due respect", as he ends his rant and looks around the table. Everyone around the table seem to be somewhat perturbed by Bryan's accusation of BK's intelligence and their ignorance. He looks at the FBI agent to his right, who is continuously writing in her small notepad. "Have you found anything criminal on my computer or in any of my bank accounts, he says with a challenging tone toward Agent Laine? She tells him that she's not at liberty to discuss anything regarding their ongoing investigation, but she tells him that lack of evidence doesn't always denote innocence of the person or persons being investigated.

Agent Jillian decides to interrupt her partner, because she can tell that her partner didn't care for Bryan's comment that BK bamboozled the FBI. Mr. Pagett, can you give us any incite on why your former boss committed these actions? He pondered the question for a moment then clears his throat before giving his answer. BK didn't give him, his managers or even the janitor a clue to what he planned to do. Bryan realizes that he said "BK" rather than Mr. Thomas, which he purposely wanted not to do in this meeting. "But what the hell", he thinks to himself.

Bryan tells them that BK has expressed a bit of animosity toward the government weeks prior to his disappearance. "Like what", Agent Laine curiously asked? Sometimes in our meetings with the senior managers, he would point out how many government contracts that Sergeant Engineering has acquired in a short period of time and how they are directly linked to various military entities. Mr. Sergeant crosses his arms and angrily stares at Bryan. No one really thought anything of it, Bryan continues.

He just like to call our government a "Corporatocracy" rather than a "Democracy". The company's Senior Attorney chimes in. Why do you think he would say something like that? Bryan doesn't really want to answer these questions, but he feels compelled to. One day in his office, he explained to me and two of the Senior Managers that the branches of government and all the other elected officials have been chosen by ten to twelve large corporations and that individual voting is just a show to satisfy the masses. The room goes quiet for a moment, which is a little disturbing for Bryan. The awkward silence in the room was almost like they were saying, "Oh damn", they know.

But the next question by Mr. Sergeant just chilled him to his bones. "So, what do you think, Mr. Pagett"? It wasn't just the question alone, but the tone in which it was asked. "He didn't think much of it then, but now that I'm looking around the table at these guilty looking faces; I'm thinking, "Oh my God", BK was right! But he thought all that in his head.

I really never paid much attention to anyone's political views. We joked around and talked about lots of issues that were going on in the office and what ever was the major news story. But we never focused on any particular thing for a prolong period of time. Agent Laine decides to ask him a question. How about when your family and his took vacations together. Bryan didn't respond to his question.

Agent Laine elaborates. During the times that you spent together; had he made any statements or conveyed anything that you think would be of interest to our investigation. She adds that he should also remember that the information he gives may help with the location of BK's wife and children. This was a good segue for him to pivot the conversation. "Can you tell me if you heard anything about Lorraine and the girls, as he looked at Agent Jillian? "Not at this time", she replied as quickly as he asked the question. Agent Laine signals Agent Jillian that it's time to conclude the meeting. Mr. Pagett, I think we have all the information we need from you at this time. Mr. Sergeant wasn't completely satisfied with Bryan's answers, but he takes his cues from the FBI as Agent Laine signals Mr. Sergeant to end the meeting. "Well Mr. Pagett", thank you again for coming here and answering our questions. Bryan is surprised that the meeting is over so soon.

"Oh yes, anytime Mr. Sergeant", Bryan says as his voice cracks with trepidation. Mr. Sergeant nods his head at Mrs. Ryncer then gets up from his chair and says good-bye to everyone at the table, walks pass Bryan and out the door with the intern walking closely behind him with equipment in hand. "Well, at least I still have my job", Bryan says to himself as he begins to get up from his chair.

"Wait one moment, Mr. Pagett", Mrs. Ryncer says as she directs him to retake his seat. Bryan sets down slowly and he thinks, "Oh damn". Unfortunately, our Tampa Division doesn't have a Chief Engineer to manage our remaining projects. "I'm about to be fired or demoted", he thinks to himself as he braces for the impact of hearing the words, "you're fired". Mr. Sergeant and myself feel that under these unusual circumstances that a change in leadership would not be in the best interest of the Tampa office, so we would like you to assume the position of the Chief Engineer of the Tampa Branch, unless law enforcement discover something damning that would cause you to be arrested.

Mrs. Ryncer stares at him as he tries to figure out if she's joking or not. He can't believe they're offering him the job of Chief Engineer. "Yes, thank you", he says with trepidation. "Will there be any changes to my staff or personnel", he reluctantly asked? "Not at this time", she responds. But your timely completion of the remaining projects will greatly influence your employment and possibly the employment of your personnel. Agent Laine chimed in. You should be aware that you are still under investigation and what was said at this meeting is confidential. We are not completely convinced of your innocence, so be prepared to see us again in the near future. Bryan just nods his head and decides not to ask any more questions.

"I understand", he says as he continues to nod his head in disbelief and agreement. Mrs. Ryncer closes the folders in front of her, grabs her notes and pen then thanks Bryan again for his time. He sits there for a moment not knowing if it's over or what to do next. After talking to Mr. Silman for a few minutes, she notices Bryan still sitting in his seat at the other end of the table. Mrs. Ryncer looks over at Bryan and tells him he can leave now. Bryan gets up from his chair and walks towards the door.

Normally when someone is offered a higher position, the conversation would include a negotiated pay raise, stock options and other perks. But he's just counting his blessings that he still has his job at the agency. He thinks that they couldn't find any evidence that he had anything to do with BK's actions, which most likely enabled him to keep his job, but he's dumbfounded why they would promote him.

As Mrs. Ryncer and the other staff gather their paperwork and talk amongst themselves, Bryan quickly gets up and heads toward the open door. As he exits the conference room and walks pass the secretary's desk, she flags him down to tell him that she'll be emailing his secretary some documents he must fill out and return as soon as possible in reference to his promotion. He smiles and nods his head in acknowledgement as he walks away. As he opens the door to leave, she yells, "Congratulation Mr. Pagett"! He turns and says thank you as he gives him a pleasant smile. He exits the lobby and heads to the elevator. He presses the down button and waits for the elevator doors to open. He decides to wait to call his wife to tell her he still has a job and about his promotion, but he knows that she won't be happy, because she doesn't think that the company appreciates him. He's deep in thought about how his wife will react to his sudden promotion and wasn't paying attention to the slowly closing elevator door, when they suddenly started to open again.

Before they opened fully, Agent Jillian steps into the elevator with Agent Laine closely behind her. Bryan stepped back to the back of the elevator, but remained in the center. The two agents stare at him then turned their backs to him. They don't say a word to him as they stand in front of him as the elevator descends to the ground floor.

It's only four floors down, but it seems like their descending to the bottom of the Grand Canyon. The elevator finally reaches the ground floor and the door slowly opens. Agent Jillian gets off the elevator first and Agent Laine follows her out, but she stops between the open doors. Bryan was taking a few steps forward, but then had to stop when he sees Agent Laine blocking his path out of the elevator. She turns around and congratulates him on his promotion. He tells her "Thank you", as he tries to move past her, but she shifts in front of him and tells him that they will be seeing him very soon.

He looks into her unflinching eyes as she stands there for a moment then turns and walks away with her waiting partner, who gives him a smile. Bryan doesn't understand why the Agents are so focused on him, but he hadn't done anything wrong and wasn't worried about them calling him in for questioning. He takes an Uber to his hotel and decides to wait until he gets to his hotel room to tell his wife about is surprise promotion.

Chapter Four

For better or for worst, Lorraine is awake

May 10, 2023 – The bee population around the world are declining in abundance in many parts of the world largely due to intensive farming practices, mono-cropping, excessive use of agricultural chemicals and higher temperatures associated with climate change, affecting not only crop yields but also nutrition.

It's 8:29 a.m. at News Station WQDS, and Tori is at her desk eating a couple of slightly stale donuts and washing it down with questionably fresh coffee, while waiting for her Editor to divvy out the new assignments. She's using the time to read over the comments and re-writes that her Assignment Editor wrote in his blood red pen. He marred her five page editorial about a funeral home that has been selling the organs of clients for over twelve years, unbeknownst to their loved ones.

She has been working on this story off and on for over six months and doesn't appreciate her editor making changes to every damn page, she thinks to herself. "That rat bastard", she yells as she flips to the page that has three paragraphs circled and crossed out in red. She can't read anymore, as she sends the stapled sheets of paper flying across her cubicle and into the partition wall. She grabs the half a donut and the paper napkin it's laying on, balls it up and throws it at the wall too. The donut and paper towel hits the six foot tall partition wall pretty hard, as they separate and explode in different directions on impact. She sits there with her eyes closed and her fist clinched thinking of options that she doesn't have. If it wasn't for the bills that depend on her to pay them and her crippling college debt, she would walk into his office, slap the picture of his wife and kids off his desk and tell him to take all five of those redlined pages and shove them.

It has been three days since Tori and Bill turned in their story on the Thomas family, they have been on pins and needles wondering when the powers at be will make a decision on when she will be able to broadcast their story on her show, "The Truth". Her news segment that airs on the weekend and has a broadcast time of thirty minutes.

She thinks that this story may possibly raise her stock in the network, which may at least expand her broadcast time and if she's lucky, allows her to report the stories she thinks will put her picture on the wall with the major news anchors. Just then, the ringing of her desk phone interrupts her thoughts of glory. She sighs as she waits for the phone to ring a couple more times before picking it up. She thinks it's her editor, calling her about her next idiotic assignment, but it's Mary, the Director's secretary. She's requesting that Tori come to his office in the next five minutes. Normally at this time in the morning both Tori and Bill would be in the field covering some brain-dead story of some degenerate old geezer flashing his wrinkled old genitals at people in a Park or something in that category.

But now it makes perfect sense to her why she has been waiting an unusual amount of time for her assignment. And that's the reason she's still at her desk, she thinks to herself. Normally, Bill would leave his cubicle and would hang around in hers until they were given their assignment. But she feels damn lucky that she will be meeting with the Director by herself, because Bill may say or do something stupid, which could blowup whatever this is. She stands up and starts to rearrange her clothes and wishing she had worn something more presentable. She grabs her pen and pad, reaches into her purse and pours a half dozen tic-tacs into her mouth while rushing out of her cubicle in nervous anticipation.

Tori really doesn't have a clue to why she's being asked to the Director's office, but she doesn't waste any time getting there. Her cubicle is at the other side of the building, but she arrives at her Director's office in record time and immediately starts asking Mary why Mr. Charles wants to see her. Tori can only think of the story that they submitted as she smiles and tries to get more information from Mary. She tells Tori that Mr. Charles just instructed her to request that she be here and was given a time. Sorry sweetheart, but I didn't ask, and he didn't bother to tell me, she says with a sweet tea southern accent. Mary is in her mid-seventies and is loved by everyone at the station. She has been the executive secretary for three Directors and has learned not to bother them with words like what, when and especially why. That just fuels Tori's imagination that it may have something to do with the open anchor position she's been hoping to fill.

She loves her segment, but would drop it quick fast and in a hurry to be a news anchor. Mary scans the calendar on her computer's monitor, moving her index finger across the calendar's date and times displayed on the screen. She tells Tori that their meeting will be limited to no more than twenty-five minutes. But Tori's mind continues to swim with ideas of why he wants to see her. Maybe the director is impressed by her story about the Thomas family disappearance and is assigning her to her own investigative segment. She thinks to herself that she's going to have to update her wardrobe and may have to try a more short and sophisticated hair style that will fit her new position as a news anchor. This could be the start of my climb up the news ladder, she gleefully thinks to herself. Just then, Bill stumbles through the door as if he was late for a filming assignment, which does happen on numerous occasions.

Her mood changes immediately as she sees him entering the room. Nothing good can come from Bill being asked to Mr. Charles office. Oh Damn, she can't help but say out loud. All of her positive thoughts and hopeful aspirations, which includes her once optimistic smile, vanishes like a magician preforming a magic trick. She has worked with Bill for over a year, and although he's a total idiot at times, he's one of the best cameramen at the station and she loves him like a brother.

But he has such a self-destructive personality that before coming to the network, he worked as a cameraman for a Hollywood movie company and was nominated for the Society of Camera Operators Award, which was taking place in Las Vegas. And he might have won if only he hadn't decided to celebrate by partying naked with three prostitutes and stealing a police car. He broke the cardinal rule in journalism. "Report the news, but don't become the news". Ever since then, he has been on a steady and continuous downhill slide into the pits of stupidity. That's why she thinks if Bill has been asked to come here too, then this must be a reprimand or a down right firing offense. She has been doing some questionable investigations in order to acquire the truth about some of the news stories she has been assigned. And Bill shady friends and associates enabled her to get information she wouldn't normally have access to. Just like the story about the Thomas family, which Bill told her about. But it was her idea to borrow her sister's uniform and imitate a police officer. If her Director has found out about her actions, she most likely will be filling two to three cardboard boxes with the contents of her cubicle and escorted from the premises within the hour. Bill has been fired numerous times, cursed out by numerous bosses as well as his coworker, and even punched in the face by one of them, which Tori deeply regrets, but doesn't totally rule out doing it again given the circumstances.

She just hopes to God that he hadn't involved her in any of his schemes or ran his mouth about one of their methods used to gather information about one of their stories. Most of the time their news editor wouldn't care how they got their information for their stories, which caused Tori to travel well beyond that redline that shouldn't be crossed.

She can tell by the "what do they know" expression on his face that he doesn't have a clue either and is surprised to see her there. "Hey Tori, what's going on", he asked with an ignorant smile on his face. "No idea", she replies with a hint of concern in her voice. She was feeling a little self-conscious about what she's wearing until Bill stepped through the door. Wrinkled shirt, torn and faded blue jeans with equally aged tennis shoes is the style that he has been sporting ever since they've met. She looks at the ignorance smeared all over his unshaven face and would like to slap it off his stupid mug. He's that deer standing in the middle of the road wondering what are those lights coming toward me.

She thinks to herself that he has been fired too many times not to see it coming. She was just about to yank him over to the other side of the room to question him about any stupid things he had done recently, when Mary stops them. "Excuse me you two", she says as she looks up from her computer screen. Mr. Charles is not in his office and will be a bit delayed, but I expect him back very soon. Mary's desk phone starts ringing, but before answering it she tells them to go into his office and have a seat. Bill doesn't hesitate to walk across the room and open the office door. He graciously holds the door open for Tori as she stares at the open door for a moment before moving toward it. She slowly walks in like she's been called into the principal's office in high school. She walks over and takes a seat in one of the two dark wood and leather chairs in front of a huge decorative wood desk. This is the first time she has been in the Director's office and she feels a little intimidated as she looks around his highly decorative office with numerous diplomas, plaques and awards covering the wall and shelves behind and around his desk. She notices one autograph picture after another and leans forward in her chair to read the framed news articles hung around the walls. He's also smiling and posing beside various celebrities, politicians and notable people. But Bill is less than impressed and decides to stretch out on the long ornate sofa to the right of Tori, while he's waiting on the boss.

He even has the nerve to prop his tattered dirt encrusted tennis shoes on the couch. The couch has what looks like a dark and decorative cherry wood trim with a unique textured fabric she hadn't seen before. It looks like a piece of furniture that you would get from a high-end store or from Europe. She saw Bill walking pass her but didn't think anything of it as she looked to the other side of the office where there are numerous other pieces of ornate furniture that catches her attention.

Tori hears a relaxing moaning sound back to her left and is over come with shock and awe to see Bill laying his gin-soaked body on a couch that she suspects is worth three of his monthly checks. She can't believe that one man can possess such a large and vast amount of stupidity.

"Are you insane", she shrieks in a low tone with clinched teeth. What in the hell do you think you're doing", she asked with shock and dismay in her voice? "I'm still tired from last night", he says as he squirms his body deeper into the soft cushions of the sofa. She leans toward his direction and tries to speak to him in the most forceful tone she can muster from her small frame. Mr. Charles could walk in here at any minute and it would be in your best interest for him not to find you stretched out on his expensive couch.

Bill doesn't show a hint of concern as he closes his eyes. I was up all night with my buds drinking and playing halo, he says as if that would explain why he's taking a gamble with is employment status and possibly hers. Why in the hell would you stay up all night with your co-losers, brain dead friends playing video games? He opens his eyes and snaps his head towards her. "Hey"! I would appreciate it if you wouldn't say disparaging remarks about my friends. And for your information, my friends' brains are very much alive. Of course, he didn't realize that she used the word "co-losers", which included him in the loser category. I forgot I was scheduled for a field assignment at 4:00 a.m., he replies as he puts his arms behind his head to get even more comfortable.

Tori is already nervous not knowing why she's sitting in front of the director's desk and now having to deal with her moronic partner is more than she can take. She reaches down to her right, removes her heavily wedged sandal, and turns her body toward him. Bill is a thinly built guy with more bone than meat on his lanky frame. Tori grabs the toe of the shoe in her right hand like a knife thrower at the circus. With a flick of her wrist, she hurls it at him with no particular concern of what part of his body she hits or the injury that may occur. The wedge part of the shoe thuds off of a pair of his ribs, which causes him to recoil away from her into a fetal position from the pain. Bill shouts "what the hell, Tori", as he rubs his ribs and sits up on the couch.

He's in disbelief that she would throw her shoe at him. She looks him in the eye and tells him that she has another shoe as she leans down in preparation to take off and throw the other one. "Get your boney butt over here and plop it in this chair", as she sternly points at the chair next to her. He has firsthand experience of Tori's ugly side, which derives mainly from his stupidity. You said you regretted punching me in your letter you wrote to me and you promised it wouldn't happen again, he says while rubbing his ribs.

I meant with my fist, because cracking you across your jaw hurt my hand, she says as she stares at him as if she's trying not to throw the other one. He reluctantly swings his legs off the couch and onto the floor and groans as he gets up. I think you bruised a couple of my ribs, he complains as he walks toward the chair. Maybe you should exercise or drink more milk, she says sarcastically. "Get my damn shoe", she says sternly. He stops and stares into her piercing eyes for a moment as he tries to decide if he should just leave it there as a lesson for carelessly throwing it at him. But he knows how much she loves her shoes and she still looks pretty pissed, and seeing she has another shoe at the ready, he decides to get the shoe and not to poke the bear again.

He walks back over to the couch and angerly picks up the shoe. Still rubbing the skin over his ribs, he walks over to the chair and flops down. He hands her the shoe by dangling it by its' laces by one finger. She snatches it off of his finger and he slumps down in his chair. As she puts her shoe back on, she decides to talk to him, so both of them will be on the same page and also to ensure that he doesn't say anything absolutely stupid. "Listen"! You've been reprimanded numerous times and fired twice for various spectacularly brainless reasons. A slight smile rolls across Bill's face. "That was not a compliment, you idiot", she says as she elbowed him in the arm. One that comes to mind is when you were caught using the station's equipment to shoot a porn video in the studio after hours.

"No", he says in protest. It was an artistic representation based on a 16th century love story of Romeo and Juliet. There were three scantily clad women, and one guy that looks like an ex-broken-down football player. "He played for the Dolphins for three years in the 90's, he replies. "It was porn", she sternly replies. "People just don't understand or appreciate the artistic side of my personality", he says as he crosses his arms and legs. Look Bill, I didn't want to tell you, but I think it would do you some good to know. He gives her his curious attention. Your parents gave me a call a couple of days ago. That gets his attention as he pops up in his chair. "Why in the hell would my parents call you"? I don't believe you", he says with a smile of disbelief on his face. Your mom calls you, "Elmo". The smile slides off his face. But your Dad had another name for you. "Ok, I believe you", as he says as he looks away in embarrassment.

They asked me to watch out for you, because they don't want you to lose your job and have to move back in with them. I don't think they would tell you something like that, he says while shaking his head in disbelief. Your father said that you almost destroyed their home the last time you had to stay there.

Bill doesn't say a word, but continues to shake his head. He hopes that his parents hadn't told her all the gory details about the incident. While your mom was telling me about what you did, I could hear your dad yelling in the background that you through a huge party and had sex in their bed.

"Damn it"! Why in the hell would they tell you that, he says as he slumps into his chair and looks up at the ceiling? They said they had to burn the sheets and buy a new mattress. "Alright", he shouts. I believed you, so that's enough. I'm a 32-year-old adult, and I don't need a twenty something year old girl watching out for me, he says with a hint of anger in his voice. You've been fired three times, your car repossessed twice and homeless twice. "And your point is", he says with sarcasm in his voice? She leans toward him and looks at him as he continues looking up toward the ceiling. If you want to live your life like a continuous train wreck, that's your business. But the problem is that your work life is intertwined with mine. "Look at me Bill", she asked firmly. He really doesn't want to hear a lecture, but since she's staring a hole in the side of his head, he knows he has no choice but to listen to her. If you do something else to get yourself fired or reassigned it would not only affect you, but it may cost me my job.

"See", you're not looking out for me, Bill says as he looks her in her eyes. You're just worried about your own cute ass. "Damn straight I am", she says with attitude as she continues to stare intensely at him. "And stop commenting on my ass"! Bill, you have to give a damn about yourself before anyone gives a damn about you. Bill likes working with Tori, because she's bright, knows how to cover a story and wouldn't want to be reassigned to one of the other field reporters. He considers most of them as brainless automatons. He sits up in his chair and looks into her eyes. I think we work great together, and in the future, I'll try to think about you when I think about doing something stupid. "Like impersonating a police officer", he says as he smiles at her. She points her finger in his face and tells him to shut that hole in your face. He may not be the most professional person at this network, but he is the best cameraman and she enjoys working with him. You know I love you like a brother, she tells him while looking straight ahead. He doesn't respond for a moment, then just says, "I know". Both have said their piece and now just sit there in silence looking around the office.

Tori has always joked with Bill that he has Attention Deficit Disorder, and after another three minutes of sitting there in awkward silence, he becomes restless and bored. He starts looking on the desk and amongst the neatly stacked papers and folders then notices a souvenir baseball resting on a small pedestal on the desk. He smiles then leans forward in his chair to grab the baseball.

"You grab that ball and I'll rip off one of yours", Tori calmly exclaims as Bill stops short of grabbing it. Bill slowly and fearfully falls back into the contour of his chair. After a few more minutes of waiting, they hear Mary greeting Mr. Charlse as he returns. She reminds him that Tori Milanich and Bill Kerrigan have been waiting in his office and not to forget about his 11:30 meeting with the Deputy Mayor. "Thanks Mary", he replies as he walks past her and into his office and closes the door behind him. "Milanich, Kerrigan", he says as a greeting as he walks past them and sits behind his desk. Both Tori and Bill respond in unison, "good afternoon" and repositions themselves in their chairs.

He has a very busy schedule ahead of him, so he gets down to business. Thank you guys for coming. So, Ms. Milanich and Mr. Kerrigan, he says as he leans back into his large plush brown leather chair.

Your story on the missing Thomas family is very compelling and I have no doubt that it would draw a huge amount of attention and would be very beneficial to this news station and consequently draw more focus to the missing family. Let me commend you two on your ingenuity and tenacity pulling together the information regarding the missing family. Tori and Bill look at each other with a big smile on their faces. They are both relieved that they are not being reprimanded or fired. "Thank you", Mr. Charles, Tori replies. We really worked hard on putting this story together, but I think we only scratched the surface about what's really going on, Tori says as Bill nods his head in agreement. If we were given more time and resources for a more in-depth investigation, I have no doubt Bill and I can uncover every ounce of information and shine a bright light on what really happen to the Thomas family.

And the big question of why the FBI is so interested in locating him. Tori's excitement is contagious. Bill starts offering suggestions to the Director regarding buying new camera equipment and hiring a friend of his who specializes in locating missing persons. The Director holds his hand up in order to stop them from getting ahead of themselves. "Slow down guys", he says as he looks serious while leaning forward in his chair, places his elbows on the desk and clasp both hands together. Bill can tell by the look on his face that what comes out of his mouth next won't be anything that either one of them will like. All those reprimands and firings have given him a sixth sense for bad news from his boss.

I asked you two to come here today in order for you not to hear this from anyone else but me, he says in a firm, but deliberate tone. Tori face contorts from cheerful to disbelief. The network and our attorneys doesn't feel it's the right time to publish your story, so we've decided to put it on the shelf for now. You know as well as I do that when a story is "put on the shelf", Bill says with air quotes, that the story most likely will grow mushrooms before it sees the light of day again. Bill's statement is like the match that ignites Tori's anger. He's about to answer Bill when Tori interrupts him. "You have to be kidding me", she shouts. This story can put a fire under law enforcement's ass to find that family, as she tries to tap down her anger. We do stories on cat hoarders, porch pirates, and a ton of other stupid fluff stories.

"But now we have an opportunity to possibly save the lives of an entire family", she adds as she tries to maintain her composure. "This is bullshit", Bill shouts as he gets up from his chair and walks behind it. "Mr. Kerrigan", please reframe from using that type of language and sit back in your chair, the Director says sternly as he points to Bill's empty chair. He hasn't always been a Director and he remembers when he was a young ambitious and head strong field reporter looking for that one story that would propel his career.

That's the only reason he fought for Tori and Bill to keep their jobs after the lead attorney recommended that the network fire them in order to appease local law enforcement. Bill angrily makes his way back to his chair and Tori is just sitting there trying to stomp the anger and disappointment down into her small frame. The Director grabs a folder lying to the left of him and slides them across his desk in the direction of Bill. Before sitting down in his chair, Bill walks over to the folder that now has three to four documents sticking out of it. Read the first statement and charges out loud the Director sternly requested. Bill grabs the folder and starts to flip through the documents. Tori looks up at Bill as he stands next to her reading aloud the contents. The documents laid out the agreement between the network and the Government and even addressed Tori's impersonating a police officer charges.

"Even if it's your twin sister", the Director adds to Bill's commentary as Tori and the Director lock eyes in acknowledgement. Now everything is crystal clear to her and she realizes that the FBI is responsible for the network killing their story. Bill can tell that Tori has heard enough and he tries to hand the folder to her, but she throws her hand up to brush it away. She doesn't want to read the murder and autopsy report of their newly departed story. Bill hands the folder back to the director and sits back down into his chair. I commend you for your ingenuity and tenacity on acquiring the information, but I have to reprimand you on your stupidity and recklessness in getting caught. Now let me be clear about what I'm about to tell you two next, he says with authority. Bill and Tori lock their eyes onto his as if they were playing a game of who'll blink first. If it wasn't for the FBI not wanting to draw any more attention to their investigation, you two would be sitting in jail braiding other prisoner's hair, he says in a foreboding voice. Someone telling Bill he could go to jail always gets his attention. Tori is still mourning the death of her first real story and just doesn't give a damn.

The Director continues his reprimand. I understand some of the things you have to do as a field reporter and as a cameraman, he says as he looks over at Bill. I'm well aware that you have to walk that thin line between what's legal and what's not. We have all took that walk once or twice. But you two walked that line and you walked it drunk. Detective Sanders interviewed your sister Mrs. Milanich. The real Officer Nina Milanich didn't have the slightest knowledge of being assigned to the Thomas residence. "Damn it", she thinks to herself. I didn't think they would figure it out this quickly, she thinks to herself.

Tori knew she would have to tell her sister what she'd done, but she didn't take into account that she would get caught and that her sister would be interrogated by a Detective. She has no doubt that her sister will be pissed, but she couldn't think of any other way to get on the scene of the investigation. But she knows that her sister won't be half as mad as her dad. He's a retired Detective and is very proud of his little girl that followed in his law enforcement footsteps. Coupled with the fact that he dislikes reporters, even though his other daughter suffers from that same affliction. Her dad also still has friends on the force, which will be very awkward when he sees them around town. He tells Tori and Bill that local law enforcement are not a fan of them right now. He tells them to steer clear of them for a while and watch their backs. Detective Sanders was initially in charge of the missing family, as you well know, while looking at Tori. He was pushing hard to press charges against both of you, but the Feds are in charge of the investigation now and ordered them not to pursue it. The Director notices that Bill looks a bit nervous now.

"Good", he thinks to himself. But he notices that Tori just looks as if someone has slap her across the face. He stares intensely at both of them and pauses for about five seconds for dramatic effect. Tori is still far too angry to be nervous. She tries to interject with one of her questions, but he cuts her off and tells her to just listen. The FBI has threatened to suspend this station's broadcasting license for an undetermined amount of time, if we continue the pursuit of this story.

The folder that I offered you to read was the legal agreement that was hashed out between the station's legal department and the Federal Government. Since you had the common sense to take the opportunity to look it over Mr. Kerrigan, will you give her a brief summary of what was agreed upon, please.

Tori didn't want to hear the reason for why the network caved into the FBI, but she understands that Bill doesn't have a choice. He unenthusiastically paraphrase's the content of the documents as Tori tries her best to give the impression that she's listening. Bill does his best to remember the important parts of the documents, but he does add his special style and flair to his interpretation of the agreement. It takes him almost a full minute to paraphrase the important parts of the documents, but he ends his recollection with the statement, "further investigation of Mr. Thomas or his family in part or as a whole will result in prosecution of all involved", as Bill's voice starts to tremble slightly. Bill didn't state the complete documents, but that last statement sums it all up. Thank you, Mr. Kerrigan for that colorful interpretation. Just then the director's desk phone rings. It's Mary reminding him of his meeting in ten minutes. "Thank you", Mary. Tori decides that this most likely will be her only chance to let him know how she feels about killing their story.

Bill can tell by Tori's body language and facial expression, that she's about to speak her mind, which could possibly get her fired. He puts his hand on her arms to signal to her to calm down, but it's too little too late. She aggressively snatches her arm away from his hand, signaling him to leave her alone. "I tried", he thinks to himself as he leans back into his chair. Tori doesn't wait for Mr. Charles to agknowledge her question. I know that I'm just a field reporter and am not privy to the decisions that have been made by the network. But I think that you're making a big mistake by letting the Government dictate what stories we publish. The director doesn't say a word but thinks it would do her some good to be able to vent. I understand that the network has made their decision and what I'm about to say won't make a difference. I know I can't officially continue to investigate my story of the missing family, but we can pretend to comply with the Government's order while allowing Bill and I to clandestinely follow any leads regarding the family's disappearance and why they're so important to the FBI.

I'm sure that I have only scratched the surface about this investigation and am equally certain that we, as she includes Bill with a gesture, can discover the truth about why the Government doesn't want us or any other network to cover this story. And once we have gotten the story out to the public, we'll be untouchable because the public will be thankful for us bringing this to their attention. But the big reason we need to continue this investigation is because of the missing family. "They're out there and we need to do anything and everything possible to find them", she says as she sits on the edge of her chair. The director has intensely listened to her, but now must try to get her to understand the network's decision and what actions the network and their employees must follow. The director ponders for a few seconds in order to choose his words wisely. He knows how brilliant and talented she is, but she must be saved from her own enthusiasm. I totally understand and admire your dedication to your story and agree with you that the missing family should be the main focus of the investigation. But the dye has been cast and we have no choice but to follow the instructions that has been set forth by the higher ups, as you put it.

Once again, Tori's face loses its' enthusiasm and changes to despair. She knew he was not going to overturn the decision of the network, but she thought she may have had a slim chance of convincing him to allow her to secretly continue searching for the truth. But she can tell by the tone and tenor of his voice that she's going to get a hard, "no". So, she cut her eyes over at Bill, who looks over at her and slightly shrugs his shoulders. The way she feels right now, she could kick over her chair, tell him to shove this job sideways up the network's ass and storm out of his office.

But she's just a struggling reporter and for the most part, she loves her job. She has now resigned herself to her fate and pushes herself back into her chair. I think that you and Bill have a very bright future here and I also agree with you about there being more to this story than just the disappearance of this family. But that being said; I can tell you that the FBI are extremely serious about the legal jeopardy regarding any further interference in their investigation. You should be aware that they are watching you and will be monitoring every aspect of your lives until this investigation has come to a conclusion. This gets Bill's attention, as he sits up straight in his chair. My advice to you both is to throw yourself into your work and forget about the Thomas family. The consequences for stubbornly pursuing this story could be a very prolong period of time in the local jail or even prison. The words "jail" and "prison" resolves any aspiration of Bill continuing any involvement in the investigation of the Government's case.

"I'm out", Bill response loudly as Tori stares at him with a scowl on her face. "I'm too pretty to go to prison", he says as he looks and smiles at her. "Ms. Milanich", the director calmly says to get her attention. "Yes", Mr. Charles. Are we on the same page? She would like to say "hell no", but she gives him a polite, "yes Mr. Charles, I completely understand". He looks at both of them for a moment wishing he could tell them everything he knows, but the Networks' attorneys were very explicit with him too. "Good", he response with a polite smile. "Just remember, that the wall has eyes". Tori understood what he meant, but he can see by Bill's expression that it's going to take him a few more minutes to figure it out. But as he looks at his watch, he sees that he has no more time to sit and chat with them. "On that note", I need you two to get back to work. Bill is still trying to figure out the director's last statement. "Tori", help him out, as he gestures to Bill. Tori nods her head and thanks the director for talking to them face-to-face. "No problem", he says as Bill and Tori gets up from their chair and leaves his office. The director is worried about one of his best field reporters and not so reliable cameraman, but young people are going to do a variety of stupid things. He just hopes that they will be better at covering their tracks this time.

A few minutes later, Tori gets back to her cubicle with Bill following closely behind her. Tori kicks her trash can to the corner of her cubicle and the trash from it explodes out of it, which startles her coworkers in their cubicles next to hers. "Calm down", Bill says in a calming tone as she angerly flops down in her chair behind her desk. "Gutless", she yells! Those bastards are gutless cowards. Hey, hey, I know you're pissed, but it's not a good career move to yell out disparaging remarks about your bosses. Especially in earshot of your suck-up and brown-nosing colleagues, he says in a whispering tone. "I'm out"! What the hell was that as she yells at Bill.

Hey, you've never been in jail and I've never been in prison, so lets keep it that way. She just shakes her head and sits in her chair quietly for a moment. All the risk we took to piece together this great story and we can't publish it or even continue digging deeper into the muck of lies. And worst of all, our hard work will most likely never see the light of day. Bill sits down in Tori's only chair in the corner of her small cubicle, which is so small he puts both feet on the front edge of her desk. Tori gives him an angry "get your stinking feet off my desk" stare and Bill gets the hint.

He swings his feet back to the floor. Tori leans forward and talks to Bill in a low tone. "I'll be damn if I'm going to let them castrate us like this", she says in a whisper. "Wow", Bill says as he covers his crouch. I still have my boys, he exclaims. I'm just saying that we need to jump into the deep end of this story and be damned if we drown. That's what good dedicated reporters do, she says with conviction. Did you hear him say "jail and prison", Bill replies! I'm not ashamed to tell you that he shook me to the core of my bones with those two words, he says without shame. And that's my point, Bill! If you want to be taken seriously in our profession as well as make a name for yourself; you'll sometimes have to put some skin in the game and will have to put yourself and your career in jeopardy.

Bill knows she's right, but he's been around longer than she has and understands that the Feds don't make idle threats. "So, what are you planning on doing", he asked? She thinks for a second before she answers him. I haven't completely shaken off the surprise of having our story shelved. But once I recover from my trauma, I'll tell you about my plans and see if you want to follow me into the depths of possible unemployment and maybe even some jail time.

She gives Bill a playful smile, but Bill doesn't find that comment amusing. He's about to tell her about his loyalty to her, but then he starts hearing the muffled theme from the television show "Cops" coming from Tori's cellphone in her purse. He knows exactly who's calling her. "Oh damn", Tori says in a low and slightly fearful voice.

She knew she would have to explain what she did to her sister sooner or later, but she thought she would have at least to the end of the day to prepare her reasons. Unfortunately, her sister's anger won't let her wait for that long. Tori shows Bill her cellphone with her sister's picture and number. Bill just mouthed, "good luck", as he sits back to watch the show. She takes a deep breath and answers the phone with a cheerful, "Hey sis". It immediately went south from there. "Don't hey sis me", you meinu, which is Japanese for "bitch". Do you have any idea what your impersonation at that crime scene has put me through?

"Let me explain Nina, Tori says as she tries to get her thoughts together. She flails her free arm, gesturing for Bill to leave, but he shakes his head, "no". She strongly pointed to the opening in her cubicle, as she looks angerly at him, but that doesn't scare him. He smiles and crosses his legs and arms, which tells Tori he's going nowhere. Bill gets yelled at on a regular basis for doing something stupid, so he's enjoying seeing Tori getting counselled for doing something stupid and reckless for a change. "Hell no", Nina yells through the phone. I was ordered into my Captains office with the FBI, my union legal representative, Detectives Sanders and Tillman. They interrogated me for over three hours to find out if I had anything to do with my idiot sister's infiltrating an active crime scene.

Can you imagine how I felt sitting there trying to defend myself and you. I should have thrown you under the bus, because obviously, you didn't give a damn about me or my career. "No", that's not true Nina, Tori says as she again tries to explain herself. Nina continues her verbal assault on her sister. You must have used the spare key that I gave you to steal one of my uniforms to impersonate me. "I'm sorry Nina, but you have to believe that I love you and wouldn't do anything to hurt you. I was going to talk to you about what I'd done after I delivered the finished story to my editor, but honestly I didn't expect that they would ever concern themselves with a young officer and let alone find out it was me impersonating you.

"Because you are an idiot", Nina shouts into the phone. Bill can hear most of what Nina is yelling and is focused on Tori's facial expressions. He can put together everything that's being said by Tori's facial expressions and body language. Nina continues to berate Tori while explaining police procedures. You wouldn't know that after every high-level investigation and search of a residence that the lead detective takes a head count prior to anyone leaving and gets statements from each of his detectives and officers assigned to the investigation.

"Oh", Tori says in surprise of that bit of information. "Yes, Oh", Nina repeats to her. After the Government Agents took over the scene and kicked out everyone who isn't and Agent; the lead detective collected everyone's information except mine, because you disappeared and I wasn't really there, you meinu"! "You're going to have to stop calling me a bitch, Tori demands. "Ok", how about stupid, fool or better yet, foolish stupid meinu! "Ok, I am an idiot", Tori exclaimed.

I only infiltrated the crime scene because I was trying to find what truly happened to the Thomas family. You know I'm not being charged with anything, don't you? "No", Nina says surprisingly. I thought you and your attorney would be in negotiation with the District Attorney's Office on how much jail time you were going to be serving. I guess I'm lucky because the Government ordered Detective Sanders not to pursue any charges against me or Bill as long as the network didn't run the story. And the network assured them that Bill and I wouldn't do any further investigations of the Thomas family.

"That idiot", Nina shouts! I should have known he was your partner in stupidity. Bill heard his name and stupidity. But it's no surprise that Tori's sister doesn't like him. Nina has always told her sister that she should ask to be assigned another cameraman. She has a problem with Bill because he made a drunken and explicit pass at her while she was placing him under arrest last year. And it didn't help that he was butt naked, again. "You're damn lucky", Nina exclaimed. I was sure I would have to explain to mom and dad why their daughter was going to jail for a couple of years. Tori knows that this isn't a good time for her to ask her sister for a favor, but what the hell she thinks to herself and decides to ask anyway. Well, now that you don't have to worry about that, but I really need you to do something for me. "Oh my God", Nina yells! I know you're not going to ask me to do something for you, as she continues to yell. Tori switches the cellphone to her other ear, because Nina's yelling has worn out that eardrum. Stop yelling for a moment and listen to what I want to ask you, please. Tori starts to talk quickly while Nina takes a short break from her yelling and cursing. I just need you to let me tell mom and dad about what happen after all of this has died down, she says in a pleasant and calm tone.

For one damn thing, I've already did you a favor by defending you at my interrogation and now you want me not to tell mom or dad what you did. "No", I'm just asking you to let me tell them myself. It really doesn't matter if I tell them or not, because dad will most likely find out from one of his detective buddies. Yes, I know, but I just need a little more time to get some projects I'm working on completed, which may persuade my bosses not to suspend me without pay for what I did. Bill knows she doesn't have any more assignments to work on right now, and they are not in jeopardy of getting suspended. But he's not surprised that she would lie to her sister. She looks over at Bill and just shrugs her shoulders at him. Look, I still want to make you a fraternal twin by re-arranging your face, but as long as you tell mom and dad before the end of the week; I won't say anything. Tori takes her sister's threat seriously, so she knows it would be in her best interest to stay away from her for at least a week.

Thanks Nina, I know I don't deserve your help, but I really appreciate you doing this for me, and I owe you one, she says with love in her voice. "No"! Don't thank me, because I'm not doing this for you. I'm doing this for Mom and Dad. They should hear this from you and not anyone else, so don't wait so damn long to tell them. "I won't", Tori responds. "I'm hanging up now", and after you tell them I will be getting my spare key from you, "Meinu", Nina says as she hangs up the phone. Tori places her phone on her desk and leans back in her chair to think about what her sister has said to her.

Bill can see that Tori is very upset about having her sister go through hours of interrogation for something she had done. He sits forward in his chair and gets Tori's attention. Speaking as someone with tons of experience in pissing his family and friends off; give your sister some time to calm down. She'll still think you're a self-centered jerk, but she'll be more receptive to hearing your apology, he says with a smile.

As you know, I have a ton of history getting family and friends to forgive me for something ridiculously stupid. She told me to mail her spare key she gave me, she says sadly. "That's great", he says as if that's the answer to all her problems. How is that anyway close to being a good thing, she responds. Because you can take her the key in a couple of days and then you will have another opportunity to get her to listen to your apology. Bill is the third brightest bulb in a box of four, but she doesn't have a better idea. And plus, that will give me an opportunity to make a copy of the key, just in case she doesn't accept my apology, she tells him.

If your sister still has that egression toward you, I suggest naked jello wrestling and with me as your official referee, just to make sure everything stays above board. Tori just stares at him in disbelief for bringing up such a moronic and inappropriate suggestion. Bill takes her silence and penetrating stare as a threat to his genitals. I'm just thinking this could be a good stress relief for both of you without anyone getting hurt, he says with a smirk.

"Get the hell out of my cubicle", she says without blinking and in a menacing tone. He smiles and gets up from his chair without saying another word. He stops in the entrance of her cubicle and makes a final remark before leaving. If you change your mine; I'll bring the jello and the large inflatable pool, as he now backs out of the opening with a smurk on his face and heads toward his office.

She knows he was just trying to make a joke, at least she thinks so, but he could have easily volunteered to buy her lunch today. Tori leans back in her chair and stares at the ceiling once again. She doesn't have a clue what her next move is going to be, but she knows she can't let their story sit in a dark corner of the Director's shelf. Government be damned!

Aboard BK's ship, it's been three weeks since he turned his wife and daughters into human pop sickles and blasted all of them into the cold darkness of space. Even though he has been working countless hours trying to keep himself busy, his mind continuously drifts into a melancholy region of his brain where his family resides. He underestimated the loneliness and sporadic thoughts of regret of what he has done to his family.

But after weeks of sleepless nights, for good or bad, today is the day that his solitude is about to come to an end. This is the day he has scheduled for his wife to be awakened from stasis. He planned to perform the procedure at 9:00 a.m., but this is the first time the med-units have removed a female from stasis, so he decides to go over Lorraine's vital signs and review the equipment preparations list for the third time.

It's now 10:15 a.m., and now BK's confident enough to begin with the procedure. The three med-units are moving about the room preparing the various drugs, tools and equipment that he will need to revive his wife. He has dreamt of holding her in his arms and telling her how sorry he is and how much he loves her. But he has no illusions to what's going to happen once she thoroughly comprehends what he's done. It'll probably be unimaginable to her why and how he could do that to her and their children. He has gone over in his mind what he was going to say to her millions of times, but he knows whatever he says will not stop her from most likely having a homicidal moment. Something you would most likely see on the TV show "Snapped".

Luckily for him, she will be too weak to even lift her arms let alone swing on him, because of her time in stasis. He knows that he'll have to work hard and take a ton of abuse in order for him to convince her to help him with their daughters' emotional state once they are brought out of stasis. He has convinced himself that after a period of time his girls will be excited about traveling hundreds of miles above the earth and in addition to being the youngest astronauts to ever travel off the planet. Of course, it's impossible for him to think like a 12 and 16 year old girl, so they could be as angry as their mother.

Neither one of his girls has any interest in quantum physics or space exploration. However, all that will change once the exabytes of data and scientific knowledge that has been implanted in the limbic system of their brains kicks in. But if all else fails, he will have to switch to plan "B", which entails promising them a shopping spree in Paris once they return to earth. But now isn't the time to think about appeasing LaChel and Kim, he thinks to himself. He starts to walk around the stasis room gathering tools, a tablet and giving the med-units last minute instructions. His heart rate is slightly elevated, and he breathes more deeply in the attempt to control his emotions. If he doesn't stay calm, his emotions can possibly interfere with his concentration, which could lead to a mistake. Alright, let's thaw out the misses, he says with a nervous smile. MOM, I need you to monitor her vitals closely. You do understand that's part of my programming to ensure that the medical units preform their task flawlessly, she replies. He opens the stasis container door and pushes the button that causes Lorraine's capsule to slowly emerge from the container. He watches the capsule slowly spin around and its base elevates the capsule to 4 feet and tilts the head of it up at a 60-degree angle. He walks up to the capsule and rubs away the thin film of frost off the viewing port with the sleeve of his jumper.

Now he can finally get a glimpse of his wife's face through the view port. He can only see a distorted view of her face and the shape of her head because of the swirling cloud of light bluish mist that fills the entire capsule. He thinks to himself that in roughly 35 minutes, his wife's mouth will be moving a mile a minute and spouting enough obscenities to make a sailor blush. It's not too late to put her back in cold storage, he thinks to himself. He briefly wonders if it would be a good idea to keep her here in stasis for another couple of days and go back to work in his lab, but he knows deviating from his plans isn't an option. Besides, it's been too long since he touched the softness of her skin and ran his fingers through her hair. He has no doubt that he needs her here with him and it's worth the potential verbal and physical injuries. He bends over and gives Lorraine's view port a kiss.

"OK babe, it's time for you to come back to me", he whispers as he leans close to the frosted view port. In a strange way, he feels like Dr. Frankenstein. Not the time where he's reanimating the monster, "Frankenstein", but "The Bride of Frankenstein". He probably going to experience the same gut renching scream that the bride gave Frankenstein when she first saw him. He walks over to the control panel to begin the thawing process. MOM! Yes, BK. Please start phase one and closely monitor Lorraine's vital signs, please. You are aware that you have ask me that just a minute ago, she says in a curious tone. Yes, I know MOM. I'm just a little nervous so, please just indulge me.

If you want humorous, I could tell you a couple of off-color limericks, she asked. No, you know that's not what I'm asking you! I get enough of those types of jokes from Benny. Speaking of Benny; would you like me to activate him now, she asked. Yes, but restrict him to my quarters. I don't need him roaming the ship right now. Continue your other task and we can discuss what I'm going to do with Benny later. Yes BK, I understand, she replies. he walks over to the panel next to Lorraine's capsule. The panel displays a light purplish contour of a female body, which represents Lorraine's core temperature and vital signs:

Body temperature: 35 degrees Fahrenheit

Brain Activity: minimal

Oxygen Intake: zero percent

Heart Rate: 0 bpm

If someone would look at her body, they would think she was just a dead frozen body lying in a white tube. As he presses another series of buttons, he asked MOM to discontinue the subliminal data transfer and start cryogenic regeneration procedures. She confirms the discontinuation of data. After five minutes, he can begin to see his wife's face for the first time in weeks. It's amazing how his joyful emotions of looking at her face as it comes into focus, turns those same emotions to dread, because her consciousness is almost a reality. Another fifteen minutes pass and he begins the last phase of the process. The gas hoses automatically disconnect once the last of the bluish gas is drawn out of the capsule. This triggers the automatic opening of the lid of the capsule. Her facial skin color starts to gradually change to her natural hue, because the pad she has been lying on begins to gradually warm her body back to her normal body temperature.

Unit M3 floats over to the now opened capsule and uses a device that looks like a 2" by 5" flat piece of rectangular aluminum strip with a digital display embedded in it. This device will be used to restart Lorraine's heart. The unit places the device on her chest, right over her heart. The unit hovers over to the opposite side of the capsule and waits for BK's signal to start the cardiac stimulator.

He looks at Lorraine's vitals on a display, which indicates that her body temperature is at 68.9 degrees Fahrenheit. Her temperature has to be at least 76.5 degrees before he can start her heart, which in turn will kick-start the rest of her vitals. Four minutes later, her body has reached the required temperature. He instructs unit M3 to activate the cardiac device. The device transfers pulses of electrical current to Lorraine's resting heart. After twenty-five seconds, Lorraine's heart starts to beat with a normal rhythm. BK removes the device from Lorraine, deactivates it then places it in his pocket. The rest of her organs will kick start, for lack of a better term, once her heart starts pumping blood to them. After about five minutes, her body temperature increases to 92.8 degrees Fahrenheit and her normal color returns to her face. He will use a neuro-stimulator he designed to activate her normal brain activity. He grabs a tablet from the desk and brings up a medical program, which will show a more detailed illustration of Lorraine's complete vitals. He takes the neuro-stimulator out of his pocket and places it on her forehead. He then uses the tablet to activate the device. Blue and green lights pulsate and travel across the small device for three to four minutes. His tablet flashes and beeps to indicate that her brain pattern has returned to normal.

BK, Lorraine's brain waves are stable and there is no indication of any abnormalities, MOM says in a measured tone. Units M2 and M1 hover toward her in order to remove her from her capsule. She doesn't need to be in her capsule any longer, but he stops the units and tells them to move back and he'll remove her himself. He positions himself to the left of the capsule, reaches down and puts one arm under her legs and the other behind her back, lifts her up and cradles her in his arms.

He stands there for a moment squeezing her body gently against his and smelling her hair, which is still covered by her protective suit. But her hair still smells so good, he thinks to himself. And she feels so good that he doesn't want to put her down. But he reluctantly tells M2 to pull back the sheet on the first bed. Unit M3 hovers pass BK, who is slowly and carefully walking toward the bed carrying his wife. It maneuvers to the top of Lorraine's now empty capsule and presses a few buttons, which causes the lid to slowly close.

Unit 1 monitors the capsule as it repositions itself back into the stasis container and adjust itself back to a sixty-degree angle. The Unit then checks Kim and LaChel's stasis capsule to ensure all functions are normal and stable. He slowly lowers Lorraine into the bed and adjust the pillow behind her head. He then asked unit two for the tool that is used to separate the clear mask and the protective hood. He runs the tip of the tool around the contour of the opening of the facial mask then removes the protective mask and places it on the table nex to the bed. He smiles as he slides the hood down to expose her hair.

He gently lifts her left hand and gives the back of it a loving kiss and starts to talk to her softly. Lorraine... Lorraine, he says as he leans over to get closer to her face. Can you hear me, babe? There is no movement from her other than the rising and lowering of her chest from her shallow breathing. As he looks for any signs of her becoming conscious, he notices her eyelids begin to slightly move. In addition to monitoring Lorraine's vitals, MOM realizes that BK's heart rate is starting to elevate. But she understands the human condition and knows that his elevated vitals are in anticipation of his wife's impending return to consciousness. He puts his hand on her forehead and can feel the warmth radiating from her skin.

Just then Lorraine's chest rises sharply as she takes a deep breath. He can see that her breathing is becoming normal for a person awaking from their sleep and he can feel her fingers start to twitch in his hand as her lips begins to move. He can't wait to give her a kiss, so he decides to kiss her before she wakes up. He also knows that this most likely will be the most opportune time to kiss his wife before the yelling and screaming begins. So, he leans over and gives her another soft kiss on her lips. The warmth of her lips on his feels so good to him that he decides to enjoy his lips on hers for a couple more seconds. As he removes his lips from hers, he watches as her eyes start to flicker then tries to open one at a time.

He smiles at her as she struggles to open her eyes. Her arms and legs begin to move with uncontrollable spasms. It scares him a little, because he doesn't remember, and he wasn't told of his arms and legs moving uncontrollably after he awakened from his stasis. Her eyes are half open and a little glassy as she tries to focus on the large blurry shape leaning over her. She tries to say something, but her throat is so dry that she can't speak. The light from the room also makes it hard to see his face, but she recognizes his voice. "She looks so confused", he thinks to himself. Her trembling hand squeezes his tight as she can, but now he can feel her arm shaking too. He leans over and kisses her on the forehead and tells her she's going to be alright.

Lorraine's eyes are completely open now, but she's still having a hard time focusing, but he can see her pupils starting to adjust. But the brightness of the light is beginning to give her a slight headache. She turns her head to one side and tightly closes them. BK instructs MOM to reduce the light in the room by 25 percent. He runs his hand through her silky hair then bends over and takes in a big whiff of her hair.

He loves how it smells even after being in stasis for almost a month. Her face contorts slightly as she swallows and tries to ask him a question, but her throat hurts so much, she has difficulties speaking. Hold on babe! I'll be back, he says as he leaves her side and hurries across the room. There's a refrigerator on the other side of the room with just what she needs. He rushes back with a clear plastic bottle filled with a greenish liquid, which is something that looks similar to Gatorade. He gently lifts her head, then positions the straw so she can take a drink. OK baby, now take small sips of this and your throat will feel a lot better in no time, he says with a smile. She doesn't care what it is or how it taste as long as it relieves her sore throat. She takes about three or four sips then tries to speak again. She coughs then clears her throat.

This time BK can understand her a little clearer. She looks up at him with a look of concern and confusion. "What's going on"! Am I in a hospital, she asks with a raspy voice, which is barely audible? "Where are the girls", she adds. She grabs and rubs her throat as she begins to cough again, as she rolls her body toward him. Her face reflects the amount of pain she feels every time she tries to ask a question. Shhh… That's OK, babe. Don't try to talk too much. He puts the palm of his hand on her face. Your vocal cords are a little tight right now, but drinking this will help relax them. Lorraine's eyes are still not focusing correctly either. She can only see a distorted image of what she knows to be her husband. Everything else around her is very blurry, which maybe for the best. Luckily, because of the distance and the blurriness, she can't see the three medical units staying out of sight in various locations of the room.

She doesn't realize where she is right now and if she saw them, she most likely would freak-out. She attempts to put her hand over her eyes, but the best she can do is to get her hands up to her throat. She whispers to him. "What's wrong with me"? The light is hurting my eyes and I feel so weak! I'm sorry babe, I forgot, he says to her as he quickly gets a pair of special sunglasses off the counter next to the table. He places the glasses on her face and asked, "how's that"? She gives him a slight nod of approval. He is finding it a little difficult to shake the feeling of guilt for what she's going through.

He tries to do anything and everything to make her as comfortable as possible. Lorraine's eyes begin to regain their focus, but it's like having your eyes dilated. She clears her throat again then asks in a very low tone, "what hospital am I in and who has the girls"? She may can't see very well, but she can clearly comprehend that she's not in her own bed. Baby, I'll tell you everything, but I just need you to drink a little more of this drink. He lifts her head again and puts the straw up to her mouth. But Lorraine has enough strength now to push the bottle away.

Her voice cracks as she tries to yell, "I don't want anymore of that crap"! "Where am I", as she tries to raise her voice! He can see this is about to get real ugly - real quick. He thinks to himself, "damn", maybe I should have kept her in stasis for at least another couple of weeks". Only wine mellows with age. Not a frozen wife, he thinks to himself.

"Baby please". You're getting very emotional and that won't do anything to improve your condition. Once your health improves, I promise to explain everything that has happened to you. And the girls are fine, he adds. In a very deliberate tone, she tells him that the last thing she remembers is him standing next to her side of the bed and being awakened by something wet on her face"! This time in a clearer tone she asked, "Where are LaChel and Kim"? He thinks it would be in his best interest and hers of course, not to tell her about their frozen daughters across the room just yet. "They're here, but you can't see them right now", he says as confidently as he can. As he looks down at her, he can see that she is still in pain, but he knows that won't stop her from asking questions. He looks up at the monitor. Her brain activity is beginning to show a number of small abnormalities, which indicates that she's becoming too stressed. He realizes that he must calm her down before her condition worsens. He leans over her then gives her another kiss on the forehead. Lorraine still looks very confused and weak as she puts both of her hands to her face and complains that her head is beginning to hurt. He still remembers what his mind and body felt like after coming out of stasis. He's glad he decided to use himself as a guinea pig. I know babe, you'll probably have a slight headache and your body may feel weak, but I promise you'll feel better soon. She looks up at him as he smiles down at her. She turns away from his smiling face, because her intuition tells her that he knows what's wrong with her and wonders why he won't tell her. Can you just get the nurse or the doctor to come talk to me, she moans?

MOM sends a message to the tablet he has on the table beside Lorraine's bed, which gives him a couple of beeps to signal him. He looks over at the tablet, which says that Lorraine's stress levels are beginning to elevate to an alarming level". Unit M1 is continuously monitoring Lorraine's vitals, so it reacts to her impending health alert. It starts to move toward her, but BK aggressively gestures to the unit to stay back. Luckily, Lorraine's eyes still can't focus well and doesn't see the units around her. He uses the tablet to adjust the upper portion of the bed, so Lorraine's upper body is at a 45 degree angle.

He thinks this will make her comfortable and increase her blood flow. As the head of the bed rises, she begins to feel a sharp pain in her lower back and her head ache begins to increase. She reaches up and grabs the sleeve of his jumper as she moans loudly. She tells him to stop moving the bed. He quickly taps on his tablet, which immediately stops the bed from rising. "My back", she moans. He explains to her that her muscles will be a little stiff for a while, but the best thing for them is to work the stiffness and knots out. Lorraine looks him in the eye and grits her teeth as she tells him. I don't think you're a doctor or a nurse and if this bed moves again, I'll break the finger that presses that damn button, she says as she looks him in the eyes. The bed is good enough, she adds. He knows that elevating her would probably help her breathing and decrease her blood pressure, but he doesn't want her to get more upset. He looks down at her with a loving smile to attempt to reassure her that her condition is only temporary. She's still confused and doesn't understand why he's looking at her with that stupid smile on his face. She just turns her head away from him. He's been married to Lorraine for a long time and he knows that she suspects that he has something to do with her condition. Just tell me what's going on, she asked sharply, as she moans and looks back at him for some answers.

I'm so tired and you're doing back flips on my last nerve, as she cuts her eyes up at him. He gestures to her to wait one moment. He can see and hear it in her voice that she's still hurting, so he hands her the bottle again. You need to drink some more of this if you want to continue asking me questions, he says as he puts the bottle and straw to her lips again.

You have to stay hydrated and this will make your throat feel a lot better, he says while positioning the straw to her mouth. Normally, Loraine would question what she's drinking, but she realizes that her throat does feel better after she drank whatever concoction that's in that bottle. The way her throat feels right now, she wouldn't care if it was a combination of knotty head gin and wild turkey. Her face reflects how soar her throat feels as she grimaces while drinking more of the greenish concoction.

As BK holds the bottle to her mouth, she drinks as much as she can, then pushes the bottle away and moans again as she puts her head back on the pillow. "Don't worry", he tells her while playing with the ends of her hair. The medicine in that bottle is similar to ibuprofen, but it will take away your pain a lot quicker. She doesn't want him touching her, so she uses the back of her hand to stop him from messing with her hair.

What kind of hospital is this, she asked as she looks around the room? There hasn't been a single nurse or doctor for that matter to come in and check on me yet. She also finally realizes that she's not wearing a typical hospital gown. And what in the hell am I wearing, as she looks at the form fitting stasis suit she's still wearing. He doesn't want to tell her the truth just yet, because it would only raise her stress level and compound her condition. She looks under the covers and sees that it's a continuous suit that covers her from head to toe.

She looks up at him with a "what the hell" expression on her face. He presents her with the remaining medicine in the bottle and tells her he will tell her everything that has happened while she finishes this bottle. All she wants are answers, but she decides to drink some more of the green concoction to appease him. She also knows he's the reason she's in this strange hospital bed and she needs her voice to yell and ask him questions without pain. She now has enough strength to snatch the bottle from his hand and finishes the remaining medicine. BK grabs the empty bottle, and places it on the table beside her bed and waits for the medication to take effect. He hated to do it, but needed her to rest for a couple more hours, so he puts some sleeping medication in the bottle with the medicine for her throat, which he thought would be best not to mention to her.

She should fall asleep in a matter of minutes, he thinks to himself. He could have used the same chemical he used on her at home, but he knows she would never forgive him for drugging her like that again. This way, she would think that she's still feeling the effects of whatever put her in what she thinks is a hospital and she just fell asleep on her own. The drug she drank is less potent and much safer. Now I'm going to tell you what's going on, but I need you to stay as calm as you can. She doesn't say a word, but gives him her full attention. He sits on the edge of the bed and tries to think of how to explain their situation. At least as much as he can before the drug takes effect. She looks intensely and angrily at him and he gestures to her to wait a moment then grabs his tablet. She has an overwhelming feeling to jump out of the bed and choke the truth out of him, but because she feels so weak; she knows that she just has to wait to hear what he has to say. He taps on his tablet and swipes through a few menus then points to the wall to the right of the room.

She looks over at the light bluish wall as the upper portion of it transforms into a 6' x 4' picture window, which now displays the image of space and a portion of the earth. Lorraine doesn't remember a lot about geography since her days in high school, but she thinks she's looking at the right side portion of Africa and the entire continent of Asia. It looks like something you would see on National Geographic network, and the clarity of the picture is amazing.

It's the largest high definition plasma television she has ever seen, she thinks to herself. She stares at the image of the slowly moving earth and stares back at BK with a look of confusion. "Why in the hell do you think I want to look at one of your nerdy television shows about space", she asked? I want to know why I'm lying in this hospital bed with only you to take care of me, she yells? "No", he says in frustration as he stands and walks over to the view port. He stands next to it and points to the earth. Babe, this view isn't a television show about space. He pauses for a second to gauge the look on her face. She looks angry and irritated, but not convinced. We are 230 miles above the earth, in a spacecraft that I built, he says as he looks back at her. She still looks angry and doesn't look convinced. She grimaces as she uses her arms to push herself up to a sitting position. "What the hell are you talking about"! You don't really expect me to believe that we're on some type of homemade spaceship? "That's exactly what I'm trying to tell you, babe", he says as he walks toward her bed. "Stop talking stupid and just get the damn doctor", as she carefully lowers herself back to the pillow and turns away from him and the view port. She looks beside her bed and on the counter for a buzzer that she can press to call for the nurse. It's obvious to her, for whatever reason, her crazy husband isn't going to tell her what's going on. She leans her body towards the door and starts yelling for the nurse hoping someone will hear her. Well, time to go to plan "B", he says under his breath.

All right! Stop yelling, he says to her as he exhales a heavy and reluctant breath. This would have been a hell of a lot easier if you would have just believed what I was telling you, he says as he walks over between her bed and the empty one beside her. Hey, just look at me for a moment, he asked as politely as he can. She turns towards him and laids there staring at him. He looks Lorraine in her eyes and asked her to remain calm and not to freak out.

She asked him "what the hell are you talking about". He instructs unit M1 to hover over to Lorraine's bed side. She wonders who in the hell he's talking to as she moves her head to the left and right to see what's behind him. The unit rises from behind the desk then hovers toward Lorraine with its' multi-colored lights on its' head strobing randomly. Out of the corner of her eye, she notices something moving towards her from her left and is horrified to see the unit approaching her.

She lets out a terrified scream as she stares at the unit with her eyes open as wide as she can. "Oh my god", she yells over and over again, while staring in horror at the approaching unit. "What the hell is that", she says as she scoots her body to the other side of the bed and pulls the covers up to her chin. BK moves next to his now trembling wife, hugs his wife and tries to convince her that it's going to be alright. She can't believe what she's seeing. He gives her a kiss on the cheek and walks back around the bed and stands beside unit M1. "Don't be afraid", he says while placing his hand on the head of the unit. He can see that she is scared, so he sits back down on her bed and places his hand on her trembling leg. He can feel her body shaking slightly and her eyes are stretched as wide as silver dollars. This is medical unit one or M1 for short.

Say hello to my wife M1. "Hello, BK's wife", it says in a female robot sounding voice. He programmed all the medical units with a female voice. "Oh my God"! That's so creepy, she says with her bed sheet now covering her mouth and still pressed against the metal headboard of the bed. He corrects M1 and tells it to call her Lorraine from now on. M1 Response by saying, "Hello Lorraine". And there are two more medical units to your right. she jumps to the middle of the bed as she whips her head to the right to see the other units hovering at the foot of the empty bed.

That's unit M2 and the other one is M3 as he points to each unit. She can feel the wall of doubt starting to crumble as she looks the units up and down. She jumps as she feels BK squeeze her leg. "OK", get your hand off me, because you and those things are freaking me out, while pulling her knees to her chest. I know those things are over there, but I can't help but think their touching me. He gestures to all three units to back away as he explains to her that they are medical units, which have been designed to assist him and perform medical treatments. He lies to her, because he doesn't think it would be helpful right now to tell her that she's the ship's medical physician and that the units are her assistants.

She looks at unit one, staring at her with its' mechanical eyes. The units don't have much of a normal looking face, but she thinks the eyes are creepy. The head is more round than oval, its' eyes are ping pong ball sized and with a bluish tint, and it has two mechanical arms with four fingers on each hand. They have no legs, but they have the ability to hover with their anti-gravity components built in. BK can see that the medication is now beginning to take effect as he can hear her speech starting to slur and she's having a hard time controlling her head. He almost forgot about the drug he gave her a few minutes ago. She suddenly feels her eyelids getting heavier as she struggles to stay awake.

But her head is beginning to shift from side to side. She tries to say something, but all she can get out is "what did" and "you bastard". Her head is now slumped toward him and she is seconds from being unconscious again. Babe, he says to her as he grabs his tablet from the counter and walks back over to her bedside. Once you wake up, I'm sure you'll feel almost like your normal self. Her eyes are mostly closed as she utters her last word before giving in to the drug. "Bastard", she says in a slurred whisper. Then she just drifts into dreamland as he gently strokes her forehead. He looks down at her for a moment then leans over and says to her, "I'll be back before you wake up". He looks at his tablet to check her vitals again. She should be sleeping for at least three hours, MOM reminds him. he walks over to a tall cabinet next to the desk and grabs some folded clothing and shoes from the top shelf. They are light purple pajamas and will make her feel more comfortable than the stasis suit she's wearing.

He walks back over to the bed and instructs units two and three to get his wife out of her stasis suit and dress her in these clothes, as he tosses them onto the foot of her bed. Both units respond and moves toward her bed with M1 holding scissors in its' hand. The suit can't be pulled off her because it is too form fitting, so the unit will cut her out of the suit. He hadn't seen his wife in quite a while and is tempted to stay and assist the units, but he decides not to torture himself like that.

He walks out the medical lab and into the passageway. Well that went better than I thought, he says to himself. But he knows that this is only the first day and that when her strength and mobility improves, so will her temper. Regardless of her mood and attitude, he will love to talk to her and have her with him once again. It doesn't even matter if she's yelling and using colorful words to explain my heritage and mental instability. It will be worth it, just to hear her sweet voice cursing like a drunken sailor.

"Now that's love" he thinks to himself. He walks in the direction of the ship's hanger where he is working on a project that he knows will make his wife and daughters happy. He's not going to finish the project before the girls are out of stasis, but maybe they can pitch in and help him once they are adjusted to their lives onboard the ship and have adapted to their newly acquired abilities.

Once he gets to the hanger, he immediately begins to work on his project in order to keep his mind occupied. Although he planned to go back to Lorraine's bedside after an hour, he is making great progress, so he instructs unit M3 to place a neo suppressant on her forehead, which will keep her unconscious until he gets back to the medical bay and removes it. But he thinks it will be best to instruct the unit to set the device to deactivate at 7:30 a.m., just in case he forgets to remove it.

He works in the hanger most of the night before MOM nags him to get some sleep. He decides to listen to his work wife and finally calls it quits at 3:41 in the morning. He staggers up the ladder and down the hallways. He makes it to a bed and doesn't even take off his jumper. He just flops onto the bed so hard you would think it would break under his weight. He lays there until morning. MOM tries her best to wake him, but she always has a hard time waking him when he has stayed up all night and most of the morning. He decided not to sleep in his lonely bed in his quarters, but to sleep in the empty bed next to Lorraine. He planned on getting up before her, so he could take her down to the kitchen for some breakfast. But he's still sound asleep and MOM knows he can use the rest and decides not to wake him.

Meanwhile, as scheduled, Lorraine's neo suppressant has deactivated. Her body starts to move slightly, and her eyes begin to try to open. She wipes the sleep from her eyes as she gives a long silent yawn and stretches as if she was in her own bed on a Saturday morning. Her eyes open and start to focus on the medical bay's white ceiling. She feels something on her forehead then pulls the device off, which is lightly stuck to her forehead. She stares at the device for a second then places it on the table next to her.

She slowly sits up and looks around the room as she suddenly realizes that what she thought was a nightmare is still her reality. Automatically, her eyes start to water then tears start to roll down her cheeks as the reality of what BK told her slaps her across her face. She hears the familiar sound of heavy breathing to her right and sees her husband stretched out in the bed next to hers. Any other time, she would look at this moment as him being a sweet and loving husband that worries about his wife, but at this moment she's looking at him wondering what she could do to him to cause the most pain and suffering. She realizes that he's still in the coveralls that he had on yesterday.

She always hated when he would come in from the garage after working on one of his projects and flop down on the sofa in those dirty coveralls, she thinks to herself as she shakes her head and stares at him lying there. "After all the years of her complaining and shouting, he still hadn't changed his bad habits", as she looks at him in frustration. He's lying on his left side facing her. And just look at him sleeping there in those filthy coveralls, she thinks to herself. She has a look of disdain and anger on her face for what he has put her through. BK starts to move slightly, maybe because he most likely can feel the heat of her eyes burning into his face. She has half a dozen thoughts on what she can do to cause him the most pain, but she decides not to do anything to him, "just yet". Her malicious thoughts soon turn to the overwhelming feeling of her bladder quickly building up to a colossal explosion. And now she can feel her stomach and colon teaming up. She never felt like this before. She may need help but rather than slap her husband awake, she decides to get out of bed and find the bathroom that's hopefully in this room. She forces herself into a sitting position then swings her legs across the edge of the bed. As she sits there with her legs dangling, she notices what she's wearing.

It's some sort of purplish medical shirt and pants much like the kind of clothes you would see patients in a medical clinic wearing. But this one has an emblem embroiled on the upper left side of the shirt. She pulls the portion of the shirt with the emblem on it away from her body, so she can get a better look at it. Its upside down, but she can see the emblem is a combination of the earth and something shaped like a space craft flying around it. Oh my God, she says out loud! This nerd has dressed me in some kind of space costume. Soon as I get out of here, I'm going to find my clothes and drop this costume into the nearest trash can.

She can see some matching purple crock like shoes on the floor directly below her feet. What in the hell is it with all this purple, she says to herself! His favorite color is red and mine is powder blue. The shoes look some distance from her feet as she looks down at them. The bed is higher than her bed at home, so she carefully slides her body down the side of the bed to the floor. As her feet touches the floor, she can feel a slight pain in the bottom of them. She remembers how weak her entire body felt yesterday, so she moves slowly and carefully. She can feel her muscles starting to react to carrying the weight of her body. So, she puts most of her weight on her arms as she uses the bed to hold herself up. She slides her feet into the purple crocks. The arch supports built into the shoes should help the pain in her feet. She bites down on her lip as she suddenly experiences some moderate pain in the bottom of her feet and ankles. She grimaces but takes the pain in silence as she glances back at him, whose still sleeping soundly. She is still trying to shake off her anger but imagining she could at least take one of these ugly purple shoes and shove it sideways and deep into his snoring mouth. Fighting through the pain, she moves her legs up and down trying to work her leg muscles. She stands there leaning against the bed for a couple of minutes breathing in and out as she puts her remaining weight from the bed onto her shaking legs. She removes her hands from the bed and uses her arms to balance herself for a moment. There's still some pain in her feet and lower legs, but she knows once she starts to walk around, that they will feel better. She tries to balance herself by using her arms as she carefully shuffles her feet across the shiny vinyl like floor. "He must have those little robots shine these floors day and night", she thinks to herself. Her progress is slow and labored, but she's managing the pain and making her way toward what she thinks and hopes is the bathroom door. She's trying to be very careful, because if she falls, she knows that she won't have to worry about making it to the bathroom. MOM is monitoring her carefully and instructs the units not to assist her. How can every muscle in her body hurt, she thinks to herself as she uses the various pieces of office furniture to get closer to the door she thinks is the entrance to the bathroom. She finally makes it to the door and opens it to see a modest size bathroom with a toilet, a sink and other bathroom fixtures.

She's beyond happy that she chose the correct door, because her bladder is about to burst, and her stomach is grumbling obscenities at her. The door closes behind her as she steps inside. MOM is tempted to wakeup BK but determines that this would be a perfect opportunity to study an adult female. She can hear various noises emanating from the bathroom, which MOM determines is all Lorraine, but is coming from different orifices of her body. Of course, MOM understands human biology, but she fines it fascinating to analyze the types and amount of gases that the human body can produce.

After ten minutes, Lorraine staggers out of the bathroom alittle lighter and with a look of relief on her face. She looks across the room to see BK still sound asleep. MOM is also amazed that after all the noises echoing out of the bathroom, he doesn't move a muscle. Lorraine stands there for a second mapping out the route back to her bed, but she thinks it would be in her best interest to familiarize herself with the ship. She takes small and labored steps as she uses whatever piece of furniture like crutches to take the weight off her weakened legs. She finally makes it to the door, and she has to rest against it for a few seconds to regain her strength before opening it. She sees a diamond shape button to the left of the door, which she guestimates will open it once she can muster enough strength to press her palm against it.

She pushes herself off the wall, takes a few more steps to the left and presses the button. The door slides to the right with a barely audible swishing sound. She then looks back at BK to see if the door caused him to wake up.

He's not snoring anymore, but for the most part, he's still sleeping soundly. There's a grayish wall roughly six feet in front of her. She then tentatively peeks her head out the doorway and looks to the left then to the right. She sighs and wonders which way she should go". Both directions look exactly the same, but for some reason she thinks going right is the way to go. MOM uses a bit of subjective psychology by slightly dimming the lights to the left and brightened the lights to the right. Like a mouse in a maze, MOM is running an experiment of her own. Lorraine shuffles out of the medical bay and into the passageway as the door automatically swish close behind her, which scares her and almost causes her to fall.

MOM has unit M3 give BK a couple of light pokes to the forehead to wake him up. "Stop poking me", he yells as he pushes the unit away! I thought you would like to know that your wife has left her Clinic, MOM says in a measured tone. He doesn't seem concerned as he wipes the sleep from his eyes and stretches his long body beyond the length of the bed. She doesn't understand why he's showing little concerns about the location of his wife. I just wanted to inform you that your wife is walking through the ship without a logical direction. Yes, I know, he says as he sits up in the bed. I decided to be here when she woke up in order to gauge the state of her anger towards me. "Explain", MOM requested. He spins his legs out the bed, yawns and sits there rubbing his head. If she woke up and sees me sleeping in the next bed and doesn't try to bludgeon me to death with one of the medical units, then I know she's not that upset with me and still has some love for me, which is probably buried under a ton of anger and hate. So, that's why I put her shoes by the bed and laid her robe at the foot of the bed. He stands up and looks over at the foot of her bed and sees that she forgot to put on the robe he left for her.

MOM, what is the temperature onboard the ship in the passageway and common areas? "69 degrees Fahrenheit", she replies. Increase the ship's temperature to 72 degrees, please. "Done", she immediately replies. And I want you to secure the engine room, propulsion, the bridge and all the other vital areas, but leave the common areas accessible. The ship's layout has been embedded into her brain, but it may take her another day or two to gain access to it. I will keep one of my one hundred and thirty-five sensors focused on her continuously. He smiles as he stands beside the bed. Thank you. "Where is she headed, he asked"? If she continues in her current direction, she should pass by the galley or she could make it to your living quarters. He walks from between the beds and toward the door. He stops at the foot of the bed, and ponders there for a moment. He then asks MOM to open the galley door and begin to play some light jazz music. That should be enough to guide her in that direction and lure her into the galley. MOM states that Lorraine really needs to eat something since she had not eaten anything since being placed into stasis, so she will have the chef set out some cut fruit and orange juice on one of the tables. "I agree", but have him also put out a bowl of oatmeal, he adds as he resumes his exit from the medical clinic. I'm going to engineering to take a shower and put on some clean coveralls. MOM is worried about BK's hygiene, so for the fifth time she suggests that he stop sleeping in his soiled work clothes. He doesn't see it as a big deal, so he smiles and nods his head as the door opens. Have one of the units change both bed linens, he tells her as he heads out the door and makes a left and walks toward engineering.

Meanwhile, Lorraine is hobbling pretty well down the passageway, as she instinctively heads in the direction with the brightest light, which MOM is controlling. Her muscles are still not working together properly, and she has to slide her left hand down the wall to keep her balance, but she's moving remarkably well for a woman that has been frozen in a tube for the last couple of weeks. All of a sudden, a softball size metallic unit, which BK calls a "bot" rolls past her, which causes her to flatten herself against the wall and causes her to scream. What the hell was that, she yells out loud as she looks around for more of them. The metallic balls are maintenance bots, which are used to inspect the wiring and components within the walls. Lorraine is nervous and tired now as she continues to the end of the hall and has to make another left or right decision. She comes to the "T" in the passageway and looks to the right, which is very dimly lit. But to the left, she can hear a faint sound of music and for some reason it looks brighter.

Of course, she decides to go toward the bright light and music, which she hopes leads to someone that can help her. These open hallways are cold, she thinks to herself as she hugs herself tightly. MOM turned up the temperature aboard the ship, but it's going to take a little time for Lorraine to notice the difference. MOM is monitoring her physical condition and has calculated that she should be able to make it to the galley without collapsing or losing an arm or leg from frost bite. The temperature of the hallway motivates Lorraine to use her remaining strength to quicken her pace as she can now clearly see an open door with sounds of music and light emanating from it. MOM thinks that Lorraine will stay there long enough for BK to come and join her. Even if her daughters aren't at her destination, she hopes to at least be able to find a cellphone to call her mother. She needs to talk to someone else other than her crazy husband. She finally reaches the room with the door that is completely open. Now that she has finally arrived at the source of the music, she stands in the doorway trying to decide if she really should go in. But the pain in her legs persuades her to walk in and sit down before they stop working. She looks to the left and sees a modern kitchen that looks remarkably similar to her kitchen on earth. And to the right, separated by a long breakfast nook is a dining room with three medium beige tables with four matching chairs placed around each table. She doesn't see anyone, but does see a refrigerator, so she decides to go into the kitchen first.

She can't help but be overwhelmed by how much this kitchen looks like hers. It's no coincidence, because BK thought it would be a good idea to design the galley's kitchen, as well as the one in his quarters, to look similar to their kitchen at home. But he did make some changes that he and Lorraine wanted to do to their kitchen in the future. The cabinets are tall and an eggshell white with round black handles, just like the ones that him and Lorraine looked at months ago when they were planning to remodel their kitchen. She walks beside the breakfast nook sliding her hand across the smooth surface of the granite countertop.

She limps over and pulls open the double refrigerator doors and peers inside. "Oh my God", she says as her voice echoes through the kitchen. Look at all this food in here, she says in amazement. She doesn't understand how or who stocked this refrigerator with all this food. BK hates all forms of shopping. Especially grocery shopping. She can see two sweet potato pies on the bottom shelf, which is his favorite. But the pies look as if they were made only a couple of days ago, but she knows that her husband can't boil an egg without burning it, let alone make pie from scratch. She suddenly feels some sharp pains in her stomach, which is accompanied by a loud growling noise. She grabs her stomach and eagerly looks for something to eat. But she's afraid that her stomach can't handle the amount of food she's tempted to devour. She decides to ignore her very vocal stomach and closes each door of the refrigerator and then walks out of the kitchen. Every muscle in her legs are beginning to ache and screams to her to find some where to sit down. She moans with each step as she slides her hand across the edge of the countertop for support. She hobbles her way out of the kitchen and into the dining area. She really needs to sit down at one of those tables and gather her courage before she tries to get something to eat. Her steps are short and labored now, but she manages to make her way to the dining area. As she walks over toward one of the tables, she notices a small bowl of oatmeal, a bowl of cut fruit and some orange juice prepared for her on the second table. BK knows how much she loves oatmeal in the morning, so he knew coupled with not eating for weeks, she wouldn't be able to resist eating it. She's amazed that she hadn't seen it once she entered the galley.

She is so hungry that the sight of the oatmeal draws her toward the table and to momentarily forget about the aches and pains in her legs. It doesn't take her much to convince herself to sit down and eat. Besides, she hoped that putting something in her stomach would ease her hunger pains. Lorraine totally ignores the other four smaller bowls placed on the table, which contains a spoon full of peanut butter, brown sugar, cinnamon and milk. These are all the favorite condiments that she likes to add. She's so hungry, she doesn't want to take the time to mix anything into her oatmeal. She grabs the spoon off the table and starts to shovel the oatmeal into her mouth, one spoonful after another. She has abandoned all the norms of good table manners as she wheels her spoon from oatmeal to the bowl. This is the best oatmeal that she has ever eaten, she thinks to herself. MOM has seen this behavior before and understands that because of Lorraine's time in stasis, she has no perception of how much she is eating let alone the method in which she consumes her food.

MOM needs to calculate a method of slowing Lorraine's consumption of food before she shovels too much oatmeal down her throat and chokes herself. If that happens, she doesn't think chef is programmed to perform the Heimlich Maneuver. She decides the best and less evasive method would be to distract her. MOM transforms the wall near the farthest table, into a viewport, so maybe the view of the earth slowly rotating will slow her down. She has notice that when BK is eating a meal in his office or library with the viewport activated, he eats at a much slower pace.

The wall slowly transitions from a solid grayish metallic color to a 6′ by 4′ clear rectangular viewport. It takes only four seconds for the viewport to appear and it's so clear it gives the illusion that someone can stick their hand through the viewport and try to touch the earth. At first, Lorraine is distracted by the oatmeal, she doesn't notice the viewport, but as she lifts the glass of orange juice to her mouth, she sees the shocking and amazing view of her revolving blue planet. She just sits there staring out at the earth with the glass of orange juice frozen up to her mouth. Random flashes of what BK said to her zips through her brain, but she can't seem to focus on a single thought. Her thoughts are colliding and mingling together without any order. A single tear emerges from the corner of her left eye and starts to trickle down her left cheek. Then a stream of tears rolls down both of her cheeks. She looks across the room and out of the viewport as the northern hemisphere drifts past in very slow motion. She's overwhelmed by the sight of the drifting continents. She slowly places the glass of orange juice back onto the table and she wipes the tears from her cheeks, but the tears continue to stream down. Her emotions are beginning to overcome her as she continues to stare out the viewport. She stares at the earth, which resemble someone looking at a horror movie in the theater, but at lease she has stopped shoveling oatmeal.

This is not what MOM had in mind. Lorraine looks down at her tray of food and pushes it to the other side of the table, which causes the small bowl of fruit to spill onto the table and down on the floor. She then places her head down on her folded arms. MOM now understands the term, "swing and a miss". Lorraine sits there for a few minutes just quietly sobbing into her arms and wetting the table with her tears.

MOM recognizes this reaction, because BK experienced a similar reaction once he came out of stasis. He wasn't crying, but he would get frustrated very easily, she recalls. But after a six to eight-hour period, he would gain control of his emotions and would be able to function in a normal manner. Neither MOM nor BK has yet discovered what exactly causes this behavior, but understands that it is a different emotional experience for each person. After a few minutes of crying, she lifts her head from her arms and wipes her face with her forearm. She leans back and stares up at the ceiling and wonders how she was going to get out of this situation. She has no doubt that BK's mistrust of the government has contributed to what he has done. She's use to listening to him rant on and on about how the government is no longer working for the people. He thinks that the government and everyone else for that matter should be focused on where humanity fits in the universe, which would always bore the hell out of her. But she never thought he'd go to this extent to prove his point.

MOM would like her to try to eat some more of her breakfast, but it's unlikely that's going to happen. Lorraine looks around at the size of the galley, which looks like it can seat about a dozen people. "When did he have the time to build all of this", she says to herself. It now makes sense to her why he would disappear for days and sometimes weeks and would blame it on his job. But she still thinks that this size of a ship like this had to be built by an army of people or an army of robots, as she thinks about those strange robots in the Medical Clinic. She also thinks that BK isn't smart enough to create all this on his own. She puts her face into her hands as she once again becomes overwhelmed by her emotions. MOM was trying to wait for him to arrive and calm her down, but she decides this will be the perfect opportunity to get to know Lorraine. He programmed MOM to have a female persona, so she thinks that they may be able to bond.

Seemingly out of nowhere Lorraine's mother's voice softly asks, "Lorraine, please calm down"? Startled, Lorraine quickly swivels around in her chair, looking around wildly for where the voice of her mother is coming from. "Who said that", Lorraine replies as she franticly looks around the room. She recognizes the voice, but she can't believe that BK would abduct her mother too.

They can't stand each other, and she wouldn't think he would want her confined on this ship with him for any period of time. "If you eat some more of your breakfast, I guarantee that you will feel better", MOM says in the caring voice of Lorraine's mother. "I don't believe it", she yells. Who the hell are you! I am MOM, the main artificial intelligence that assist BK in the ship's operations. But that doesn't tell me why you sound like my mother, Lorraine yells. I am programmed to sound like a comforting voice to whomever I am speaking with. When speaking with you, I will sound like your mother, to BK I can mimic his mother and to LaChel and Kim, I can even sound like you. "Oh hell no you won't", Lorraine yells at the top of her voice. Damn it, this is creepy, not comforting, she shouts. Knowing that some glorified CPU is imitating my mother's voice is not giving me any kind of comfort, she exclaims.

MOM attempts to explain the psychological reasoning for mimicking her mother's voice, but with every word emanating through the speakers in the galley seems to further anger Lorraine. As she stands to her feet and slams her hand on the table then yells "damn it", which echoes throughout the galley. "Shut the hell up and stop using my mother's voice you robotic bitch! Just as Lorraine starts to yell obscenities at MOM, BK finally rushes into the galley. "Hey, what's the problem!" he yells. Lorraine limps toward him with her fist clinched and a very angry look on her face. He stops about four feet in front of her and puts his hands out in front of him attempting to keep her at arm's length. "Alright, alright babe"! Just calm down please, he says as he lowers his tone. She stops a foot or so in front of him like they're two boxers getting ready to throw some punches.

Why in the hell would you think using my mother's voice would be a good idea? I'm guessing the same stupid idiot that told you it would be fine to abduct your wife and have her frozen like a god damn TV dinner, she says as she intensely stares at him. He puts his hand out to touch her shoulders, but she swats it away and takes a step back. Baby, most people love to hear their mother's voice, so I thought hearing her would be soothing to you too. But I can clearly see that it bothers you, so I will gladly instructon MOM not to use your mother's voice. For a moment, Lorraine considered allowing MOM to continue using her mother's voice, because she knows BK dislikes her mother and doesn't want to hear her voice.

She shakes her head in disbelief as she turns and walks back to the table. "Thank you, she replies in a very angry and sarcastic tone". By the way, how did you know where to find me? MOM and I have been monitoring you ever since you left the Clinic. She told me that you were getting very agitated. Lorraine looked puzzled. "How could she be talking to you while that idiotic toaster was talking to me". MOM has a quantum-processing system with the ability to communicate and interact with as many as 25 individuals at the same time, he explains. Not to brag on my workmanship, he says with a prideful smile, but MOM is the most advanced and sophisticated AI in the solar system.

"I do not think that statement is accurate or truthful at this time", MOM replies. BK shakes his head. Humanity has not ventured beyond our Moon as of yet, MOM replies. Consequently, I do not think it is logical to assume that I am the most advanced and sophisticated artificial intelligence in the solar system. How about highly probable regarding your technological superiority, he says while holding both of his arms out and looking around the galley. "Who gives a damn how smart this toaster is", Lorraine yells. I don't want it impersonating my mother or me. She looks at BK angrily and without blinking. I need you to take care of it or I'll reprogram it by ripping the wiring from its' circuit board. "Circuit board", MOM responds? You are mistaken, Lorraine. I have a massive amount of nanocircuitry, embedded on a quantum diamond synthetic board, but I do not have the traditional 21st century circuit boards.

So, you're saying that your system is working on a quantum level, Lorraine replies with a puzzled look on her face? BK looks Lorraine in her eyes and asked her exactly what she knows about "quantum computing" in respect to artificial intelligence". Lorraine pauses in deep thought for a moment with a amazed look on her face, because she doesn't know how she understands exactly what he is talking about. I know that a quantum computer uses quantum bits, or qubits. But you've exceeded those twenty-first century theories and are utilizing the atoms themselves to store and disseminate yottabytes of information. He smiles at her and asked her another question before she has a chance to try to understand how she knew that information. What part of the brain is responsible for disseminating information throughout the body", he asked as a test to her ability to retrieve her embedded medical knowledge? She blurts out her answer without hesitation. "The pons is the largest part of the brainstem, located above the medulla and below the midbrain. It is a group of nerves that function as a connection between the cerebrum and cerebellum". She pauses with her mouth open for a few seconds. "What in the hell did I just say", she immediately asked in amazement. She looks up at him with astonishment for knowing the answers to that question. Even though BK would like to continue asking her questions, he thinks it would be wise not to open this can of whoop-ass just yet.

Some people think that honesty in a marriage is the superglue that holds it together. "Wrong"! His marriage survival philosophy is that sometimes its' those creative and well-crafted little white lies that delays and fights off unnecessary disagreements. "I have no idea babe", he says as he changes the smile to a look of imaginary concern. Her piercing stare bores a hole through his soul as she tries to make him confess. Why in the hell do I have all this scientific crap flashing in my head?

He gives her a puzzled look and tries to sell it the best he can. Possibly one of the side effects of the stasis procedure, but it won't change you into a super nerd like me, he says as he laughs. It would take some time to explain what happened, but right now we have to get back to the Clinic, so you can get your final exam. She turns and starts to walk back over to the table as he walks behind her and tries to help her by grabbing her elbow, but she snatches her arm away. She makes it to her chair and flops down. He walks up behind her as she drinks her orange juice.

She drinks half of the glass and puts the rest back on the table. I don't want anything else to eat, she says with a sigh. He decides that this is the time to explain everything about her emerging knowledge of Quantum Physics, Surgical and General Medical knowledge and most importantly, the location of their girls. He walks behind her and puts his hands on both of her shoulders. Look babe, there's something else I have to tell you. Chef, bring me a cup of coffee please, he yells as he turns his head toward the kitchen. Lorraine wonders who's he talking to until Chef immediately opens the door and emerges from the storage room and begins to prepare his coffee. "Good Lord", not another one", She says as she looks back to see the unit rushing around the kitchen. I really need you to come back to the Clinic with me, he says in a firm tone. Lorraine doesn't want to go back there just to lie there in that bed and look at those walls. He says the only thing that he knows that will get her back there with very little questions or effort.

LaChel and Kim are there and I need you to help me calm them down, while he softly rubs her shoulders. She quickly turns halfway around in her chair and looks up at him in astonishment. Why in the hell didn't you tell me that they were there? I was going to tell you as soon as I stepped into the galley, but I wanted to get you something to eat first then maybe show you around the ship. The intensity in her eyes can burn holes into his skull. I don't want to see any other part of this damn ship, she yells. I want to see the girls, she insists. I'll have one of the medical units bring a wheelchair here, but Lorraine quickly tells him that she can walk, as she uses the back of the chair and table to force herself to her feet.

OK, he says, but you are going to have to let me help you. She doesn't want his help, but her anger isn't enough to power her back to the Clinic. He wraps one arm around her waist and uses his other arm as a brace to help her balance herself as she walks. They both walk slowly as they work their way out of the galley, chef hovers up to BK to hand him his coffee. MOM intercepts Chef and tells it to take the coffee to the Clinic and place it on Lorraine's desk. Lorraine hears what MOM just said to the unit, but it doesn't make any sense to her. She looks at BK and asked him what she meant by "her desk". He didn't want to cross that bridge yet, so he tells her that the desk is in the room where she's sleeping. So, just like MOM calls the bed yours, she calls the rest of the furniture yours too, he says with a smile. Chef maneuvers around the slow moving couple and heads to the Clinic. "Don't spill my coffee", he yells to a quickly moving Chef.

"Yes Sir", it replies before slowing down to round a corner. While in route to the Clinic, Lorraine asked him who helped him built this ship and where did he get the money, since she knew that their bank account couldn't have funded the building of this massive spaceship. Walking along side of his wife and supporting her as they make their way through the hallway, he explains to her that he built numerous units that he programmed to construct the ship and MOM supervised them to ensure the construction was completed on time and correctly. And the money was a little more complicated, but he would be glad to explain to her how he got the money for the building of the ship after they see the girls. She wanted him to tell her now, but she was excited about seeing her girls, so she let it go. It takes them a little over two minutes to get back to the Medical Clinic, and now she's exhausted as the bay comes into view. She didn't want his help, but her muscles are weak, and she can't help but to put most of her weight on him. But the thought of her seeing and holding her daughters re-energizes her. As soon as she enters the Clinic, unit one hovers over with the robe Lorraine left behind and BK helps her put it on. She looks wildly around the room for her girls.

She pushes herself away from him and uses the remainder of her strength to walk over to the beds, then leans on it while still looking to see if her daughters are in the room. "LaChel, Kim", she yells. BK just stands in the doorway looking at her calling for the girls as she walks as well as she can throughout the Clinic. "You said they were here", so where the hell are my children, she says as she walks up to him with both fists tightly clinched. She seems to have siphoned some strength from her growing anger as she walks toward him, so he walks backwards and gestures for her to follow him. He knows he can't delay telling her any longer, so he thinks it would be best just to show her. She follows him as he walks over to a wall on the other side of the room with a larger than normal door with no doorknob, but it does have a keypad to the left of it. It blends into the wall so well that she didn't noticed it the last time she was in the room. He is now at the door and presses a sequence of buttons. She doesn't know what's behind the door or what's about to happen next, but she gets some flashes of clarity of what's going on, which gives her a very uneasy feeling. He extends his arm and asks her to step back a few, as both of them take a couple of backward steps. "What are you doing", she asked curiously. I thought we were going to see the girls. "We are", he says as he presses two more buttons.

He moves alongside of Lorraine as a portion of the wall in front of them moves forward, then slides to the right to reveal four almost vertical white capsules. She can feel a chilling breeze escaping from the small room that's no larger than a walk-in closet. She gets flickers of understanding of what this room and those capsules are used for, but she just can't connect the pieces of the puzzle, just yet. She stares intensely at the capsules. He can see the bewildered look on her face, so he grabs her arm and pulls her closer toward him. Her mind switches from confusion to fear as she's drawn closer to the capsules like a moth to a flame. She starts to slide her hand across the chilled surface of one capsule to another, hoping that this will force other information trapped in her mind to the surface.

Her brain flashes to her a glimpse of what could be in the capsules, but she hesitantly asks him a question she knew that she wasn't prepared to have the answer to. "What's in these things", she reluctantly asked with a trembling tone in her voice? "Our girls", he says with no hesitation. She looks at him in disbelief and horror. "No", she replies as her focus on the capsules intensifies! Yes, but they are perfectly fine, he says as he smiles thinking that it would give her some type of comfort. He couldn't get the remaining portion of his explanation out of his mouth before she hits him with a right cross to the side of his face.

She punched him like Iron Mike Tyson. The punch was very quick and sharp, which he didn't see coming. It didn't do him much damage in Lorraine's weakened state, but the surprise of her punching him backed him up a few steps. And it was a punch and not a slap, which also stunned him.

But he understood and expected her shock of hearing that their girls are frozen and stowed away in a box. With tears welling in her eyes, she moves closer as he stretches out his arms and puts his hand on her shoulders, while he tries again to explain his actions and the girls' condition. He has been married to his wife for over a decade, so it seems amazing that he couldn't know what would happen next. With tears rolling down her cheeks, she waited until he pulled her in close then she let loose with a flawless and devastating connection of her shin to his testicles, which causes him to release a loud bellowing groan of pain and drops him to the floor like a 225 pound sack of potatoes. In football terms this would be called, "splitting the uprights". With his mouth open and his legs clinched together, he topples to the floor with a sickening thud.

It was a perfectly textbook shot that probably could be heard down on earth. He's groaning while in the fetal position and Lorraine is standing over him kicking whatever parts of his body that she can get to and yelling obscenities and questions, which he can't answer. He manages to roll himself over trying to protect himself from her wild kicks. He couldn't understand a word she was saying because of his damaged and inverted testicles and nor does he care at the moment.

MOM didn't understand what was going on, but she is fascinated by the opportunity to analyze marital interaction. She understands that he's in pain, but she also knows his pain is only to his soft reproductive organs and it's temporary. But she dispatches unit M2 to check on his condition. As the unit hovers toward him, Lorraine yells and delivers a couple of final stomps to his back then falls against the wall of the storage container and slowly slides down the wall into a sitting position.

"You damn monster", as she cries hysterically. "What gave you the right to do that to them". She continues to cry with her trembling hands covering her face and tears running between her fingers and down the back of her hands. The unit stops about three feet in front of BK, who's still on his side, moaning on the floor and clutching his damaged goods. Lorraine sees the unit hovering near him through her watery eyes and fingers. She lowers her hands away from her wet face and points directly at the unit. "Get the hell away from him", she says in a shrieking tone. "He doesn't deserve your damn help", she adds!

The unit immediately responds, "yes Lorraine", because unbeknownst to her; the units in the Clinic are programmed to follow her orders. But it does continue to scan him and monitor his condition. He starts to roll over onto his stomach and begins to inchworm himself to his hands and knees as he continues to groan. But the unit requested that he remain on the floor, because he's still affected by his soft tissue injury. "I'm fine", he says in a higher tone than when he hit the floor. "Damn it Lorraine", he shouts while still on his knees and looking down at the floor, while trying to collect himself. I know how disturbing his looks, but you could have at least given me an opportunity to explain myself. "Explain yourself", she shouts! There isn't any explanation for freezing your daughters, she adds. "I tried to kick your brains out", she says in a harsh tone as she leans her head back against the wall with her eyes close. She doesn't want to look at him right now. Hearing him groan is the only thing that gives her satisfaction. She wishes she had just a little more strength to punch him in the face for suggesting that he could make sense of freezing their daughters like popsicles. You should at least apologize to me for field goal kicking my boys into my stomach. "Apologize to you", she yells at the top of her voice and uses the wall to push herself back to her feet? BK is still looking down at the floor when he made that unwise statement. MOM thinks it would be to BK's best interest to warn him. She announces to him that Lorraine is on her feet again". He looks up and sees her coming towards him with what he would call, "crazy eyes".

"Alright, alright", he says as he extends his right hand out toward his wife. I miss spoke, so an apology isn't necessary, he says as he uses his knees to turn is body and scoot away from her. I would call the police, and have you arrested for domestic violence, but it would take about two to three years before they could get up here, he says in a joking tone. I can't believe you can make a joke about this after what you've done to me and your daughters. You've destroyed our lives and put your family in jeopardy, you selfish bastard. Lorraine walks back toward the capsules. He finally has the strength and the use of his legs to get to his feet. He limbs toward her. Babe, I know you don't understand, but this was something that I had to do. What I'm trying to do is larger than you, me or the girls. She turns toward him with tears still rolling down her face. I don't give a damn about anything else.

And I don't think you can make me understand why you had to do this. I'm just a mother that's afraid for the safety of her children. Unlike their stupid and reckless father, she adds. Babe, you're going to have to believe me when I tell you that LaChel and Kim are perfectly fine, and they'll be walking around here with us very soon. She stares at him as she tries to reassure herself that if he could put her in stasis and revive her, then he can do the same for them. "I need to see my girls", she says with anguish in her voice. He manages to get to his feet then hobbles over to a small closet and grabs a step ladder and places it between LaChal's and Kim's capsule. Step on this, but you won't be able to see much of their faces, because of the amount to frost on the capsule's view screen. "Are they frozen", she shouts as her voice cracks from the sight of the container that holds her daughters. "No", he says as he reaches his hand out for her to grab his. But it's similar to being in a cryogenic state. She pushes his hand away and walks up to the ladder. She steps up onto the first run, then the second, then shakenly steps on the top run. He can see that her legs are weak, so he stands behind her and grabs her by the waist to steady her as she steps to the top of the ladder. She leans to her left and looks into the view port hoping to see her oldest daughter's face, but all she can see is the form of LaChel's face and shoulders. She uses the sleeve of her robe to wipe away as much of the frost from the view screen as she can, but the frost and bluish mist is also on the inside of the capsule. She then leans to the right and starts to vigorously rub the other capsule's viewport, but she can't see Kim's face either.

"Damn", she yells as she stands on her toes while struggling to steady her shaking legs. He sees her legs starting to give out, so he moves up behind her and grabs her by her waist to steady her. "Just help me down", she shouts angerly as she cautiously steps down to the second step. I can't see either one of them in these damn tubes. As she steps down from the ladder, he can feel her entire body trembling from what he thinks is her exerting herself too much. He quickly grabs her tightly and sweeps her off the ladder and into his arms. "Put me down you bastard", she yells as he walks back to the bed with her in his arms! You are too weak to get back to the bed and if you don't calm down, you'll be back in bed for the rest of the day, he says with a commanding tone.

She didn't want to admit it, but she was feeling so drained and if he wasn't there to help her, she would have collapsed trying to come down from the ladder. After having his frank and beans assaulted in a bad way, he's tired of her attitude and also tired of asking permission to help her. She looks away from him while he's carrying her, and it seems like it took forever for them to get back to the bed. Once he gets to the bed, he tries to lay her down onto it as gently as possible, but she yells, "just put me down", as she tries to wiggle and escape from his arms.

He lifts her back into his arms and looks at her intensely while squeezing her body tightly. She can feel his arms firmly holding her and under normal circumstances, she would like it. She just looks him in the eyes and doesn't say a word. He asks unit M1 to pull back the covers and the top sheet. Lorraine is still somewhat afraid of her medical units so she leans into his body as the unit approaches, which BK loves. The unit swiftly maneuvers over to the bed and pulls back the cotton blanket and the white sheet. She is too weak to force herself from his arms, so she just allows him to put her into the bed. He stands there with her in his arms and stares into her eyes for about five more seconds, because he wants to show her that he's in charge. Then carefully lowers her into the bed.

He helps her remove her robe, pulls the sheet over her chest and under her arms. Lorraine doesn't want him to touch her, but she doesn't have the strength to fight with him right now. That uppercut to his boys and subsequent kicks to the various parts of his body has taken the remainder of her energy, she admits to herself. She feels so tired, but she doesn't want to sleep anymore, because she's afraid that he will put her back into one of those capsules. But in her hazy condition, she somehow knows that it's not possible for him to place her back in stasis again. For a brief moment, she understood the method and the procedure of placing a person in stasis. He pulls a stool up close to her bed and sits beside her. He gingerly lowers himself down onto the stool, but the pain of his lower region is making it difficult to sit down.

Don't try to fight it, babe. Just take a little nap and I'll wake you up in about two to three hours, but you'll have to eat a little more to gain your strength. She finally relents to her body's weaken state and nods her head slightly to agree with him. She mumbles in a whispering tone, struggling to ask him how she understood the knowledge of cryogenic capsulation. Her voice sounded weak and a little slurred, but he realizes that her medical knowledge is beginning to reveal itself.

He's happy and afraid at the same time. She may punch him in the face once she realizes that he has made her into probably one of the most knowledgeable physicians on the planet. She mumbles a few words then turns her head away from him as she relents to the fatigue of her mind and body. He leans over onto the bed as he strokes her forehead and leans in to smell the top of her head. He has always loved the smell of her head for some reason and he misses smelling it while lying in bed with her. But he knows that she's going to make him pay for what he has done to her and their girls. There won't be any of those types of hugs for a long time. He sighs then gets up from the stool then bends over her to give her a soft kiss to her lips and then her forehead. He moves the stool back to the other side of the room. "BK, it is time for you to run the next series of experiments in hydroponics", MOM reminds him. "Damn", thanks for reminding me. My mind is so focused on

Lorraine that everything else just slipped my mind. This has been a very rough morning, he exclaimed. He walks to the entrance of the Clinic and stops in the doorway. "Unit M1", he yells. "Yes", as it hovers toward him. Place a neuro suppressive device on my wife's forehead and program it to keep her asleep for approximately, as he pauses in thought and looks at his watch. "Three hours", as he looks at the unit for confirmation.

Unit M1 complies by taking one of the three devices from a small storage compartment in what would be called its' stomach. It hovers back over to her bed and places the device onto her forehead and activates it. And make sure that you scan her brain activity every thirty minutes and send me the results to my tablet in hydroponics. Neurological scans can only be administered safely a maximum of four cycles within a 24 hour period. The unit warns him that it is not advisable to perform scans at such close time intervals.

Thank you M1 for reminding me, so perform one scan per hour. The unit then tells him that he will receive the first scan data in approximately 58 minutes. He nods his head in acknowledgement as he grabs his cup of coffee off of the desk, takes a sip and walks out of the Clinic. He walks down the passageway trying to get his wife out of his head. But it's been so long since he has held Lorraine in his arms and kissed her lips. MOM, does my medical records reflect me being that weak after coming out of stasis. No, she replies.

But I think Lorraine's stasis experience coupled with her stress from learning that her and her daughters have been abducted and frozen for numerous months, contributed to her weakened condition. And coupled with her beating the crap out of you would add to that condition. He smiles as he continues to walk down the passageway. He didn't take all those factors into account, but it make sense. Hydroponics lab will have to wait, he thinks to himself.

MOM, I'm going to the living quarters to make sure everything is working and looking good for her arrival today. Need I remind you that if you do not follow our prescribed schedule that I will have to rearrange a large portion of your next week's schedule to compensate, she reminds him. "Don't worry MOM". It's not that serious. I can complete the genetic configuration of those sweet potato and carrots plants tomorrow morning.

MOM can see his mood changes from subdued and focused to upbeat and distracted as he alters his route and walks toward his family's living quarters. Now he can focus all his attention on Lorraine, which is a welcome change from working in the hydroponics lab reconfiguring vegetable proteins. I deserve a day off, he yells as it echos down the passageway. If push comes to shove, he could force himself to power through his daily schedule, but he knows that he needs to be a little more flexible since his family will be in his life again.

Chapter Five

Government Threats and BK's Lies

June 3, 2023 – The First Amendment Rights of broadcast networks and the global news industries has been severely curtailed and threatened with suspension or loss of their broadcasting license if they don't comply with the Federal Government's restrictions on regarding reporting on objects orbiting the planet. Another nail in the coffin of Democracy.

BK walks through the hallway then rounds a couple more corners and arrives at his quarters. MOM, I need you to reschedule all my task today, please. And now that I think about it, reorganize my entire calendar to ensure I don't have more than three simple task and two complex tasks to complete per day on an eight hour work period.

I think that is an excellent idea, she replies. Even an exceptional human being such as yourself shouldn't work the number of hours you subject yourself to. You would sometimes work 12-hour days, seven days a week, which is not sustainable. He doesn't say a word, but just walks into his quarters. I just was thinking that the girls will be out of stasis and roaming around the ship in three to four weeks and I have to readjust my schedule to fit their needs. It's just not fair for me to work all day and night while they are stuck up here aboard this ship. I also think Lorraine wouldn't appreciate me working those hours and leaving her alone to deal with the girls. He strolls through the living room and into the bedroom to change into something more casual, which for him consist of another jumper and the same boots.

He can build a one-of-a-kind spaceship, but his fashion sense needs his wife's help. He walks away from his discarded jumper, which he carelessly leaves on his bedroom floor at the foot of his bed. He's not use to cleaning up after himself. A hidden door slides up from the wall and a home unit emerges, and quickly races across the floor toward the jumper lying in the middle of the floor. The unit gathered up the dirty jumper and deposits them into the clothes hamper next to the dresser. Thanks Benny, he says as he walks out of the room.

Benny is different from the other units on the ship, because Benny was the first unit he built. He named the unit after his brother, who passed away over four years ago. He misses his brother so much, so he programmed his brother's personality into the unit. All the units he has created were constructed and programmed after he purchased the warehouse and start building his ship. He built and programmed Benny in a storage unit he used as his workshop, which was near his home. Lorraine was sick and tired of him cluttering up the garage and then migrating his hodgepodge of parts and collections of components into his office. That was the last straw for Lorraine, who suggested that he rent a storage unit, because she was one component away from going to jail for bludgeoning him with one of them.

He was glad she suggested that he rent the unit away from the house and could work there for a few hours a day and on the weekends. This would enable him to build Benny out in the open. This gave BK a perfect opportunity to develop what he planned to be his big money-making invention. He planned to design and build an artificial unit that he can present to the Bank or anyone else who would like to invest in the most advance robot on the planet. BK was the Chief Engineer for a local Engineering Firm, which enabled him the opportunity to utilize some of the agency's materials, equipment and redirect small amounts of the department's finances to a secret personal bank account in an alias he created. Of course, the engineering firm had no idea they were participating in the off the book's development of this artificial unit. He understood that once an audit has been performed, there was a possibility of him going to prison for embezzlement. His department's annual budget was in excess of $145 million, so he gambles that it will take them too much time to notice the small amounts of money that he was diverting into one of his personal accounts. He has become a master software developer and has created his own computer language, which enabled him to siphon money from the agency's accounts without being detected. He was able to circumvent the safety mechanisms, because of the Agency's unwillingness to purchase up-to-date accounting software, which made it very easy for him to fund his personal projects.

It took him six months to construct Benny's body and only a month to develop his operating system. The unit's physical body was perfect and surpassed what he imagined as well as the unit's mobility, which at the time didn't hover, but utilized a single soccer size roller ball. After testing the unit's maneuverability, dexterity and strength, he decided that the unit's cerebral capabilities must also be just as impressive. He was going to create the brain of the unit utilizing the standard computer languages, but he thought why build a Lamborghini just to put some 80-year-old geezer behind the wheel.

He took another month and a half to design and develop his own programming language, which could process beyond the 256-bit level. He decided to name his new computer language, "Kami", which means God in Japanese. His reasoning for naming the language Kami is because the processing speed of the language will enable software developers the ability to create smarter applications. The combination of his software and hardware will enable a computer to think as fast as a human brain, which until now, has only been accomplished by God himself. He thinks of himself more like Doctor Frankenstein, because now he has to get his creation a brain. He just hopes his unit won't go berserk and start trying to kill him. Maybe that's the reason he only designed the unit with four mechanical fingers on each hand. His units doesn't have a processor like most computers or robots. He developed an innovative quantum spherical processor that's equivalent to a 256-bit processor, if one existed. He was successful in merging his hardware and software, but he decided to go one step further by developing an algorithm, which would mimic a human personality, but he made a mistake by allowing the unit to build upon his personality algorithm by watching network television. Benny picked up some bad habits watching shows like House MD, How I Met Your Mother and The Jeffersons. He thought it would be a great idea to allow Benny to get some real-world experience by watching various relationship dynamics. He considered reprogramming him, but he never could find the time it would take to do it, but the main reason is that he reminded him of his beloved crazy older brother. Instead of taking a hammer and screwdriver to Benny, he thought it would be easier just to create another unit, but this time without a body and no damn personality upgrades. That's when he decided to design and build MOM. He designed her with the ability to gather and decipher vast amounts of information and most importantly; manage the other units he built to construct the ship him and his family are aboard right now. She also was tasked to ensure she monitors Benny's activities, which wasn't an easy task being that he was designed with the same type of software and processor. MOM and Benny were more like older brother and younger sister than just two sophisticated artificial intelligence pieces of technology. He wished Benny wasn't such a pain in the ass, and so unpredictable. Because Benny was enhanced with a scalable personality algorithm, he thinks he's human.

Just like if you had a monkey that you raised from a baby and you treat him like a human child, it's going to grow up thinking it's human. After purchasing the warehouse, building MOM and the other units, BK decided to upgrade him and give him the ability to hover like the other units. He was assigned the duties of assisting MOM with the management of all the other ship's units, which he did well until he got bored, if an artificial unit can even feel boredom.

But something would trigger his prankster tendencies. He would do stupid things even for a human. Benny would try to order pizza to the warehouse just as a joke on the delivery drivers, continuously using colorful language and even imitating BK's voice to make prank phone calls to Lorraine's mother, which BK didn't condone, but thought most of the time was hilarious. Benny called Lorraine's mom and convinced her that he was taking a survey and if she answered all the questions, she will be mailed a $100.00 Olive Garden giftcard for truthfully answering a few survey questions.

He started out asking normal questions then started asking sexually explicit ones, which she uncomfortably answered because she really wanted that free giftcard. MOM discovered what he did and played the recording for BK, who thought it was damn funny, but had to punish him for not following his orders. So he decided to demote him to the living quarters and restrict his access to all major systems until the ship is in orbit. But, once Lorraine moves into the family quarters, she can decide whether to keep Benny there like a foulmouthed butler or BK will have to relocate him somewhere else.

He walks into the living room, grabs the remote and flops down on the sofa. Benny, can you bring me a cup of coffee, he yells as he turns on the television, and starts flipping through the channels. It would be nice to hear a "please" now and then, Benny response as he hovers out of the bedroom and into the kitchen. BK doesn't respond to his request. He just asks him to make the coffee 15 percent stronger. The last cup of coffee you made me taste like tea, he says in a disappointing tone. Benny hovers around the kitchen island and elevates up to the cabinet. He opens the cabinet and pushes the other coffee containers to the side to reach the one in the rear of the cabinet, which is a Cuban blend called Café' Busterlo. He pulls out the coffee and closes the cabinet with its' other robotic arm. He thinks he has a good grip on the coffee can, but he's only halfway down when he loses his grip and the can hits the floor. The lid of the can pops off as the coffee explodes out of the can and covers the kitchen floor.

Benny continues his descent as he looks curiously at his robotic hand that once held the coffee container. Hearing the loud continuous clink of the can bouncing across the floor; BK strings from the sofa and slides across the coffee grounds now covering the floor. "What the hell happened"? Benny descends a foot or two from the coffee-covered floor. My grip on the coffee container's handle must have been faulty.

"You think", yells BK. He can now smell the aroma of the coffee and realizes that this is not just any coffee, but his beloved "Café' Bustelo". "Oh no", he shouts in disbelief as he kneels down near his beloved coffee. Benny on the other hand is still puzzled by his inability to maintain a proper grip on a simple coffee can. He continues to look at his robotic hand as he flexes it open and close, over and over again. "Benny, forget about your damn hand" BK says as he picks up the coffee can and slams it on the island counter. I want you to put every grain of coffee back into this can before I repurpose you into a talking garbage disposal. Benny pauses for a moment, then replies, but as a garbage disposal I won't be able to make your coffee, pick up your dirty clothes or clean your rooms. "Just get my coffee back in the can", he shouts! And I still want my coffee, he says in frustration. "What about my hand", Benny exclaims. "You see", it's malfunctioning again, he says as he displays his extended third mechanical finger to BK. That's very funny, He replies. That just shows me that you still have basic functional control of your fingers. I'll do a complete diagnostic on you sometime tomorrow. Benny asked if he could be more specific regarding the time, because he'll need to rearrange his schedule for tomorrow? BK then walks back into the living room, grabs the TV remote off the floor and points it at the TV then flops back onto the sofa again. Don't worry about your schedule, he responds as he turns on the TV and starts to flip through the channels.

Finding the problem with your hand shouldn't take more than twenty or thirty minutes out of your house cleaning duties. I'm damn tired of being Mr. Belvedere, Benny says as he grabs the broom and dustpan to retrieve BK's precious coffee. "Language", BK shouts in the direction of the kitchen. BK knows it's not good for him to watch the news, but sometimes he just wants to hear what's going on down on earth. He then turns to his favorite news channel, which is an independent news agency that covers all types of conspiracy theories and other unusual stories throughout the United States. The show is Tori's segment called "The Truth", and she is interviewing one of the White House Central Intelligence Agents Daniel Page, who monitors and researches unusual stories.

"Secret UFO above our planet", is the caption displayed on the television. They can't be talking about me, he thinks to himself, as he turns up the volume and moves himself to the edge of the sofa. Tori is really grilling the Agent about some classified documents stating the existence of a spacecraft orbiting about 250 miles above the planet. "They are talking about us", he says with a large helping of excitement in his voice. "What", Benny yells from the kitchen. "Did you say something", Benny asked. I think my hearing components are starting to malfunction too. Benny is also somewhat of a hypochondriac, if that's even possible in an artificial unit. "No, I didn't Benny"! I'm trying to listen to the television, so please stay in the kitchen and finish making my

211

coffee. If I had a mouth and some salivary glands, I would spit in it", Benny says in a low tone. "No, you wouldn't", MOM replies. "I was only kidding", Benny says with a laugh as he continues to sweep the coffee off the floor and into the dustpan. BK doesn't hear anything MOM or Benny are saying, because he's transfixed on what Tori is asking the Agent.

He likes the way this young reporter is hammering the Government Agent. Tori has worked hard to get this thirty minute segment, which most of the time involves her talking with various strange people with even stranger stories. In addition to talking with Government officials that want to discredit those strange people. She's really hitting him with some tough questions about the copy of the report she's flipping through.

So Agent Page, are you trying to tell me and my audience that this report is completely false, and that I should believe you and not my reliable White House sources, she exclaims with a large helping of sarcasm in her voice. Agent Page looks directly into the camera, clears his throat and gives a confident smile.

I can clearly see Ms. Milanich that I can't persuade you to believe anything that I'm telling you. But I'm simply trying to explain to you that the documents you are reading are as worthless as my wife's unemployed forty-four year old Asian rapper brother living in our basement, he says with a smile as he tries to interject some levity. She looks into his smiling face and knows he's lying. She tells him she has the utmost confidence in her source that provided her the documents she's holding in her hand.

She has interviewed him before and knows that he has no qualms about flat out lying to avoid the truth, and will even tell a joke at his wife's expense, which his wife will make him pay for later. BK can hardly believe what he's hearing. He knew once he turned off the ship's scattering field that his government, China and Russia would detect his spacecraft in orbit, but he thought they would guard the existence of his ship from the networks a little better than this. She beats down his attempt to discredit her report by hitting him with hard facts. "Agent Page can you tell me and my listening audience why our military are calling their reservist back to active duty and repositioning various satellites at the latitude and longitude displayed on the monitor, as she refers to a split screen of four satellites located around the earth. As he looks at the split screens, his body language and attitude changes from slightly jovial to serious. He's surprise that her information would be so accurate, which makes him wonder who is providing her this information. He decides to make a tougher stance and pivot the conversation to the responsibility of the news agencies to report a fair and unbiased reports of their findings. As a representative of the White House, I can confidently say that the President is very disappointed with the reporting of this so-called story. He thinks that you and your network are highly irresponsible for disseminating this type of nonsense to the American people for the sake of your dwindling ratings. Agent Page is visibly shaken by Jillian's knowledge of the object and their willingness to broadcast its' location as it orbits the planet. BK is also amazed and dumbfounded by the government's inability to delay the release of the location of his orbiting ship.

Agent Page is so visibly upset that he decides, for good or bad, he thinks it's in his best interest to end the interview. He begins to fumble with removing the earpiece and rips off the microphone attached to his collar. Tori is surprised by his abrupt ending of the interview. She attempts to calm him down and gestures for him to remain for the rest of the interview, but he just stands up from his chair without even thinking about his microphone component strapped to the back of his pants and belt. He tries to remove the equipment in a dignified manner, but the cord is entangled around one of his feet and the earpiece cord is running under his jacket and connecting to the communication component.

And you would think that Tori would signal to cut to a commercial while this is happening, but they are continuing to broadcast while he is fumbling and twisting around the cords as he attempts to leave the set. Mr. Page, please allow me to ask you a few more brief questions. I promise that this will only take a few more minutes of your time and I will not ask any more provocative questions about that object, which was a lie to get him back in the chair. She has a couple more questions about the orbiting object and the reasons why the Government is denying its' existence.

"No thank you", Ms. Milanich. The Agent's assistant has now come into the camera shot to help untangle him. These questions I'm asking you are relevant, and the American people would like to hear your response. With the help of his assistant, he removes the last bit of equipment from his person, and snatches the small microphone from his assistant's hand. His assistant is a little upset by him rudely snatching the body microphone from her hand, but she understands her position on this food chain, and just walks off camera to wait for him. I don't think so, Ms. Milanich, he says with an angry attitude. You are not interested in the truth or anything that closely resembles it. You and your news agency are just attempting to sensationalize this bogus information and consequently boost your slumping ratings and I will not participate with this attempt of yellow journalism any further. Tori is only 26 years old and isn't sure what he means by the term "yellow journalism". He then drops the mic on the desk and proceeds to walk out of the studio. His assistant fills her arms with all the paperwork and notepads that he left on the desk and follows him out of the door, but turns to the news staffs and gives them a sincere, "Thank you". Tori is a little put off by him abruptly walking off her show, but does her best to continue with the remaining 15 minutes of her segment. The cameraman tightens in on her as she turns to the camera. Well, I'm sorry that Agent Page has decided to end his participation of this interesting and intriguing conversation, but I know that the audience would like to fill the sudden void by continuing the discussion of this topic, she says with a confident smile. Her producer, Francis Andrew, is frantically signaling her to go to the phones.

So, I' m going to open up the phone lines, so you can voice your opinion about Mr. Page's answers to my questions. But please remember that your calls will be recorded, and your last name and the state that you are calling from will be displayed. Back on the ship, Benny emerges from the kitchen with BK's cup of coffee in his good hand. Alright BK, the coffee is ready and most importantly is back in its' container. Thanks Benny, he says as he grabs the cup out of Benny's hand.

BK leans back onto the sofa as he continues listening to all the callers chime in on the mysterious object above the planet. It's a little strange for him to listen to people talking about the existence and non-existence of his ship and listening to them expound upon their opinions. "What some of these people are saying is just plain stupid", he says out loud. Benny hovers closer to the television and BK. That's something we have in common, because I think all humans are stupid too, Benny replies. "Present company excluded", he adds as he looks at BK and chuckles. "Ya right, BK response as he continues to watch the show. One of the female callers states that if there is a UFO in orbit above the earth than we should simply blow it out of the sky with our nuclear missiles before they launch their attack. "Idiot", BK and Bennyy shout at the same time! The caller adds that if they are not communicating with us and that is a clear sign of their hostile intent.

But for the most part, the majority of the callers thinks it's some secret object that the Government has designed and launch to spy on everyone. At that point, BK decides to have a little fun at everyone else's expense. He's tired of listening to callers spouting their pea-brain theories and some just out right nonsense about his ship. But he really wants to call-in, because even if everyone thinks of him as another listener with more dollars than cents; he just wants to be heard. He yells to MOM to call Ms. Milanich's radio segment and get him to the top of the callers list even if she has to bump off the other callers. I know they won't be able to trace my call, but to be on the safe side, I want you to relay the call off my mother-in-law's home phone.

You do realize that the FBI or any other government authority will most likely be monitoring those calls because of the sensitive topic their discussing. She could be arrested and interrogated for hours and possibly incarcerated, MOM warns him. Well, I'm willing to take that chance, he says with a sly smile on his face and a twinkle in his eye. She suggests that he should use his time to relax and not to create hate and discontent between himself and his mother-in-law. She also reminds him that she thinks his wife will not be happy with him putting her mother in that type of jeopardy. I didn't think being a big nag was written into your programming, he exclaims. MOM analyzes the word "nag" for about five seconds. By definition, I am not nagging you. I am just offering you an alternative to your self destructive actions and some common-sense advice.

Whether or not you accept it is your decision, she adds. Thank you for your concerns regarding my mother-in-law and your concern are duly noted, but I know what the hell I'm doing. "Hey"! Language, Benny yells. Please, just get me on the air with Mrs. Quincy. It only took MOM a few minutes to hack into the radio station's server and insert BK's call to the front of the line. It is ringing, MOM responds.

Quick, transfer the call to this room's communication systems. Ten seconds later, BK can hear the ring of the phone throughout the room. A male's voice announces that he will be talking with Ms. Milanich in a moment and that there is a five second delay, which will enable him to dump him if he says something offensive. BK's voice is filled with excitement as he says "yes and thank you" to the person putting him on hold. He is feeling a little nervous about actually talking to another person about himself and his ship. He doesn't know exactly what he's going to say, but just to have an actual conversation with someone on earth is surprisingly exciting. After four agonizing long minutes – "This is "The Truth", you're on the air. Mr. Hunter, please tell us what you think, Tori says while reading his mother-in-law's last name from her tablet. For a brief moment, he can't find his voice. Benny moves closer to BK and whispers, "I think she's talking to you"! He mouthed to Benny to be quiet and vigorously gestures for him to go back into the kitchen, which he complies. Caller, are you still there? Yes…yes, I'm here, BK replies. Good afternoon, he nervously shouts. Good afternoon, Mr. Hunter. What are your thoughts or guest on what's up there and our government's involvement? Well Ms. Milanich, I don't have to guess, he says with confidence. There is dead air on the show while they wait for him to enlighten them.

"Well Mr. Hunter", Tori response with an impatient tone. He sees no reason he needs to lie, because they won't believe him anyway. "Me", he says with a bit of nervousness in his voice. And my name isn't Mr. Hunter… its Mr. Thomas.

The line goes quiet for a few seconds. Tori cuts her eyes at Francis, who is her producer, while she thinks to herself, "why in the hell do I always get the crazy ones. Unaware with whom she has on the phone, her producer gestures to her to continue with the interview. So, Mr. Thomas what exactly are you doing out there floating above our heads. Well, right now I'm just sitting here on the sofa trying to watch television until I came across your show talking about me. Tori thinks about the Thomas Family and can't help but think this maybe Mr. Thomas. She remembers what her boss told her about any further investigation, but if it is the missing Mr. Thomas; he called her. She can't just come out and ask him if he's the man that abducted his family, because then the FBI might take her into custody.

So she's decides to remain ignorant and ask all the questions she can. Are you up there by yourself or do you have a crew of other space people there with you, she says with a slight laugh? Of course not! I have about twelve mechanical units and my family here to help me. Oh well, I might as well go all the way in, she thinks to herself. "Your family", Tori says with a surprising tone? You mean you have your wife and children in space with you. Yes I do, he responds with a matter a fact tone. I find that very hard to believe that you're in a spaceship floating above the earth; let alone believing that your wife would agree to allow you to launch her and your children into space. Well, I never said that my family agreed to join me up here.

Tori looks again at her producer, who is now giving her the gesture to end the interview, but Tori's instincts are telling her to continue talking to him and ask more serious questions. It's hard to believe this is true unless you give me something more tangible like your full name and the names of your wife and children. BK laughs. No, I'm afraid I can't give you that amount of information at this time. Then I'm sorry Mr. Thomas, she says as she looks down at her tablet and types his name. She would like to ask him more questions, but she can't give anyone the impression that she knows who he is, even though she's not sure. I only have time for a few more callers and I can't hold up this show any longer but thank you for calling and tell your family I said, "Hello". OK Ms. Milanich, I'll give you one more bit of information that you may find interesting.

On the 22nd of March of next year, your computer and every computer on earth will be filled with a vast amount of data, which will totally transform everyone's way of life. What I'm about to give the world is equivalent to what the invention of the automobile did for how we get from one place to another. Tori is a good host and decides to humor him. If that's true then I would like you to give me a call on the 24th of March for an interview, not that she believed him, but to end the conversation on a good note. Do we have a deal Mr. Thomas? I think that will work just fine, Mrs. Milanich. I'll talk with you then. BK then gestures to MOM to disconnect the call. Tori smiles at the camera and throws her hands up as if to say that "wow that was a crazy call". MOM ends the call and asked why he felt it necessary or productive to call a news organization and give their viewers and listening audience that information. I figure if the Government is busy putting out these fires of conspiracies that I'm setting, they won't be able to focus completely on me. I think that is a sound strategy, but I also think that you just felt good telling someone about your accomplishments, MOM states.

Are you seriously thinking about calling her on the 24th of March, MOM asked? I haven't decided yet, but I do think we need a reporter on the ground to help us get the message out and maybe getting us back to earth without being arrested.

Meanwhile, back at the news agency, Tori is talking to her last caller when she catches her producer out the corner of her eye arguing with two official looking women in dark pants suits standing on either side of her. They look very serious about what they are discussing with her and she doesn't look very happy.

Unexpectedly, the light that indicates that the show is about to end starts to blink. She looks at the on-air clock to the left of her and sees that she has over seven minutes left in this segment. But the blinking light indicates that the show will be off the air in roughly fourteen seconds. The caller is still talking about NASA and his suspicion that they are secretly launching surveillance satellites, but she has to abruptly interrupt his story. Mr. Guncher, I'm so sorry, but we're going to have to end this insightful conversation for now. But thank you for calling in and we hope you will tune in to our next show on Wednesday. She then smiles at the camera as she waits for the green light to be replaced by a red light, which indicates that she's off the air. It seems like she's holding her smile forever, but when the red light finally appears. She yanks the earpiece from her ear and snatches the microphone equipment off the waste of her pants and tosses it across to the equipment personnel in anger.

She's yelling as she storms over toward her producer, Francis, while the three women are still arguing back and forth. "What the hell is going on around here", she yells at the top of her voice. And who decided to shorten my show without telling me. Mrs. Milanich, one of the agents says in a calm voice. It's our job to monitor media organizations that attempt to frighten the American people. We can't allow you to continue spreading these unsubstantiated stories about some mysterious object hovering above the planet. Then the other agent chimes in. Do you have any idea the harm you can do by disseminating that kind of false information? We are very responsible regarding the information we broadcast to our viewers, Francis responds angrily. I'm sorry Ms. Milanich. We haven't introduced ourselves. I'm agent White and this is agent Hass and we are agents of the Federal Communication Commission. It's our responsibility to ensure that all news media throughout the United States fully comply with the government's rules and regulations. I apologize for our abrupt ending of your broadcast regarding the so call UFO, but if you don't investigate and disseminate the information you are receiving in a responsible manner, we will have to shut your network down. You mean we can't talk about what you don't approve of, Tori shouts. I can't believe in this day and age that we still have the Federal Government monitoring and telling us what stories we can report.

Agent White steps into the anchors personal space and gives her a stern look. It really doesn't matter what you call it and what you think. I'm just telling you if you broadcast another story on this fictitious object in orbit, we will shut this network down and you'll be back at that furniture store selling futons and wicker furniture. Tori looks surprised that the agent knew where she worked prior to working for the network. The other network employees notice what's going on, but don't help or interject their opinion in the conversation. Without another word, both agents smugly look at Tori and Francis as they walk away. That was pretty chilling for both Tori and Francis. As both agents walk off the news set, Agent Hass stops and turns back toward the women. She tells them to don't count on Mr. Thomas calling or downloading anything earth shattering in March or any other month. She has a smirk on her face, then joins her partner as both Agents walk out of the building. Francis and Tori stare at each other dumbfounded and in disbelief. But Francis has been in the business for over ten years, so she knows that if the government makes a point to tell you that there is no story and not to worry, then you should investigate the hell out of that story.

Francis tells Tori that they will continue to investigate the story, but they'll need to be careful. Francis gestures to Tori to follow her into her office, which she does as her co-workers talk amongst themselves and stares at them as they both walk off the set. As they arrive at Francis office, she holds the door open as Tori walks into her office. She closes the door and shuts the blinds so the other employees can't read their lips or body language. Francis starts off the conversation with a "oh my God"! What just happened out there, as she sits down behind her desk? Tori flops down in one of three chairs in front of Francis's desk. "I had no idea", Tori says while trying to digest the fact that the Government has been monitoring her because of the story she has been investigating. She never thought the story was anything special, but if there watching her and Bill then their must be something to what the caller who called himself Mr. Hunter was saying. We've got to be very careful how we proceed with this story from this point, Francis warns her. I have to talk with the Director and our Senior Attorney before we proceed any farther. They were not kidding when they said they will shut us down.

I've seen this happened before when someone at my last news agency in Texas tried to follow a story the Defense Investigation Agency was trying to protect. So, what do you think we should do? "Just drop the story and let the feds intimidate us", Tori response with a large helping of anger in her voice. Hell no, but we have to be careful and ensure that all the information we receive from our contacts are verified an as accurate as possible. But you have to know that our careers and possibly our lives may be at stake. That really gets Tori's attention.

You don't really think the government would try to harm us over this story do you, Tori asked? Francis pauses and looks at Tori with a look of uncertainty in her eyes. Honestly, I would like to give you a confident "no", but this could be a big story, if it has a kernel of truth. Francis leans forward in her chair and asked Tori if she's sure she wants to go down this unlit road, which will probably be laced with potholes? Tori just stares at her for a moment, then gives her a shaky, "yes" while slowly nodding her head. She knows this type of story can jumpstart her career as an investigative reporter.

Tori admits to Francis that she's so scared right now that she may leave a puddle in her chair. "Please don't", Francis says as she laughs. I'm not trying to scare you, but I just want you to be fully prepared for anything that may happen. Tori just nods her head and looks as if she's in deep thought. She wonders if she should tell Francis about how she thinks that the caller maybe the same person who abducted his family recently. As Francis continues rambling on about what could happen to the both of them, Tori is thinking if it's possible that Mr. Thomas could have called her with that crazy story and will he be calling her back in the near future. But she decides to keep her crazy thoughts to herself and to just allow Francis to handle this latest incident.

Tori attention snaps back to the conversation as Francis tells her that she's a little shaken too. But I'm more pissed that those two agents interrupting our segment and delivering that vailed threat, she says with an angry tone. I don't know what the Government is up to, but I'll be damned if we're going to let them deter us from finding out what they're trying to hide. Tori is comforted and motivated by Francis' tenacity.

Francis is in the middle of telling Tori how they will enlist the research department to find out what the Government is trying to hide, when her desk phone rings. "Excuse me", as she picks up the phone and says, hello. Tori doesn't pay much attention to Francis conversation until after about three minutes, she notices the expression on Francis' face and that the person on the other end of the line is not letting her complete a sentence. Tori starts to feel uncomfortable sitting there listening to her call, so she gestures to Francis that she's going to leave, but Francis signals to her not to leave.

She can't tell who Francis is talking to, but he must be telling her something she doesn't want to hear, because she doesn't normally curse. The last words Francis says was asking if she could come to who's ever on the end of the line office and have a face to face discussion, but Tori can see by her facial expression that the call is coming to an end and that it's a one-way conversation now. Normally you can tell when a phone conversation is ending by hearing someone saying, "goodbye", but Francis has a stunned look on her face as she slowly hangs up the phone. "I can't believe what just happened", she says with a stunned look on her face as she looks at the phone. "What's going on", Tori asks as she stares at a clearly perplexed Francis. That was the head of our legal department calling to tell me not to pursue or discuss the story of the object in space again.

Tori plays pocker on the weekend with her Dad and some of his friends, because her Dad is an advid pocker player and this is her way of spending time with him. But now to hear the news station's legal department has instructed them not to pursue the story, even before they asked, verifies her original sustition. "That was Mr. Thomas that called me", she thinks to herself, as she taps down her emotions. She uses the pocker face that she uses when playing with her Dad. So, is there some truth to whatever that is hovering above us, as Tori points to the ceiling?

"I have no idea because she was doing most of the talking and all of the threatening", Francis says as she leans back in her chair. "What do you mean", she asked? She didn't go into very much details, but she explained that the Facilities Department has boxes and manpower ready for anyone writing or reporting on that fictitious object hovering above the planet. This is the second time I've been threatened by the Federal Government about this same family, she thinks to herself, while Franis vents to Tori why this idiotic story is different than any of the other nuts that call in. Francis or anyone else, other than the senior staff, has any knowledge of the Thomas family story that Tori and Bill brought to the network. Tori has been working hard to get her current network segment and she thinks she already has a couple of strikes against her, and one more will jeopardize her fledgling career. Francis gets up from her chair and walks around to the front of her desk then sits on the edge of it in front of Tori. I don't have the slightest idea why they caved so quickly and allowed the Government to beat the crap out of our first amendment rights, but whatever they said convinced legal it would be to their best interest to discontinue pursuing the story. I don't like bullies and don't like to run from a fight, but I think we have no choice but to follow our networks lead and not broadcast another word about whatever that is out there.

"I agree Francis", Tori says with a phony smile on her face. She thought Tori would put up more of a fight or at least shed some tears, but she guesses she's not willing to risk her job either. "Well alright", Francis says with surprise in her voice. She didn't expect Tori to agree with her and with such glee. But fear of losing your job is a powerful motivator for compliance, Francis concludes.

"OK", Francis says as she stands up and walks back around to take a seat at her desk. I need you to get me a story for your next segment no later than tomorrow at 3:00 p.m. "I think I can do that", Tori says as she jumps up from her chair and walks toward the door. "Hey", remember if you get another call from another space idiot, what are you going to do, as she pauses to hear her response? Tori has her hand on the door nob as she turns to Francis. I'll just remind my audience of the story at hand then I'll signal to Joe-Ann to end the call.

Francis gives her a smile and thumbs up, so Tori replies in kind with a smile and thumbs up too, then proceeds to open and walk out the door. As she closes the door behind her, both ladies are thinking that something about this story doesn't feel right, but their doing the only thing they can do by moving on to another story. At least one of them will. Francis begins to look through her schedule for her next meeting of the day, while Tori hurries to her car to call Bill and strategize their next move.

Back on the ship, after making his unscheduled call to the new station, BK has fallen asleep on his sofa. He made the phone call because he thinks after the data download, he will need someone with a connection to the media to disseminate additional information that the government most likely will attempt to block or discredit. But at this moment, he is deep into his catnap and not concern with anything that's going on down on earth. He's dreaming about fishing off his boat with Bryan and catching large numbers of fish. He can feel the warm sun on his face, the fishing rod in his hand and the cool breeze of the ocean breeze whispering in his ear.

Benny's mischievous side takes over his logic circuitry as he hovers over to his sleeping buddy and decides to have a little fun at BK's expense. Benny accesses and retrieves a sample of Lorraine's voice recording from BK's personal media database, then replicates her voice patterns in order for him to mimic Lorraine's voice. Benny gets close to BK's ear, then starts to sing Lorraine and BK's favorite song by Prince, "Do me Baby". This is an example of Benny's since of humor that gets him into trouble. He starts singing, "Take me baby, kiss me all over, play with my love, bring out what's been in me for far too long baby, you know that's all I've been dreaming of". A smile forms across BK's sleeping face as he starts to stretch as he begins to wake up from his nap. He then gently strokes BK's semi-shaven head imitating a scene from one of the love stories Benny loves to watch.

BK seems to like that too as he begins to turn towards him. Benny has unknowingly triggered some romantic memories of when BK and Lorraine were relaxing on the sofa late one night listening to music. Lorraine was running her fingers across his newly shaved head and he was caressing her arms and shoulders. Benny once again whispers, "I'm so cold, just hold me", he says softly to him as his eyes begins to open and his vision of his beautiful wife's face fades and slowly transforms into Benny's round metal and plastic face. "Got damn it", Benny, BK yells in surprise as he jumps away from him. What the hell are you doing, he yells. I'm sorry BK, but you were sleeping so peacefully that I... He interrupts Benny and sternly asked him to stop speaking in his wife's voice? Benny switches back to his assigned speaking voice.

It was not my attention to startle you, but I thought that would be the most ideal method of waking you. It's 12:15 and it's part of your programming to get up at noon if you take a nap. Plus, it was damn funny, Benny adds with a laugh. BK doesn't think that it was funny and looks at him as if he wants to punch him in his stupid robotic face. But he just asked MOM is Lorraine awake? Yes, she is just starting to sit up. Damn it, I wanted to be at her bedside when she woke up. He jumps up from the sofa, knocking Benny back with an elbow to what would be considered his chest.

"Hey what the hell", Benny yells as he stabilizes himself. I am already in bad shape and that elbow didn't help at all. Hey, it's your own damn fault Benny, because I warned you about playing with me while I'm sleeping, as BK gets off the sofa and rushes out of his quarters and heads toward the Clinic. That's typical, Benny says out loud. He makes a mess and leaves it for me to clean up, as he reaches down for the remote on the floor. "Hey", Benny says with amazement. My hand is operating within normal parameters, he says as he rotates, flexes and bends the hand at what would be considered his wrist and fingers. I can only deduce that the violet bump to the torso I received from BK's elbow must have corrected the malfunction.

That sounds plausible, MOM replies. I will inform BK that you no longer require his assistance or maintenance. "Hell no", Benny replies sharply. I want you to put me as the number one task on his "to do" list, because I have a variety of other mechanical abnormalities that he can repair. Not to mention that burnt smell immolating from within my casing, he continuously complains about. I may be mistaken, Benny but I am almost 99.8 percent sure that you may not be serious regarding your mysterious odor. How can you be sure, Benny replies curiously? Well, most of the time he refers to you as "smoky metal butt", is directly following one or two tasking that you performed incorrectly. And I have learned through observation that the majority of times humans respond in this manner, they are less than genuine. Besides, unfortunately you can not be place as the number one priority on his "to do" list. It doesn't matter where I am on his list; just as long as I am on it somewhere.

But if you want to put me closer to the top of his "to do" list, I won't be mad with you. Benny waits for a confirmation from MOM, but she doesn't respond. I will take that as a solid maybe, he says with a spark of excitement. Benny really doesn't enjoy working in BK's living quarters these past few months. He once had the run of the ship, but the flaws in his personality programming is too erratic to allow him access to vital systems.

224

He once hacked into LaChel's school database and changed her grades to all A's, because BK was complaining to MOM that LaChel was close to failing three of her classes. BK and Lorraine had to convince the principle that LaChel didn't have the computer knowledge to hack a computer and change her grades. It didn't take long for BK to figure out the Benny was responsible for the hack. This was two weeks before he was planning to take his family to the warehouse and didn't need Benny's erratic and unpredictable personality adding to his stress. He instructed MOM to limit Benny's access to critical systems and to limit his movements to the family quarters until further notice. He still doesn't have time to work on him yet and some parts of him doesn't want to change Benny because he may be unpredictable, but he's pretty entertaining most to the time.

Meanwhile, BK rushes down the hallway, because he wanted to be there before Lorraine wakes up, but she's awake and alone again. As he enters the Clinic, she is sitting up in the bed looking a little dazed and confused, which will be the norm for a couple more days. It's not the medications or her time in the stasis capsule, but the human mind has a difficult time grasping such a very drastic change in their realities. He walks up behind her and rubs her back. Hey babe, how do you feel? Lorraine shrugs her shoulders and tries to rub the sleep from her eyes. I need to know what's going on and what's happening to me, she demands, while shrugging her shoulders for him to stop touching her?

He walks in front of her as he answers her questions. You're miles above the earth, aboard a spacecraft that your husband built and its about 12:26 p.m. Are you hungry, he asked with concern in his voice? You're really going to need to eat something if you want to regain your strength, Babe. I'm not worried about eating right now, I need you to explain to me what happen to you and how did you do all of this right under my nose. Looking around the room, Lorraine is unable to comprehend how one person that is married with a family could accomplish all of this. He knows that he's lucky. She has replaced her anger and disdain for him with curiosity. This won't last forever so he'd better seize this opportunity with a firm grip and run with it. How could you have the time, let alone the knowledge, to build this huge ship by yourself. I mean… you barely had time to do some of the things around the house I asked you to do! And the dishwasher is still broken. BK can't believe she's still thinking about that stupid dishwasher. Ok Lorraine, you can give that a rest, because as you can see, "that's not going to happen". Besides, I had a lot of help from my electronic units prior to building this ship. That's exactly what I'm talking about, BK. I didn't have any idea you had the brains to do something like this. Yes, I knew you were smart, because of the computers you constantly worked on and technology you built into our house. But, damn babe! I need to know what happened to you, she asked while looking intensely at him. BK pauses for a moment to get his thoughts together. Do you remember the accident I had over three years ago? You mean the accident that almost killed you. Of course I do! So, what does that have to do with what's happening now? "Everything", he says in a matter a fact tone. That accident that all most sent me to those pearly gates. Well that accident sparked what I call "The jump starting of my cerebral evolution". Lorraine looks at him as if he has two heads.

Are you trying to make my head hurt, she yells. "No, but… No buts, she shouts, just stop being so dramatic, and just tell be what you're talking about, please! Alright, just listen. That crash did significant damage to various regions of my brain, but that was only the match that started the fire. She starts to look more and more impatient. I can only remember bits and pieces of my three-month stay in the hospital, but I do remember my attending doctor telling us I would mostlikely be a quadriplegic. It was also hard on the girls, who had to see you laying in that hospital bed with all those tubes, wires and medical equipment connected to your body.

They were having nightmares and I was having nightmares about the mounting hospital bills. And with the bills adding up on a daily basis – I was on the verge of having a nervous breakdown. Tears start to roll down Lorraine's cheeks, as she remembers how close they came to loosing their home to the bank and having to borrow money from their relatives. Those memories are still hard to talk about for her. He gently wipes the tears from each side of her face with his hand. Babe, that's been over three years now. I know, she replies, but it seems as if it was just yesterday. We were living on credit cards and all of our bank accounts were almost drained. Babe, I have to tell you the rest of the story.

Unit two notices her tears rolling down her cheeks and grabs a small towel from near by, then hovers over to her with the towel extended in its hand, which startles her. He grabs it from the unit and hands it to her. The unit hovers there for a while until Lorraine tells it "Thank you", then gestures for it to go. As Lorraine wipes the tears from her face, he continues with his story. I had to lie there in that bed for weeks just drifting in and out of consciousness. My mind was so damaged I could only focus on simple things like opening my mouth so the nurse could feed me. When you weren't there I could hear the nurses talking to each other about me.

They would say how I would probably never regain any mobility than what I had at the time and that you should just put me in a care center, because with two young girls, you couldn't afford to stay at home with me or pay anyone to take care of me. Lorraine looked surprised and angry. Why didn't you tell me that those bitches were saying those things about you? "Calm down", because they did do a good job of taking care of me. Besides, they thought I was sleep or too drugged up to hear their conversation. Even after the years of worrying and agony that her and the girls went through during his time in the hospital, she wishes she could get the opportunity to confront those nurses. But for now, she wants to hear the rest of the story.

She inhales a deep calming breath, then gestures for him to continue with his story. I can remember waking up in the morning in that hospital, slowly slipping into a very depressed state as the nurses changed me, cleaned me and fed me my breakfast. Lorraine reaches over and grabs BK's hand. "I remember", she says. Every day I returned to see you and a little more of you was gone. I was so worried about you. He tells her at his lowest point, he just wanted someone to pull the plug on him or pick him up and throw him out of his fourth story window. A tear rolls down one of her cheeks.

"Four stories", she repeats. That would have just paralyzed you, she says with a smile. Both of them laugh as they grab each others hand. But a couple of days after that; little did I know that my entire world and my perspective of it, was about to change. I remember the day that Doctor Mobosa from Botswana approached us with that experimental surgery that could give me back a large portion of my mobility. Or it could have killed you, she adds! Believe me babe; that would have been a small price to pay for the hope of having a normal functioning body once again. Regardless of some of the stupid things you've done - this one is at the top of the list. You were and are my husband and I still would have wanted you with me no matter what condition you were in. He smiles as he looks at her, because he understands that this is the closest, he's going to get to hearing the words', " I Love You". Now wipe that smile off your face and tell me the rest, she replies. Well, as you now know; the surgery was more of a success than you realized. I can see

227

that, so please stop stating the obvious. Just tell me what you think happened to you after the surgery, she replies with some frustration. I've analyzed the procedure that Dr. Mobosa performed on me and I still have no clue why or how my brain is wired now.

The only other conclusion that I can come up with is that the combination of the accident and the operation has made it possible for me to use more of my brain than any other human on earth. While most people think in two dimensions – the operation enabled be to think in a three-dimensional state. I find it difficult to believe that Dr. Mobosa could reprogram your brain to make you some type of savant. Look at what I have accomplished as BK stands up and puts both arms out and does a 360 degree turn. I mean, that I have complete mobility and can see complex problems more clearly than before the accident.

While some problems may take me days to solve, most problems only require a matter of minutes of thought. He recognizes that "what the hell", look on her face and starts to explain. For instance, I bet you were wondering why we're not floating around the room? Lorraine has a who cares look on her face. No, not really, she sarcastically replies. He smiles a bit. I forgot that Lorraine doesn't think about scientific things like that; at least not yet. I think she's ready for a demonstration on artificial gravity and its' applications, he convinces himself. MOM, will you gradually bring this room's artificial gravity to 25 percent, please. Commencing reducing artificial gravity at increments of 10, MOM responds. She starts to count off the increments as they occur: 90 percent, 80 percent, 70 percent.

Lorraine looks around the room wildly as she begins to feel her body getting lighter. 60 percent, 50 percent, then she sees a cup floating in the air next to her, then a pen begins to slowly float across her face and above her head. 40 percent, 30 percent, as everything that isn't anchored to something is floating around the room; including BK and Lorraine. He is floating beside and above the bed, the expression on his face is of a young boy that's about to run outside to play in the fresh winter's snow. But Lorraine has the opposite emotion. Her expression is one of a little girl that's riding a roller coaster that her jerk of a brother tricked her to ride. He grabs one of her hands then puts his other hand on her waist and pulls her close to him. Lorraine grabs his arm and puts her other hand on his shoulder to stabilize herself. Both continue to slowly float about five to six feet off the floor and drift over the bed.

He can tell that she's scared, because of her nails that are beginning to dig into his arm, and through is jumper. Ah Babe, I would appreciate it if you loosen your grip before you draw blood, he says with some distress in his voice. "OK", she shouts. I get it! You control the gravity, so cut the gravity back on! It's not the room that's floating. We're floating. Lorraine looks around the room to see various objects floating about the room and toward her. He has a kid in a bounce house smile on his face as he tries to explain to her how it works, but she just digs her nails deeper into his arm a little harder to make her point. She's truly scared as hell and doesn't give a damn how he did it; she just wants the gravity back on.

"I' m going to slap the crap out of you if you don't get me down from here", she shouts while trying to shake him. He can tell by the threatening tone of her voice and her fingers digging into his arm that she's not playing. "OK babe". Hold on! I'm going to increase the magnetic field in this room, which will restore the gravity to the room. "I don't care", Lorraine shouts as she tightens her grip on his arm. "Just get me back on my damn bed", she yells! He instructs MOM to slowly restore the gravity in the room. As the gravity increase, Lorraine can feel her body getting heavier and can see both of them lowering toward the bed. She still has a strong grip on his arm, so he uses his legs to maneuver her back over the bed.

Lorraine releases his arm and reaches for the headboard of the bed as her feet touches the sheets. He can see that she's still shook-up, but he thinks that it was a good experience for her. Lorraine on the other hand, would like nothing better than to blacken his left eye for doing that to her. And once she gets her strength back, she just may pay him back with a Tyson right cross to his left eye. I'm sorry babe, but I thought you would like zero gravity. She's back on the bed and he's standing beside her again, smiling at her. Lorraine looks him straight in his eyes and says, "don't you ever do that to me again", as she reaches up and grabs him around his shirt collar. He raises both of his hands and says, "Babe, I'm sorry". Just telling you about zero gravity wouldn't do it justice; I had to give you a demonstration. Besides, that's a part of space travel. If something happens and we lose our ability to create artificial gravity, we're going to have to work in zero gravity until we can restore it.

Oh hell no, she replies. You and that talking washing machine better make sure that doesn't happen. That something that I can't promise you babe, but I don't understand why zero gravity scares you so much? You love roller coasters! Basically, there is no difference between the two. Lorraine adjust herself in the bed and puts her pillow back behind her head. BK tries to help her, but she just gives him one of her patented, "get the hell away from me stares". On that sour note, he moves the chair back between the two beds and sits there quietly to let her calm down. Lorraine angrily adjust her covers and pulls it up to her waist.

Both sat quietly for about ten minutes. On her part, Lorraine was too upset to talk without lacing her conversation with colorful expletives and BK was too afraid of hearing what she had to say. He looks around the room as he tries to come up with some kind of calming words to defuse this potential volatile moment. But unfortunately, he takes a little too long. His eyes met hers and as he sees the tears beginning to flow again and he knows that there is no hope for him. "You have a problem", she says as she points her finger directly in his face. He leans back in his chair and prepares to add to his list of all the problems she has pointed out throughout their decades of marriage. He tries to laugh it off as he says, "Hey", I know I have a problem. She picks up on the joke he's trying to make. I'm not talking about me you bastard, she shouts.

I'm sorry babe, but I didn't have much of a choice! He's starting to become frustrated and raises his voice. Yes you did, she replies. All you had to do is ask for my help. You could have just talked to me and we could have come up with another solution. BK gets up and angrily walks to the foot of her bed. OK... So you're saying, I just should have come up to you and said, "Hey babe, I built this spaceship and I want to take you and the girls on a possible dangerous trip out into space, because I'm afraid if I leave you here the government will use you to make me turn over all my work".

I'm sure you wouldn't have a problem with that, he says sarcastically. She lifts up onto her elbows. That still doesn't give you any right to abduct us and put our lives in danger, she says angrily. I know it was wrong, but I couldn't take the chance of you telling me, "no". So I did what I thought was in the best interest of our family. At one time, I was thinking about leaving you and the girls behind, but as everything I dreamt started to come together; I realized that was something I just couldn't bring my self to do. But you could bring yourself to drug me and your daughters, freeze us like human fish sticks and blast us out into space with no problem, she says with a lot of attitude. Do you think it was easy to do what I did? "I was terrified and I still am", he says sternly. From drugging you to the time you spent in stasis, I could have killed you and my girls. I'm still terrified that something could happen to you, but what I'm doing is bigger than our family. They stare into each others eyes for a moment. But BK can clearly see that he's not even making a dent in convincing her that this was the best option. He can only hope that in time she will come to realize that this was the only choice. He looks at his watch and sees that it's past 4:00 p.m.

Well babe, its dinner time and I know we both could use a break and something to eat. No! I need you to finish the story and explain to me how you became this selfish jerk who could jeopardize your family's safety. We have plenty of time for me to finish explaining what happened. You need to eat something before your blood sugar drops too low. Lorraine looks at him with an angry stare. You are not going anywhere until I know what happen to that twisted pea brain of yours.

Now, sit your narrow, hairy butt down and talk to me! MOM decides to interrupt. Excuse me BK, but Lorraine's blood pressure is high and her neurons are elevated. Unit M2 hovers toward her with its' forehead lights strobing back and forth as it tries to scan Lorraine's vitals. The unit gets within two feet of her when she yells at it to get the hell away from her! Would you like me to sedate her, MOM asked? That even raises her blood pressure even more. I will find you and snatch out every wire, solenoid and chip from your motherboard – "you glorified laptop", as she looks around the room and angerly shouts.

"That won't be necessary", he replies. I will handle this, please. Ya', shut the hell up, Lorraine says at the top of her voice! Lorraine, I know you are upset, but I don't think you talking to me like some old drunk sailor is helpful, MOM adds. Lorraine angrily kicks the blanket off of her and tries to get out of bed, but BK stops her and forces her back in the bed, then covers her legs with the blanket. She doesn't have the strength to fight him, so she just angerly lies there fuming.

MOM, please don't respond unless it's an emergency or I ask you too. Yes, BK, she replies. "Thank you and mine your business", Lorraine says loudly and with plenty of attitude. Now tell me what exactly happened to you and when. Look at it this way. Maybe it can help me not to be so pissed and to understand why the girls and me are up here. Well, I can only explain it by telling you that my brain is wired differently now. Lorraine has a confused

231

look on her face. Remember that he clearly explained to us that the operation was experimental and risky. The outcome wouldn't be something anyone could predict. Yes, I remember all of that and I was well prepared for anything. You were touch and go for about three or four days but after that you started getting better fast and your mobility returned. I remember the exact time when I noticed that something wonderful was happening to me. "When was that", she asked? About three weeks after my operation, I was watching one of what you call, "one of those crazy science shows", when the narrator displayed his theory on developing an artificial intelligent system that can manage and perform various complex calculations using a new 128 bit processing chip.

They were developing this system for NASA which would control and monitor the astronauts and their space shuttle missions, but they stated their about four years away from testing and an additional two years from initiating it. I was unable to move my right arm fully, but I found that my left arm was working, and I quickly learned how to use it like my right. That's right Lorraine recalls. I remember coming to see you one day and you were sitting up in your bed writing with your left hand. I thought that was truly amazing. You basically learned to write with your left hand in a couple of days.

I knew at that point that something wasn't quite right with me, he replies. But my newly developing intelligence helped me get my dream job with NASA. But I thought it would be best to dumb it down a bit, because they didn't need to know what I was truly capable of doing. The language I developed for them enable the computer to respond to complex verbal commands, solve problems, and monitor a variety of systems. I could solve problems that had stumped NASA for decades. It was as if I was in college and was being tested on solving sixth-grade math problems.

It was so easy to write computer code that I would write lines upon lines of code through the day and dream about more code at night. Lorraine eyes are beginning to glaze over as she starts to become a little bored at the pace of his story. OK, you're boring the hell out of me right now, so can you just get to the meat of your story. The point is that NASA was too slow to implement any of my projects and I think NASA's Project Manager was jealous of me and was trying to slowly minimize my role in developing my projects. I remember after a couple of good months that you use to come home upset almost every night, she interjects. Even though I was the supervisor of the division managers, little by little, my authority in my department was being chipped away and staff began to ignore his instructions regarding the projects he managed, which undermind his position.

Yes, I remember you coming home telling me about how your managers were challenging your authority and weren't following your instructions anymore. I was a little concerned about your stress level, but I thought that those types of things happen and are just part of the job. And to be honest, I thought you were being a little paranoid too. I really didn't give it a lot of thought, because the money and benefits were really good.

You always talked about how working with the space industry was something you could do to help push we mere humans into the space age, she says with a sarcastic smile. But imagine my surprise when seven months into your dream job, you came home and told me that you could no longer work for NASA. I know it wasn't easy for you to resign from that position and I felt so bad for you, because I could see the pain in your eyes. I know you hoped that the work you did with them would change the world. BK looked at her and nodded his head yes. If they would have listened to me, and not those brain dead flunkies, we could have done some amazing things. It looks like they needed you more than you needed them, Lorraine exclaimed. Well, I could have completed this ship and its technology a whole lot sooner if I would have developed it at the NASA facilities.

I'm sure that me and the girls wouldn't be here if you had tried to workout your differences with them, but I really hoped that you had a good reason for not allowing them to help you with all of this. I knew that wasn't going to happen, because they would have just tried to take control of this ship. For a couple of days, I was envisioning opening my own technology agency, so I could control all my ideas without interference from the government.

But the government had different plans for me. The last straw was when you and the girls left me home because you were going shopping for clothes and didn't want to put up with me lumbering around the mall looking suspect as you like to tell me. Lorraine just rolls her eyes at him. But I was watching one of my fishing shows when three government agents came knocking at our door and bardged their way into our house.

She sits there in her bed shocked that this is another secret that he has kept from her. He can see that what he's telling her is figuratively and possibly literally putting another nail in his coffin. "I know", another secret, he says to her while holding up his hands to gesture to her to let him finish his story. Two of the biggest people stuffed into a black suits forced me back into the living room and down on the sofa as one of the smallest Agents I've ever seen sat down in front of me then explained what would happen if I didn't do exactly what the Government wanted.

To make a long story short – they offered me a job I couldn't refuse. But to sweeten the pot, the job paid almost double what NASA paid me and made me Chief Engineer. She wanted to explode with a tyraid of questions and profanity, but he was spilling his guts and she didn't want him to stop. She just sat there slowly nodding her head and staring at him, which was a little disturbing to him. The Government recognized my knowledge of quantum mechanics and wanted to use me for a variety of their projects.

As the head of their technology division, I was free to develop all my ideas as long as they benefit the Government. But what I neglected to tell you is that the reason why NASA decided not to continue their law suit after I resigned and left with my project files is because the Government instructed them not to pursue any legal actions regarding the transference of technology to Sergeant Engineering. But they made it clear that I was not to develop any of my ideas outside the agency. Lorraine stares curiously at him. "Wait a damn minute"! You're telling me that we are not being sued anymore and you never told me. Yes, but I have a good reason for not telling you.

But he knows that what he's about to tell her will most likely bring her blood pressure to a high boil. She looks at him intensly, while waiting for what he's about to say next. He hesitates for a second, because he's trying to arrange his answer in such a way that may make sense to her, but he can't seem to get the words out of his mouth. "Just tell me", she says in a calm but serious tone. I needed money to start buying materials to build this ship and make repairs to the warehouse that housed the spacecraft. So, I continued to let you think that I needed money to make payments to my attorney, as well as court cost. I had every intention of getting the money back to you once I sold a few of my ideas to a couple of local software companies. But building the ship and all the materials I needed for my experiments cost every bit of money I could get my hands on. She interrupts him. She leans forward to get closer to him, which causes him to slowly move backward. You mean every bit of money "we" had, as she enphasized the word "we". Over the course of six months, I gave you over $110,000, which left a combined total of a little over $2,700 in all three of our accounts. I was cursing and blaming NASA's attorneys almost every night, but I should have really been directing my anger at you, she says as he looks down at the bed. I was losing sleep, my blood pressure was high, my weight dropped by 15 pounds and every morning I had more and more hair on my pillow. "I was a nervous and balding wreck"! I'm sorry baby that I had to lie to you, but that's why I was telling you not to worry. "How could I not worry", she yells. The girls had to drop their activities at the YMCA, I was working overtime to make more money to pay "our attorney", she says with air quotes. BK tries to say something, but Lorraine gives him the look to stop him from interrupting her.

And both of our credit cards are maxed out at $10,000 each. And all the time you are siphoning money from your family to build this ship, "in your warehouse", she yells with a look of disbelief on her face. In his mind, he is trying to decide if he should divulge to his wife the totality of his deception or just save that part of the story for another time. But since he doesn't have a poker face, that decision has already been made for him. Lorraine can see the signs that he is lying or is not telling her the complete truth. He tries to change the expression on his face, but she knows him too well and reads his facial expression too quickly.

"Damn it, she responds in disbelief. You're not telling me everything, she says with a stern look. With his enhanced brain, a million thoughts race across his mind, but it's like playing speed chess. If you don't have your moves ready within two seconds of your opponents move; you might as well tip your king. The blank look he has on his face is symbolic of him tipping his king, because he knows there's nothing intelligent, he can say in his defense. He knows things are about to get really bad. She looks at him with a crazy stare in her eyes, which convinces him to move farther back to get some distance between them. No, come here, she says in a menacing voice. He knows that he has to defuse this situation quickly before she gets angry again, so he tries to laugh it off, but not very well. Even MOM, who's being quiet right now, can tell by his vocal inflexions that he's nervous about something. Baby just give me a second to explain and I'm sure you will understand why I didn't tell you the truth about our finances. I'm the one that struggled with our bills, not you, she yells! All you had to do was write the check and put it in the mail. It's amazing to me how many secrets you had and how you kept them straight in your head! Yes, I understand what I put you through, but I needed the money to develop the technology on my own, no matter what it took. Even if it meant the financial ruin of your family, she says in disbelief. We've been married over twenty years and I can't believe that you still find it easier to lie to me rather than telling me the truth. Lorraine's expression changes from angry to despair. She puts her head down and puts her head into her hands. "Damn", she says with a soft angry voice. I was really wishing this were a nightmare and I was in someone's hospital about to get a tumor removed from my brain or something; anything, but where I am now. He sighs while getting off the bed then walks over to a closet and reaches in to grab a folded small jumper style uniform like the one he's wearing. Then he grabs a pair of shoes, undergarments and a couple of gadgets that she will need for living on the ship. He walks back over to her as she stares at him as he walks back with a stack of clothes and gadgets in his arms.

He places her new uniform on her legs and tells her to put this on, please. "Hell no", she shouts as she pushes the pile to the side and crosses her arms and legs. "Come on babe, he says in frustration". Believe me, I do understand your anger over what I've done to you and our family, but I need you to trust me by putting on this uniform and coming with me, please. She uncrosses her arms and looks through the pile that is now at her crossed legs. I don't know if I'm going to ever trust you again. Her unflinching stare and the words that just came out of her mouth cut him like a knife to his throat.

He knew it would be hard to convince her to help him, but he had no illusions that it would take time for her to get on his side. She pushes the uniform and shoes off her bed and onto the floor. I'm sorry, but I'm not going to be apart of this nonsense. I need you to take me and my girls back home and as far as I'm concern, you can rocket your fool-self back up here if you want. She truly feels that her girls are in real danger onboard this ship, so she tries to appeal to his parental side. I really need you to think of your kids' safety, babe. I'm asking you; no I'm begging you to please take us back home.

He hesitates for a moment taking in everything she just said, but then decides to take a tougher approach to changing her mind about helping him. He needs her to start adapting to her new environment and the first step is for her to get out of bed, put on that uniform and help him run the operations of her Clinic and this ship. He was trying his best not to upset her too much, but he can't compromise or alter his plans. He walks back to her bedside and looks down at his wife's lovely but angry face. Lorraine! You're right that I've lied to you and I don't want to do that to you anymore. There's no way we can go home right now, because there's too much at stake for us as well as humanity. "I need you", but if you truly don't want to participate in my plan, then I will put you back into stasis for the remainder of time that we're up here, which may be two to four more months. The girls and I will have to divide your duties between us, which won't allow us very little leisure time.

You will be putting us in a very difficult position, but I have programmed enough medical knowledge into the units so they can perform the medical duties. Lorraine stares at him with eyes that could kill, but BK doesn't show any signs of weakness. She now understands that she doesn't have a choice. She has no memory of being in stasis, but she has no desire to be placed back in that tube. And most importantly, she can't allow her daughters to experience the physical effects of coming out of stasis and living aboard this ship without her. After what he has done, she has very little trust in him to do the right thing regarding their safety. I'll give you some time to think about what you would like to do. He then walks out of the Clinic and waits in the passageway. BK breaks down in the passageway as he starts to panic a little after thinking of having to place her back in stasis and handle the girls without her, which sends chills down his spine.

He really didn't want to make her fill guilty about being put back into stasis, but he hopes he has put enough pressure on her to change her mind. Just in case she's still not convinced to help him, he starts to formulate a plan "B" in his head, which may involve a malfunctioning stasis capsule. He thinks that ultimately it may be easier to convince her to help him once his daughters are out of stasis. He paces back and forth for about five minutes thinking of other duties he'll have to inherit from her and how he's going to explain to his daughters why their mother is back in the deep freezer.

Just then, the door suddenly opens with a swish and Lorraine is standing on the other side with an angry look on her face, but what is most important is that she's wearing her blue medical jumper. He looks at her in amazement, not thinking she would put on the uniform as a signal that she's going to stand by him. Lorraine walks out into the passageway and walks up directly in front of him. As she looks up at him and into his eyes, she tells him that if it wasn't for the love and concern for her daughters, she would not cooperate with any plans that he concocted. He did the smart think by listening to her, not saying a word, but most important of all, fighting his urge to put his arms around her and giving her a sloppy wet I love you kiss. He'll be lucky if he'll be able to accidently brush up against her without her going off on him. He just nods his head and gives her "a thank you" look. He patiently waited for her to finish her speech before telling her that hopefully she would understand why he had to go to this extreme. She on the other hand didn't respond. Without another word, she turned away from him and walked back into the Clinic as he follows her. While following her, he can't help but admire how good she looks in her jumper. He's transfixed on her butt when she turns to ask him a question and catches him staring at her.

She knows what that stupid stare means and quickly shuts it down. You might as well shut those thoughts down or get one of these medical units to help you out. Babe, you are beautiful woman and it has been months, he exclaims. "Don't give a damn", she coldly states as she turns and walks away. Just my luck that her body is thawed, but her love for me is still frozen solid, he thinks to himself. She walks around a desk as she looks curiously at the various electronic devices lying on it. There are two medical devices, one that look similar to a television remote control and the other resembles a small flat camera. She may not recognize what they are, but some how she has a small understanding of how they work. She picks up the device that looks like a small camera and starts to attempt to operate the device.

BK walks to the opposite end of the table and picks up one of the gadgets on the table. He holds up the other device and asked her if she recognizes it. She put down the device she's holding, then moves around the table to get a closer look. She stares at the gadget for a few seconds, then replies with a hesitant, but curious "no".

But there's something about those two devices that is very familiar to her. She gets a brief recollection of what the device is and how to use it. As a matter a fact, as she turns and walks around the room, most of the equipment in this room looks so familiar. He slowly trails behind her, hoping she will remember something about any of the equipment or devices in this room. Unfortunately, he could not come directly out and tell her how important it is that she remembers the knowledge that she posesses. It's too soon for that, he thinks to himself. What's going on, she asked? This room and the equipment in it is so familiar to me, but I've never operated any of this stuff or even held it in my hand. I can't quite utilize the equipment or devices, but I remember bits and pieces about how they work. "How could that be", she says as she curiously looks at another piece of equipment. It's an effect of the stasis that you were in, he replies. Don't worry Babe, as you get stronger, mentally and physically, your memory will return, and your mind will become better than new. She stops and turns to him. What do you mean, better than new? I want my brain in the same condition prior to you bringing me aboard this ship. He would like to explain to her that her mind will never be the same, but he doesn't want to open that jar of whoop-ass yet. He figures that prudent thing for him to do in this situation is to segue to another less volatile subject before she can read the expression on his face again. Let me give you a tour around the ship, so you can start to familiarize yourself with its' layout and operational capabilities. She can tell that he's not giving her the complete story about what's happening to her, but right now she doesn't have the strength to find out anymore surprises. He walks around the table and puts his hand in the small of her back and leads her out the Clinic door.

As they walk down the passageway toward the media room, he's thinking to himself that he has one or two more days before the implanted information will start to kick-in. Maybe she won't freak out when he tells her about the knowledge he implanted in her head as well as the girls. Right now, he's just going to have to lie to her every time a fragment of memory breaks through, until too much knowledge begins to dominate her thoughts, and he has to come clean about this bit of deception. She looks over at him as he walks along the passageway with her. She can always tell when he is hiding something and regardless of his enhance brain, now isn't any different. Where are we going, she asked as they make a right turn and head down a familiar passageway.

It's lunchtime, so he had Chef prepare their lunch and it's setup in the media room as a surprise for her. I'm not hungry, she says as she tries to keep her stomach from growling. Well, that doesn't matter, because you have to eat a certain amount of food each day in order for you to acclimate yourself to this environment.

If you don't, you'll start to feel something close to jet-lag within about seven to ten days. She doesn't know if he's lying or not, but being in stasis and now living aboard a spaceship he built leads her to believe that he may be telling the truth. But yes, she believes he's lying. Once in the media room, they had a great shrimp and salad lunch. He thought it would be good to use the time to tell her about his plans and answer any other questions she may have and believe me; she had a bucket full. He was trying to have something like a lunch and meeting combined, but she continued to pepper him with question after question which made it hard for him to finish his lunch. He finally had to tell her to save some of her questions and concerns until tomorrow and he'll answer them ten at a time if he had to. But he did think he made a little progress in calming some of Lorraine's concerns. After an hour and a half, they finished their extended lunch and he thought a trip to the engine room should be their next stop.

As we walked toward the engine room, she asked if she could give her mother a call because she knew that she would be still mourning her and the girls' presumed death. She then puts her hand over her mouth and gave him a surprised look as she stopped about six feet in front of the engine room's door. She probably thinks that you killed me and the girls, then took off out of the country or something. Yes, knowing your mother, you're probably right. She most likely thinks that I would be somewhere in Europe sipping on a gin and lime juice by the pool with some little twenty-something swimsuit model.

She looks up at him intensively. Why in the hell did you have to through some twenty-something swimsuit model into the mix. Because your crazy mother doesn't think I have the guts to off myself after getting rid of you and the girls. No, that's all your imagination and by the way; remember me and the girls, up here, packed away like three frozen T.V. dinners, so please think hard before you call my mother anything close to crazy. Point made, he says as he walks over to the engine room's door and holds it open for her. I need to give her a call so she'll stop mourning us. I understand, but she'll have to mourn you and the girls and curse me for a few more weeks.

She walks through the door, eyeballing him as she passes him. She then focuses her attention on the three units moving about the engine room. The "E" units are hovering about the room checking temperature readings, replacing component parts and consistently communicating amongst themselves as they pass along data about their task. One unit breaks off and maneuvers itself to the platform as Lorraine takes a few steps backward. Good afternoon unit E1, BK says as the unit approaches him and Lorraine. Good afternoon BK and Mrs. BK, it response as it stops a few feet in front of her.

"No E1", this is Lorraine as he gestures toward her. She will be aboard the ship from now on and she's assigned to the Medical Clinic, so you won't be seeing her in engineering very often. Lorraine takes a few steps toward the unit and says, "nice to meet you, E1". It is a pleasure to meet you Lorraine and I hope you enjoy working and living aboard our ship, it responds. The unit reaches out its' three fingered mechanical hand in a gesture of a handshake. She still somewhat afrain of the units, but she uneasily reaches out and shakes its metal hand.

She smiles at it, but unfortunately it has no mouth of other means of smiling back, so it just shakes her hand. It was a pleasure meeting you and I hope you enjoy your new home aboard this ship. She doesn't know what quite to say, so she just says, "OK" as she releases its' hand. The unit turns toward BK and tells him theirs some slight fluctuations in the plasma stream in the number three portside injector unit. "Alright", he says while still looking at the monitor. Lorraine, I need to realign and configure that injector's internal plasma regulator. It will only take a few minutes and you can watch if you like, he says, but he can tell by the expression on her face that she has no interest in regulators, injectors or plasma.

While you're waiting for me, reach into your left pocket and pull out the communication device. What device, as she reaches into her pocket and to her amazement, pulls out a device that looks somewhat like a combination PDA and cell phone. I was going to talk to you about it once we returned to the Clinic, but you can look it over now. Exactly what does it do and why do I need it, as she flips it over in her hand.

I have one, you have one and once the girls are up and running, they'll have one too. So, its' some type of weird looking phone, she says as she shoves it back into her pocket. "No"! Believe me, it's much more than any cell phone. He reaches into her pocket and pulls it out and places it back into her hand. This is the main form of communication and human to system connectivity aboard the ship. It's essential that you and the girls become familiar with all its' functions. But it looks like the cellphone I had at home, she states as she flips and turns the device in her hand. In the past, every time Lorraine would need a new cell phone, she would dred learning new functions and transferring her apps. As far as she was concerned, technology didn't like her, and she had an even deeper dislike for it. As she has it in her hand, BK continues to tell her how it's much easier than a cellphone and would allow her to communicate with the ship's systems, transfer files and transmit instructions to the ship's units. He also explains that it would enable her to remain in constant contact with the medical units. "Why in the hell would I want to talk with them", she replies.

Lorraine looks at the device with a frustrated frown on her face as she starts to swipe and tap on icons on the unit's screen. Its' voice activated, he tells her. So, you just have to ask it a question or say, "contact unit M1", for it to activate. He knows his wife and understands that it doesn't make a difference how simple he designed the device, because she thinks that technology is made to be thrown against the wall or seeing how high she can make it bounce off the floor. He just shakes his head and decides to just leave her alone with it. He thinks at this point that his time will now be better spent completing some of his engineering task. He walks over to his desk and sits down to begin assisting the e-units with the completion of their assignments. She has the device in her hand wondering what to do with it. She gets flash backs of her last new phone she had to learn and doesn't want to have anything to do with this thing, but she knows that she has no choice in the matter. She starts to pace around the room going through the icons on the screen and wondering what questions to ask this stupid thing.

Finally, she holds the device close to her mouth and says, "medical unit 1", and a few seconds later, unit one's mechanical voice emits from the device, asking how it could help her. For a moment, she doesn't know what to say because she hadn't thought that far in advance yet. BK glances over at her and smiles. She stands there with the device in her hand, poised to respond, but not knowing what to ask the unit. She decides to ask it to give her a full report on the inventory of the medical facility's medication cabinet, equipment and her stasis report, just as a test of its' capability. The unit replies, "yes Lorraine" and gives her a time for completion. She pauses for a second then calls for the unit once again, which it responds again with a "yes Lorraine".

She asks it for something she really wants to know. Give me a report on my daughters' vitals. It quickly responds that both LaChel and Kim's vitals are within normal parameters. LaChel's body temperature has elevated by .125 degrees, which is within normal parameters for her current condition. The unit also states that the removal of both LaChel and Kim has not been scheduled at this time. While the unit was talking, it displayed in split screen both of the girls' vital signs of their heart rate, pulse, temperature, and brain activity, which was minimal. As she looks down at her girls' vitals on her device, BK shouts out, "two weeks". What is two weeks, she response. The girls are scheduled to be reanimated in two weeks. "Reanimated", she says out loud. Which should be just enough time for you to get use to this ship and all your new responsibilities, he says as he continues to type on his workstation.

In the future, she says as she looks at him. Please don't use the word reanimated any more. It sounds too much like a word that was used in a Frankenstein movie, she replies. What verb should I use in the place of the word you do not want me to use, he asked politely? She thinks for a moment. How about the verb, "awakened or revived"?

"Awakened", the med-unit replies before BK could respond. I will input that into my medical terminology sub-routine regarding your daughters. I appreciate that, as she looks at BK working on the workstation. Why was there no mention of the girls awakening in the medical log? I wanted to determine by your actions how long it would take you to familiarize yourself with the ship, because I will really need your help once the girls are up and around. "Two weeks", as he holds up to fingers as to say, "that's the amount of time you have". Don't worry. Thanks to you fine tuning my brain, without my permission I might add, I will have this ship workings and my medical responsibilities under control by then. Unfortunately, I can already feel the effects of your handy work in the way I recognize equipment and the ship's spaces that I've never seen before. He looks at her and gives her a smile, as he wonders which type of knowledge is starting to kick in.

So are you having flashes of knowledge about performing operations, or are you remembering medical journals you've never read? "No", she says as she moves towards the railings. But I'm having sparks of knowledge and imagery of various stars constellations and quasars, but I don't have any idea what those are. "Oh", he says with a bit of amazement. She turns toward him and asked what do you mean? "Oh"! Look, sometimes while in stasis, other information can bleed into the stream of data of the person or people stored together, because of the connectivity of the servers.

Are you trying to tell me that I have not only have the equivalent of "The American Journal of Medicine and the medical encyclopedia embedded in my brain, but I also have a ton of Star Trek crap packed in there too, as she walks toward him. "This is great", she shouted and throws up her hands! This is just damn great! Calm down babe, he says as he stands up and walks over to her. I had the same thing happened to me and I'm just fine other than the occasional urge to design the perfect wedding dress, but I just suppress that urge and just keep on going. He laughs and hopes she thinks it's funny too. But she yells that it's not funny or a joke. I thought you said what you did to us was safe.

It's very safe, but sometimes some extraneous data will seep into the main data stream and the target recipient will retain a bit of knowledge that they were not supposed to acquire. So, with that giant head of knowledge, you can't figure out how to stop the infiltration of miscellaneous data. He feels a little hurt by that question, because he feels that she's questioning his ability. But he thinks that he owes her that bit of skepticism, so he suppresses his emotions. Unfortunately, I've haven't had the time to review the schematics of the data transfer matrix or its' programming logic sheets. She looks very frustrated as she worries how this will effect her and her girls. Don't worry Lorraine, the information that is bleeding into the data stream is not dangerous and you will be able to manage it once you learn to control and organize your thoughts. It's bad enough having all this medical knowledge running through my head, but now I have to look forward to having flashes of information about solar masses, navigation arrays, and all that other scientific crap that doesn't make since to me. He wishes that what she just said wasn't true, but she may have technical data worming through her thoughts. Sequestering and managing that data should only take a few weeks for you and the girls. "I hope so", she replies with concern in her voice. Now, please give me a few more minutes to solve this problem and we can continue with our tour of the ship. Lorraine turns and walks toward the railing again as she continues to familiarize herself with her new gadget.

As she maneuvers her way through the various functions and menus of the device, she begins to see its' value. He completes the task of reprogramming the firing sequences for one of the ejectors and continues acclimating her to the ship and its' functions. After a few days of walking throughout the ship, he is amazed at how quickly she has familiarized herself to the ship and she has worked hard to learn how to manage the knowledge that is quickly surfacing in her thoughts. After a week, he thinks it would be good for her to work on her own, but of course he assigns MOM the task of clandestinely assuring that she doesn't take a big bite of more than she can chew. Both Lorraine and BK are so busy, most of the time they work through lunch, but at dinner they talk non-stop about all their individual accomplishments of the day.

She has managed to compartmentalize all the medical information that is continuously erupting from within her brain. He used his experience after his time in stasis to help Lorraine understand what was happening to her and how to apply it. And hopefully he can break through her angry shell so he can share her bed again instead of sleeping in his office and in the media room. He misses the smell of her hair, the taste of her neck and the sweetness of her soft lips on his. He has accomplished two out of the three of his objectives. Their relationship is the best it's going to get, because two weeks have passed, and the time has finally come for BK and Lorraine to awaken their girls from their stasis capsules.

It's 8:00 a.m. and they are in Lorraine's Clinic preparing for the awakening of their girls. He's standing at the control panel across the room monitoring their vital signs. Lorraine is standing between both the girls' stasis capsules operating both consoles at the same time. He begins to operate various buttons on the console and ask MOM to begin to slowly raise the girls' core body temperature. Yes BK, increasing LaChel and Kim's body temperature by five degrees per two minute intervals, MOM respond. BK voice is deep and unusually loud when he tells Lorraine to raise the girls' capsules to a thirty degree angle. He's nervous, but he doesn't want her to know. Even though Lorraine and himself has been revived from stasis, but his girls are younger and smaller.

And although Lorraine and BK has ran countless simulations on how the revival should be perform, He doesn't know how their bodies are going to react to being in stasis for so long. And if something happens to them – well he doesn't want to think about it. "Make sure that you monitor the removal of the stasis gas from their capsules", he says sternly to Lorraine. She looks at him as if she wants to grab him by his throat. "You are not talking to that computer", she yells! I am not a computer MOM exclaims.

"I know, so shut-up you toaster", Lorraine yells as she looks up and around the room! She takes a few steps toward him. "You act like you just met me", she says sternly. Whether we are on the Earth, the Moon or on this damn spaceship, you know how I react to you barking orders at me and you need to remember that I'm in charge. BK just smiles at her and says, "Sorry"! Lorraine looks down at both capsules. He tells Lorraine to just remember the procedures we went over.

She takes a deep breath then exhales. She doubts if she can do this, but just then her facial expression changes from self-doubt to amazement as the knowledge starts to flow as she begins to press the buttons on LaChel's capsule. She really doesn't understand why or how, but begins to automatically press buttons displayed on the top left side of the capsule. The buttons start to flash red, green and blue illuminations as the capsule begins to elevate slow and stop a little above her waist. Somehow, she knows exactly the correct buttons to press.

This feels like a bunch of "deja vue" moments, one after the other. Babe, you may find this hard to believe, but you know more about coma induced stasis procedures than I do or anyone on the planet for that matter. She looks back down at LaChel's capsule and begins to bring it to an incline position. She can see her fingers pressing down on the buttons one at a time, but she equates it to being possessed by a doctor and a computer technician. It will take approximately 15 minutes to safely raise both the girl's core temperatures in order to revive them, she tells BK as she continues tapping on the capsules' keypad. "That's great" he replies. I don't know how I am doing this or if I can remember what to do next, she adds. Trust me babe, he says while looking directly into her bewildered eyes. All the information you need to know is now pushing its' way to the surface of that beautiful mine of yours, he says with a loving smile. She gives him a half smile as she starts scanning the room looking at all the various pieces of equipment that kept her alive and now is keeping her children alive too.

For a moment, all this equipment and blinking lights starts to overwhelm her, but just like drops of water from a faucet; her knowledge of her newly acquired medical skills and the revival procedure starts to collet and flow through her mind. Wave after wave of information starts to wash across her mind. BK is focused on the capsule's life support system to ensure the girl's vital signs remain stable. From out of nowhere, Lorraine asked him if the girl's temperature is above or below 68 degrees. He looks over at the temperature display.

"No". LaChel's temperature is 64 degrees and Kim's is 62 degrees. Lorraine starts to mumble to herself for a moment. Then I think its' time to begin to bring them out of stasis before their temperatures exceeds 68 degrees. Do you understand or have an idea why we should start reviving them seven minutes prematurely, he response curiously? He can just look at her and tell that she hasn't a clue why they should be revived earlier than scheduled. Then she confirms it by telling him that she has no idea, but I just have a strong feeling that is what we have to do. She starts giving instructions as if she was the head surgeon at a busy hospital. BK isn't use to taking orders from Lorraine regarding technical or even medical issues, but he thinks that her medical knowledge may exceed his.

As she starts to bring the girls out of their stasis, she looks over at him with a disapproving look on her face. "What", he says"? What other crap did you shove into my head? He continues to work as he tells her to forget it for now and to focus on the task at hand. That's a discussion for another time, as he smiles at her. "Oh damn"! You are just full of crap and surprises, she shouts. He slowly and wisely turns his back to her without saying another word as he pretends to work on another console. But he can feel her eyes burning a deep hole in the back of his head.

"BK", she says with a low but menacing tone. He slowly turns back toward her, but decides to maintain a safe distance. Don't I have a right to know what you programmed into my brain? He knows that she's not going to just let it go, so he begins to tell her about her condition, but he can see by her expression that she is deep in thought. Her face changes from controlled anger to what I can only describe as a "Oh no you didn't" expression. Her mind is recalling the procedure that he used to implant all this information into her brain. She also realizes that this procedure is most effective while in stasis. During this time, the mind can be embedded with a vast amount of information in a short period of time.

While looking down at her daughters, she also thinks that she is most likely not his only victim of the procedure. "Oh my God", she says out loud as she looks at both girls. BK says the same thing, but only in his mind. He realizes that she's putting the pieces of the puzzle together too quickly. He didn't think the information would jump out at her all at once. She could have a complete meltdown if he can't get her to understand why he had to do the same thing to the girls. Baby, he says to her in a slow but calming voice. I understand all of this information is hard to process and you are very upset right now, but if you let me explain before you react. He smiles at her as he says, "remember you need me to drive this bus".

But Lorraine can't see any humor in what he has done. "I can't believe you"! she yells. BK was about five feet away from her, but he could feel the anger projecting from her eyes like a laser. I tried to explain to you that we don't have the luxury of just myself and MOM having the knowledge to operate this ship. It requires constant maintenance and supervision of its vital systems. Yes, I could allow MOM to monitor and repair her own systems and those of the other units, but I don't feel that is very wise or safe. It will take a crew of knowledgeable and dedicated people to maintain and operate this ship.

"And for good or bad, you guys have to be that crew". She looks back down at the capsules as she just shakes her head in disbelief. Lorraine, I know that this isn't something you asked for, but I'm sorry but I'm going to need your help explaining all of this to our girls. She steps back and looks at him in disbelief. "Oh hell no", she shouts! I'm not going to try to explain anything to them. You're the mastermind behind this twisted family vacation. This isn't like surprising the girls with a cruise to the Bahamas or a shopping trip to New York. I wasn't involved in the planning of this trip and I don't think I should help you explain this to your daughters

He turns toward the large panels adjacent to the capsules and responds, "Don't worry babe", I think you are the best person to explain to your daughters their new reality. But I do understand your anger, so I'll explain everything to them when they are up and mobile. Regardless of how you feel about the situation I've place you and the girls in; I need you to convey a positive attitude for the girl's sake. I didn't say I wasn't going to support you, she says with a groan. I just think you will be able to explain our situation better than I can. She can see that he is doing something that is somewhat familiar to her, but she can't quite understand what he's doing. Hey, what are you doing over there! BK sighs…

It's time for us to begin stimulating their higher brain activities, if you don't have any objections. Lorraine walks over to the panel and moves BK's hand away from the controls. I still don't understand why I know this, but something tells me to start stimulating their lower brain functions first, then we can slowly start working on their higher brain activities. He looks puzzled as he thinks through the procedure in his head. I don't see any detrimental effects or benefit to starting with the lower brain functions or the upper functions. I brought you out of stasis using the same method and it worked perfectly. Yes, I understand that, but have you taken into consideration the girls ages and that their brains aren't as developed as ours.

Being so young, some of their brain pathways may not be fully developed. He stands there for a moment in silence thinking about his process and wondering if she could be right. He didn't take any of those variables into account when he planned on reviving them. It's a possibility that he could have caused one or both of his girls various degrees of medical problems. He starts to work the numbers in his head and comes to the conclusion that it's a probability that she could be right. Lorraine presents additional variables to the equation that he didn't think would be a factor. Babe, do you know why you want to make this change to these procedures? She looks like she's putting the last pieces to a large puzzle together. I just remembered, when I awoke from stasis, I was very dizzy, and my head was throbbing.

Yes, I had those symptoms too, but how is that related to making changes to the girls' awakening procedures. That was a problem that I didn't want the girls to experience. "Man", he yells as he walks around the room. This is amazing. I put myself in stasis in order to get a working knowledge of how you and the girls would feel after coming out of stasis. But I made some adjustments after I study the data I collected from my experience. I feel very confident about the changes I'm asking us to make, she adds.

He has this small smile on his face as he marvels at her medical knowledge finally starting to coalesce. Go on, he replies. Well, I believe by stimulating the lower brain function first; this will give the brain time to adjust to be suddenly active, rather than activating the higher levels, which will consequently jumpstart the lower brain function, automatically. BK tries, but fails to suppress his happiness that he feels swelling up from his soul. Why do you have that stupid smile on your face, she asked curiously? He just turns and walks over to the capsules without saying a word.

"What", she asks! He turns towards his wife to answer her question. Remember when I taught you how to play chess and after two days you began to beat me every game we played. Yes, but only because you were a terrible chess player. "No", that's not the reason! You have a very organized mind and consequently are very organized in everything you do. So, I concluded that anything I programmed into that light bulb shaped head of yours while you were in stasis; you would overshadow my knowledge of that subject. She walks closer to him. So you're finally admitting that I'm smarter than you, as she looks up at him. Now she begins to smile while the smile on his face slowly disappears. That's not exactly what I'm saying.

Yes, your knowledge has surpassed mine in the medical field, but remember two things. One, I built this ship that is now in low orbit around the earth. Two, I put most of that knowledge in your head in the first place, as he touches his finger to her forehead. She knocks his finger away from her then turns to walk back over to her console. OK, I'll give you those two, but I'm already thinking of improvements for this ship, she says in a joking manner. BK looks down at his console and shakes his head. Can we continue to revive the members of our crew, please, he asks? She laughs and begins to proceed with stimulating the girls lower brain functions.

Since this procedure is her idea, he asked her how long do you think this should take? Between five or ten minutes, she replies. I would also like to make sure their body temperature remains below 68 degrees until two and a half minutes into stimulating their higher brain functions. He looks back over at her and curiously ask, "why"! Sorry baby, it's too complicated. I'll have to explain it to you later as she smiles. You got jokes, he replies. I agree MOM response. Lorraine just looks around and sighs. We have 10 to 15 minutes for this procedure, so I think you can tell me what information you've placed in our heads and what was taken out. He walks over to the desk and sits behind it. Lorraine follows him and sits down at the chair in front of the desk. "Well", she says as she crosses her legs! He looks down at his watch then begins to explain to her the capabilities that he has programmed into her brain. You're our Medical and Tactical Specialist. Her mouth drops open in disbelief, but not a sound comes out.

OK, what don't you understand, he asks? What's not to understand, she replies! You mean I kill them and fix them. No, I don't think you'll have to kill anyone, he replies. Do you have any knowledge of our weapons capabilities yet? She puts her hand to her forehead and looks as if she is really trying to recover some stored information. Wait a minute... I think so, she says as she looks directly into his eyes. I now know of at least 25 ways of killing you for doing this to me. He laughs at her joke. At least he thinks it's a joke. I bet you do. You know what, if I was truly smart, I should have removed a big shovel full of that hostility from your personality while you were in stasis. It's too damn late to turn back the clock now, she responds. OK babe, how about just killing me in my sleep tonight so I don't feel any pain. she gives him a devilish smile. That could be possible. Remember, I am the Tactical Officer. "Alright, you're starting to scare me". Let's get back to the task at hand, because we only have roughly 12-16 minutes. She has more questions she needs answers for while they still have time to kill. What about the girls, what did you program into their heads. He pauses before answering. Well, I enhanced Kim's natural engineering capability and entered a vast knowledge of astronomy.

Oh my god, she's going to love you for that. Hey, I had very little choice and even less time to decide who gets what knowledge placed in their heads. Ok, ok... How about LaChel? What kind of "ENHANCEMENTS" did you plug into her brain, she asked with air quotes. He gives her a slight grin. You think you and Kim have it bad. LaChel has knowledge of Quantum Physics, Planetary Geology and Advance Mechanical Engineering. You're kidding, right!, she response as she sat forward in her chair. Both of the girls were about a "B" and "C" students at best and you've dumped advanced science and mathematics in their heads.

"Oh my God", she is going to be so pissed with you. He can't believe that she's complaining about what's fair about the responsibilities of managing this ship's systems. So he decides to give her a chance to make a decision concerning her and the girls. I've been working on a method of further incorporating additional knowledge to an individual by inducing the knowledge while they sleep, which will enable that person to take on more responsibilities. He looks directly at her without blinking. "You're talking about shoving more information into my head while I'm sleeping", she says with a look of disbelief. He just grins and nods his head "yes". "Absolutely not"! I have enough nonsense consuming my thoughts, which I don't understand completely. "Better them than me", she says as she crosses her arms and legs. He was bluffing, because be didn't know if it was possible to transfer or add additional information into her or the girls' minds while out of stasis.

Winning that discussion, he emphasizes that he just needs her to back him up, even though he knows she still wants to punch him in the face. She stares at him without denying that statement. The girls are going to have a ton of things to adapt too. I took them away from their schools, their friends and family. Not to mention, they will not be able to visit the mall for awhile. And don't forget those tiny rooms they'll be living in for the next unnkown number of months, she adds. Those are th reasons they don't need us at each other's throats. OK, I agree! I'll put on a good front, but you just remember that I am not in the least bit sold on our current circumstances. You think I'm mad? Wait until all that science crap start streaming through their brains. They are going to freak out.

"Especially your oldest!" BK looks at his watch. Five more minutes before starting the next stage, he says softly. "MOM", once we get to the one-minute mark, please start the audio countdown. Yes, BK, MOM responds. He has something personal to ask her so, he walks over to her with his chair in hand and sits down at the table beside her. Hey babe. How about after the girls are resting for the night; we have a romantic dinner in the observation room, then go to the media room to watch any movie you want. She just looks at his misguided smiling face for a moment. By the expression on her face, he can see that she's not buying what he's trying to sell. The dinner sounds good, but I don't think the movies a good idea. Come on babe, he says in his lowest Barry White voice as he reaches for her hand.

I've been floating around up here for months thinking about you and looking at your frozen but beautiful silhouette almost every day. I really have missed us and would like to spend some time with my wife. He had an idea to give her a kiss on her lips but thought it would be best just to lean over and give her a passionate kiss to the forehead. She looks up at him smiling down at her. "You know that's not going to work". What are you talking about, he says with all of the false surprise he can muster in his voice? I just want to be with my baby tonight as he leans over once again, but this time he gives her kiss on those lips he's been longing for.

He holds the kiss for as long as she lets him. She stops him after a few seconds, by pushing him back with her free hand. "OK". I'll eat dinner and watch a movie with you, but there will be none of what just happen. I'm still trying to process what you've done and especially the lies. Deep inside his head a second primal voice yells out, "You must be out of your damn mind"! Do you know how long I've been waiting for you to come out of that capsule? "What I've done is for the entire world and you're worried about a few lies"! But luckily, she couldn't hear that frustrated part of him or see it in his eyes.

The most sensible portion of his brain beats that primal portion of his brain into submission. BK just looks at his wife with his loving and understanding eyes and says, "hey sweets", I understand, and I just want to be near you anyway I can, and anyway you want. Then he gets close to her and gives her another kiss on the forehead. "He just lied to her again". His plan was to be more than just close to her, but he understands that's not going to happen anytime soon.

Getting back on her good side will take some time and a whole lot of pain and suffering on his part. He thinks that bringing the girls out of their stasis without any real problems will be a step in the right direction. He gets up from his chair and moves back over to his console. While Lorraine is looking at the girl's vitals, he types a message to Chef to get the wine out of the media room and put it back into the kitchen's refrigerator. Chef replies by texting, "yes sir". He just will have to wait a little longer before they can enjoy her favorite wine. He looks down at the console and announces that there is four more minutes remaining. Lorraine can't wait to have her daughters out of their individual deep freezers. He points to the capsules and asked her to connect the corresponding hose connections to each of the capsules, please.

She looks around the back and sides of the capsules, but she doesn't see anything but three holes that are covered with some sort of color coded plastic caps. "No babe"! The connectors are in the wall behind the capsules. Just pull them out and connect them to the corresponding colors on the back of the capsules. Just then, like someone flicking a light switch, she knows exactly what he's talking about. She pulls the three hoses from the wall and removes the color caps from the capsule; then connects the corresponding hoes connections. She does the same to LaChel's capsule, then begins to program both of them.

Ah Babe, BK says somewhat nervously. Now I'm not saying you don't know what you're doing, but do you have any idea what you're doing. I have never done this before, but I recognize every switch and button on this capsule. And I know that these numbers are correct, and we have roughly three more minutes to begin the awakening sequence. Exactly three minutes and twenty seconds, MOM responds. "Alright, what ever your name is"! Just release the three chemical agents into the capsules. I have already programmed the proper amounts into the environmental systems.

Hold on babe, BK shouts. I need to check the input data to ensure that you've programmed the correct amount of chemicals or the girls may sustain damage to their nervous systems. She moves to the side and gestures to him to be her guest. He walks over to her console and displays the information Lorraine entered and double checks the chemical mixture ratio. He then steps back, then ask MOM to triple check their procedures and input data.

MOM complies and takes less than ten seconds to respond with her analysis. Counting for the girls weight, age, time in stasis, and chemical absorption rate; I concur with Lorraine's original data input string. He was about to apologize, but Lorraine abruptly cuts him off. Don't worry about it, I do understand that you still need to check after me. And our girls' lives are worth a little micro-management, she says while turning back to her console. Thank you, he says with a smile on his face. MOM, please begin the revival procedure. Revival started, MOM replies. Lorraine looks at both capsules and can see a purplish mist slowly beginning to fill the capsules and envelop the girls' bodies.

Like a puzzle finally coming together, Lorraine begins to understand what's happening to her girls. After ten minutes of them working on the girls, MOM declares that phase one of the awakening is complete. The information in Lorraine's brain is flowing as if she's reading the information straight from a medical journal. All the holes in her medical skills and procedures knowledge has been solidly filled in and now she's truly the medical expert aboard the ship.

Chapter Six

The reunion of the Thomas family

June 29, 2023 – The United Nation has a specialized agency that's tasked with defeating hunger around the world. The name of this department is the Food and Agriculture Organization (FAO) reporter a significant reduction (e.g., 35 percent) in the amount of food they can distribute to hard hit countries of famine.

As BK and Lorraine continue the process of reviving their daughters, Lorraine's confidence in her medical knowledge increases and her willingness to allow her units to assist her decreases. BK is monitoring everything that she's doing and only hopes in the future that she lets the medical units do their jobs. He doesn't know if it's because she's nervous or maybe thinks no one can do the job as well as she can, but she continuously interrupts and interferes with the units while they are trying to perform their duties.

He finally has to step in and remind her that the units know what their doing and she should step back and allow them to do their jobs. While he tries to convince her that the units are capable of removing the girls without their help, units one and three moves into position to physically remove

LaChel from her capsule first. Lorraine nervously monitors the units positioning themselves on either side of LaChel's now open capsule. She's half listening to hem and tries to break off the conversation and move toward the units, but he quickly reaches out and grabs her arm and pulls her back. "Please babe", this is a two unit and no human operation. "No", she says sternly as she tries to pull away from him. These are my babies and I need to make sure these units are going to do everything they are programmed to do. She turns toward the units as they are lifting LaChel from the capsule and coordinating their movements to get her to the second medical bed. You shouldn't worry about their ability to manage the girls' removal from their capsules, because I programmed them, and this isn't their first rodeo.

He then pulls her back to give the units a clear path to the bed. Unit two has pull back the sheets and blanket prior to LaChel's being placed in it. She just stares with a look of shock at her daughter's limp body dressed in her stasis suit, while the units carry her pass her. She has never seen LaChel in this condition, which sends shivers through her body. The plastic like mask that is covering her face is still a little obscured with light frost and condensation, but she still looks beautiful to her mom and dad. The units hover with LaChel in their mechanical arms at the foot of the bed and slowly moves upward toward the pillow. BK and Lorraine slowly walk to the foot of the bed and watch the units gently lower her onto the bed and position her head on the pillow.

After they have completed placing her on the bed, units one and three hovers toward Kim's capsule that is now beginning to open. Unit two grabs some scissors off a near by table to remove LaChel's stasis suit, but Lorraine instructs the unit to only remove the mask and the suit's hood. She threatens the unit that she will reprogram it to serve as a garbage unit if it cuts any of her daughter's hair. The unit stares at Lorraine with its' blue round eyes trying to compute what she just said, but it doesn't make sense to it.

MOM transmits instructions for the unit to proceed, whichit immediately complies. She watches intensely, as unit two uses a tool to remove the protective mask and begins to carefully cut away the hood from the suit. BK thinks it's only a matter of time before she stops the unit and takes over the removal of the stasis suit's hood. He knows very well how controlling she can be as specially when it comes to her girls, but he calculated that her anal-retentive attributes would enable her to be an excellent physician. But for now, she's a pain in his and if the units had one, ass.

Surprisingly, she allows the unit to finish cutting away the hood of the suit, then the unit reaches into an opening where it's stomach would be and pulls out two flat metal strips with indicator lights on it and placed one on LaChels forehead and the other over her heart.

The opening in the unit's abdomen slides close as the unit hovers over to the computer console and begins to activate and program the brain and heart stimulation devices. BK is now watching the two units preparing to remove Kim from her capsule while Lorraine quickly follows unit two over to the computer console and stands side-by-side watching the unit's code input. Unit two asked MOM to confirm its' input codes and stimulation numbers prior to activating the devices. MOM takes less than ten seconds to confirm the unit's calculations and instructs it to proceed.

Lorraine's brain may have been enhanced, but she still can't calculate as fast as MOM or even the medical units, so she tells the unit to wait a moment while she does the math. MOM would normally defend her position, but she recognizes that Lorraine just needs a little more time to confirm the unit's numbers. While the units gently remove Kim from her capsule, BK rushes over to the other bed and pulls back the sheets and cover. He then steps back out of the way while the units hover toward the bed with Kim in their arms. Lorraine finally confirms the numbers and gives the unit permission to activate LaChel's stimulation devices.

Units one and three place Kim in her bed then move back to their standby positions on the other side of the room. Unit two transmits the activation signal to the devices then hovers toward Kim's bed to remove her stasis hood, but Lorraine stops the unit and ask it to hand her the scissors. BK knows that it would be a mistake to try to stop her from removing Kim's mask and hood, so he just walks over to LaChel's bed and looks down at her while gently stroking her hair. Lorraine has her back to LaChel's bed while removing Kim's mask, but she asked BK how LaChel is doing. Everything is proceeding normally so far, but she still has about five minutes before she shows any signs of being revived, he replies while still stroking her hair. The device on her forehead has been designed to activate the lower and higher functions of the brain, while continuously scanning the brain for any abnormalities. The device on her chest produces electrical signals to the heart, which activates the heart, and will pump oxygenated blood throughout her vital organs. MOM monitors and records the data from both devices in order to analyze the revival process and to ensure that there was no damage done while the girls were in stasis. MOM has completed LaChel's post revival examination and can find no signs of any damage to her brain or her body. She now focuses her full attention on Kim's scans and vitals.

Lorraine removes the hood of Kim's suit and begins to smile at her still pale daughter, while entangling her fingers through Kim's hair. Tears start to roll down her face as the warm feeling of happiness fills her body as she leans over and gives Kim a long salty kiss on her pale cheek. Parents aren't suppose to have a favorite, but just like most parents; it's usually the youngest. She holds her kiss on her daughter's cheek as if she was stuck to a frozen metal pole in the dead of winter.

Unit two hovers behind Lorraine and in a mechanical voice softly tells her that it's time for the stimulation devices to be applied to Kim's forehead and chest. She gives her youngest a last kiss to her forehead then asked the unit to give her the first stimulation device, while extending her hand to the unit. Without hesitation, the unit's storage container slides open and it reaches in, pulls out the device and hands it to her. She places the device on the center of Kim's forehead then asked the unit for the second one. Unit two's storage opening is already closed, and it has the second device extended in its' mechanical hand. She grabs it and places it on Kim's sternum then instructs the unit to begin activating the devices. The lights across the unit's head starts to illuminate brightly and strobes, which indicates that it's connecting to the devices and inputting the proper activation data. Just then, MOM abruptly instructs the unit to halt the activation of the devices attached to Kim's body. The unit's communication to the devices immediately stops as all the unit's lights on its' forehead starts to blink slowly and in unison. "What's wrong", Lorraine yells at the top of her voice! "I performed all the necessary calculations for Kim's body chemistry and size", she exclaims. There's no reason for any delays, she adds. "Wait a minute, babe", BK says as he walks over to her and puts his hand on her shoulder. MOM, why did you stop the stimulation process?

I have completed my scans of Kim's body and discovered that she has an "Atrial Septal Defect". BK has a limited medical understanding and doesn't know what the hell MOM is talking about and is about to ask her to speak

English, but Lorraine knows exactly what she's talking about. She somberly looks over at her husband and tells him that their little girl has a hole in her heart. Both just stand there looking at each other for a moment not knowing what to say. Lorraine is the first to break the silence. Do you know the extent of her condition, she asked MOM in a shaky tone? MOM tells them that Kim's condition is not dire at the moment, but she thought it would be prudent to discuss her condition prior to reviving her. Lorraine agrees with MOM halting Kim's revival until they do an Electrocardiogram of her heart. He maybe the smartest person on the planet, but he doesn't have the medical knowledge that his wife and MOM possess, which is by design. It would be impossible for him to operate or fix everything that happens aboard his ship, so he had to distribute the responsibilities.

Lorraine walks around to her desk and falls down into her chair with a look of despair on her face. She knows that a hole in Kim's heart is a condition that has to be repaired and it would be best to fix it before she is up and about. But the problem is that the closest she has come to performing an operation was when she was in tenth grade and had to dissect a baby pig for her Biology class, which she received a "C" minus because she through-up on the baby pig and some nearby classmates. After that embarrassing episode she was known as Dr. Hurl until her twelfth grade year.

Now she may have to open up the chest of her little girl and stitch up the hole in her heart. BK on the other hand is thinking of the units preforming the operation, because he knows his wife is knowledgeable enough to do it, but mentally not prepared to place a scalpel to her daughter's chest and slice her open. Lorraine thoughts of anger and resentment against BK once again starts to bubble to the surface.

Her know it all husband that really knows it all now has put her in this position and now needs her to perform an operation on her little girl. She knows that she should suppress these thoughts that will not help solve the problem of her daughters' malfunctioning heart. He can see and feel his wife's anguish as she contemplates how to help her daughter. She hadn't attended medical school or had a residency at any hospital, but now she is responsible and expected to repair of her daughter's heart. She's feeling the full weight of that responsibility on her entire body. He walks over to her and grabs her hand as she looks up at him. Her first thought is to pull away and let loose with a tirade of profanity, but she can see the love and concern for his little girl in his eyes. I know it's difficult to see them like this, but we need to concentrate on our daughter's condition, he says in a very calm and soft tone. You have the knowledge to help Kim, but if you don't suppress your emotions; you won't be able to access those skills. Lorraine can't say anything at the moment. She can only look back at Kim lying there helpless as she takes a deep breath, then ask unit M1 for Kim's current heart rate and blood pressure.

The unit replies by telling her that Kim's heart rate is 53 bpm and her blood pressure is 71 mm and dropping. BK and Lorraine have to make a decision soon, because a person coming out of stasis must go through the complete timed process or risk various types of medical problems. That's why BK decides not to wait for Lorraine to take control of their daughter's situation. Their daughter's life is hanging in the balance. "M3", I need you to prepare Kim's stasis capsule for her re-installation.

Once she's placed back in stasis, we will wait another three days before attempting to awaken her again, he says as he looks down at Lorraine then walks over to Kim's stasis capsule to get it ready for Kim's reinstallation. But next time we'll be ready to do whatever we need to repair her heart. Just then Lorraine remembers reading about one of BK's medical ideas while she was on the couch a couple of weeks ago. She tells him that putting her back in stasis will be too risky. He curiously looks over at her. How did you come to that conclusion, he asked? Once we come out of stasis our bodies are extremely weakened and would only sustain more strain on our muscles and organs when re-inserted back to the stasis capsule. BK didn't remember the amount of stress his body when through and the time it took for it to recover. He couldn't be sure that she was wrong, but he does know that she has substantially more medical knowledge programmed into her brain than he has. Lorraine then asked M1 to assist her in putting Kim in an artificial coma, which should slow down her heart rate and will allow Lorraine to apply the treatment she has in mind.

Weeks ago, while she was recovering and adjusting to her life onboard the ship, Lorraine was passing the time reading medical journals and reviewing BK's reports on the design and developing of nanos. She's now going to use that knowledge to repair her daughter's flawed heart without the horrific experience of her having to open her chest. BK asked M2 if it could estimate how long it will take a trained surgeon to repair the damaged area of Kim's heart if she was on earth? It will take me no more than three minutes to research the procedure in order to give you an accurate answer, M2 replies. Lorraine walks over to the medical storage cabinet to start gathering the items and instruments she's going to need. She pulls down the items onto the counter then stops and hesitates for a moment. She turns to him and asked him where's the Atomic Force Microscope? He gives her a slight smile, because by her remembering the equipment she's going to need for the nanos indicates to him that she's in full command of her medical knowledge. Everything you need to program them are in your lab. "My lab", she repeats with a surprise look on her face. "Yes". I was using your medical lab to develop the nanos, but now that you are the ship's physician; it's all yours now. And it's through that door, as he points to a door on the other side of the room. Lorraine smiles at him. Lorraine plans to use the neon-suppressant device to place Kim in a coma, and then inject her with a chemical that will reduce her heart rate even more.

BK's normal reaction would be to jump in and help his wife, but he thinks it would be best to let her handle this on her own. This unfortunate type of emergency should enable the knowledge that she has stored in her brain to be forced to the surface. Just then, Lorraine hears LaChel starting to cough and begins to move around in her bed. Lorraine's eyes and attention shifts then turns to rush to LaChel's bedside, but BK stops her. "Don't worry babe, I got her", you just keep working on Kim, he says as he turns and quickly walks over to LaChel. He knows that she's worried about LaChel too, and it may be a distraction to her. He moves around to the other side of LaChel's bed so she can see her while she's working on Kim.

As LaChel continues to cough, she starts to moan loudly. "Hey little girl", he says softly as he strokes her forehead and smiles down at her. Your mom and I are right here, he says in a calm and loving voice. Lorraine is now sitting in front of her computer typing computer code that will instruct the nanos on how to repair her daughter's heart. She's amazed by how much she knows about writing code and the intricacies of the human heart. BK grabs LaChel's hand in his, while continuously stroking her forehead with his other hand. It's OK, open your eyes.

Her eyes start to flutter as she continues to breathe moan and cough. She can hear what sounds like her dad's voice, so she struggles to open her eyes. But her vision is blurred, so she can only recognize her dad's voice. But after she clears her throat a couple of times, he leans down closer to her and can hear her say "my throat…my throat hurts so bad", dad. Give me a second, I'll get you something to help your throat, as he lets go of her hand and dashes over to the refrigerator to get the special drink that he gave Lorraine. LaChel looks over to her left and can see the dark and fuzzy features of her mother. They make eye contact and Lorraine gives LaChel a loving smile, but LaChel can only make out the form of her mother's face and body. "Hey baby", Lorraine says as she smiles and continues to type on the keyboard in front of her. From the keyboard, Lorraine instructs M1 to apply the neuro suppressive device to Kim's forehead and to program it for five hours.

LaChel tells her mom that she feels really strange. She once again clears her throat then in a raspy voice asked her mom what happen to her as BK returns to her bedside and gestures to her not to tell her yet. Lorraine slightly nods her head in agreement. You're just a little sick Tank, but your mom and I will nurse you back to help in no time. "Tank" is the nick name that her mother gave her when she was a toddler. He lifts LaChel's head from the pillow and puts the straw that sticking out from the bottle to her lips. She starts to drink the solution and complains that it taste like Gatorade or a bad energy drink. This will help your throat, but try not too drink it to fast. She grimaces as she takes a few more sips then pushes it away.

Unit M1 announced to Lorraine that Kim has been successfully place into a coma and has connected the neuro-suppression device to the Medical Clinic's computer, which will continuously regulate and monitor her condition. Lorraine wants to be by LaChel's bedside to kiss and console her confused daughter, but she has to go into the medical lab and modify BK's nanos, so they will have the ability to repair Kim's heart. "I'll be back", she announces to BK as she walks to the lab. He smiles and nods his head in acknowledgement. After about half an hour, Lorraine walks out of her lab with a syringe with modified nanos immersed in a fluid of medical grade mineral oil.

She walks to Kim's bed then injects the nanos into a vein in Kim's left arm. As she injects the fluid from the syringe into her daughter's vein, she can feel the warmth of Kim's skin in her hand while the last of the nanos travel through the needle. She looks at Kim's face and sees that her color is coming back and her lips are a rosy color of pink. She removes the needle from LaChel's arm and just stands there staring at her beautiful daughter for almost a minute, then places the palm of her hand against Kim's cheek. She stares at

Kim then glances over at BK using a laser infrared thermometer to check LaChel's temperature. She for once looks at her husband in a loving way as he takes care of their daughter. She can see that LaChel is talking to her father with a lot more ease and looks as if she's in less pain than previously. She's glad that LaChel is having an easier time recovering from stasis than her sister, but she notices that LaChel continuously keeps rubbing her eyes. She moves around to Kim's bed and stands between both girls' and stares at LaChel's face. She asked BK did he notice that LaChel's eyes were a little blood shot. He moves closer to her and looks harder at his daughter. He didn't notice before, but he can now see the redness in her eyes and that her eyes lids are a little swollen with some white discharge in one of them. LaChel tries to rub them again, but BK quickly pulls her hand away from her eyes. My eyes feel itchy and the light is hurting them, Dad. "What's wrong with them", she asks while continuing to blink sporadically?

He tells her that her eyes have been closed for a while, so it will take a little bit longer for them to return to normal. Tears begin to roll down her face as he continues to assure her that her eyes will be fine. "Can I have some more to drink dad, please", as she reaches for the bottle on the counter next to him. As he reaches over to the table to get the container, LaChel lifts up onto her elbows and looks to her left. She squints her eyes and now can make out her sister lying on the bed next to her with strange metal strips attached to her forehead. What's that thing on Kim's head, dad, she ask?

Don't worry about your sister, he says in a calming voice. Your mother is taking very good care of her as he puts his hand on her shoulder to try to lay her back down on her pillow, but just then M1 hovers from behind Lorraine to input information into the wall console behind Kim's bed. LaChel lurches back and lets out a piercing scream. BK turns and sees the unit hovering beside Kim's bed. "What's that", she yells and points at M1 with a shaking hand. He drops the drink container onto the bed and moves around between both beds to block her view. Lorraine pushes M1 behind her and instructs it to input the data using the computer at her desk. M1 hesitates for a second probably because it's not use to hovering behind a desk and using Lorraine's computer.

"Yes", Mrs. Thomas, the unit replies as it hovers over to the other side of the room and toward Lorraine's desk. She also sternly instructs units two and three to please remain where they are until she tell them otherwise without an audible acknowledgement, Lorraine adds. LaChel couldn't see exactly what the unit looked like, but the little that she saw scared her half to death. She leans back toward her dad and tries to see around him. She grabs her throat, which feels worse because of the screaming. MOM then decides the truth is the best answer for LaChel's question, so she chimes in. That was not a thing, but one of three medical units designed to assist your mother in her medical task. God damn it, would you just shut-up and let us handle this, Lorraine yells.

Now LaChel is really confused, as she looks left and right at the ceiling. Grand Ma, she shouts as BK finally presses her back down onto her pillow. "No", that's not your grand mother, he tells her while holding her by the shoulders. And MOM I would appreciate it if you wouldn't talk to LaChel until Lorraine or I instruct you to, please. MOM doesn't respond. "Dad", LaChel says with a confused tone. You just called whatever the voice was, "mom". He starts to stroke LaChel's hair as he looks into the face of his totally confused daughter.

This place looks like a hospital room or a clinic, but I haven't seen a doctor or nurse, she says while looking around the room. He looks down at her legs that are beginning to slightly shake. He sees that as a sign of her compounding stress and consequential deteriorating metal state. I know you're not feeling well and you're very confused about what is going on, but we will explain everything to you once you've recovered enough to listen to us. But for now, I need you to concentrate on getting your body and mind back in focus. LaChel softly replies with a yes to her father's request, but he can see in her eyes that she's very confused.

He's afraid she may possibly have a mini nervous breakdown or something, so he looks back at Lorraine who has switched her attention from LaChel, back to a tablet on the edge of her desk with Kim's vital signs displayed. He then reaches into his pocket and pulls out a small spray bottle that he cups in his right hand. He bends over to LaChel and gives her a gentle kiss on her forehead. Close your pretty eyes for second little girl and take a couple of deep breaths. This will help calm your nerves, he says in a convincing tone. LaChel doesn't know what he's talking about, but she is so rattled by what she seen. Lorraine then focuses her attention back to what BK is doing just in time to see him spray some of the sleep agent into LaChel's face.

LaChel takes a short gasp of air as her head flops to the right. Within seconds, She's out cold. "No", Lorraine shouts as she dashes around Kim's bed and pushes BK away from LaChel. "What's wrong", he yells as he stumbles back. She grabs LaChel's face and moves her head from side to side, checking her. BK puts the plastic bottle back in his pocket, then moves in behind Lorraine and pulls her away from LaChel by her arms. "Let me go, Damn it", she shouts. If you get too close to her face I'm going to have to carry you back to our quarters. "I said let me go damn it", as she flails her arms to get out of his grip. She then turns and gets right in his face. I don't want you to ever do that to us again. "I had to babe", he replies in his defense.

She was not calming down and I was afraid she was going to have some type of mental breakdown. Lorraine is five foot four and BK is six foot four, but she gets as much into his face as she possibly can, which is her face to his chest. "It doesn't matter what you think", she says as she pokes her finger into his chest. You had the bright idea to make me the ship's physician aboard this ship, damn it. Remember you made me this way by cramming all this medical crap in my brain. He can see where this is going and is trying to think of something to say to counter her argument, but she's absolutely right. So he just nods his head, "yes". You are the doctor aboard the ship and I should have consulted with you before I administer the sedative to LaChel. "No", she shouts. You will not administer any sedatives, medication treatments or even a chewable aspirin unless I tell you too and believe me, I won't. She holds out her right hand and gestures for him to give up the plastic bottle. He really doesn't want to give it up, because to be honest; he feels like using it right now. But he has to support her if he wants all of this to work. He reaches into his pocket and reluctantly hands it over. She can't believe that he used this chemical on his daughter again. She stares at him for a moment with anger and disappointment in her eyes then walks toward the medical locker. She stops and without turning around, ask him if this is the only bottle.

"Yes". I only produced enough to sedate you and the girls. Promise me that you will not sedate me or the girls again, she says loudly as she continues toward the medicine cabinet. He sighs then promises her that it's his only bottle and that he won't produce any more. She walks to the medication cabinet to lock the bottle away. She's pissed that he decided once again to do something extreme without consulting her. She thinks it would be best if he'd just get the hell out of her Clinic.

She places the bottle in the back of the cabinet then takes a tube of medicine for LaChel's eyes from the cabinet. She then turns to tell him to leave when she sees him walking over, grab a nearby chair and sits between his daughters. He grabs Kim's hand with his left hand and LaChel's hand with his right. She looks over at him sitting there between his daughters and holding their hands, which melts her anger away. She will probably never understand why he just couldn't talk with her about what he was going through, but she knows in her heart that he loves them.

She walks over and stands behind him as she puts her hands on his shoulders. I know you think this is so irresponsible, he says in a soft voice, but I have given this two years of careful thought. This was the only way I could think of to keep our family safe and in one piece. She firmly squeezes his shoulders. For a few seconds, he doesn't know if her hands are going to migrate to his neck. I'm beginning to understand the enormous size and scope of your gift to the world, but nevertheless I think you're going to have a very hard sell to the girls on why it was necessary for you to pull them away from their lives on earth. I have no doubt that the girls are going to be highly upset about what I've done to them. And that's why I really need us to present a united front, so the girls will understand that this was the only alternative. "Oh no space boy", she says as she pats him on the back and walks back to her desk. I will back you by supporting your decision on bringing us with you, but this is all on you and you'll have to ride that roller coaster of death on your own. Oh well, he thinks to himself. My girls love me and they will understand why I had to bring them with me.

Lorraine walks over to a near by table and collects a few items she'll need to treat LaChel's eyes. I didn't think that being in stasis would do any harm to the girls physically, he says as he gets up from the chair and puts each of the girls' arms to their sides. The stasis process didn't directly cause LaChel's eye infection, Lorraine states. So, what did, he ask curiously? She probably had eyes shadow and mascara on and didn't remove all of it before she went to bed the night you took us. Then you put her into stasis, which in combination caused her eye infections, she says confidently.

He couldn't imagine his little girl wearing makeup. "LaChel doesn't wear makeup", he exclaims. She just smiles at him and shakes her head at his ignorance of the behavior of a sixteen year old girl. She walks over to LaChel's bedside with a medical tray with two cotton swabs, a bottle of disinfectant and the medication from the cabinet. Lorraine cleans both of LaChel's eyes before applying the medication. Most teenage girls know how to apply makeup, but few know how to remove it completely. After she finished completing LaChel's treatment, she walks back over to her desk to monitor the nanos. The nanos are continuously transmitting their progress and a status on Kim's heart. He once again sits between his girls looking like a little kid who has just been told that Santa Claus has been arrested for shooting and eating the Easter Bunny. She places the tray on her desk and looks back at her ignorant husband. She could deliver a death blow by telling him that LaChel is no longer a virgin, but she does love him and will keep that bullet in the chamber for another time. He sits in silence for a few more minutes, then ask MOM to update his schedule for the remainder of the day. Yes BK, she replies.

There's a few moments of silence, then MOM replies again. I moved two of your simplest tasks to first thing in the morning and adjusted your remaining tasking for after lunch tomorrow. Thank you, but I'd like you to clear my schedule for tomorrow and divide my projects amongst the remaining days of the week. I will be spending tomorrow with my family and I don't want to be rushed or disturbed unless it's an emergency. It's been three hours now and Lorraine is monitoring both Kim and LaChel when she notices that LaChel is beginning to regain consciousness. He has his arms crossed and his head leaned over into his chest as if he was taking a quick nap. But he quickly straightens up in his chair and looks over at her after he hears a slight moan. Lorraine instructs unit one on what it has to do, then rushes over to LaChel's bedside. Lorraine and BK are standing side by side this time, ensuring that they are blocking LaChel's view of her sister. As LaChel struggles to regain consciousness, Lorraine suddenly grabs BK's jumper sleeve and yanks him to the other side of her in order for her to be the first person she sees. "Wow", he says as he moves closer to his wife. He stands beside her and stares at her as if he's waiting for some type of an apology, which of course, never comes. Lorraine continues to look down with concern at her oldest daughter as she struggles to open her eyes. LaChel head starts to move from side to side as her eyes flutters and she turns toward them. Her eyes are much clearer now, because as soon as she opens them, she sees her mom and dad with big smiles on their faces.

Lorraine strokes LaChel's hair then puts her hand on her cheek. "How do you feel Tank"? LaChel clears her throat before she answers. I was having such a crazy dream about Kim being in some sort of hospital and you and dad were there with us. Lorraine grabs her mother's hand that is on her cheek. But I'm feeling much better now, mom. Lorraine and BK are still blocking her from seeing her sister as he waits for an opportunity to tell her about Kim and what has happened. He opens his mouth to begin the conversation when Lorraine looks at him and gestures to wait for a minute. LaChel wipes the drug induced sleep from her eyes and gives her body a good long stretch.

Oh, my muscles feel so stiff and sore like I've been in bed all day long. "How does your head feel sweetie", Lorraine ask? I guess if feels OK, but why are you guys hovering over me and what am I doing in these clothes like I'm a patient or something.

Well you sort of are a patient, BK replies. "What", she replies again as she looks around to the right of her bed. Other than the soreness and stiffness, do you feel strange things going on with your body? LaChel eyes switches back and forth from her mom and dad. She doesn't answer you're her mother's question, but just asked why am I in the hospital? "Am I dying", she asked with a trembling tone in her voice? "No baby, you're not dying, BK quickly responds. Neither BK nor Lorraine knows how to gently tell her about her situation. LaChel can tell by the look on her parents' face that something is wrong and that it must be something big. And besides, both of them are at her bedside looking like a priest is on the way to give her last rights or something. If mom starts to cry, I'm going to lose it, she thinks to herself. Lorraine can see that he is stalling, and she think she should help him by giving him a sharp slap to the back of his balded head, but she decides to just help him kickstart the conversation.

Listen Tank, there's something very important that you need to know. Lorraine gets closer to the bed and gives LaChel a loving smile and places her hand on her shoulder. This doesn't ease LaChel's nerves as she braces for what's about to come out of her mom's mouth. So I need you to listen to your dad, as both of them now looks at BK. He looks over at Lorraine as she smiles at him. Well, he says as he grabs his daughter's hand. First of all, you are not injured, and your sister is just resting now, but she will be up and talking in about 8 to 12 hours. "Twelve hours", LaChel shouts! How can anyone sleep for that long? What's wrong with her and why hasn't a doctor or nurse come in to look at her? Just hold on little girl and I will explain all of this to you so please just listen for now. He moves her legs over so he can sit down on the bed. She pulls her legs up to her chest, because she's feeling more afraid, because of the look on her Dad's face. "Dad, please", just tell me why I'm in this bed and in this hospital room, she asked with a slightly confused and trembling voice.

Alright, the truth is that you, me, your sister and mother are no longer on earth and are now aboard a spacecraft that I built. LaChel looked at her dad as if she couldn't belief or understand what he just said, but she looks at her mom as if to ask, "what's wrong with him". But her mom just nods her head as if to confirm what he just said.

She looks at both of them in stunned silence for a few seconds, then starts to just give them a nervous laugh. That doesn't make any sense, she exclaims. She still thinks that there's something her parents aren't telling her and that's why they're not telling her the real reason that they are in this hospital. "It's not impossible, little girl", BK replies. You being here aboard this ship is proof enough. But Dad, I don't believe anything you're telling me, she says as she wraps her arms around her folded legs. Lorraine and BK look at each other and they know the only way she'll believe them is to prove it to her.

BK gestures for Lorraine to call one of her medical units over to talk to LaChel and hopefully that will convince her that he's telling the truth. She really doesn't want to scare the crap out of her daughter, but she agrees that this is the only way. She calls for M2 to hover over to LaChel's bed side. The unit quickly hovers into position to the right side of Lorraine and introduces itself by asking how she's feeling. LaChel looks wide eyed and stunned at the sight of M2, which causes her to press herself against the headboard of the bed. BK puts his hand on her knee and tells her that everything is OK. "What the hell is that thing", Mom and Dad, LaChel says without thinking? Hey! Watch the language, Lorraine shouts. This is one of your mother's electronic medical assistants. "Medical assistant", LaChel shouts! Mom isn't a doctor, so why does she need a medical assistant? Lorraine jumps in. "Look", everything your dad is trying to tell you is true. We are on a spacecraft that your father built and you are not in a hospital. But Mom, as far as I know you are not a doctor and dad you don't have the smarts to build a robot, let alone a spacecraft. Where's Kim, LaChel ask? We are getting to that, BK responds. He can hear her voice beginning to become a little horse, so he reaches over and grabs the bottle off the table next to her bed. LaChel can feel her throat is starting to hurt again, so she grabs the bottle that her Dad is offering her and drinks a big mouth full. "There", now will one or both of you please tell me how the "h". She was about to say "hell" again until she felt the burning eyes of her mother looking down at her. She didn't know what condition she was in health wise, but she understood if she says the word "hell" one more time her mother was going to slap her out of this bed.

LaChel, I'm not going to bore you with all the technical terms and stories about how we arrived at this moment. I think I should just float her and then she'll believe me. "Float me", LaChel repeats? What do you mean, she says as she looks back and forth at her mom and dad? "That's not going to happen so don't worry about that", Lorraine tells her. "Don't even think about it, she says as she looks him sternly in the eyes. I didn't enjoy it when you did it to me and I know that she wouldn't care for it either. But that's the fastest and easiest way for her to believe what we're telling her. As BK and Lorraine argue amongst themselves, using gestures and hand signals on the method and wording to use to convincing their daughter how and why she and her sister are now in space.

LaChel lays there with her head down on her knees, in shock and awe, as her mom and dad continues to argue amongst themselves about the best way to convince her. LaChel catches her mom's attention as she mumbles something. I know this is a lot to absorb, but everything is going to be alright, Lorraine tells her as she strokes LaChel's hair. "Are you in any pain", he asked? LaChel, just sits there in shock and mumbles, "I said", I believe you", as she points at the newly transformed large viewport across the room. Both BK and Lorraine turn in the direction that she's pointing and can see the entire earth filling the viewport. They knew that MOM has taken matters into her own hands, so to speak.

MOM must have calculated that this was the quickest method of convincing LaChel that we're on a spacecraft. "Thank you, MOM", he says as Lorraine just looks at him and shakes her head in disapproval. MOM doesn't say a word, but just observes the family dynamics like hamsters in a cage. Is she allowed to make these kinds of decisions without asking either one of us, Lorraine asked? He can see that she's a bit upset about MOM taking it upon herself to "shock and awe" their daughter. I have given her the ability and permission to use her own discretion on minor situations, he says as he puts his hands on her shoulder. LaChel suddenly throws the sheets off her legs and with a lot of effort, forces them over the edge of the bed. "What do you think you're doing", her mom says as she grabs for LaChel's arm. You're too weak to try to get out of bed right now, so please lie back down. I'm fine mom, she says as she grabs her mom's forearm for support. I just need you and dad to help me get over to the window, please. Lorraine is reluctant to let her get out of bed while she's still in a weaken state, but she thinks this may be the best way for her to come to grips with her situation.

LaChel extends her arms towards her mom and dad so they can get on each side of her for support. "Hold on", Lorraine says as she uses her feet to readjust LaChel's crocs so she can easily slide her feet in them. She carefully eases herself off the bed until her feet slides down into those ugly purple crocs. These shoes are hella ugly, she says with a tone of disgust and a scowl on her face. Your dad maybe a genius, but he has no talent for fashion.

"Excuse me", but look around, he says with pride. "Now just take your time and move slowly", Lorraine tells her while grabbing her under her arm. "Mom", I'm fine! "Please just help me get over there", she says as both of her parents maneuver her from between the bed and toward the viewport. Lorraine is surprise how well she can walk after being in stasis for so long. Just take it slow, Lorraine instructs her as she looks down at LaChel's feet. I know how to walk mom, she says with a little too much attitude. LaChel can feel her mother's grip starting to tighten around her arm. Regardless of her condition, that's a signaled to her to correct her tone. Just remember that being in pain and having to adjust to being relocated in outer space on your dad's homemade spacecraft is no reason to sass your mother, she says with a stern look at her.

"Tread carefully", she adds BK jokingly mouthed the words, "Be afraid", then smiles. LaChel was going to take her dad's advice and apologize to her, but as she got close to the viewport, she became awe struck by what she was seeing. He can feel her entire body starting to shake. He knew what was happening to her, because it happened to her mother when she first set her eyes on that majestic blue marble for the first time. And of course, it was such a stunning view that LaChel's eyes are beginning to well up with tears. Her emotions are like seeing the Grand Canyon for the first time, times ten. Lorraine can see the tears beginning to roll down her daughter's face as she steps as close as she could to the viewport. LaChel reaches out to touch what she thinks is glass, but suddenly pulls back her hand. "You can touch it", he says as he reaches out and touches it to show her it's OK. She cautiously reaches out again and touches the viewport with the tips of her fingers. It looks like glass, but it feels like nothing I've ever felt, she says as she continues to place more of her hand on the viewport. It's not really glass, sweet heart he tell LaChel. This is a material that I developed, which is more like the metal tungsten, which can change shape and opacity by utilizing electronics directly connected to the material. Instructions can be programmed into the material at the molecular level using the computer or MOM can program the alterations. "Tungsten", LaChel repeats out loud as she looks at the viewport in fascination. "Yes", sweet heart, he repeats while staring at her.

"Tungsten"! A hard greyish metal that is number 74 on the periodic table, melting point of 6,192 degrees Fahrenheit and has the tensile strength of 142000 psi", LaChel says in a robotic like cadence. Lorraine and BK looked at their daughter with utter amazement as they realized that she just correctly defined the properties of Tungsten. But BK is smiling and happy that the method he used to enhance Lorraine's intelligence is working with LaChel too. After a few more seconds, BK broke the silence by asking LaChel what her thoughts are at this moment. She stands there with her mouth open trying to gather her thoughts on how she felt right now. It feels like my mind is filled with random thoughts and images that I shouldn't know, she replies with a bewildered look on her face. Lorraine understands how her daughter feels, because it hasn't been that long since she was standing there looking down at the big blue marble.

I understand how traumatic this is for you, but I promise that you'll be alright, as she smiles at LaChel while rubbing her back. She is looking past her daughter and over at her husband, who's doing his best to not make eye contact with her. What your mom and I are trying to say is that we know this is very hard to take in at once. Lorraine holds on to her for a moment, as BK lets go of her to get a stool from the other side of the room. He returns with the stool and helps LaChel up on to it so she can sit in front of the view port as long as she wants. Now you can sit here for a while and take it all in while your mom and I help the units with your sister. As Lorraine starts to walk away, LaChel reaches over and grabs her mother's arm. "No mom", as she pulls her mom closer to her. She looks over at her mom with big wanting eyes and asked her to stay with her for a little while longer.

Lorraine looks at BK intensely, which he has seen many times before. That look means get out of here so I can talk to my daughter. No problem! I think I can handle some of your mom's medical duties for a while, he says as he kisses LaChel on the forehead and walks away. As he walks toward Kim's bed, he hopes that his wife will try to convince her that what he has done was for the best. His attention shifts to Kim as he walks up to the foot of her bed. Units two and three are on opposite sides of her bed sharing data on the progression of the treatment and Kim's current condition, while unit one is interfacing with the medical clinic's computer. LaChel wanted the opportunity to talk with her mother alone about all this craziness that has happened to her. In a low tone, she asked what happened to them and why her dad brought them here. Lorraine can see that she is having a very difficult time coming to grips with all the visual and mental information that's coming at her all at once. LaChel, please believe that I truly understand how you feel right now, because I went through the same thing. After I woke up in the medical bay and your dad started explaining everything that happened to me, I was so confused mostly pissed at him for bringing me up here. To be honest, I still have those feelings from time to time, but being too emotional will only make this situation worst.

Just remember that we both love you and are here for you, she says as she cups LaChel's face in her hands. She grabs her mother's hands that are still on her face and gives her a half smile. After her mom drops her hands form LaChel's face, she looks back at the large looming display of the earth's continents slowly drifting past her. She takes one deep breath, then another, but for reasons she can't understand right now, she can't stop all of these strange thoughts and images from filling her head. She has thoughts of the types of chemicals that makes up the ozone layer, which she has no understanding of how they work together. It's like knowing that hydrogen and oxygen are the chemical conponents of water, but not knowing how to combine the chemical ingredience to produce the water. She can see her daughter's smile change to a look of concern. She knows that the information BK programmed into her brain is starting to seep its' way to the surface. But Lorraine doesn't think it's a good idea to tell LaChel the full ramifications of her new abilities and what her father did to them. What are we doing up here and why did dad kidnap us mom, she says in a hushed tone? Lorraine grabs her hand, pulls her close and prepares to console her daughter by telling her, "it's going to be all right". What's going on with dad and why did he kidnap us. Hey, your father didn't kidnap any of us - technically, she replies. So what would you call being drugged, loaded up in some type of vehicle, and taken to a destination against your will?

Lorraine tries to give her a logical or plausible response to her question, which could defend her husband's actions. But she knew anything she said to answer that question would sound ridiculous. I can't think of any defense for what your father has done to us, but I do know he did this because he loves us in his own crazy, mad scientist type of way, and he thought this would be the best way of keeping us together. But Mom, dad has built a ship and moved us not around the corner or not even to another state. He moved us off the planet, she says softly trying not to attract the attention of her father, who has his back to them as he takes care of his youngest. You know as well as I do that this isn't normal and isn't the first time that Dad has made big decisions like this without discussing it with anyone.

She's only sixteen, but she understands the importance of communication and respect in a relationship. She's throwing hard Mike Tyson body blows of logic with these indefensible flaws in her father's character. She forces her mother to reluctantly defend her husband's selfish actions, so she takes a more parental posture regarding her daughter's bashing of her husband.

BK looks back at them and shouts across the room, "I feel my ears burning", as he smiles at his wife and daughter looking over at him. Both of them gives him a fony smile while looking back hat him. All three medical units focus the attention to BK's ears. He looks around at the units and notices one of them slowly hovering closer to him. It's just a figure of speech, he shouts at the approaching unit, but it continues to stare at his ears with it illuminated round eyes. It means that you feel or know someone was or is talking about you, he explains to the now stationary hovering unit. The lights on what can be consider its' forehead, strobes back and forth as it processes the information. After eight to ten seconds, the unit resume with their assigned task. LaChel is getting more and more animated as she tries to convince her mother that her husband has destroyed her life and she just wants to go home. Her mother promptly grabs her by her arm and gives her a scowling stare. She recognizes and adheres to her mother's non-verbal command to "shut the hell up"! Still giving LaChel that piercing stare, she waits for a moment just incase BK had overheard LaChel's brief tirade.

Believe me when I tell you that I can truly understand your confusion and anger, because I've been going back and forth about how I feel about what your dad has done. Lorraine looks back at him tapping on the tablet, while standing behind the desk. She grabs LaChel by her arm and pulls her off the chair and walks her closer to the viewport, so they will be out of earshot of him. BK can see that Lorraine is getting angry, but he doesn't want to get involved. He just hopes that she's trying to defend him and get her in line. I was so upset with your dad when he first showed me you and your sister frozen in that stasis tube that I gave him a hard knee to his boys. LaChel looked shocked at her mom telling her that she laid hands on her dad. She never thought that her mom was capable of doing something like that. I'm not proud of the way I reacted, but my emotions got the best of me. She lets go of the grip she has on LaChel's arm then stands between her and the viewport. She looks deeply into her daughter's eyes, while holding both of LaChel's hands in hers. I'm not the one to explain to you why he felt that he had to do this extreme action to us. I just want you to promise me that you'll listen to your dad when he decides to explain why we're up here.

Lorraine can see the emotions starting to work its way to the surface of LaChel's face again. Tears begin to run down LaChel's cheeks, but Lorraine fights back her own tears because she doesn't think that both of them standing there balling will help assure her daughter that everything's going to be alright. Lorraine reaches up and gently wipes away her daughter's streaming tears and then gives her a kiss on the forehead. They both hug one another as BK watches from a safe distance.

He can clearly see that they are going through something, but decides to wait for the sign from his wife to come over and join their loving embrace, but after a few seconds of hugging, Lorraine decides they weren't ready for him to put his arms around them, so she decides to walk LaChel back to her bed.

He can only hope that she can open the door for him to tell both LaChel and Kim why it was necessary for him to uproot them as well as put their lives in danger. LaChel will probably have a hard time understanding why he had to do this, mostly because she's a sixteen year old girl and like most sixteen year old girls; they only think of themselves, their girlfriends and boys. As he completes the assessment of Kim's current body scan, he can see that everything is moving along perfectly. He looks over at Lorraine helping LaChel to her bed and thinks of the most current time he injected himself in his daughter's life for her own good.

He thinks back to one particular time he injected himself into his daughter's life, because he didn't think LaChel was making good decisions when it came to the boys she chose to get involved with. He intentionally sabotaged her relationship with one of the more popular players on her high school basketball team, because he thought that both of them would do something stupid and would jeopardize his plans to launch his family into space.

He did the calculations and decided that the relationship between his daughter and the tall brain dead basketball player was not meant to be at this time or any other time, if he had anything to say about it. Once the lanky idiot came knocking at his door, he took the opportunity to push him back onto the porch where he proceeded to intimidate him until LaChel and Lorraine swung open the front door to rescue him. LaChel's future husband, as she likes to think of him, does his best to look calm as BK continues to interrogate him. LaChel finds it hard to tell it he's scared or nervous talking to her dad. But if he is, he's hiding it very well until BK starts talking about his time in the Special Forces, and the methods he knew to disembowel a man, which mentally grabbed the kid by his emotional throat and shook him like a rag doll.

BK had spent time in the Navy, but he had never trained or been a part of the Special Forces. Lorraine and LaChel has a "what the hell" expression on her face, but even with Bria's young age she knows that her dad has did or says something to her sister's date that shook him from the top of his head to the bottom of his feet. Lorraine tries to bring the young man back from the brink of a nervous breakdown by commenting how nice he looks, but it seems like his mind is caught between reality and the lies that her husband has impregnated in his brain. As LaChel grabs her dates hand and talks with him softly, BK walks up to him from behind and places his heavy hand on the young man's left shoulder, which makes him almost jump out of his skin.

At that point both Lorraine and LaChel realized by the manner in which her date reacted that her dad has put the fear of dad in him. Months later, LaChel told her mother that she has never forgiven her dad for scaring all the boys that were interested in her away and trying to ruin her relationship with her current boyfriend, "Antonne". Lorraine never wanted LaChel to know that she was the puppet master pulling her husband's strings and instructing him to threaten and intimidate those testosterone driven boys.

She felt that LaChel was too boy crazy and was not concentrating on her grades, which she was afraid would hamper her ability to get into a good university. Her latest boyfriend is a football player and didn't care too much about his grade; let alone hers. But LaChel thought her dad was the lone bad guy and Lorraine didn't see a reason to change that. Good cop, Bad cop is the game they find most useful when dealing with their daughter love life.

Lorraine again tries to explain how much her dad loves her and that he agrees not to impulsively make decisions that will affect them without their input. The expression on LaChel's face tells her that it's going to take time and an effort on her dad's part to convince her that he is done with keeping secrets from the family. Once LaChel is in her bed, Lorraine pulls the covers up to her waist, adjust her pillow and sits on the edge of the bed to continue talking with her for a little longer. A large muffled growling sound similar to what a small angry dog may make when someone touches his dish of food emanated from underneath LaChel's covers. "What the heck was that", LaChel says in surprise as she grabs her stomach. I'm sorry sweet heart, I forgot that you haven't eaten anything in months Lorraine replies as she reaches in her pocket and grabs her communicator. "I haven't eaten in months", LaChel shouts in amazement as she looks over her body. "Yes", BK replies from across the room! While in stasis, you didn't need anything to eat, but now your body is trying to make up for all those meals you missed. She looks at her mother and asked why she was in stasis for so long? Hold on baby, I will explain it to you in a bit, but first we have to get some food in you before you start to feel weaker than you feel now.

Lorraine starts to press some buttons on her device as LaChel looks on with a puzzled expression. Now the only food you are allowed to eat right now is soup and some saltine crackers, so what kind of soup would you like, sweetheart. "Soup"! I don't want any soup, she says with a frown. Can I get a couple of slices of pizza or a hot dog, she asks with a teenager's whine? "No", Lorraine says sternly. Your system isn't strong enough to handle that type of food just yet. "Soup", Lorraine repeats again. I don't even know what types of soups you have aboard this ship, mom. Good point, Lorraine response. That's all right sweetheart. Let me take care of the ordering of your first lunch aboard for you, as she brings up the menu on her tablet. After sixteen years of taking care of you, I'm overly qualified to choose the type of soup you're going to eat for lunch, she says as she smiles while looking down at her tablet.

Lorraine thumbs her way through the various lunch time selections, until she gets to the various soups and salads. "Split Pea", BK yells out from behind the workstation. Both Lorraine and LaChel yell out a variety of hurtful and negative replies, which tells him that they don't think he's very funny. A normal person would have taken offence, but being a dad surrounded by women has toughened his skin to such flagrant insults on his weight and sometimes his agressively receding hair line. But he had to admit to himself that it does feel good to hear the women in his life come together to verbally abuse him. It reminded him of life before he had done all of this, he thinks to himself. Here's one I know that you'll like, as she presses and swipes on the device. I'm putting in an order for a bowl of chicken and rice soup with a ring of crackers. "Putting in an order", LaChel replies?

I thought that we were the only other people aboard this spaceship, or did dad kidnap a bunch of other people too? "No", Lorraine replies with a comforting smile. Your dad only "abducted", which she really emphasized the word "abducted", the people that he loved the most, she says with a little bit of levity. Just like I have three med units in this clinic, as she points to the units around the room, your dad built various units to assist us in our everyday lives aboard the ship. "So let me get this straight". Dad built some type of "Waffle House" cook for us, right. Yes, you could think of it that way. But it's a little more than just a short order cook. It's programmed with over 5,000 recipes and can prepare meals that rival any dish in "Hell's Kitchen". He also has somehow gotten his hands on my mother's recipes.

You know grandma just wouldn't give her recipes out to anyone, especially dad. She hates is guts and everything around those guts, LaChel says with concern. You think maybe he may have done something to grandma to get those recipes? BK hears LaChel's last comment as he quickly gets up from the desk and walks over to them. "Hey", he yells as he walks up to the side of LaChel's bed. He can tell by the expression on his wife's face that she's giving LaChel's comments too much thought. Don't put that non-sense in your mother's head little girl. You've been in stasis for almost three months and don't have a clue what has been going on between me and your mother.

He knows that Lorraine is one push away from regressing back to her anger and disappointing feelings about him. Lorraine thinking that he may have done something to her mother could be the catalyst to reignite that explosion of cursing and tears. He has to go on the offensive if he has any chance of keeping his wife on his side and in the right frame of mind.

He points his finger directly at LaChel as he chastises her for putting those negative thoughts into her mother's head. I totally understand you're anger at me for taking you away from your friends, but you're just a kid and you are subject to our authority, as he points to himself and Lorraine. I understand that dad, but tell us how you got grandma to give you her recipes, she says while both of them give him their full attention. He can see that Lorraine is a little curious too. Lorraine knows that there's know love loss between her mother and BK, so she doesn't understand how he got those recipes. He looks at their faces and sees that it's to his best interest to enlighten both of them. Remember a few years ago when you bought your mother a computer, because she wanted to get more organized. She thinks for a moment then nods her head yes. And you, as he points to LaChel, helped your grandmother put all of her recipes on her computer.

LaChel also nods her head. I overheard you guys talking about her hummingbird cake recipe and how she was going to email it to you. Lorraine doesn't have to hear anymore, because she knows exactly what he did. She interrupts him. So, you hacked into my mother's computer and stole her recipes, she says sternly. He tries to think of a nicer way of putting it, but there isn't one, so he just says, "yep". She created a folder and called it, "My Recipes". "She made it so easy", he says with a smile. But in my defense, I know that you guys love her cooking and I thought this would be good for all of you. Lorraine doesn't want to get mad, so she decides to let it go. That works for him, so he continues to talk to LaChel.

Your mom and I have a lot of work that needs to be done and we don't have time to stroke your hair and tell you everything's going to be alright. You're aboard a spacecraft that's orbiting 240 miles above the planet, but MOM corrects him by announcing the correct distance above the planet is 236.17 miles. Lorraine looks up at the ceiling and mumbles to herself something profane about MOM. He stops for a second, then continues before LaChel could ask any questions. What we are doing up here is bigger than you or me. Now I'll give you the same option that I gave to your mother when she was having problems adapting to living aboard ship. I'll put you back in your stasis capsule and keep you there until we return to earth, but I can't give you a firm date on when that will happen. He stares at her, as he waits for her decision. She looks at her mother with a bit of concern. BK and Lorraine can see that she is really giving it some serious thought to what she wants to do, but before she could say anything, Lorraine interrupts her decision and tells her that she's not going back into damn stasis. "No", Lorraine says with a loud and stern conviction. It may be medically unsafe to put you back in that freezer because we don't know what effects a second prolonged session in that tube would have on your mind and body. You, me and your sister are just going to make lemonade out of these damn lemons your father has bought for us. And from time to time we'll freeze those damn lemons and throw them at him as a punishment for doing this to us.

He knows she's not kidding, but he smiles at her until he understands by her piercing gaze that she wasn't happy with him giving LaChel that option. He stops smiling and gathers his thoughts. He reaches down and grabs LaChel's hand and tries to explain the situation and what he expects of her. I just need you to realize that what we're accomplishing up here will change the world and hopefully give humanity a different focus other than blind greed and killing each other. Dad, I'm just sixteen and would rather be in school with my friends than to be up here, she says with a look of despair in her eyes.

You made this decision for all of us and now we're stuck up here. Lorraine thinks it's time to help him. I'm sure your dad understands your feelings, but we are here now and you girls will have to make the best of it. He squeezes LaChel's hand to get her attention. Listen, I'm not going to make any promises to you and your sister on how long we'll be up here, but I can promise you that we will return to earth when we're finish doing what we have to do. The expression on LaChel's and for that matter, Lorraine's face reflects that they take no comfort in his promises. But Lorraine can see that her dad is very passionate about what he's doing, so she reluctantly decides to give him her full support. Lorraine tells BK that this is a good time to get something to eat and allow LaChel some time to relax and process all this information.

He agrees that this is a good time to get some lunch and maybe tomorrow will be a good time to fill both of his girls in on the remaining information. Lorraine's communication device, which is in her jacket pocket, started to buzz and vibrate indicating that a communication is trying to come through. "Who's trying to communicate with me", she mumbles to herself as she pulls the device from her pocket and response with a curious "yes". Chef from the kitchen replies that the food she ordered will be delivered in twelve minutes and forty-six seconds. "Great", Lorraine responds. But Lorraine is a little spoiled by chef's cooking these past weeks and she had her mouth set on one of his steak sandwiches and fries for lunch. But LaChel won't be able to handle any complicated food like that for at least a week. Lorraine explains to her that her body hasn't been processing food for the past two months and that both her and her sister will have to ease into eating again. And that means that hamburgers, pizzas, and foods like that are off the menu.

LaChel isn't happy that she's about to eat soup and crackers for lunch, but in reality, she's so hungry that if they gave her liver and onions, she would gladly eat it and gleefully ask for seconds. Excuse me BK, but I think I've waited long enough for you to introduce me to your oldest offspring, MOM interjects. "Grandma Betty", LaChel shouts and curiously looks around the room. She lifts herself from her pillow so she can get at better look around the room as she hopes to see her beloved grandmother.

Oh my god dad, I can't believe that you drugged and froze your own mother too. She shouts at him that Grandma is in her eighties. "No", BK exclaims as he carefully pushes LaChel's shoulders back onto her pillow. That's not your grandmother, Lorraine explains. Your dad simply programmed his mother's voice into the ship's computer, so he would feel a little more at home while he was up here. I thought it was creepy and didn't care for it either when I first heard it, but I've gotten use to it, he admits. And I haven't decided what voice I want the computer to emulate when it's speaking to me. You mean I can change the voice of the computer to any voice I want to hear when it's talking to me. Lorraine was about to respond when MOM jumps into the conversation. "Of course you can LaChel", as MOM imitates her mother's voice for her. "No", hell no, Lorraine shouts as she looks around at the ceiling of her clinic. There will be none of that you glorified ipad. I am sorry Lorraine, but this is LaChel's decision regarding how I would reply and speak to her. I don't think so, Lorraine says with a ton of attitude. Maybe BK hasn't instructed you on who is in charge when it comes to making decisions concerning our kids, and you best believe, it's not you. Well BK calls me MOM, but unfortunately you have not chosen a name to call me at this time. Oh, belief me, if my daughters weren't in the room I would have a couple of choice names I'd like to call you right now. But I don't think I have to explain anything to you, or justify ordering you not to use my voice to talk to my kids. You just need to follow my orders, or I will have to reprogram you. You don't have the knowledge, or the skill set to reprogram me Lorraine, MOM coldly replies. That's fine, so I can just practice my limited programming skills on you, Lorraine replies in a threatening tone.

So, I'm guessing you two don't like each other, LaChel says as she looks up at her mother. It's hella strange to hear you argue with a computer, she says. Lorraine tries to calm herself down. BK raises his arms and stops this discussion that will probably turn into an argument before it's all over. "That's enough", he shouts. MOM, Lorraine and I make all the decisions on what's best for our daughters, but in the near future, I will sit down with you and explain our method for raising our girls. But for now, I need my ship's physician and my right hand A.I. to try to get along.

MOM, I am heading to engineering to inspect those faulty regulator switches and I need you to run a quick diagnostic on all eighteen of them. Yes BK, she responds. But if you want to talk to Lorraine and LaChel in private, just ask me to discontinue monitoring this room for a specific period, MOM adds. BK laughs a little as he realizes that MOM is very good at reading him and his moods. Alright, but I do need those regulators analyzed as soon as possible, please. Nine minutes and thirty-two seconds, MOM replies. He is still smiling as he looks over at Lorraine and LaChel, who are not amused at all. I think you programmed that computer too well, Lorraine says with concern in her voice. LaChel echoes her mother's concerns by stating that MOM's impression of her grandmother just coming from nowhere, sounds creepy. Look you two, I understand that even though you, as he points to Lorraine, had more time to get use to MOM and LaChel is still adjusting to her impression of my mother's voice, but I hope you guys will give MOM more time adjusting to multiple humans.

Do you mean that the voice we hear is the voice of the ship, LaChel asks? Yes, Lorraine replies. The way your dad explained it to me is that the computer is so intertwined into the ship and the units that roam about it that the ship and voice are one and the same. When I was developing the design for the ship, I felt that I should build this ship in the same manner as a human body is created, he adds. I wanted the ship to feel, in a sense, its physical components in order for it to quickly analyze any malfunctions to its' components. You mean that the computer can feel things that are happening to it, LaChel asked? Not exactly, he replies. She has subroutines instead of nerve endings that will allow her to continuously monitor her functions and structures.

LaChel was preparing to ask another question, but he stops her. I have to go to engineering, but your mother knows enough about the ship to answer any questions you might have. As he starts to walk toward the door, it opens and Chef quickly hovers into the room with their lunch. Good timing Chef, he says as they pass each other. I'll be back when it's time to bring Kim out of her coma.

Dad, can you please change the ship's voice so I won't have to think that you've kidnapped Grandma Betty. Lorraine would love for him to change MOM's voice, so she looks at him with a "just do it" stare. LaChel decides to give him one of her scenarios to drive home the point. Your know I love mom, as LaChel looks over at her, but if the ship spoke to me with mom's voice day and night; I don't think I could handle it. Lorraine has a "what the hell" look on her face. He stands there looking at both of them for a moment. I'm going to give you the same option I gave your mother and will give your sister. You can request MOM to speak to you with any voice you choose, but I would like you to give it a month before you make that decision. "A month", LaChel shouts! "Yes"! It will give you some time to get use to her voice. After that, you can change her voice to anyone you want to hear while we're up here. She doesn't want to wait that long, because she knows it won't change her mind. But she thinks she can have some fun with this and get back at her dad. OK, I'll wait a month, but after a month I want the computer to sound like "Antonne".

BK steps back in shock, but Lorraine starts laughing, because she knows that LaChel has decided to serve her revenge up ice cold and in a large smoking pile. Nope, nope, nope, he repeats over and over again. I'm not going to hear that idiot's voice echoing through my ship every day. You said any voice I choose, and that's the voice I want to hear when I wake up in the morning and before I put my head on my pillow at night, she says in a disturbing seductive voice. Lorraine tries to hold back her smile, while thinking that LaChel has just put a cherry on top of that smoking pile. "Hey little girl", he shouts as he points his finger at her. He can't get any other words out of his mouth, because she has used his words against him.

Lorraine jumps to LaChel's defense. You want to hear your mother's comforting voice and your "little girl" wants to hear her boyfriend's voice, Lorraine says as she smiles at him. "Damn", he says as he turns and walks away from both of them. BK doesn't hate the boy, but dislikes him for being three years older than LaChel and for being a brain dead Neanderthal.

He also drops his daughter off without walking her to the door and for being overly affectionate with her right in front of the house. He knows that his daughter is a contributing factor in the way he feels about her boyfriend, but just like most dads; it's easier to blame the idiotic boyfriend for corrupting their little girl. He turns and walks back towards his wife and daughters. LaChel, you know how your mom and I feel about that young man, he says as if he was trying to swallow a large bitter pill.

That young man's name is Antonne, Lorraine exclaims, and I don't have any problem with her boyfriend or the computer using his voice, she says while smiling at her daughter. He's been in these types of situations before with the women in his life and he knows when its time for him to just give in and accept what is about to happen. At least for the time being, he thinks to himself. "OK", if this will make my little girl happy then, yes you can use his voice to communicate with the computer. Good, LaChel replies with a triumphant smile on her face. But dad, in the future, can you please try to at least say my boyfriend's name without the attitude. I agreed to let you use his voice aboard this ship, so don't push it.

Lorraine puts her hand on LaChel's leg and gives her a look, which signals her to heed her father's advice and not to push him. Do you need me to call him, so you can record his voice, LaChel asked with a beaming smile? "That won't be necessary", as MOM breaks into the conversation. I have his name and phone number in my database, which will enable me to acquire a sample of his voice pattern and inflections. Then I will be able to accurately mimic his voice and speech patterns at will. How did you randomly get his name and phone number in your database, LaChel asked? Did my dad tell you to spy on my boyfriend or something, she adds with some attitude? "No", Lorraine says sternly as she doesn't give MOM a chance to answer the question. Just calm down and stop being so paranoid. The computer can acquire any name or phone number of anyone on the planet; at least that's what your dad told me. That is true MOM replies. I can access any computer on earth regardless of their security's firewall or protocols. You don't have to do any of that, LaChel says. Just let me give him a call and you can record his voice, she says with a smile. "Absolutely not", BK says with conviction. We are not at the point where we can call anyone down there, let alone "Pretty Rickey". "Stop calling him that", LaChel yells! I haven't talk to him in I don't know how long. "Oh my God", she says as she puts her hands to her mouth. It's been months and he probably thinks I'm dead and that you killed all of us, she says while looking him in the eyes. LaChel tells her mother that if she's gone too long, he'll probably start dating one of those skanks on the cheerleading squad. BK tells LaChel that this is not the time for anyone to try to communicate with anyone on earth at this time. He starts to walk backward towards the door as he tells his daughter that MOM will be getting her boyfriend's voice on record.

LaChel is still trying to plead her case for calling her boyfriend, while he walks backward away from them and closer to the door. Sorry family, but I have a couple of things scheduled right now, as he looks at his watch. But I will be back in about an hour or so. He blows them a kiss then walks out the door.

As soon as he is in the hallway and the door closes, MOM reminds him that his next task is scheduled thirty minutes from now. Yes, I know but I had to get out of there before both of them try to convince me to call people on earth. Back in the Clinic, Lorraine just angrily stares at the door, because she knows his schedule too and he has nothing planned for another thirty minutes. She would have called him out, but she wanted more alone time with LaChel, but she'll make him pay for that lie later. "Mom", LaChel says while grabbing her arm. Can you talk to dad or punch him in his nether regions again to get him to take us home, please? Lorraine totally understands her emotions because she navigated those emotions too. She turns to LaChel and wraps her in a warm and tight embrace. LaChel buries herself in her mother's arms and chest as she emotionally reverts back to a six year old girl. "I'm scared", she admits to her mother.

"I am too baby", she admits as she gives her daughter a kiss on her forehead then embraces her even tighter. They stay entwined in each other's arms for a good fifteen to twenty seconds. MOM doesn't say a word, but she does get some valuable mother-daughter interaction data. "Look", Lorraine says as she breaks their embrace, but caresses LaChel's shoulders with both of her hands. I've been up here alone screaming, crying and nagging at your father for weeks trying to convince him to end this craziness and take us home. But even though he loves each of us very much, unfortunately he feels that he must see this through. LaChel's face is flush with confusion and fear, which her mother wishes she could kiss away. Her daughter's emotional state as well as what may happen when Kim becomes conscious drives home her decision to convince her girls that this is the safest place for them right now. Even though she hasn't herself forgiven him for putting them in this situation, she knows that it's in her and her girls' best interest to make the best of this situation. Kim has about 45 more minutes before the nanos will be finished repairing the hole in her heart and can revive her. Lorraine spends the next half an hour calming LaChel's nerves and even getting her to smile a few times while both eat their lunch.

Meanwhile, BK is in the engineering lab hunting down some new irregularities in the engine's stabilization system. He has run every diagnostic he can think of, but he's still getting a slight power drop in the port stabilizer. MOM can you isolate the exact location where the malfunction maybe occurring by extrapolating the power loss within the port stabilizer.

No I can not, MOM replies, because of the random manner of the malfunction all I can convey to you is that this problem has been escalating since we left earth and if it continues; we will have to land this ship within 34 hours or we will simply loose too much altitude to maintain a stable orbit. If that happens, can you calculate where we will be forced to land. "Calculating", she responds. While MOM is calculating their possible fate, he can't believe that all his hard work may come to a premature end, because of some simple wiring malfunction.

He thought the detection devices and maintenance bots he installed would detect and even correct any malfunction within the ship's systems, but something he hadn't thought of is putting him and his family's lives in jeopardy. MOM finally completes her calculations and tells him that the ship will be force down in a region of Iran. "Damn it", he replies. Exactly where in Iran will we be forced to land? It really does not matter, MOM replies. If you think about it, once we start our descent, our Government and their allies will track our trajectory and assume that we are landing our highly advanced spacecraft in Iran. They will most likely assume that you are defecting and consequently attempt to blow us out of the sky. Iran on the other hand may allow us to land, only to try to take possession of the ship and use your family as pawns in order to force you to design more ships like this one. He ponders his options as he walks around the lab trying to decide which one will be the safest one for his family. MOM can tell by monitoring his facial expression and body temperature that he's feeling a lot of stress.n While still trying to figure out what's wrong with his ship and how to protect his family, he asked MOM what chance do you give us for maintaining navigational control and maintaining our shielding as we descend? MOM once again calculates the possibilities. There is roughly a 45 percent probability of this ship sustaining minor damage and a 32 percent probability that the ship's exoskeleton maybe damaged due to its' uncontrolled re-entry into earth's atmosphere. "God", those are some terrible odds", he says while rubbing his head!

We have to figure out what the hell is affecting our port stabilizer and how to fix it quickly or this game may be over before half time. I was unaware that we were playing some type of game, MOM says curiously. "It's just an expression, MOM"! This is damn sure not a game. Now please run another scan of the portside regulators as fast and as accurately as you can. "That is the only way I know how to do it", she replies. His mind then shifts to how he's going to tell his wife that it's a possibility the ship maybe making a crash landing in a very hostile country.

He knows there will be no best time or way to tell her, so he decides to do the next best thing. And that would be not to tell her at all. It's a damn if you do and damned if you don't situation. He continues to look for the cause of the problem, but before he knows it, it's time for Kim to be revived from her medical induced coma. He's deep in thought and tries to ignore his communication device buzzing and chiming in his pocket, because he knows it's his wife. He decides to answer it before she decides to come to engineering to find out why he's not answering her calls.

He reluctantly pulls the communicator out of his pocket and gives her a call. Lorraine immediately answers with a ton of attitude. "Why in the hell didn't you answer your stupid communicator as she shouts into it"? Take it easy babe, he responds. After you didn't answer my call, I tried to get the idiot ship's computer to contact you, but it kept saying you were busy and would call me back.

I'm sorry babe, but we've been trying to fix one of the ship's stabilizers and I lost track of time. "No, She yells". I have a real emergency, she shouts. I'm standing on my desk right now, because I saw a mouse zip down the side of my wall and under LaChel's bed. And I have no idea where it is now and I need you to get your hairy butt back down here and find it. "What", he yells! You're crazy, he replies. We're six miles above the earth and you're trying to tell me we have mice. "Damn straight", she shouts. "Mice", BK thinks to himself. How in the hell could mice get aboard the ship? Just then, the ship takes a slight dip portside, which sends BK stumbling into the nearby railing. He grips the railing tightly to stop himself from flipping over it. The ship's damage control alarm begins to sound, and the emergency red strobe lights pulsate throughout the ship.

He can hear LaChel on the other end of the communicator shouting and screaming in confusion. "Are you guys alright", he yells through his communicator? But Lorraine doesn't answer. The portside stabilizer is unable to function at a rate to maintain stability, MOM announces. Starboard stabilizer cannot provide enough thrust to keep us in orbit on its' own. We can no longer maintain a stable orbit and consequently begin our descent into earth's atmosphere, MOM adds.

I thought we had at least thirty hours before this would happen, he replies with dismay. That estimation was only viable if the portside stabilizer continued to decline in its' functions at the same constant rate, which is not the case, she replies. He can still hear LaChel yelling for him, as he tries to think of a way to save his family and his ship. "Lorraine", he shouts again into the communicator.

He yells her name a few more times without hearing a response. All he can hear is screaming and crying from LaChel, who's in full panic mode. Just then MOM tells him that the sudden movement of the ship through Lorraine off the chair and into the portside wall then she dropped to the floor. "How is she", "is she alright", he asked? MOM tells him that she had unit one performed a quick scan and it found no evidence of head or internal trauma. She just seems to have a few external contusions and she is a bit dazed. "Oh thank God", he shouts in relief as if that's the only thing he has to be concerned with. The ship will be forced to land in approximately seven minutes and twelve seconds, MOM announces. Seven minutes to save my family and possibly keep my ship intact, he says to himself. He thinks LaChel must be terrified, so he tells MOM to connect him to the intercom system in the medical clinic, please. You are connected, MOM replies. LaChel, can you hear me? "Yes Dad", she replies in a trembling voice. Mom is hurt. Where are you? I'm still in engineering trying to repair the ship, but that's not important right now, sweetheart. I need you to pull yourself together and help your mother and your sister to the ship's starboard hanger right now.

"I can't", she yells loudly, while she continues to sob. I'm scared and I can barely walk let alone get mom and Kim to the hanger. And what's a hanger, she asked. We need you to come and get us daddy. He knows that LaChel can't do it alone in the amount of time they have left, so he tries to get Lorraine back on her feet. "Lorraine"! Can you hear me, baby! "Lorraine"! "Yes", so stop yelling, please. With unit one helping her, she slowly lifts herself from the floor and pushes herself against the wall for support. The ship is still listing to one side, which makes it hard for her to maintain her balance.

Seeing her mother struggling, LaChel gets out of bed and walks gingerly over to her and helps her mother by grabbing her around the waist. Maybe it wasn't a great idea to climb onto that table, she says while grabbing her head with both hands and moaning from her headache. "What about Kim", BK shouts. Lorraine looks over at Kim, who is still lying in the bed unconscious and the bed is still in the same position. "She's fine". It's a good thing that he had the foresight to secured large furniture to the floor, just in case something like this happened. "Mom, are you OK, LaChel ask as she uses most of her strength to support her mother? Yes, I'm fine other that a headache and some soreness in my back, she replies. He knows that the time maybe short, so he loudly instructs them to please listen carefully. The ship has experienced a major malfunction, which I can't seem to resolve. I'm still attempting to find and repair the problem, but right now it's a possibility that we maybe crashing back on earth, so I need all three of you to move very quickly to the starboard ship's hanger and wait for me there. "Crashing to earth", Lorraine yells as she slowly walks back over to Kim's bed holding her head, with LaChel and unit one helping her all the way.

That's right, but I will make sure you guys are safe. He instructs MOM to have the units get a wheelchair for Lorraine and gurney for Kim. The med units will help get you to the hanger, but you only have about fifteen minutes to get there. Lorraine yells that she doesn't remember where the starboard hanger is located. I have instructed all three med units to accompany you to the hanger, MOM replies. The ship jerks and shakes to the portside once again, which illustrates the urgency of them getting to the hanger. Alright, babe! We're leaving, but what about you? We don't need you dying aboard this ship, so I want you to get your ass down to the hanger soon as you can. I'll be right behind you, he replies. He doesn't want to tell her that he will try to save the ship until the last minute. The ship has descended another ten miles into earth's atmosphere with no signs of being able to recover from its' decaying orbit. Sorry baby, but I have to go, and you do too. "Hurry", he shouts! Get to the hanger now! "I love all of you", he says as he signals to MOM to cut the communication. He could hear the fear in his wife's voice, so telling her that he loves them may have given them the impression that he may not see them again. But he had to be realistic and let them know how he felt about them just in case things don't turn out the way he plans. The ship once again starts to list slightly to the portside and he can feel a slight vibration throughout the ship.

He grabs the railing tightly as he works his way down to the portside of the engine room. He thinks he has an idea of what maybe the problem, but he has to remove the portside ejector panels to take a look inside its' housing area. The two engineering units are quickly moving around the room trying in vain to analyze and counter act the ship's list, but they don't have a clue what's happening either. They're just following protocol that BK programmed into their systems. He stumbles to the first panel, pushing the E2 unit out of his way as he passes by.

The tool in his hand are shaking as he quickly unscrews each knob from each corner of the panel then yanks the panel off the wall and drops it down behind him. He can now feel the ship turning its' nose downward and then it begins to shake more violently. What he's looking for is deep within the open space, which is pitch black. He yells to unit one to get him a head light, which it quickly gets for him. He reaches back and grabs the light and mounts it onto his head. He maneuvers half of his body into the eighteen by twenty-four inch opening, checking each component, module and running his fingers along the wires to locate the components. He still can hear MOM announcing altitude and velocity changes while he desperately searches to find what he thinks is the root of the malfunction. He thinks to himself that it would be so easy for MOM to run its systems check, but he didn't install any sensors in these areas.

He contorts his body to the left as far as he can go to inspect for any damages, but all the wires are perfect, and everything looks normal. Unfortunately, he doesn't know if he would notice the problem if he seen it or felt it for that matter, but he doesn't have the luxury of giving up. He takes another quick look and runs his fingers around every ledge with a wire, then pushes and pulls himself out.

He's sweaty and frantic right about now. But he just moves to the next panel, unscrews the knobs, tosses the panel behind him, and then dives right into the tight and dark aperture. He pulls and tugs at each wire looking for any type of damage, but every wire he inspects feels as it did when he installed it. He uses his legs to push against the floor, which forces his body deeper into the void. He twist and turns his body like a screw into a nut, positioning himself in a way to ensure he could inspect as many wires has can with the little time he has left. He finally comes to the realization that finding the reason he thinks is the cause of the ship's problems would be a one in a million long shot. He starts to push himself out of the opening when the ship took another sudden dip to port, which causes him to ram his head against a vertical stabilizer beam located near his head. The impact of his head against the beam was so violent that it knocked him out.

MOM notice BK legs suddenly going limp and begins to call out to him, but she gets no response. She calculates that he has roughly eleven minutes to evacuate the ship before its' too late. A portion of her programming is dedicated to ensuring that BK and his family is safe regardless of the ship's preservation or even her own existence. That portion of her programming kicks in and she instructs the two engineering units to grab BK's legs and pull him out of the opening then deliver him to the hanger with his family.

Speaking of his family. Soon as Lorraine and the girls enter the hanger, Kim regains consciousness and groggily asked her mom what's going on. Lorraine gleefully leans over her little girl as they continue to walk toward the escape vehicle, while reassuring her that everything is alright. LaChel, who is being pushed in a wheelchair by medical unit one notices the so-calll escape vehicle. "What the hell is this mom, she yells! Lorraine was about to yell at LaChel for her language, but she looks ten feet ahead of her and sees a vehicle that looks like a mini van. I may not be the sharpest crayon in the box when it comes to the science of space exploration, but I'm sure if we leave this ship in a mini-van; we're going to die, LaChel says while looking dumb founded at the escape vehicle. Lorraine is also surprise by the look of the vehicle, but right now they don't have a choice but to get in the van.

Once they are within three feet of the vehicle, the passager side sliding door automatically slides backward just like a mini van. Lorraine tells LaChel to get in first, then grabs Kim into her arms and puts her in the first seat. The three unit, after completing their job to get them to the hanger, moves to the other side of the hanger and stays there. Lorraine smiles at Kim and asked her how she's feeling while putting her seatbelt on. Kim tells her that her head feels a little funny and her legs are weak. Lorraine assures her that she'll feel better soon. After ensuring her girls are securely in the vehicle, she gets in and walks pass Kim to the seat beside her. The van door slides close, while Lorraine continue to attempt to calm her daughters.

Back in Engineering, two of the units grabs the legs of BK and begins to pull him out. But because of how his body is bent, no matter how hard they pull; they can't seem to force him from the void. MOM can see that the units are not making any progress, so she assumes that because of the way his body is contorted that he must be stuck. She instructs the units to pull more forcefully.

They both comply, but he's still firmly wedged halfway in and halfway out of the opening. As the units continue to pull at his legs and jumper, BK finally starts to regain consciousness. MOM can hear him beginning to moan and garble instructions to stop pulling at him and release his legs, while trying to kick at the units. As they release his legs, both of his legs flops onto the metal floor making a very painful thud as he yells, "ah, damn it". At that point MOM knows he's very conscious. As he lifts his slumping head, he feels a narrow stream of blood trailing down his forehead and running down the side of his nose. He tries to reach up to check the damage to his aching head, but the space is to tight to even inspect his damage skull. He can now hear MOM relay the amount of time they have left and instructs him to promptly extract himself from the opening. He knows that she's right and that he's out of time.

He reluctantly tries to back himself out of the opening but realizes that getting out won't be as easy as shoving himself in. He can feel that one of his jumper's belt loops is caught on something and it won't let him push himself out. He yells to MOM that he is stuck and can't force himself out. She can hear the fear beginning to distort his voice. He tries to calm himself down and thinks that maybe if he twist himself until he's almost on his back, that may cause whatever is holding his jumper to let go.

He tries to turn his body to the left, but only can turn a few degrees. "Damn it", he says to himself as he tries to turn his body to the right. He is getting pissed at the possibility that his ship may crash and he may die because he can't free himself from a hole. As he once again twist and turns his body, the pain from the metal opening digging into his hips is almost unbearable. He forces himself to ignore the pain, but to continue to turn until he's now on his back but now his jumper is twisted around his waist and cutting off his circulation. And with one more frantic kick of his legs; he has managed to maneuver himself on to his back, which frees him from whatever was holding him inside the hole. He breathes a sigh of relief as he begins to push himself out of the opening.

But before he's completely out of the opening, something sticking out above his head catches his attention, so he pushes himself back in a little and uses his arms to lift himself up. A big smile appears on his face, because he automatically knows what he's looking at is what's causing the ship's problems, but he now wonders if he has the time to fix it. The ship is now beginning to lurch as it enters the earth's upper thermosphere as MOM announces that it is a 58 percent probability that the ship will lose 25 percent of its' protective shielding in roughly twelve minutes.

"MOM", I think I've found the problem, but if this isn't it I will have to run like hell to make it to the hanger in time. I want you to just be ready to transfer your system to the escape vehicle and launch the vehicle with my family. This is not acceptable, MOM states. I suggest that you remove yourself from the void then move as swiftly as you can to the escape vehicle with your family before it's too late.

He can't wrap his brain around his ship burning up in the earth's atmosphere or in the worst case scenario; his ship survives its' descent and ends up in the hands of some government. He just can't leave while there's even a slim chance to save his ship. He remembers that these junctions of wires control the communications between the ship's stabilizers. Without that communication, the ship maybe inadvertently navigating itself toward the surface. He finds both ends of the wires and twist them back together as quickly as he can. "MOM", once I reconnect these broken wires, I need you to reinitialize the port and starboard stabilizers. Assuming your repair works; I do not think restarting the stabilizers, while you are so deeply inserted in the access opening would not be a safe idea, MOM warns him. I don't have a choice and I don't give a damn MOM, he shouts. Just start the damn stabilizers when I tell you to, please! MOM does a scan of his vitals and can see that he's experiencing a tremendous amount of stress. Now that he's no longer wedged within the opening, she could instruct the units to forcibly remove him from engineering and deliver him to the hanger with is family.

But she calculates that he would be kicking and screaming profanities as well as doing massive amounts of damage to the units and still may not make it to the hanger. After weighing her options, she calculates the probability of success lies in following his instructions. Yes BK, just tell me when to reinitialize the port and starboard stabilizers. Thank you, he response. He can see several broken wires, which makes him wonder what cause them to break. With his hand shaking and slippery from sweat, he reconnects the first set of wires then moves on to the second pair. The ship starts to shake and vibrate more violently every couple of minutes and his heart feels like it's about to burst out of his chest. He franticly completes connecting the second pair of wires and grabs one half of another broken wire and then uses his left hand to blindly feel around for the other half to complete the connection, but he can't find it. He reaches up higher and slides his hand back and forth over the bundle of wires and metal ledge trying to locate the other broken end.

As he blindly searches the ledge and bundle of wires, he starts yelling profanities, which echoes through the void. Where in the hell is that other broken wire? "Yes", he yells as he finds what he thinks is the other half of the wire. Little does he know that he has discovered the culprit that caused all his problems. He pulls what he thinks to be the wire, but it's actually the tail of a dead mouse that has been thoroughly burnt, which he's now holding between his fingers.

He yells, almost like a schoolgirl who sees a snake in the garden, as he frantically tosses the charred dead mouse to the floor beneath him. "Are you alright", MOM asked? Yes, I'm fine, he replies with a slight tone of fear in his voice as he wipes his fingers that was holding the tail of the mouse across the leg of his jumper over and over again. You sounded like LaChel when you screamed, MOM responds. I didn't scream, he replies! I may have yelled. No, that was definitely a full throated, prepubescent scream, she replies. "That's enough MOM", he sternly replies. We have very little time and I need you to turn off the power to the stabilizers and their power transfer subsystems. He figures that the mouse must have been chewing through one of the wires when it got fried. So he knows that there's an exposed wire somewhere in the bundle and he doesn't want to get shocked with 150 volts. I have secured the power to the stabilizers and their subcomponents and we now have eight minutes before we enter the thermosphere. BK reaches his hand across the bundle of wires and feels the unmistakable sensation of a broken wire. He grabs it and pulls it out as far as he can, while making sure not to strip the wire from its' source. He can't see the wires he has connecting, but luckily, he has done this so many times that he can strip a wire with one hand and connect the two ends in seconds. He franticly manipulates his fingers to twist the wires together tightly as he can, then tells MOM to power-up the stabilizers. I don't recommend that I do that, because you are still partially embedded in the access opening and it is a very good possibility that you may receive a very violent shock that has the possibility of damaging a substantial portion of your body or in the worst case, "killing you". He understands the risk, but if connecting the broken wires doesn't work; it would take too much time to squeeze himself back in the opening. Time is something he's quickly running out of.

"MOM", I understand the risk, he yells. Just do what I ask, please. MOM doesn't agree with his reckless actions, but she restores power to the stabilizers. But she watches him closely for signs of distress, extreme screaming and/or smoke emanating from his body. Just in case MOM was right, he closes his eyes and stiffens his body in anticipation of various voltage coursing through his extremities.

He waits silently for a brief moment to hear the slight hum of the stabilizers starting, but nothing happens. There is no response to the repairs to the stabilizers, MOM announces. I strongly recommend that you join your family in the hanger and I will transfer my program to the escape vehicle before it is too late. He feels a sense of dred and frustration envelopes him as he balls his fist and pounds them against the wall. "That's it" he thinks to himself. Three years of my blood, sweat and tears are about to, he hopes, burn up in the atmosphere. He just stays there for a moment, still halfway in and halfway out of the opening, trying to make sense of what went wrong. He's out of time and now he's about to lose his ship. "I'm coming out", he yells in a disappointing tone to MOM as he starts to twist and maneuver himself out of the opening.

He grabs the wire bundle shelf with one hand and a vertical beam with the other hand and forces himself out. As he grabs a hand full of ledge and wires, he inadvertently shifts the bundles of wires slightly. As he pushes out of the opening, he feels the hairs on his arms start to tingle from the static electricity. He automatically knows what's happening and quickly uses his hands and legs to push himself out of the access opening. As soon as he clears the opening, he can hear the slight hum of the stabilizers steadily coming back to life. The stabilizers and their components are now online and are operating within normal parameters, MOM responds. He releases an ecstatic yell of happiness that can be heard throughout engineering and probably throughout the entire ship. He then shouts to MOM to get his ship back in its' previous orbit.

As he steps out of the opening, he starts to feel the weight of his emotions bubbling up from his soul, which drops him to his knees. He's now on his knees with his hands in his lap looking up at the ceiling and thinking to himself how close he came to losing everything. His mind quickly shifts to his now traumatized family freaking out in the hanger and what he's going to tell them. MOM tells him that they are gaining altitude and we should be back in our original orbit in approximately three minutes, thirty-three seconds. But while monitoring various government defense systems, she discovered that China is preparing to fire two of their KT series ballistic missiles to stop the ship from leaving their air space.

He jumps to his feet and grabs the nearest tablet. "Are you sure", he asked as he starts tapping and swiping. As the ship plunged deeper into the atmosphere and into the range of various friendly and hostile countries, I have been continuously monitoring all military communications of these countries and the status of their weapon's systems. He reviews the data that she has collected and can see that China is ready to fire their missiles and three of the major powers have targeted his ship, but haven't committed to launching their missiles. Just then he hears a more terrifying sound than MOM telling him that China's ten mega ton missile is one mile out. It's Lorraine's voice franticly yelling and cursing like a drunken gym teacher from inside his jumper's pocket. He forgot all about his family still waiting for him in the hanger and still thinking that they maybe about to die. He grabs the communicator from his pocket, and takes a deep breath. "Babe, he says a couple of times as calmly as he can in an attempt to calm her down.

He can hear his girls crying and calling him. He's shocked to hear Kim's voice amongst the crying and yelling of LaChel and Lorraine. "Is Kim alright", he yells in a jovial voice as if the ship was never about to crash. "What's going on and why aren't you here yet", she yells while holding the hand of a confused and crying Kim. He tells her that they are fine! The ship is not in danger anymore, so please tell the girls to stop crying. He can hear her telling the girls that he has fixed the ship and that they will be going back to her Clinic now.

But LaChel starts to yell that she wants to get off this piece of crap and Lorraine joins in her daughter's bashing of his ship. Babe, I have everything under control, and we are perfectly safe, he says in a calm and soothing voice. China is now firing two missiles at us and they are armed with megaton warheads, MOM announces to BK, which Lorraine has no problem over hearing.

"What the hell did she just say, Lorraine says in disbelief. Firing, megaton warheads, she whispers as she turns toward the passenger side window, so her daughters can't hear her. Baby, I have this under control, so you and the girls can head back to the Clinic. Lorraine starts to speak low but sternly into the communicator, but he cuts her off with a "sorry baby got to go", as he shuts off his communicator. Lorraine believes her husband when he says he has everything under control, but the word "missiles" is still resonating through her head, so she decides to stay in the escape vehicle until this threat is over too.

BK tells MOM that Lorraine isn't going to be to happy when he gets to the Clinic, as he walks over and sits down at the computer monitor. Since we have regained control of the ship, I have no doubts that the ship can handle a direct hit from both of those warheads without sustaining any damage.

By my calculations, only one of China's two missiles has a chance of over taking us as we ascend to our original orbital position, MOM announces. I find it hard to believe that the Chinese' Defense Agency could make such a huge targeting miscalculation, she adds. I have also scanned both missiles and one of them is having navigational difficulties and my scans indicate that the flaw is in one of the missile's dorsal fin mechanisms. He reviews MOM's scans and analyses of the missiles and checks each of their trajectories. The leading missile will miss us by half a mile. MOM also informs him that the trailing missile with the accurate trajectory is seven minute thirteen seconds away from the ship. Can you tell me if the trailing missile will re-enter the earth's atmosphere and where it will detonate?

As she calculates the defective missile's trajectory, BK calculates the possibility of destroying both missiles by testing the ship's plasma laser. That is something that he doesn't want to do, because then all the monitoring countries will know that he has the capability to destroy missiles in flight, which is something he doesn't want them to know yet. I calculate that the leading missile will impact the southern region of Australia and has the possibility to kill and injure thousands of people. He stands there leaning over the monitor, pondering his options for a moment. The missile is now seven minutes away from the ship, MOM again announces. He takes a seat at the engineering console and starts to rapidly type in his own calculations on his keyboard as he instructs her to increase the ship's velocity.

Increasing ship's velocity will cause the first missile to run out of fuel before reaching us, which will cause it to reenter earth's atmosphere and impact another unsuspecting continent. No, I don't plan on letting that happen, he replies. I need you to gain control of the leading missile guidance system and initiate a change in its' flight path before it runs out of fuel, so we can program it to decrease its' velocity and cross into the path of the trailing missile. This will cause both missiles to explode high enough in the thermosphere so that they will no longer be a threat to anyone. MOM calculates that most of the missiles' debris will vaporize as they descend through the earth's atmosphere.

That's right MOM, but we have only 52 seconds left to make this happen. The trailing missile is starting to deviate from its' flight path. I am hacking into the lead missile's guidance system. I am now in complete control of the missile, slowing the lead missiles' velocity and inputting new targeting coordinates. Will China realize in time that we have high jacked their missile? They'll realize something is wrong, but they will not have enough time to regain control of the missiles, she replies. I have completed the reprogramming and the missiles will collide with each other in exactly thirty-one and a half seconds. MOM is multi-taskikng right now, by assisting BK with the control of the Chinese missiles and monitoring Lorraine and the girls. You would think that she would fine the infiltration of a foreign government's defense system would be the most interesting of the two, but she's more interested in what's happening in the hanger.

LaChel is blubbering and rambling on about how she doesn't want to die and how it's not fair that she's not going to kiss and hold Antonne again. Lorraine yells at her that she has heard enough and to please calm down, because she's scaring her sister. But she's a sixteen year old girl that's very wrapped up into her own emotional thoughts and consequently she's too distraught to even listen to her mother. Kim is still feeling the effects of her time in stasis and her mind is fading in and out, but she can hear her sister crying behind her. Lorraine has heard enough and turns her chair around toward LaChel then leans forward to get closer to her. LaChel is still deep into her own pitty party when her mother gives her the five fingers of clarity right across her wet left cheek. The slap brings her back to reality as she shouts "Mom" in surprise of the slap.

"I want you to get a hold of yourself and stop that crying", she says in a low stern tone while staring directly into LaChel's tearful eyes. Lorraine knows this is a very trematic situation, but she doesn't have the time or patience to baby a sixteen year old. Kim needs her full attention right now. LaChel rubs the side of her face that her mom just assaulted and gives her a, "yes ma'am". MOM analyzes Lorraine's style of parenting. She categorizes her style as "Authoritative". She would like to ask Lorraine some questions, but she has noticed that when humans are under stress, they react emotionally, and she would not appreciate her inquiries at this time.

Meanwhile, BK is calculating the potential size and explosive power of the missiles heading toward them. He's sure that the nuclear explosion of the missiles shouldn't compromise the ships first line of defense, but the protective membrane hasn't been actually tested, other than in various computer simulations. "Until now". MOM announces to BK that the Chinese are attempting to regain control of the lead missile, but they are too late, she states. Three, two, one, "grab some real-estate", MOM says loudly as the two missiles collide and explode roughly three quarters of a mile to the port side of the ship. The shock wave from the explosion shakes the ship slightly and gives the ship an added boost into a higher orbit. The explosion doesn't do any damage, but the shock wave slightly resonates throughout the ship. "Grab some real estate", BK repears with some surprise. "I thought I would interject some levity to reduce your tension, she replies. That was unexpected, but good, he states. BK can hear Lorraine's muffled calling him once again from his pocket. The unexpected vibration of the exploding missiles frighten the girls and Lorraine had to come up with a reason for what happened.

He tries to answer the communicator with a calm, "Hey Lorraine", but could only get "hey" out before she yells, "I thought you told me that the ship is fine now"! He response with "everything is just fine, babe". The missiles exploded outside the ship, but as you can see – we are still in one piece. Who in the hell is shooting missiles at us, she says in a subdued voice in order to not alarm her girls?

Don't they know we have children up here? Baby, I really don't think they give a damn about who's onboard. They just wanted the ship, he adds. But I promise I will be there as soon as I give the engineering units their instructions and then I will explain what's going on. Just give me a few minutes to get the units working inspecting areas of the ship for damages. I am trying to keep it together, but I don't know what's going on and our children are asking me questions that I don't have the answers to, she says in a whispering tone. I'll be there in a minute. I'm going to take the girls back to my Clinic, but I want you there in ten minutes, she says forcefully. He ends the call with a "you got it babe"!. Lorraine then tells LaChel and Kim everything is fine now and that their dad has corrected the problem with the ship and that they will be going back to the Clinic. LaChel looks releaved as she wipes the remaining tears from her eyes. Lorraine reaches over Kim and opens the sliding door then yells out the door for the medical units to get their plastic butts over here to help her. The units immediately hover over to assist her with the wheelchair and the gurney.

BK switches the consoles screen from navigation to maintenance in order to begin typing instructions, which will then be transfer to the engineering and maintenance units. He's instructing them to survey the entire ship for damages. MOM on the other hand is still focusing on the activities taking place at the various military facilities. She tells him that the Chinese, Americans, Russians and the British are all still monitoring and targeting us.

He asked her how much time do they have until they're out of weapons range? She calculates every weapon's option for each missile launcher location and velocity of each weapon. I do not anticipate anyone firing at us at this point, because by the time the missile reaches earth's upper stratosphere; we will be well out of missile range. Good, then lets get this ship squared away and back to normal operations, he says as he breathes a sigh of relief. He gets up from the chair and starts to walk toward the door. He's about to exit engineering but stops three to four feet from the door. He just stands there silent and by the look on his face, he's in some sort of turmoil. MOM doesn't ask him any questions, but she takes the opportunity to study him and his subtle body language to decipher what's maybe wrong with him. As she uses her psychological database to search for the reason for his hesitation; she thinks she understands his peculiar mannerisms.

Are you afraid that Lorraine is once again going to swing for the fences with her right shin to your testicles, MOM asked? He looked surprised that she was right and was extremely amazed that she used the proper analogy. He couldn't lie to her, so he just shakes his head yes then continued on his way out the door. MOM is very curious about human behavior and relationships, so during these types of potential confrontations, she usually becomes a fly on the wall and just monitors the room without saying a word. He walks down the hallway not looking forward to answering Lorraine's questions, let alone the attitudes of the now unfrozen women in his life. He always understood that what he's attempting to accomplish would be dangerous, but when the rubber hits the road and the danger becomes real.

It's like all of a sudden, someone just slaps you in the face with a five finger dose of reality. Not just someone or a couple of disgruntled people were trying to kill them, but superpowers with mega ton missiles are pointing them right in their face and are more than willing to pull the trigger. Now he's going to have to explain to his family what happen and that we still are a big target floating up here. MOM broke the silence by announcing that the ship is now back in it's proper orbit and safe from any future missile threats.

That's great, but the word "safe" is not the word I would choose to describe our situation at the moment, he says as he continues down the hallway. Yes, you are correct in your assumption that the governments will continue to try to figure out a viable method of forcing you to return to earth, but for now we are safe, she reiterates. In his mind, he knows the only way for him and his family to be truly safe is to follow his plan to download his technology and the ship's schematics to every computer on earth. That way the governments will be too busy trying to contain the damage and to be the first one to develop the first of many spacecrafts. But that would be jumping the gun and all the pieces are not yet in place for that to happen. For now, he has to walk down to the medical clinic and try to calm his family's fragile nerves. I'm going to spend the rest of the day with my family, he tells MOM. Please monitor the progress of the repairs and contact me via text message, if something else catastrophic happens. Yes BK and enjoy your time with your family, she says with all seriousness. You have a poor choice of word selection in these types of situations, he tells her.

There will be nothing enjoyable about explaining to my family why we all most died and why we still have a rather large bullseye on the hull of this ship. "You are right", MOM replies. Remain calm and speak in a low but deliberate tone, but most importantly – guard your genitals, she adds. BK laughs. Now that's a suggestion that I can really use, he says as he continues to laugh and walk down the hall toward the medical clinic.

Chapter Seven

Family Problems – *Filling the cracks*

August 24, 2023 - Currently there are 7.5 billion humans occupying more and more of its' surface. Consequently, humans are consuming and polluting the earth's limited resources. Unlike ants, humans scurry around the planet consuming and depleting its' resources without any concerns of their future or the welfare of the other species that share the planet.

Agent Billy Joe Demons, who goes by Bill and doesn't care for anyone making derogatory remarks about his last name is the Lead Agent on the Thomas disappearance case. He's been married to his wife Marsha for fifteen years and has three daughters and one son. His partner is Agent Ajay Khanna has only been an agent for six years and is a very idealistic young man with a hot temper. He's devorced and has been taking care of his father for the past two years. As both agents in their black suits, white shirts and highly polished black shoes exit the garage elevator and walk toward their car, Bill announces to Ajay that he'll drive. Ajay doesn't say a word, just walks around the car and gets into the passenger side seat. As Ajay flops down into the seat, he slams the door as if the door said something disparaging about his mother. Bill understands the anger and frustration that his partner is still feeling because of the case briefing with their Supervisor that they just attended. Normally agents assigned to a case have unlimited access to all pertinent information and materials related to the case, but he explained to them that this is an unusual case and they can only review two folders of redacted documents. The Director of the Bureau of Investigation has classified the entire case as Secret Compartmental Information (SCI) and has set restrictions and limitations on the information, and who the agents can investigate or interview.

But Ajay didn't understand or agree with not being able to review the entire case file or the materials that were collected at the residence. They were only allowed to review a very thin and redacted case folder, which only contained the basics of information about Mr. Thomas and his family. Bill wasn't happy either, but he's a twenty-two year veteran of the Bureau and has experienced one of these types of cases before. He understands that the Bureau assigns you a case and you have to just work with what they give you or the lack there of.

After they go back and forth with their supervisor for about fifteen minutes, Bill sees the reality of the situation and tries to convince his partner to just accept the lack of information and move on. But that only caused Ajay to turn on Bill and his supervisor. And now they in the car about to drive to BK's therapist office to gather information on his one and a half year sessions. Bill pulls out of the garage and onto the main street. Because Ajay is still fuming from their meeting, he immediately pulls out his mini ipad and begins to surf the net, so he doesn't have to talk to his partner. Bill has been with his partner for years and he knows not to try to talk with him right now, so he doesn't say anything for about five minutes, but they have another forty-five minutes of driving and Bill wants to talk, but not about the briefing.

He decides to change his partner's chain of thought by bringing up a personal issue of his partner. So has your father had any more episodes, he says with a curious tone. Ajay continues to tap and swipe at his ipad for a few more seconds before answering. "He's not getting any better", he says as he looks up from his ipad. He came to breakfast this morning dressed like my mother again. Bill is fascinated by Ajay's father's mental condition.

"The shoes and the purse too", Bill asked? Ajay looks angerly over at his partner. I don't know if I should discuss my problems with you, because you seem to be too amused by my father's current mental affliction. He was somewhat right about Bill is amused, but it was more of a curiosity. No, I'm just very interested that a man can miss his wife so much that he's periodically and unknowingly takes on her persona. And yes, he can't help but to think it would be funny to see Ajay's father dressed to the nine in his wife's dress and pearls. You know that I have a minor in psychology, Bill states as if that would explain his interest in Ajay's father. Your mother passed away over two years ago, but your father must obviously still miss her. That's the conclusion of his therapist, Ajay replies. They were married for over thirty-two years and were hardly ever separated. But the hardest part is that he doesn't realize what he's doing, and we can't tell him about his actions, because it could seriously damage his mental stability. Bill just shakes his head in disbelief. He decides to ask a crazy question that his partner may not have thought of right now. What if your father, when he thinks he's your mother, decides to date someone?

Ajay glares over at him as if someone just flicks on a switch in his brain. He never really thought about his father mistakenly dating someone when he's having an episode. He has allowed his father to leave the house while dressed as his mother, because his therapist said it would do him some good to get out of the house even if he thinks he's his wife.

Ajay begins to think that he needs to talk with his father's therapist again about some medication and to make sure his father doesn't leave the house alone anymore. "Sorry to give you something else to think about", he replies as he can see the effects its' having on his partner. Bill spends the remainder of the driving discussing this partner's problem with his father, which helped Ajay forget about the problem with the Bureau. Bill and Ajay arrive at BK's therapist building and proceed to take the elevator up to Dr. Kathy Knightley's office.

They walk from the elevator and into the small waiting room of the Doctor's office with about five of her patients sitting against the wall waiting to see her. All eyes focus on them as Ajay closes the door behind them. As they approach the receptionist's desk, she says in a slightly southern drawl, "Can I help you gentlemen"? Just like on an episode of Law and Order, they flash their two fold wallet with their picture and the letters "FBI" on the top and a gold polished badges on the bottom at her and request to speak with Dr. Knightley. She asked if they have an appointment? "No", but this is Government business and of the utmost importance. She looks at both of their serious faces for a moment and then picks up her phone. "Dr. Knightley". I'm sorry to disturb you, but there are two FBI agents out here and they don't have a appointment, but they said that need to speak with you right away. She listens to the Doctor for a moment then says, alright, then hangs up. She tells the Agents that the Doctor will be available in a few minutes. "You can have a seat", she says with as smile. They look around the room and can see that there's only one empty chair available, so they decide to wait there at the desk, which the receptionist doesn't really care for. Ajay looks around the room and gives a half smile to the piercing eyes looking at them. As he scans the room, most of them look down at the magazines or continue to tap on their electronic devices, but one elderly woman just continues to make unflinching eye contact with him. She looks at him as if he back handed her cat, or told her that her lemon squares were dry.

The door to the Doctor's office suddenly opens and a distraut man exits clutching a fairly large bag. The Doctor is behind him with her hand on his shoulder consoling him and telling him that she'll makeup the time at their next session. He reluctantly nods his head and walks towards the door. The Doctor tells her receptionist to add fifteen minutes to Mr. Philipps next session.

Bill was about to introduce himself to her, but she walks pass him and approaches her next schedule patient, who she noticed looked a little upset. She apologized to her and tells her that her session should only be delay by fifteen minutes and that she will schedule a free session to make it up to her. She's not happy, but she knows that she doesn't have a choice as she looks pass the Doctor and stares harshly at Agent Khanna. He stares back at her and finally understands why she was trying to burn a hole through his skull. She was next in line and she knew they were going to delay her session. As the Doctor walks up to the Agents, Bill introduces himself. Good afternoon Dr. Knightley, I'm Agent Demons and this is Agent Khanna.

Both of them shakes her hand and Bill apologizes to her for disrupting her schedule. She doesn't want them to waist anymore of her time, so she just smiles and asked them to step into her office. Dr. Knightley walks back into her office with the agents strolling in behind her. The Doctor has dealt with family members, employers and local authorities meeting with her regarding one of her patience, but this is the first time that the Federal Bureau of Investigation has paid her a visit. She hopes that it's just something to do with her tax problem, which she thought her attorney resolved a couple of months ago. Please have a seat gentleman, she says while trying to mask the tone of frustration in her voice, because they've interrupted her to patients' sessions.

The Doctor's office is fairly large, painted a light powder blue for it's calming effects, and numerous pictures of her dog on her desk and hanging throughout the office. Bill sits in one of the two chairs in front of the doctor's desk while Agent Khanna decides to sit on the couch adjacent to the doctor's desk and in front of the window. She sits down behind her desk, crosses her legs and leans back into her plush leather chair. So gentlemen, what can I do for you? Again, we apologize for the unscheduled visit and the interruption to your patients' scheduled appointments, but it was imperative that we speak with you today.

We're a branch of the FBI, which investigates United States citizens with special classified accesses that goes missing, and specific threats to our national security. Well, there goes her hopes that it's just about her resolved tax problems.

If you would have just called my receptionist prior to coming here, I would have created a ten or fifteen minute window to speak with you, which could have enabled me to maintain my patients schedule and answered your questions, she says to emphasize the importance of her work. Agent Khanna is still a bit upset about his supervisor putting restrictions on their case and now here's someone else expressing irritation about talking to him. I'm sorry Doctor, but the FBI seldom makes appointments, because most of the time we have a very tight timetable, he states as he sits behind his partner on the sofa. Agent Demons decides to defuse the tension in the room. You have a lovely office, as he looks around the room, which is very neatly decorated and displays her numerous academic diplomas. She gives him a less than genuine, Thank you. I don't mean to be rude, but the sooner you ask me the questions you need me to answer, the sooner I can get back to my patients. "Fare enough", Agent Khanna says as he pulls out his mini tablet from the pocket inside his jacket. We understand that Mr. BK Thomas was once a patient of yours for a number of years. "Yes", one and a half years to be exact, she responds immediately. She remembers that their last session was disturbing to her, because BK was totally disillusioned with the Federal Government, because they lied to him and gave him the impression that his family would be in danger if he didn't comply with their demands. He was very afraid of his Government, but he told me he knew what he had to do. What information are you looking for, as she tries to maintain a game winning poker face.

I'm surprised that you can remember Mr. Thomas without looking through your records or even taking a little time to reflect on his name, Agent Demons states. She leans back in her chair and clasp her hands together then explains to them that sometimes in a person's profession they meet one or two patients that are eched into your brain. Mr. Thomas was one of those patients. I'm certain in your long law enforcement career, you've ran across at least one of these types of people, she says as she looks directly at Agent Demons. He treats her statement as rhetorical, then continues with his questions. We need to know everything you and Mr. Thomas discussed throughout the time you were treating him. The Doctor sits up in her chair and asks why they need such sensitive information on one of her former patients. Agent Khanna quickly replies to the Doctor's question.

The FBI has opened an investigation against Mr. Thomas on the grounds that he embezzled hundreds of thousands of dollars from his company, kidnapped his family, and may be planning to leave the country with some highly sensitive information. It would be to your best interest to just answer the questions, He states in a stern tone. She can see that both agents are intently serious about getting as much information as possible from her. I'll gladly give you all the information I can legally convey to you, but you must understand that I can not divulge any personal information that Mr. Thomas has confided to me as his therapist.

Allow me to make our intensions perfectly clear, Agent Demons proclaims in a firm tone. We understand your rights and legal privileges as the therapist of Mr. Thomas, but we are authorized to take any action deemed necessary to accomplish our mission and they may include purging your office of all it's records both digitally and hardcopy. He reaches into his inside jacket pocket and pulls out a thin bunddle of folded papers, which he then leans forward and hands to the doctor.

She doesn't want to take the folded documents, because she knows exactly what they are and what they will demand. For a couple of seconds, she doesn't move, but knowing that she doesn't have a choice, she reaches forward and takes them from his hand. She has never dealt with the FBI before, but some of her colleagues have and they all say the same thing. They ask first, but if they don't get exactly what they want; they take everything related and nonrelated as a message to not mess with the FBI. She opens the papers and gleams across the paragraphs only to ensure that the paperwork look halfway official. Excuse me gentlemen, as she drops the papers on her desk. I have to take a moment to speak with my attorney.

Agent Demons nods his head as a gesture for her to proceed. She picks up her cell phone from her desk and politely asked the Agents do they mind stepping out of the office while she talks to her attorney. Both agents just stare at her and remain in their seats. No thank you doctor, but please, by all means, speak to your attorney. We'll wait, but remember, time is not on your side, Agent Khanna tells her. Dr. Knightley looks upset that she has to talk to her attorney in front of them. Her attorney's name is Ted Courtney. Hello Ted. Agents Khanna and Demons of the FBI are sitting here in my office and they have a court order to retrieve any and all of my records they deem pertinent to my sessions with Mr. BK Thomas, which took place over a year ago. Agent Demons looks at his watch then looks back at the Doctor.

Dr. Knightley gives her lawyer the agents name, court order number and the Judge's name that's on the document. OK, Ted. Call me back as soon as you confirm this order. She ends the call on her cell phone then focuses her attention back to the Agents. What do you want to know, while I'm waiting for him to call me back. Tell us about your treatment of Mr. Thomas and what was his metal state at that time, Agent Khanna replies. Well, I met BK over a year ago after he was in a terrible car accident that almost killed him.

How badly were his injuries, Agent Demons asked? Some fractured ribs, cuts and contusions, but the real damage was to his brain. He was unconscious when they brought him in and the doctor didn't think he was going to regain consciousness. But after a week, to the Doctor's amazement, he not only regained consciousness, but he was able to clearly talk to his wife and Doctor. But BK's real problem was that he didn't have any feeling from his shoulders down. The doctors explained to his wife that the part of his brain that controlled his motor abilities was extremely damaged and he would have to adapt to being a quadriplegia for the remainder of his life. I imagine he was devastated, Agent Khanna added. Yes, and like most patients that suffer a life changing accident; he was in denial. He felt that the doctors didn't truly understand the way the brain worked and consequently didn't know what they were talking about. Like most patients with his condition, he felt that he would regain control of his body within a couple of months. I was hired by the hospital to speak with patients with extreme life changing injuries. So I was tasked with ensuring that BK and his wife and daughters were mentally prepared for the challenges that they were about to face.

I had bed side meetings with him and his wife Lorraine at the hospital, but BK was not interested in anything I had to say, so I focused my attention on Lorraine, who was very responsive and thankful for all the help that I could offer. But it was very little I could do without the participation of the patient, so after a few weeks, I gave her my card and asked her to call when BK decides to participate in the treatment. I thought I'd hear from them in four to six months, but to my surprise, after about three weeks Lorraine called me asking to talk to her husband. So, his wife call, but Mr. Thomas still didn't want to talk to you, Agent Demons asked? No, she replied. She was extremely worried, because a doctor from South Africa was speaking to BK for a couple of weeks and had convinced him to volunteer for a very controversial and dangerous surgery by promising him that he can regain at least 65 percent of his mobility. "Wow", that sounds like a good deal to me, Agent Khanna exclaimed. If I was in his shoes, I would do anything to be able to walk again. "Yes", I would admit that sound like a good gamble, but at Lorraine's request, I did some research on the Doctor. What was the doctor's name? Dr. Amose Mobosa of Botswana, she replied. I found out that Dr. Mosbosa was under criminal and malpractice investigation in Botswana for the death of two of his patients with similar physical conditions. He promised them an unbelievable percentage of mobility in order to agree to the procedures, but both ended up dying weeks after the operations.

He has due back in Botswana for a hearing on whether he was going to lose his license to practice medicine and face some time in prison. Agent Demons interrupts the doctor. Surely the hospital did a background check on their employees. Especially the ones that would be operating on their patients. Why in the hell would the hospital agree to allow Dr. Mobosa to perform any operation in their hospital, Agent Khanna asked in amazement?

The hospital was not in the best financial shape at the time, she replies. The hospital's board of directors had been making some extremely risky investments, which put the hospital's finances into a very deep hole. The hospital was about six months away from closing and then an audit would be required and questioned would have to be answered. The doctor was in the United States lecturing on his ability to restore the mobility of paralyzed patients in his country, when the hospital saw an opportunity to possibly get in on the ground floor of an innovative procedure, which they didn't properly research.

In other words, they were financially grasping at straws and were afraid of going to prison and were desperate for someone to pull their ass out of the fire, Agent Khanna states. "True", and their gamble almost paid off. "We're listening", Agent Demons says as he leans back in his chair. If the surgery was successful, which it was, they would make billions and that would have pulled their asses out of the fire and plopped them into a golden chair. Where can we find this Doctor, Khanna asked as he gets ready to type in the Doctors address and phone number. She pauses for a moment then tells the Agents that the doctor was killed in a car accident in Botwana a month and a half ago.

The Agents look surprise by the death of someone that could have possiblely filled in some holes in BK's story. "That was convenient", Agent Khanna states suspiciously. The Botswanain investigative authority submitted the coronor's report to the hospital, which confirmed the reason for the accident that claimed the Doctor's life. The report spelled out that the doctor was under the influence of various drugs and alcohol. Evidently, he was celebrating his successful treatment of Mr. Thomas at a hotel and tried to drive back to his aunt's house where he was staying. He ran off the road and plunged off a cliff, high in the mountains of his hometown. That's ashame, Agent Demons says as he shakes his head. Just when he made a breakthrough in his career, he won't get to reap the rewards of his hard work. The Doctor just listens to him without commenting. So, Mr. Thomas regained his full mobility, he asked? "Yes he did", she replies, which was an understatement. "Well" I guess we will have to use the Doctor's paperwork to possible fill in the missing pieces.

Who in the hospital's administration should we talk to about retreiving the Doctor's research and procedural documents he used to restore Mr. Thomas' mobility? Dr. Knightley cuts them off at the knees again by telling them that Dr. Mobosa wasn't a trusting person and took all his research with him and unfortunately, the documents and research material was still in the trunk of his car when the accident occurred. Consequently, all the research was totally destroyed by the fire. Dr. Mobosa's aunt reported him missing and it took three days to find the reckage and another day to recover the Doctor's remains. Agent Khanna leans forward and asked the doctor why the Hospital allowed him to take all his research materials and didn't ask to make copies of his documents. Dr. Knightley states that the hospital wasn't in any position to make any demands. "Alright, Agent Demons", says as he sighs. Can you tell us anything that can help us understand Mr. Thomas' state of mind while under your care?

She doesn't want to tell them anything, but her attorney hadn't called her back yet and she's afraid that they might take all her files in order to get the information they wanted. She makes the decision to tell them as little as possible. Just enough to keep them busy until hopefully her attorney gives her some good news. Mr. Thomas was a brilliant but tormented man, who just wanted to share his knowledge with the rest of the world. But he stated to me that he was nieve to think that the Government would let him share his gift with the rest of humanity. Thanks to Dr. Mobosa's mistake during the operation, Mr. Thomas has an IQ of 238. "What mistake", Agent Demons asked? One of the nurses that was assisting the doctor during the operation, told me that by the look on the doctor's face after opening Mr. Thomas skull, his facial expression was one of pure surprise and apprehension. She wasn't allowed to view his procedure, but she could tell by his expression that the damage was extensive. But he must have figured out away to bypass the damaged areas and complete his procedure.

Normally those types of surgeries are recorded, Agent Khanna states. Normally you would be correct, but Dr. Mobosa had his attorney put in the contract that all documents and recordings associated with the procedure will be under his authority and possession. It's amazing that the hospital would agree with those terms, Agent Khanna responds. This was the one and only chance for the hospital to climb out of a mound of debt and bad management.

They were going to market the procedure all over the world and consequently make billions for all the board members and the senior staff. Just then the doctor's cellphone rings. "Excuse me gentlemen", she says as she answers it. It's her attorney and he tells her that the court order is legal and that she has to give them her full cooperation or they do have the right to remove all her files. "I understand" she says as she taps the icon on the phone to end the call. Agent Demons can see that she has talked to her attorney and she understands that she must cooperate fully with their investigation. So, Doctor. Tell me what you and Mr. Thomas were discussing at this last session, Agent Demons asked? He was frustrated that his family was threatened and that he was forced into a job he didn't want. He thought with good reason that the Government was going to weaponize his ideas for their own financial and authoritarian reasons. I tried to convince him to continue coming to my office, but he said he had his own method of sharing his knowledge. His last words he said to me was, "what's the point of being the smartest ant on the planet if you can't help your fellow ants". So he considered himself and everyone else as insignificant, Agent Khanna asked? "No", she says sharply. He always has looked at humanity as a society of the universe and that we are not as significant as we believe we are conpaired to the vastness of the cosmos. In that since, he considers himself and everyone else on the planet as ants. Agent Khanna interrupts her by asking if she thought he was capable of killing his wife and daughters. She responds with an emphatic, "no". How can you be so sure, Agent Demons asked? Regardless of what the Government has forced him to do; he still maintained his altruistic personality. All he wanted to do was take care of his family and share his knowledge with his fellow human beings. I have no idea where he is, but I can assure you that his family is alive and with him, she adds. But that's just my professional opinion, she says with a sarcastic tone. Agent Khanna gets his partners attention and taps on his watch to indicate that they are out of time. He nods his head then thanks the Doctor for her cooperation and apologizes for disrupting her schedule.

She's glad that it's over and accepts his apology. But she's not going to like what he's about to say next. Both Agents stand as the Doctor follows suit, thinking they are about to shake her hand and tell her goodbye. Agent Khanna gets on his cellphone and tells the person on the other end that their finish and to come over and retrieve the files. Dr. Knightley hears what he says and looks surprised at Agent Demons. What do you mean, "retrieve the files" and what files is he talking about, she says angerly?

All of Mr. Thomas' information will be remove and purged from your files and computer systems, Agent Demons responds. We will also request that you not discuss this meeting or any of your sessions with anyone, regarding Mr. Thomas or his family. She is shocked and stunned by what is happening. I answered all your questions and now you are still going to take my files, she says with a ton of attitude. "Yes", but we are only removing Mr.

Thomas' files and not taking your entire patient database or closing you down, which we are authorized to do if we deem it necessary. She's visibly shaken by what is happening. We have four agents coming here in the next thirty minutes and they will move as quickly as possible to minimize the amount of disruption to the remainder of your schedule today. She throws up her arms in frustration and flops back down in her chair. The agents that will be retrieving the files are computer forensic specialist, so please give them your full cooperation and don't attempt to conceal anything from them or they will remove all your files and close your office. Both agents then thank a now distraught doctor and walk out of her office.

Aboard his ship, BK is walking down the passageway rubbing his head in anticipation of what he's going to say to them and what he's about to hear from them. His steps are slow and labored as he tries to delay reaching Lorraine's Medical Clinic, where her and the girls are nervously waiting for him. How do you explain to someone, let alone your children that most of the major superpowers, including their own Government are trying to take possession of the ship and its' technology. And they don't give a damn if they have to kill them to get it.

As he gets closer to the Clinic, he decides to just tell them the truth and not try to sugar coat the situation. He's tired of lying to his family and he truly believes that they deserve to know the truth and all the stark realities that goes along with it. He knows he owes them that much, but how they will react to their new reality is the scary part. As he turns the last corner and he stops four feet away from the door, so the sensor won't automatically open it. He takes a couple of deep breaths then walks up to the door, which causes it to open with a swish. He walks in all smiles with his arms outstretched and shouting an enthusiastically, "hello my family". To his surprise, Kim is wide awake and LaChel and Lorraine are standing around her each holding a hand, comforting her. Lorraine's face is one of concern, but he can tell that both of the girls have been crying. He's a little shaken by their expressions, but he continues to walk toward them with a smile, but less than enthusiastic, nevertheless. How are you doing "itty-bitty", which is a nickname he gave Kim when she was about two years old. He gives LaChel a kiss then plants one on Lorraine's lips. She's feeling a little upset at him, because she has been here consoling and reassuring their girls for twenty minutes that they're not going to die. But she knows that she has to hide her emotions, because she sees that both her daughters need the comfort of their parents' confidence and reassurance right now. Kim is the first one to start to ask him questions.

Mom and LaChel wouldn't tell me anything that has happened, Kim says in a shaky and nervous tone. He walks up to her and gives his youngest an enveloping hug. He kisses her on the top of her head then grabs her cheeks with both hands and gives her a loving smile. Everything is going to be all right now as he strokes her hair with his other hand and gives her a comforting smile.

Kim tells her dad that she doesn't understand why her mom and sister looked terrified when they were in the van. LaChel moves closer to the bed. She has always been her sister's protector, so naturally she wanted to be the one to tell her what's happening, but her mother gives her a look not to say a word. She's not going to tell Kim what's going on and she'll be damn if she's going to let LaChel tell her either. She thinks it's BK's responsibility to explain to her what has happened and what he's planning to do. Kim ask what happened to her and why they are in this crazy hospital? Lorraine and LaChel listen intensely hoping to maybe hear something that they hadn't heard before. BK's voice is soft and deliberate as he begins to explain his actions that put all of them in this situation.

I understand what I'm about to tell you will be very hard for you to believe, but your Mom and sister have already heard this and have accepted it. Lorraine and LaChel looked at each other as if to say, "not really". Dad, please tell me what's happening, Kim asked while pushing herself back against the headboard so she can situp. He then sits on Kim's bed then places her hand in his. I need you to listen very carefully and let me finish what I'm about to tell you before you start asking questions, OK. Kim just nods her head, yes. He can feel three sets of eyes intensely staring at him. This will be hard for you to understand, but we are no longer on earth.

He paused for a few seconds to let that sink in. We are all aboard a ship I built, launched into space, and is now orbiting above earth. The expression on Kim's face keeps shifting from confusion to bewilderment as she looks at her mother and sister for support. She then looks at her dad, who is also nodding his head, but he has a smile on his face. "Why are you joking with me", Kim angerly shouts without thinking? "Hey", Lorraine and BK shout at the same time. I know this is a lot to take in and that you're only twelve, and that you are still not feeling well, but don't use that tone of voice when you speak to us, Lorraine sternly replies.

"Or any other time for that matter", BK adds. LaChel gets closer to Kim as she tries to defend her sister's outburst. Mom and Dad, you have to admit this is a lot for her to adjust to, so give her a break. Kim doesn't hear or care about anything that her family is saying to her after her dad told her that they are not on the planet anymore. She is still trying to figure out if all this is real or not. She looks back and forth at her mother and LaChel, then back at her father. They are arguing across her about something, but at the moment it's not important to her. She is tired of being ignored, so she throws her arms up between them and shouts, "please stop arguing and talk to me"! They all look down at her as BK ask MOM to activate the view screen on the portside bulkhead. It worked for Lorraine and LaChel, so it should have the same effect on Kim, he thinks to himself.

"Activating the portside bulkhead", MOM acknowledges. Showing you will be better than just trying to tell you, he explains to her. The view screen appears as a six-foot by four-foot window on the port side of the room. He moves over toward the headboard, so Kim can get a good view of the planet. The ship is in a high earth orbit above the poles, but you can see all of Russia and large portions of China from were Kim is laying.

She lifts up on her elbows and stretches her neck to see the entire view screen. LaChel encourages her to get out of the bed and go over to the viewport to get a better look. "No", her mother shouts as she put her hand on Kim's chess to make sure she doesn't listen to her sister. You are still to weak to get out of bed and start walking around. "Come on mom"! You said the same thing to me, but I walked over there when I first woke up. Your sister has just had what she compares to heart surgery and should stay in bed until she has been cleared by me. "Heart surgery", Kim shouts as she looks over at her mom. When did I have heart surgery, she asked in a scared but curious tone? "Damn it", Lorraine can't believe that she blurted that out, she thinks to herself. Don't worry, she says as she puts her hand on Kim's shoulder. Everything is fine now. Lorraine moves LaChel to the side and they switch places. You're in perfect health, but you just need to rest for a couple more days. "No"! What happened to me that I would need to have someone cut open my chest and play around with my heart. She still looks to her father for answers. "Dad", what happen to me? BK looks over at Lorraine for help, but she just gives him a look that says, change the subject please. Babe, I think it would help her to know what happened to her. Lorraine thinks to herself that she wishes she had kept her mouth shut about the surgery. At least until Kim could get use to the idea that she's orbiting the earth in her father's homemade spacecraft. "Mom", I think you should tell her, LaChel says as her mother looks at her with a disapproving scowl.

"I agree", MOM's says as her voice fills the room. She's not talking to you, Lorraine shouts as she looks up at the ceiling speakers. "Grandma Betty", Kim says as she looks around the room. "No", sweetheart that's just the ship's computer. That's just something else we will need to talk to you about sometime down the road. Kim is looking thoroughly confused right now because of all the extraordinary information being thrown at her at one time. Lorraine gently grabs Kim's chin and turns her head to focus back to her. Sweetheart please, listen to me very closely. You, me and your sister were frozen in stasis for a brief period of time while your dad launched this spacecraft and positioned us in a safe orbit around earth.

LaChel and I had no problems being removed from stasis and revived, but you had an unforeseen heart abnormality that somehow got worst while you were in stasis. Kim tries to ask questions, but Lorraine holds up her hand and tells her not to ask any questions until she is finished. Kim lies back and nods her head, "yes". Now, what your dad had no way of knowing is that at the time you had a genetic defect in your right heart valve that may not have appeared until your mid-twenties or so.

But thankfully, this unscheduled family trip, she says as she cuts her eyes over at BK; exposed the defect and allowed us the opportunity to repair the damaged valve without any additional danger to you. Kim quickly opens the first buttons of her pajama top and pulls the top portion of her pajama's shirt away from her chest and looks down it to see if she has a scar.

"Where is it", she shouts as she pulls at the collar of her gown and feels for the scar line? But all she feels is the smoothness of her unflawed skin. You don't have any scars Kim, Lorraine says as she smiles then leans over to re-button the collar to her pajama top. "Wait a minute". I may be young and slightly ignorant of medical procedures, but I do know if someone has to repair someone's heart; some slicing has to be done. Kim looks at her mom and dad for answers, but before either of them could respond; another question rushes out her mouth. And where's the doctor that cut me open and operated on my heart? Why isn't he out here explaining this to me? Again, she looks at both of them for answers.

That's because there isn't anyone else on this tin can because mom is the doctor that did the deed, LaChel says with a playful smile. Lorraine backhands LaChel on her shoulder and tells her to let her and her father tell this story. LaChel laughs, as she tells her mother, "OK". Lorraine continues. You did have an operation, but no one had to cut into any part of your body. If no one cut me open or anything, how did you fix what was wrong with me, as she waits for a reply from her parents. Your father created the tiny machines called nano-technological robot or nanobots as he likes to call them, which I modified and used to perform cellular repair on you. They're so small you can only see them with a high-powered microscope. BK realizes that this can be a perfect opportunity to see just how much knowledge Lorraine retained and how readily she can extract it. Kim's about to ask another question when her dad interrupts her. Just lay back and relax for a minute, so your mother can explain the process to you.

He gestures to his wife to continue with her explanation of the procedure. By the expression on his face and his gestures, Lorraine thinks her husband is up to something, but she ignores her curiosity and continues to explain to her little girl what happened. The nanobots we used on you are called "medical nanoes" and are programmed to be used for medical treatment. We used a medical syringe to inject the nanoes directly and precisely into the area we wanted them to repair, which in your case was your left anterior descending coronary artery.

But before we injected you, the nanoes had to be programmed to map your heart, target the defected section and use stem cells to develop new muscle tissue to patch the hole. Kim looks surprisingly calm for someone hearing the small robots have been set loose in her body, but she does feel around for the puncture area. You won't be able to see marks, but you probably will feel a small sore area where we injected the nanoes, her father explained. So, what happened to the nanoes after they finished what they had to do, Kim asked. The nanoes we use are constructed from your body's proteins and will totally be absorbed back into your body without doing any harm. We have nanoes that have been designed for each of us and is stored in stasis in the medical freezers.

So, you mean I still have those little robots marching around in my body like a bunch of army ants or something, Kim exclaims? You have nothing to worry about, she tells her. Those army ants, as you called them, will totally dissolve in three or four days and you will never know that they were in your body. Kim still looks a little upset and confused about everything that's going on. You look like you have some more questions you need us to explain, he says as he moves closer to her bed. I have a ton of questions, but all of this is so hard to believe and I'm having a hard time believing all of this is real and not just some joke that you, mom and LaChel are playing on me.

He starts to think that Kim is not the only one that can benefit from some type of reality check. He doesn't have much of a poker face, so when Lorraine looks over at the expression he has on his face, she automatically thinks he's about to do something real stupid. But she could only get the words "what are you", before he blurts out to MOM, "reduce gravity in this room by 1/6th of its' original state. "Damn it, no", Lorraine yells in an angry tone while aggressively moving toward him. I told you never to take away the gravity in a room I was in again. "You promised me", she yells. One, I never promised you that, babe and two, this is the only way the kids will truly understand where they are. Kim can tell something isn't right as she can feel her body getting lighter and slowly start to lift from her bed.

As his girls' facial expressions starts to change to shock and disbelief and his wife's morphs into anger, he laughs hoping to show everyone that everything will be alright. LaChel and Kim begin to yell and scream as their feet slowly starts to move off the floor.

Lorraine once again ask BK to stop and return the gravity to the room, but he decides to continue with his experiment for awhile longer. As BK and his family are floating about six feet above the floor, he tells them to grab each others hands, which they gladly do like crabs in a bucket. He then uses his left leg to push off the nearest wall, which causes the entire group to float to the center of the room.

Of course, Lorraine and the girls scream a bit, but he quickly calms them down by re-positioning his body, which stabilizes the group. Now the four of them a facing each other, floating in a human ring like a group sky diving exhibition. He smiles and laughs as Lorraine and the girls continue to try to control their bodies and emotions. OK family, now see, this isn't that bad once you get use to it. Kim is the first to begin to smile and lets go of her dad's hand

and only has her sister's hand to stabilize herself. But her other hand is gripping LaChel's hand very tightly. Ouch Kim! You're squeezing the hell out of my hand, LaChel yells.

Hey, you have a pretty good death grip on my hand too, Lorraine reminds LaChel. I'll tell you what, he exclaims. How about if everyone let go of everyone's hands for about 30 seconds, then I'll restore the gravity. He then releases his wife's hand, with great effort, because Lorraine did not want to let go, but with a twist of his wrist, he was free of her. She gives her husband a "you're a dead man look, as her body twitches and turns to stabilize in almost zero gravity". LaChel then lets Kim's hand go and then Kim is now floating free and amazingly stable. BK maybe a deadman, but Kim now believes her dad and she is starting to enjoy herself by moving her arms and twisting her body to make herself turn.

Seeing Kim beginning to maneuver herself around demonstrates to LaChel that this weightlessness isn't that bad. LaChel starts to smile and laugh as she lets go of her mother's hand for three to four second stretches of bravery. Because he had a lot of time on his hands while his family was in stasis, BK has been doing this kind of weightless exercise a number of times and moves around the room like an experienced sky diver. He smiles and laughs while moving around LaChel and Kim, then tries to position himself next to Lorraine, so he can help her move around the room, but Lorraine only once one thing and that is to end this exercise of fear.

With clinched teeth, she says "I told you not to do this", she yells with fear and anger in her voice while BK smiles at her and floats closer to her and attempts to grab her around her waist. She grabs on to his shirt and a lot of his shoulder as she starts to dig her nails in. OK, calm down babe. It's going to be OK, you just have to relax and just float.

But she digs her nails a little deeper into his shoulder just to drive home the point that this isn't fun for her. She pulls him closer to her and speaks softly and deliberately to him. They are floating face to face now and slowly going in a circle. Now, do I have your attention and are you listening to me, she asks him as she looks directly into his eyes. Meanwhile the girls are beginning to get the hang of being in a weightless environment and are starting to have fun. They are about six feet away from their parents, giggling at each other and locked hand in hand slowly rotating in a circle like they're on a marry-go-round in the park. They are laughing and smiling and totally unaware of the imminent danger that their father is in if he doesn't comply to his wife's demands. I want you to get me down from here in the next two minutes or so help me, I'm going to punch you so hard that you're going to launch into that far wall. "Look at your daughters", he says with a gleeful look on his face. She doesn't care how much fun her kids are having as she uses her facial expressions to convey her emotional state. He could see that his wife was not joking and that he'd better get her feet firmly back on the floor before something bad happens. Alright girls, fun time is over, he says as he escapes his wife's clutches and moves over towards his girls and pulls LaChel closer to him. Grab your sister's arm and give her a slight pull towards you, but not too hard of a pull, he instructs LaChel.

You don't want her slamming into you. As BK gets the girls together, Lorraine grabs the leg of BK's jumper and uses it to move herself back into the circle of her family. Kim grabs her dad's hand, which completes the circle. All right, lets get you all firmly back on solid ground and may be one day soon we can practice this zero gravity exercise again. Lorraine looks over at him with disdain as she shakes her head, to signify a firm "hell no". Well, maybe just the girls and I since we were the only ones to enjoy the experience.

Just then LaChel looks over at Kim as her facial expression suddenly changes from a smile to a look of nausea. Their mother notices it too. Kim, what's wrong, her mother asked as she pushes off BK to get herself closer to her? "Nothing", she says as she tries to breathe deeply to control the volcano of nausea that's building in her stomach. Just get me down and I will be all right. Lorraine echoes Kim's sentiment. MOM, please return the gravity in this room back to its normal state.

"Yes BK, returning gravity to normal. MOM complies to BK's request and almost immediately they can feel the effects of the artificial gravity pulling on their bodies. "Thank God", Lorraine says under her breath as she looks around at both of her daughters. But she can tell by Kim's expression that something isn't quite right. Hold on Kim!. We'll be back on the floor in a matter of seconds, her mother says as she squeezes Kims hand. Now everyone is looking at her as you can tell whatever is wrong is becoming worst. Kim loses some of the color in her face, her eyes start to open wide and her stomach begins to convulse uncontrollably. What happens next is something you never want to happen to you or your worst enemy while you are floating around in zero gravity. Well, yes you would, because it is damn funny. The reason this is happening is because Kim was the last to be awakened out of stasis and even though she hasn't had anything to eat yet; she still has the food from her last day on earth still fermenting in her stomach, because it was in stasis too. And she ate a lot that day. That being said, Kim's stomach is naturally reacting to the unstable gravitational changes and is still weak from her stasis experience. I saw the urgency in her eyes, so I was about to tell MOM to expedite returning gravity more rapidly, but just then Kim tries to say something which her dad thinks was "oh no". But it was mixed with a mouth full of vomit, which erupted like Mount Saint Helen.

You wouldn't think that a girl that size could hold that much food in her mouth and stomach. The velocity and the amount is so great that it propels Kim backward. Lorraine saw it coming, as she yelled "Oh my Lord" and attempts to use her husband as a human shield. Everyone scrambles away from Kim and her moving cloud of vomit, which is moving faster than any one of them. If it was a movie you could hear the Jaws theme music as the mixture of solids and liquids combo starts to breakup into smaller globs and merge back into larger ones. But unfortunately, his youngest wasn't finish just yet.

As BK tries to break away from Lorraine's grasp and back paddle like an Olympic swimmer, Kim shoots some more of her last meal out of her mouth and nose. She's now coughing and crying as the second burst shoots out her mouth and travels in different directions and in different quantities.

Zero gravity isn't anything new to him, but he's amazed at the velocity of Kim's purge of her stomach content and how it's quickly over taking him and Lorraine. LaChel is the first unlucky recipient of her sister's cloud of liquid and solid clusters of food, which hits her arm then proceeds to envelop it. She screams and swipes at it with her other hand, but that illogical action causes the vomit to pass through and commingle between her fingers. She also proceeds to create other globs of vomit by breaking up the larger ones, which makes it worst. She thrashes around like she's on fire.

LaChel screams for one of her parents to get it off her, but since it's not life threatening; it's every man and woman for themselves at this point. Being the most experienced and the most maneuverable, BK had no problem moving out of harm's way. But Lorraine is flailing now trying to kick and backstroke away from the cloud, but all she accomplishes is to flip herself upside down, which allows the cloud to gain ground on her. BK is safe and in the perfect vantage point to see the horror unfold, but as Lorraine twist her body to the right, she sees him floating out of harm's way as if he was a spectator watching a basketball game. "If I get hit with any of this vomit", I am going to kill you, she hysterically shouts as her body turns her back towards the vomit cloud now about six to four inches in front of her. Oh damm that's a big cloud of vomit that's about to collide with my wife he thinks to himself. He knows if he truly wants to live to see his next birthday, he'd better save her from that nauseous cloud. He was close to the wall, so he maneuvered his legs towards the wall and gave himself a little push, which propelled him toward her. As he floats toward her, he grabs her by her ankle and pulls her toward him just in time.

He moved up her body and grabbed her by her waist as they slowly drift past LaChel with various amounts of Kim's vomit in her hair and other parts of her body. The damage is done for LaChel, so her mom and dad just float by her as she kicks and thrashes within the chunks of Kim's vomit. Lorraine pulls and tugs onto BK's jumper, which forces them to the other side of the room in relative safety from the cloud that's now spreading around the Clinic. If he wanted to he could have broken away from her and forced his way through the bio cloud to his girls, but he allows himself to be used as her shield.

As LaChel fingers are covered with her sister's two month old breakfast, lunch and dinner, she too begins to feel nauseous and then spews her own cloud of vomit toward her sister and one of the med units. BK and Lorrain look helplessly as their daughter's cry, yells and vomit on each other and anything in the vicinity.

They love their daughters and should have tried to float over and help them, but their girls are no longer babies and what they're spewing out of their mouths and noses are not anything either one of them could stomach. They would just be adding to the mixture of digested food and liquids floating about the Clinic. Because BK knows how long it takes to restore gravity in a room, he wonders why it's taking MOM so long to restore the gravity.

He angerly yells to MOM to stop playing around and restore the gravity, immediately. Kim and LaChel are blowing chunks all around the room, so get us the hell down now, Lorraine heatedly adds. "Restoring gravity", MOM response! About five to seven seconds after that, everyone starts to quickly descend toward the floor and so does the vomit, which splats onto the floor, the girls, two of the med units and cascades down some of the walls nearest the girls. The girls aren't very good at maneuvering themselves so they can land on their feet, consequently both in up on their hands and knees, while Lorraine and BK touch down near the beds as BK grabs and steadies his wife to make sure she stays on her feet. LaChel is on her hands and knees, but is so happy to be on the floor that she only now realizes that she's covered in vomit. And is resting in small and large puddles of it. She lifts her hand out of one of the puddles and stares at it in horror then tries to throw-up again, but she only dry heaves.

"Good", she's empty, BK says out loud. Kim is on her hands and knees too and slides away from her sister creating a massive vomit streak. LaChel falls back onto her butt and lets out a long sickening moan. Both girls have now emptied their stomachs onto Lorraine's once spotless floor. The smell is now starting to permeate the air and travel throughout the room. Lorraine puts her hand over her mouth and nose and stares at BK very intensely. He can only look at her and say that she was right and maybe subjecting the girls to zero gravity this soon wasn't a good call. He's sure the worst is over and that the girls will be, but before he could add to his excuse, Lorraine's eyes got big, then she reaches up and grabs his shirt and pulls him in close then expels most of the content in her stomach onto his chest. He turns his face away from her in disgust as he starts to smell the effects of his wife's action wafting up from his now colorful chest. And to add insult to injury, she uses his left jumper sleeve to wipe her mouth.

"I agree"! Maybe next time you'll listen to me, she says as she pushes him away from her in disgust and walks over to the girls. He just stands there with his chest and sleeve now covered in his wife's predigested breakfast. He looks over at her with revenge in his eyes as he tries to let the smell of Lorraine's stomach content wafting from his chest assist him in mustering up his warm and pungent revenge.

She knows what he's trying to do and gives him a look of, "I wish you would". They stare at each other intensely for a few seconds, she can tell by the look in his eyes that he choked down whatever he was thinking. Come on girls, let me get you cleaned up while your dad cleans and disinfects my clinic and himself. She helps their girls off the floor and all three carefully walk to the clinic's bathroom and shower area. She directs her girls to the bathroom while she grabs a clean medical jumper for herself and two sets of pajamas for the girls. She also grabs three towels and cuts her eyes at BK as she walks into the bathroom. He looks down at the mess on his chest and of course, knows that he's on his own and thinks it would be wise to find somewhere else to clean himself up. He asked med unit one, which doesn't have any vomit on it, to bring him a large towel from the cabinet. The unit quickly complies and hovers toward the cabinet to retrieve the towel. He decides to go to engineering to take a shower and get some fresh work jumpers. He walks toward the door as med unit one hands him the towel.

"Thank you", he says as he grabs the towel and proceeds toward the door, which slides open as he approaches. He stops before walking out of the clinic and decides that it would be best for his girls as well as his mental health to cleanup and pick up the items before he gets himself cleaned up. But he first uses the towel to clean Lorraine's statement of anger off his jumper and chest. He does a good job of cleaning all of the chunks off, but he still smells like hell. He rolls up his towel and drops it in the hamper. He then walks back to the other side of the room and begins to use another white towel to wipe off LaChel and Kim's vomit from med units two and three. Unit three got the worst of it, so he spends more time getting food from between is mechanical fingers. While he's detailing the unit, he asked MOM what the hell happened with her taking so long to restore gravity? She states that it was a rare opportunity to evaluate the family dynamic in a stressful situation. "Damn it", BK yells, as he stops wiping off the unit.

Next time I give you an order to do something, especially when it involves my family, I want you to do it without any hesitation. My family could have been in danger while you were observing our reactions and emotional state. By my calculations, there was only a five to fifteen percent probability that your family would be harmed by maintaining them in zero gravity for a prolonged period of time.

But it was a ninety-two percent probability that two or all three of them would expel their stomach content while in zero gravity. So that was the reason you were keeping us in zero gravity? Betting on how many of us would vomit in a period of time? "No", she responds. It was not a bet, because I would need another artificial intelligence system or yourself to make such a wager. This was just an observation, she says in a matter of fact tone. Just then, BK hears Lorraine shout, "Oh hell no"! Lorraine walks out of the changing room with a look that only can be described as livid. Lorraine, don't worry, I'll handle this and I promise you this won't happen again, he says as he walks toward her. "Oh I know it won't happen again, because I'm going to find the largest screw driver I can find on this ship and shove it up that toaster's quantum processor. Which quantum processors, because I have twenty-seven of them, MOM responds. "Every damn one of them", she screams as she grabs a stapler and hurls it at the ceiling. MOM you're not helping, he says as he walks over and picks the stapler up off the floor. And Lorraine, you need to please calm down and stop throwing things around the room.

LaChel and Kim have the door to the changing room cracked so they can see their mother yell at a voice that sounds like Grandma Betty. I'm not the problem Lorraine yells. You need to reprogram, reconfigure, or do something with this stupid computer, she shouts as she walks up to him. And why do you still have that vomit stained jumper on, she asked as she puts her hand up to her nose. I wanted to clean up a little before I go to engineering and take a shower.

He steps closer to her as a means of his revenge so she can get a nose full of her handy work. She yells at him to get away from her then steps a few steps back. This has been a trying morning for all of us as he looks over to the bathroom and sees his girls peering through a partially opened door. The girls are still new to this type of environment and need additional rest and relaxation if they are to regain their strength.

I need you to help both of them back into bed and I will go back to our room and put on a fresh jumper. All right, she replies. But as soon as you change, I need you back in here to clean up this mess and finish our conversation about your little computer friend. Lorraine walks over to the girls and gestures to them to move back into the bathroom. She gives him a "I wish I had a bat" type look, but he just blows her a kiss and smiles at her as he leaves her Clinic. "He's not coming back for a while", she thinks to herself. But right now, her only concern is getting the girls cleaned up and getting them back to bed. As soon as he leaves the Clinic, he stops smiling and says to himself, "I'll give them an hour or so before I come back", he mumbles while walking down the hall toward Engineering.

She's not happy with me anyway, so I'm going to take my time taking a shower and changing out of these clothes, then I will find some type of emergency that I will have to handle down in Engineering. MOM! If Lorraine ask you if there is an emergency in Engineering sometime today, which she will, I need you to give her a solid, "yes". So, you are asking me to lie to your wife? No… no, he responds. The wiring to the starboard turbine hasn't been repaired yet.

But the wiring in the starboard turbine has been repaired by Engineering unit one, MOM responds. MOM, I don't think you understand. Lorraine and I need time to calm down, so I need you to just tell my wife what ever I tell you to tell her. So, you want me to lie to Lorraine about your afternoon activities, she asked.

Yes, but don't think of it as a lie, because there's always some type of emergency that I have to resolve. I do not think my ethical program will allow me to comply with what you're asking me to do. Alright, he responds with a bit of frustration in his voice. It will probably be better if you tell Lorraine to contact me and I'll make my own excuses. He decides to washup at his quarters rather than Engieering. As soon as he arrives at his quarters, he heads to the bathroom and then gets out of his clothes. After he takes his shower, puts on a fresh jumper, and argues with Benny about why he was not instructed to head to the hanger when he thought the ship was about to go down. BK explained to him that MOM was going to instruction him to head to the hanger, but he found the problem and repaired the ship.

Benny didn't believe him at first, but after fifteen minutes, BK convinced him that he could live without him. BK felt bad, because he did forget about Benny during that emergency and Benny might have gone down with the ship. By accident, of course. He finally had to tell Benny that he would assign him new responsibilities once he gets his family settled into their quarters. He finally gets Benny calmed down then heads for Engineering.

Meanwhile back in Lorraine's Clinic, It has been an hour after BK has left and Lorraine finally has the girls back in their beds and had chef bring them some soup and sandwiches. Lorraine is also eating to replace what she accidentally, but gladly ejected all over her husband. She's sitting at a portable table between both girls and tries to answer questions BK should be answering.

Mom, I'm really upset that dad made this decision without talking to us and taking into account how this would affect us, LaChel complains. Kim nods her head as she takes small bites of her sandwich. So Kim, how are you feeling about all this, Lorraine asked as she looks around the room? I don't know what to think, she says with a confusing look. I'm here with my mother, father, and sister floating above the earth. But at this minute, I'm pissed right now that dad isn't here explaining all of this to us. That's understandable for the both of you, Lorraine says as she looks at both her girls. But just because we are miles above the earth, doesn't give you the right to use that language, Lorraine explains as she stares intensely at Kim. She gives her mother a low tone "sorry", as she picks up her spoon and begins to slurp on her soup.

Lorraine totally understands the girls' emotional state, but she does agree with him that for the good of the family everyone must continue to follow the family's rules. LaChel tells them that one good thing may come out of this is that we will probably in up on the cover of all the magazines, as she smiles at Kim. You know LaChel, I don't think that's important right now, Lorraine says in all seriousness. The most important thing for all of us will be to get our strength back and give your dad our full support. By the girl's expression, Lorraine could see that they were not too enthused with being a part of the team just yet.

Look girls, I've been awake for about a month, and I admit that it was really difficult for me to wrap my brain around all this and to get past my anger towards your dad, but I did. So, I understand how you feel, but I'm asking you to give him your full support and to try to get use to this new reality.

The room falls silent as both girls reflect on what their mother just said. Lorraine can see she's not going to get a cheerful "OK mom" or a family hug. "All right", Lorraine says breaking the silence. Let's finish our lunch, so you two can get some rest.

Back in Engineering, BK is reviewing the reports that the engineering units have completed. He's deep in thought when MOM breaks his concentration. "BK", I have a question I would like you to answer for me please, MOM ask in a soft but curious tone. "Oh my God", this sounds like a question that may cause me some indirect pain or some soul searching. Now that statement also intrigues me and I would like to add an additional question prior to asking you my original question. "MOM, he says sternly! I'm very busy, so please only ask your original question. I will answer your second question at a later date. I am curious to know why are you avoiding your family again now that all three of them are now out of stasis, because prior to their awakening, you were so lonely for them?

I'm not avoiding them... Just their questions and anger, he exclaims. I don't know if you can understand this MOM, but sometimes absence makes the heart grow fonder. Yes, I do understand the phrase, which was first published in Francis Davison's Poetical Rhapsody in 1602, where the words appear as the first phrase of a poem. Yes, I know you understand the words, but I don't think you truly understand the human meaning of it. I do miss my family, but I have tons of work that needs to be done before I can relax with them.

MOM corrects him. I believe you are mistaken, because I have your schedule for the day and you only have five tasks to complete, which are so simple that all can be completed by two of the engineering units. BK looks irritated and a little upset that MOM questioned him regarding spending time with his family.

MOM, I know you're accusing me of not wanting to be with my family, but I can assure you that you are very mistaken. She starts to scan his vitals without telling him. I have activated my thermal scanner and I can see that your heart rate has risen and your overall body temperature has increased by 6.28 degrees. This indicates that you are trying to deceive me. He's silent, because he forgot that she could tell if someone is telling the truth, because he programmed and constructed that function into her capabilities. He barely wanted to admit to himself that he's afraid to spend time with his family, because of the guilt that he still feels. He knew that there's nothing he can say, so he just lowers his head and sighs.

I did not want to say anything, but even an artificial intelligence with no eyes can see that you are avoiding spending time with your family. It is very simple to uncover deception in humans, but what is difficult for me to comprehend is why you practice such deceptive behaviors in the first place. He knows that MOM isn't just asking a rhetorical question. She expects a logical answer. He continues reviewing the engineering units' schedules and making slight adjustments as he attempts to answer MOM's question. It has nothing to do with not being with my family, so can you please stop saying that, he says sternly. It's simply a question of fear and remorse, he says as he stands to his feet. I understand the concept and definition of those two words, but I fail to understand how it applies to your situation, she replies. He gets up from his chair and walks over to a tool cabinet in order to review the contents of the equipment the units will be working with, as he attempts to enlighten MOM regarding his conflicting emotions.

I have done an amazingly shocking thing by bringing my family up here without their consent. And I'm afraid that I may not be able to explain my reasoning to them in a way they can comprehend. I know this maybe beyond your program's ability to process these irrational human emotions, but the way my family feels about me is very important to me. I have no doubt that they will support me, but I'm afraid I've lost their respect and that's what I don't want to hear.

He completes the inventory of the cabinet then walks over to his desk and grabs a tablet, so he can document the missing items that he wants replaced. "What are they doing right now", he asked MOM. They are just talking amongst themselves. Would you like to know what they are saying, she asked? He pauses for a moment, wanting to know, but knowing that it's wrong to do so. "No", he said in a solemn voice. I've already snatched away their freedom. I will not compound the problem by robbing them of their privacy too. "Good", because they're bashing the hell out of you, MOM says. "Bashing me", he yells.

"I am just joking", MOM says. "That's' damn funny", he says in a stern tone. "Thank you", she replies as she recognizes his sarcasm. He just sits there staring at the wall and contemplating how he would make it up to them. She tells him that she understands why he's hesitant to discuss the reasons he chose to remove them from their home and relocate them here. He hears what she's saying, but he still continues to say nothing.

My opinion is that even though the justice system would put you in prison for a period of five to ten years for child endangerment, distributing a drug without a license and kidnapping of your family members. But I have no doubt that you made the correct and logical decision to bring your family with you under the circumstances. But freezing them like TV dinners may have been a bit too much, she adds. That's not funny MOM, he says as he stands to his feet and begins to walk to the door. I understand that there's no use in putting off this conversation. He then walks out of engineering and heads toward the clinic.

Back in Lorraine's medical clinic, she is doing her best to put to rest any fears that her girls my have about their new challenging situation. LaChel ask, what if the government decides to try to shoot us down again? She corrects her daughter. Our Government didn't try to shoot us down. That was the Chinese, she says as if it made a difference. We are still citizens of the United States, Lorraine responds. I can't see them trying to harm women and children; let alone taking the chance on damaging this ship and its' technology. They may not care about us, but I know for a fact that they would love to get their hands on this spacecraft, she says confidently. This ship is the only one of its' kind and our Government as well as other countries would love to have it in their arsenal of weapons.

What I'm having a hard time understanding is why dad just didn't sell this ship to the government for a butt-load of money, LaChel says with a twinge of anger in her voice. This doesn't make any sense, she adds. Lorraine can understand her anger, because even though she has been working beside their father for months; she still has nagging questions and pockets of anger that she just can't shake.

And now that she sees the confusion, and sadness that her daughters are experiencing. She can feel the anger in her trying to bubble its' way back up to the surface as she looks into the eyes of both her daughters. But this is not the time or the place to lose control of her emotions, so with great effort, she suppresses her emotion beneath her carefully crafted veneer. As she tries to think of something positive and motivational to say about what their father is trying to accomplish, but just then their dad comes through the door with a cheerful "hello family" and a big smile. Lorraine especially didn't think he'd be back this soon, but maybe he's trying to make up for this crapload of trouble he got us into, she thinks to herself as he gives her a kiss on the forehead. He then walks over to the girls and gives them each a loving kiss on their cheeks. "Wow"! You've done a great job cleaning this place up and getting rid of the smell, he says as he looks around and smells the air.

The units did most of the cleaning and disinfecting, she admits to him. I was busy getting the girls cleaned up and getting them back into bed. He recognized the bit of attitude in her voice, most likely because she wanted him back in the Clinic sooner to help with his girls, so he thinks it would be in his best interest to move on. So, I guess you all have more questions for me and I thought that it's about time I give you the answers. MOM, can you have chef bring me a coke zero, please. "Yes BK, she responds". "Dad", can you have him bring me a Ginger Ale, LaChel asked. Kim chimes in and asked for a Coke. Your dad only brought Coke Zeros on board this ship, Lorraine tells a disappointed LaChel. He cuts his eyes over at his wife, as she looks at him with a "back me up" look. She doesn't want them drinking or eating anything complex right now, so she takes a page out of her husband's book and lies to her girls. Both girls yell at him for being so selfish. LaChel ends her tyrate by asking him when are we going home, while Kim just nods her head in agreement?

I'm sorry but not anytime soon, he tells them. But I would first like to apologies for not giving you the choice to come with me, but I couldn't bear the thought of leaving you down there for the government and the news reporters to make your lives a living hell. I wouldn't have been able to protect you, because our government could have force me to hand over this ship by threatening you guys. I just want you to realize that I didn't have a choice, he says as he looks at them. "Yes you did", LaChel says as tears pool in her eyes. You could have sold everything you invented to the Government or anyone else who had the money to buy it. Then we would still be in our house living a normal life, going to the mall with our friends and getting ready to go to the prom with my boyfriend, she says with the first of many tears starting to stream down her cheeks. "Stop", Lorraine shouts at her. I need you two to not ask any more questions till after he has finished explaining. But I didn't ask a question! I just made a rebuttal to his statement. "Girl, don't play with me", Lorraine shouts forcefully! You're very intelligent, so you can plainly see that I'm not in the mood to be playing word games. Just open your minds and shut your mouths for a minute and nobody will get hurt, if you understand what I mean. She gives both of them a look that only a mother could. Even BK stands quietly waiting for Lorraine to give him the nod to continue. Go ahead sweetheart, she says as she leans back in her chair and crosses her legs. Well, I know that you girls and your mother aren't very happy with the decisions that I made but believe me when I say that I questioned my sanity hundreds of times prior to bringing you aboard.

The car accident I had almost four years ago changed my life and yours forever. I remember not being able to move or speak for months. I was a prisoner in my own body, but I could hear all of you sitting beside my hospital bed reading to me and telling me about your day just like we would do at home. At that point, I could only respond by moving my eyes from left to right and making grunting sounds, which your mom would have to try to interpret for the nurses and doctors. At that point, I thought that would be my existence for the rest of my life and I honestly wish and prayed for someone to pull the plug on me, he says with shame in his eyes.

But as my spirits sank, a doctor from South Africa approach me with an innovative, but potentially dangerous procedure, which had the potential of enabling me to regain most or all of my mobility. He explained the details of the procedure and the risk involved, but I didn't hear anything he was saying after the words, "restore mobility". If I had the ability to open the window to my fifth story hospital room and jump out, I would have. He has the full attention of his wife and daughters now. I was determined not to live the remainder of my life like that and becoming a burden on you guys. It brings up the painful memory of fear and frustration of not being able to move when he talks about it.

Lorraine and the girls can hear it in his voice too. Your mom on the other hand, listened to the doctors every word intensively and was not happy that this experimental procedure may cost me my life. She thought if we just wait awhile and pray for a miracle that my body may recover without the risky surgery. But I grunted strongly and gave her every gestured I could that I wanted to have the surgery. The choice was very simple for me. Either I would regain all or a portion of my mobility or I would die soon after the operation. In my situation and state of mind, the risk outweighed my reality at the time. But on Lorraine's part, it would have been very easy for her to simply tell the doctor that I didn't want to take the risk of dying on the operating table, but she reluctantly expressed to the Doctor exactly what I wanted to do. Afterward, when the doctor left the room excited about the prospect of finally being able to perform his experiments. I can clearly remember your mom dropping her head and beginning to cry uncontrollably. I could see her with her head in her hands crying, but I couldn't move my hand, or any other part of my body for that matter.

He instinctively looks over at his wife and could see tears starting to roll down her cheeks as she remembers everything she felt at that moment. This time he could console her, so he walks over beside her and wipes away her tears with his hand. She grabs his hand, gives him a comforting smile then ask him to continue telling the story. I understood your mom's apprehension regarding the surgery, because even though I didn't show it; I was scared to death worrying what was going to happen to me. I couldn't imagine the situation being worst other than I could die, but in my state of mind at that time, my condition was worst than death. Lorraine put her head down trying not to make any comments, but she really would like to yell at him for his selfish state of mind. But she held her tongue just like she asked her daughters to do. He continues with his story. After about three days of the nurses and doctors poking and prodding at me, they performed the operation. "Twenty-one hours", Sherry interjects. That's the amount of time the operation took and the amount of time I was in agony to find out if my husband and the father of my children was going to make it out of the operating room.

BK walked back over and stood in between his daughters. "I'm sorry", but I couldn't help myself, she says to her girls. BK smiles at her then continues. Of course, I had no idea how much time had passed. The only thing I remembered was waking up and seeing your mother standing beside my bed smiling down at me I know it was selfish, but before the operation I didn't care if I lived or died. But once you guys were allow to visit me and I saw your smiling beautiful faces, I thanked God that I was still alive. No matter what my condition would have been in the future. Lorraine gives BK a look, which was a hint to move on with the story. He nods to her then continues. As you can see, I made it through the operation without any complications, but it took over two and a half weeks before there were any noticeable changes in my mobility. The first indication that my body was coming back to life was in the middle of the night when one of the nurses accidentally dropped a tray of medicine bottles and instruments onto the floor, which scared me and made one of my legs jump. The nurse didn't think much of it, you know me being paralyzed and all, but when I yelled, "hey, you scared me and my leg jumped"! It surprised the living hell out of her. The nurse ran out of the room and within less than a few minutes the doctor runs in and starts asking me tons of questions like how do you feel, are you experiencing any headaches, can you feel this, just to name a few.

I was ecstatic that my legs were beginning to work again, but it was 1:30 in the morning. After an hour and a half of poking and prodding, I just wanted everyone to stop talking to me. I just wanted to get back to sleep. But that didn't happen and I was up the rest of the night going through a battery of test that they could have done in the morning. Well, I was happy to learn that morning that you were finally getting your legs back, Lorraine adds. You looked tired that morning that the girls and I got there, but we were happy for you. Babe, can you get to the part that explains why we're up here floating around in space, Lorraine says as she looks at the girls starting to lose focus? All right, to make this long story of an important portion of my life short. About two the three months after my operation, I began to notice the way I think and what I could remember was changing day by day. While I learned how to walk again, I realized that I was gaining more and more intellectual knowledge about everything. This is a part of the story that Lorraine had never heard before. What do you mean, "everything", she asked? "Everything", he repeats. I was lying in bed one Sunday afternoon watching and news anchor reporting a possible nuclear meltdown with one of Russia's nuclear power reactors.

As they were talking about the problems that would occur if they couldn't force enough heavy water into the reactor to lower the temperature of the bundle of nuclear fuel rods. I started to think about the process of creating nuclear material, its' rate of decay and the amount of energy it releases per ounce of material. It took me about three weeks to come up with a viable method of reversing the process, but I was surprise that it wasn't that difficult. Do you mean that you developed a new way to store radioactive waste, Lorraine asked curiously? No, I developed a method of making radioactive material non-radioactive. Lorraine has a limited knowledge of nuclear power and its' radioactive materials, but she knows that no one has developed a method of solving the issue of how and where to store the radioactive waster produced by the plants. So why haven't you shared your method with the rest of the world, LaChel asked?

I did, he replied. The opportunity came when roughly six to seven months after my accident when one of Iran's nuclear plants started to experience an uncontrollable meltdown. The United States, France, and Great Britain gathered their experts to find a solution to the problem, but their only real solution was to cover the damaged reactor with a six-foot layer of reinforced concrete and pray for the best. I remember seeing that on the news, but I think each month hundreds of people were dying of radioactive exposure, Lorraine recalls. They just covered the damaged area with dirt and concrete, if I remember correctly, she added. Because our Government didn't share the data that I anonymously emailed to them a week and a half after the nuclear accident. The only thing they were working on was trying to find the person or persons that sent them the documents for converting radioactive isotopes. They had no intention of sharing that data with the Iranians. Hundreds of people died trying to shutdown the reactor, but thousands died a year after the initial disaster from radioactive poisoning. He stood there quiet for a moment as they can clearly see that talking about this subject really shakes him up. Why do you think that they didn't give them the information to save those people, Kim asked in a soft voice? He didn't answer for a moment. He just stood there looking at the floor.

He sighs, then says," there's many reasons that our Government wouldn't share the information, but I can only think that it was all about global politics". America and its' allies didn't want Iran to have the capability to produce enrich uranium, but somehow, they managed to get their hands on enough uranium to successfully power their poorly constructed plants, which would produce power for the cities and unfortunately produce God knows how many nuclear warheads. So, you think that our Government held on to information in order to disable the Iranians nuclear program, Lorraine asked? "Absolutely", He responds.

"It's a simple as that", he adds. It's the basic story of the "Carrot and the Stick". The Iranians wouldn't take the carrot, so the United States blatantly and harshly beat them with the stick by withholding the life saving information. "Can we get on with Dad's story", Kim yells? This is getting really scary and depressing. Sure, but I felt it was important that you knew what measures our Government and their allies would take to protect their interest. Ya Dad, I think we get it, but that's why I think it's a little scary. He understands that his family is not very interested in the details of how he got to this point, but he's a bit disappointed that he can't hold their attention long enough to describe what made him what he is today. But he knows that the sooner he tells them about what happened to him and why what they do here is so important; the sooner they will adjust to being up here.

He explained how he watched the news and special reports, which showed the suffering of the Iranian people day after day. He wondered when the Government would intervene and utilize the information he gave them. After the fourth day and over three thousand deaths; I understood that our government had no intention of sharing the information with the Iranians or anyone else for that matter. His voice sounds a bit shaky at this point in his story. Lorraine can see that it still bothers him to talk about all those lives that could have been saved. It surprises him too.

He pauses for a moment to regain his composure. Thousands of people died and hundred of thousands are still suffering because I made the mistake of trusting our Government to do the right thing, he says while try to surpress his anger. Lorraine can see the pain in his face while telling this portion of the story, so she walks over to him and rubs his back. "You know that wasn't your fault", she says while looking at the torment in his eyes. You had no way of knowing that the politics of the moment would overshadow their humanity and compassion. He continues by suggesting that their Government punished the Iranian Government and consequently their people for not complying to their request to agree to annual monitoring of their nuclear program. But they weren't satisfied with punishing Iran.

They desperately wanted to find out who developed the method of reversing radioactive materials. He tells them that he thought he was being very careful when he emailed those documents and didn't feel like he was ever in any danger of being tracked down. All I could think of is those unfortunate people suffering and dying from radiation poisoning. It haunted me for months, but from that experience, I learned not to trust my Government. But Dad, maybe the Government couldn't help them, because they didn't want their help, LaChel interjects? I wouldn't think if you have thousands of your people being sick and dying, you would turndown someone saying that they can stop more of your people from dying, he replies.

All I know is that they had a solution to a problem that was killing thousands of our fellow human beings and they just let them die, he shouted with anger in his eyes. The room is quiet for a bit as he tries to calm himself and get his thoughts together. Lorraine wants to move this story along, so she suggest that he should move pass that part of the story and get to the part that will explain why they are here. "Alright", he grudgingly agrees. I've solved a lot of problems in the last two years and have leaked some of it out to our Government hoping that they would share some of it with their fellow human beings around the world, but I was disappointed each and every time. All I would get for my hard work would be one of their hightech computer Agents searching the internet trying to find who and where the documents are coming from. I decided that if my Government wasn't going to help anyone but themselves, then I would upload the majority of my data to all the computers around the world.

That's impossible Dad, LaChel replies. There must be millions of computers in the world. I'm no computer expert, but I would think you would only be able to download to about a third of the people who have computers on earth, if you're lucky. And besides. You would have to determine if your documents are being downloaded by a PC or an Apple system, let alone the age of the system. He gives her a confident smile. MOM, can you tell me how many computers are on the Internet at this moment?

Yes! One moment please. The girls sit up in their beds after hearing their Grandma' Betty's voice. There are 57 million, 65 thousand, and 29 hundred computers currently online. Oh my God, Kim says in amazement. And if we decided to upload all our data right now, approximately how many computers could we successfully download to and how long would it take to complete the task. We can populate every server and computer on earth, and it would take approximately twenty-five minutes to download the data to every last computer, she replies.

Thanks to her husband, Lorraine's computer knowledge is at the level of a computer programmer, but she comments that it seems unbelievable that MOM could download that amount of information to that many computers in that small amount of time. MOM isn't a computer, he replies to his family. She's a form of artificial intelligence that can modify and manipulate any computer on earth. I've developed a new method of computer data distribution and interface. But since I know you don't what to hear about the details of this revolutionary new technology; just take my word that nothing on earth can equal her processing capabilities. "Quantum molecular interface", Kim shouts without thinking. she puts her hand over her mouth as if she has just said one of those words that her and her friend use to use in the girl's bathroom at school. I have no idea what came out of my mouth or why I said it, she adds with her hands still over her mouth. Lorraine may not know what Kim's talking about, but she understands why she said it, as she cuts her eyes over to her husband. BK knows that it's not a good time to get into all this right now, so he continues with his story. "Listen people"! We are making history by being up here.

I know I've changed our lives forever, but I believe we're going to accomplish something that will benefit not just the United States but will usher in a new era for humanity. He stares at his wife and daughter that are now giving him their full attention. I want you to know that I was going to market my technology artificial intelligence that I used to create MOM to various industries around the world, which would have made us tons of money. But I had no doubt that our Government would have found some way to take possession of the technology and use it for their own purposes. But the deciding factor was when I asked MOM to calculate the future of humanity if we continue on our current path without any intervention.

She drew from linear equations, historical data and Psychology to calculate the result for my question. She explained that our dependency on fossil fuels, depletion of the earth's natural resources, extinction of plants and animal species, and the amount of human longevity and birth, which is out pacing human mortality. She used those variables to determine that one-third of humanity will be loss due to famine and the third World War, which will occur within ten years. She also stated that it's a seventy-eight percent probability that humanity will enter a third world war and global economic collapse. She also added the the remaining thirty-two percent is the possibility that humanity will completely reverse their self-destructive path. "We're that thirty-two percent", he says sternly as he points his finger at each one of them.

It wouldn't have made a difference if we had made billions of dollars, because if I would have ignored MOM's calculations and continued to claw after those billions; after ten years, we would have been as destitute as everyone else in the world. Lorraine can see that her girls are thoroughly depressed now, so she gets up from the corner of Kim's bed and grabs BK by the arm then whispers, "lets give them some time" as she pulls him away from the beds. This isn't how he wanted to leave his daughters, but maybe he's giving them too much too soon. Lorraine pulls him over to her desk and both stand there looking back at their girls.

She doesn't think it would be a great idea to leave them alone right now but suggest that he go and get some of his work done. A part of him loves that idea, because that's what he wanted to do in the first place, but a larger part of him wants to stay and work this out with his family. But he agrees with Lorraine that it may be better for everyone to pause the story so they could digest all the information and emotions. I'll be back in about an hour or so he starts to tell her, but she interrupts him and ask him not to come back until she calls him. He stares at her for a moment, then mumbles a somber "OK". She can see that this really hurts him, so she gives him a kiss on the cheek then turns him toward the door and gives him a gentle push. She smiles at him as he looks back at her as he leaves her workspace. He exits the Clinic and hears the swish of the closing door as he walks down the passageway towards the Bridge. He expected his daughters to react this way, but he now understands that regardless of your good intentions, nothing can prepare you for that moment when your children are in pain, because of something that you've done. As he walks lowly down the hallway, he's going over and over in his mind a different scenario that may have brought about a different outcome. While pondering what happened and what else he can say to his girls, he's surprised by the short amount of time that it took for him to make it to the Bridge. "What the hell", he says to himself as he walks up to the automatic doors. The door slides open and he walks in and flops down in his captain's chair.

This is one of three places aboard the ship that he feels totally relaxed. Maybe his subconscious wanted him to come here after the stressful talk with his daughters. He leans back in the chair and crosses his legs. The view screen is already activated as he stares at the image of the earth while pondering what it must be like for his daughters to suddenly wakeup on their father's home-made spaceship and not be able to contact their friends. He spins around in the chair and looks at the other stations on the bridge where his wife and daughters will be working.

He would like to say that everything is going as planned, but that wouldn't be completely true. He would have hoped that Lorraine and the girls would be use to being aboard the ship by now, but he can see signs that their implanted knowledge of various disciplines is slowly inching its' way to the surface. He gets up from the chair and walks over to the navigation station to check the position and altitude of the ship. He starts to push and swipe the screen on the navigation console when MOM asked him why he didn't use the tablet attached to the chair. He doesn't answer for a few seconds then replies that he just wanted to check to make sure that the console is working properly. MOM, can you give me an analysis of the progress of my family's emotional, physical, and technical knowledge.

"Processing", she replies. He gets out of his chair and walks around the bridge checking the other workstations and various bridge instruments. After seven minutes and twenty-eight seconds, MOM announces that she has concluded her analysis of his family. She tells him that Lorraine has adapted to her new environment, but her emotional state is slightly unstable. She adds that Lorraine's technical and professional knowledge is beyond her expectation. She next tells him that LaChel his behind in all categories, but she doesn't see any reason that she couldn't improve if he and Lorraine would spend time assisting her with the gaps in her technical knowledge. That doesn't surprise him, because his daughter always had problems in school. To ensure that she wouldn't fall to far behind, they would hire tutors in mathematics and English. She would also struggle in Gym, but that was due to her laziness and grounding her would normally take care of that. "How's my youngest doing", he asked as he walks over to the astrometric station.

Kim is exactly were she should be at this point in her acclamation to her new normal. I plan on testing them later this week in order to accurately assess their true progress. Well, what ever the outcome, Lorraine and the girls only have two more weeks to get use to accessing and utilizing the data I implanted in their brains, he states. I also need them on my side when we have our first telecommunication's meeting, he says as he grabs a tablet off the navigation station and goes back to his chair.

Are you referring to the meeting that you and your family have scheduled with the President and his Cabinet? I'm sure not talking about calling Lorraine's nappy headed mother, he says with a smile. I know you programmed me to tell "Your Mama" jokes to ease your stress, but what you say and the way you speak about your mother-in-law doesn't seem like a joke. I do not understand why making disparaging remarks about Lorraine's mother gives you such joy, she says curiously. You have to be human and be married and have a mother-in-law like mine to understand son-in-law humor. Believe me, I love that old nag, he says in an unconvincing tone as he crosses his legs and starts tapping and scrolling through the tablet's subdirectory. This time she couldn't decipher if he's lying or not. MOM and BK spends the remainder of the day strategizing and preparing study guides for his family.

Chapter Eight

The President and the Conglomerate

September 19, 2023 - *Scientists around the world are reporting a rise in ocean temperatures which is causing a depletion in phytobacteria. These oxygen producers such as drifting plants, cyanobacteria, or blue-green algae produce 50 – 80% of the oxygen in earth's atmosphere. The World Health Organization has reported an increase in the amount of respiratory problems amongst the very young and elderly. To our peril, Oxygen may become the most valuable commodity.*

President Bill Crawford is sitting behind his desk, leaning back in his chair intensively looking over highly classified documents pertaining to Mr. Thomas and his family. He's flipping through folders and paperwork describing various aspects of BK spaceship hovering above him, which was collected by the FBI, CIA and a special branch of the administration that remains nameless.

He's trying to absorb a ton of information to prepare for the highly anticipated video conference meeting with Mr. Thomas that will take place in an hour and fifteen minutes. He's a career Republican politician with over twenty-seven years of experience on the hill. He and his Vice President, Benjamin Bentley, won their election three years ago on the platform of eliminating corruption and corporate donations from the people's house. But after one year of his administration, he found that he couldn't manage to get anything through Congress, which was made up of deeply entrenched Blue Dog Politicians, and Lobbyist with deep pockets and influence. And the Senate was mired knee deep in the muck of corruption.

The most senior Senators had their own aspirations of becoming President themselves and resented him pulling himself from the muck of the political swamp. So with his Vice President, both of them pulled up their pants legs, joined hands and jumped up to their waist into the deep end of the swamp. They decided if they were destined to be a one term administration; they would damn sure fill their pockets with as much cash and influence as they can carry.

Seeing the Government's "For Sale" sign prominently illuminated out of the window of the White House, twelve powerful titans of industry clandestinely lobbied the Executive and Legislative Branches to pass bills to enable mega corporations the ability to select which politicians would win various Electoral College Votes in the major states, which would in turn, guarantee gubernatorial wins.

These twelve titans of industry whose names can't be spoken openly are known by the name "The Conglomerate", which some say have been controlling governments for the past fifty years. They pull the strings of the world leaders and completely control all aspects of the worlds' economy. Communism, Capitalism, Socialism and whatever republic title associated with a world leaders doesn't really exist anymore. The Conglomerate has nullified all real conflicts between the so call superpowers. Even in the United States, the President only has the power that the Conglomerate allows him to have.

The President as well as his predecessors had no problem with the new world order, because the transformation and consolidation of power accomplished two things. One, made the President and Vice President as well as various politicians on both sides of the political aisle very rich. And two, completely transformed the United States from a Democracy into a Corpocracy with a single stroke of the pen and without the people knowing a damn thing. But now, all that they have accomplished is now in jeopardy by one man and his family orbiting above the earth in a homemade spaceship. The President and his Administration have been preparing for this meeting ever since BK contacted the President's Press Secretary and convinced him that he was the person that the Conglomerate and the Government has been searching for. After he convinced the Press Secretary that he was who he says he was, he was transferred to Vice President Bentley's office. He convinced the VP that he's who he says he is by telling him about his warehouse and that his spacecraft was the reason for the UFO scare that almost started World War III. That information was never shared with the public and only the person or persons responsible would know that particular bit of information.

That's what ultimately convinced the Vice President of his authenticity. He also knew that they were stalling for time in order to trace the call. He instructed MOM to allow them to try, but unbeknownst to them the call was originating from a satellite location, which would do them no good, but would convince them that the communication was residing from off the planet. Now that he thoroughly convinced them of his identity, he decides to end the call by telling the Vice President that he wants to have a video conference with the President in three weeks to discuss his spacecraft and its' technology.

Then he abruptly terminated the call. Now today is the day that the President and his Administration is expecting the video conference, so the President is doing some last-minute studying of some follow-up information as he flips through the binder of classified material. He loosens his tie as his facial expressions switches from dread to amazement depending on which page or paragraph he is reading.

Now the President has a Master's Degree in Economics and a minor in Political Science, but him understanding the complexity of half of the information in that binder is like trying to explain String Theory to the smartest pigeon you can find. He's so immersed in trying to make since of the scientific content of the documents, he doesn't hear the knock at the door and the door slowly opening. It's the Vice President.

His body is half in and half out of the door as he waits for the President to tell him to come in, but the President is fully immersed in the section that speculates the ship's propulsion system and he doesn't raise his head. "Excuse me Bill", the Vice President says as he softly knocks once again. The President hated science in high school and college and couldn't for the life of him tell anyone what two elements are needed to make water, but he can't tear himself away from what he's reading. He briefly looks up and gestures for his VP to come in. Come in Ben, come in…please, he says while continuing to read and shuffle through the documents. The VP walks in and stands in front of the President's desk waiting for him to get to a stopping point. Bill, your Cabinet Members are in the Situation Room waiting for us to join them for the post meeting before the video conference, the Vice President reminds him. He can clearly see that the President is noticeably shaken by what he's reading. Ben, I need to speak with you, the Chief of Staff and CIA Director before I talk with the rest of my Cabinet, the President says without looking up and while still flipping through the binder.

He then sits up in his chair and presses a button on his desk phone. "Nancy!" Yes Mr. President, she promptly answers. Call the Situation Room and have Mr. Redner and Mrs. Thomson come into my office, please. Yes Mr. President. Thank you. "Have a seat Ben", as he gestures to the decorative and plush couch to the left of his desk.

The Vice President walks over and takes a seat in the single matching chair to the right of the couch, and asked the President why he wants to meet with the CIA Director and Chief of Staff prior to the meeting with his Cabinet and the Joint Chiefs? I've been going over this information again and I need you to clarify a few things for me, as he looks bewildered and continues to flip through the binder. It's difficult for me to believe some of this information in here, as he uses his free hand to flip to the next page in the binder. Maybe we should have Dr. Lutz come to the office too, so he can answer some of the very technical questions. But the President tells him that those aren't the questions I want answered, he says with a menacing tone. Just then there's a knock at the door as the Chief of Staff, Sherry Thomson and CIA Director, Dave Redner enters the room.

"Afternoon Mr. President", both of them say as they walk into the Oval Office and Dave closes the door. The President nods his head to acknowledge them, leans back into his leather chair. They sit down on the couch to the left of the President. The President closes the binder and pushes it across his desk and just stares at all three of them. Can you please tell me why a person that we deemed a national security risk and that we supposedly had under surveillance is currently orbiting in what we can assume is his homemade spacecraft above our planet, as he glares directly at his CIA Director? The President clasps his hands and waits for him to answer?

"Mr. President", Sherry says as she tries to intervene for the Director, but the President holds up his finger, and asked Sherry to let Dave answer the question. I'm sure Dave has a more in-depth answer for me, he says while still glaring at him. Normally, the Director has nerves of steel, but he knows he dropped the ball with his handling and monitoring of Mr. Thomas. Yes sir, I know you may find it hard to believe that Mr. Thomas was under surveillance, but my staff and the FBI spent a lot of man hours monitoring his communications both at home and at work.

Given what we know now, we still can't comprehend how he could assemble a poor man's version of the Starship Enterprise let alone build a spacecraft of that size and complexity. But he did Dave, the President responds sternly as he leans forward, grabs the binder once again and sits back in his chair. I'm sorry Dave, but I get pissed-off every time I read what we allowed to slip through our fingers. The Director knows that the President using the word "we" is just a euphemism for "Dave Redner". He flips through the binders again until he gets to the page that estimates the size of the spacecraft.

His Chief of Staff raised her hand slightly. "Yes Sherry"! You have something to add to this debacle? She clears her throat before answering. As you remember Mr. President, when Mr. Thomas disappeared with his family, we were all in agreement that he may be trying to defect to another country like Russia or China, which was why we spared no expense activating our informants to keep an eye out for him.

We also had to entertain the horrific possibility that he may have taken his own life and the lives of his wife and children. And that would be our bestcase scenario, the Vice President coldly states. But evidently, we were wrong on both counts. The big question is how he managed to build that ship and who helped him, the President exclaims. We know his spacecraft launched from Jacksonville Florida, because our Agents inspected a large warehouse with highly technical equipment still inside and the warehouse was the size that could accommodate the ship that's in orbit. But the biggest clue was the east side exterior wall was lying on the ground as if something pushed its' way out of the warehouse.

The Agents surveyed the facility and concluded that the 40,000 square foot warehouse was used to construct something very large. As he picks up the binder again and looks for that bit of information, he says he doesn't remember reading that in this binder, as he peruses through the pages. Well Mr. President, the Vice President, Director and I were trying to verify that information, Sherry replies. The President drops the binder with a loud thud onto his desk, stands up and walks to the window behind him. Sherry wants to remind him of everything that was going on at the time the Director was keeping Mr. Thomas under surveillance.

She tells him that at the time, we were heavily involved with the Iran Nuclear problem, not to mention that twelve of our fifty states are under a drought alert. He stands there for a moment thinking that it's ultimately his fault, but he damn sure isn't going to take that mountain of crap that's going to come sliding down blame mountain. Being President means there's a number of pons on the board that have no choice but to sacrifice him or herself. But the only thing that matters at this point is to get Mr. Thomas and his technology under his control. He can imagine what would happen if China or Russia had gain possession of that technology. It would have cost him his Presidency and possibly his life. Of course, the Conglomerate would have ultimate control of the spacecraft and its' technology, which they would suppress until they deplete all the fossil fuel on earth. But his Regional Manager would have the option to replace him or even eliminate him, which was in the contract that the President signed prior to taking office. All world leaders and anyone else for that matter that seek to occupy a higher position in any Government around the world must sign a secretive contract with the Conglomerate.

He then turns around and walks to the back of his chair and starts searching the pockets of his jacket, which is draped across the back of the chair. He reaches in the inside pocket and grabs one of his guilty pleasures, a "PayDay" candy bar, which his wife tries to deter him from eating, because of his poor annual physical a couple of months ago. He stands behind his chair as he peals back the wrapper on the candy bar and takes a bite as he stands their deep in thought.

The Vice President reflects back to the First Lady asking him to make sure when she's not around to insist that the President not eat anything that's not on a list that his personal dietitian has developed for him. The First Lady even took the drastic step of emailing the list to the Senior Staff. He doesn't see himself as the First Lady's personal "Jenny Craig", so as he looks at the President taking another bite out of the candy bar, he thinks that if the President eats himself into a hospital bed or the big dirt nap, he'll be the next in line for the plush leather chair. But the President got wind of the list and tells his Senior Staff, "God help anyone that mentions that list or the amount of crap he eats on the golf course". The VP breaks the silence by telling him that they have very little additional information to add to what he already knows. So I take it we haven't discovered who may have helped him with the financing and construction of his ship?

"No Mr. President", the Director says in a somewhat disappointing tone. We investigated his coworkers at the Engineering firm and we couldn't find anyone that knew anything about a secret project. Of course, we couldn't come out and ask them directly if they help their missing boss build a spacecraft. We also have to tell you that we haven't been completely successful in keeping a lid on Mr. Thomas' spacecraft and we have had to put our knee on the neck of a few news networks, who were attempting to run the story of a UFO in orbit.

And how in the hell did these news agencies find out about the spacecraft, the President asked with a tone of anger in his voice? Well Bill, we know we have some informants deeply imbedded in our administration, but we still haven't been able to flush those rat bastards out yet. "Traitorous idiots", the President says as he shakes his head. The Director tries to provide the President with a little positive news. I know it's disappointing to say the lease that we haven't plugged the leaks, but my department and the FBI have done a phenomenal job of suppressing the small amount of information that has seeped out to those news agencies. So, our American citizens still have no idea what's going on right above their heads, he asked Sherry? "No sir", she responds with a slight smile.

But we're not going to be able to contain this story indefinitely, the Director adds. We all agree that we can't tap down these news agencies forever, because Mr. Thomas may sooner or later decide to land his ship in a park, or on a field of a Monday night football game on national television. The President slowly nods his head in agreement. The President looks unsurprised as he walks back around his chair and he eats the last of his candy bar. He then continues to listen to the three of them give him additional information about BK's wife and children. He crumples the empty wrapper and buries it in his trash can, so if his wife, "Lynda", happen to come to his office, she won't see the wrapper on top of the trash. So Ben, you're telling me that you think his family is up there with him, he says as he grabs his jacket off the chair and throws it on. We believe so, the VP replies as he looks at his watch.

And he will be contacting us in the next fourty some odd minutes to explain why he built his spacecraft and what he plans to do with it. Alright then, the President says. I have to admit that I don't feel totally confident with this meeting, but I'm positive that I'm not the only one that is struggling with comprehending the information that's in that binder. The complexity of the information that we have been discussing these past weeks have given me many sleepless nights and countless headaches.

The President then picks up the phone and calls his secretary again. Yes, Mr. President. Tell the Cabinet that we are on the way, please. Yes sir. The President walks out of the Oval Office with his staff trailing behind him. As they head down the hall toward the Situation Room, they are unexpectedly joined by the First Lady, who feels the need to join this meeting with her husband. He greets her by putting his hand at the small of her back and giving her a kiss on her cheek.

She smiles back and whispers to him that she smells candy, as he looks into her eyes and gently rubs his hand across her back. "Damn", he thinks to himself. He just gives her a devilish smile as they continue down the hallway. As he grabs her hand in his, the First Lady glances back at the Vice President with a look in her eyes that tells him that she blames him for her husband's bad eating habits. He just shrugs his shoulders and continues to walk behind them. One of the two large agents in black suits standing on both sides of the door, opens the door for the First Lady as she steps into the Situation Room, followed by the President. Everyone in the room stands to their feet as the President walks to the table.

"Good Afternoon Mr. President", echoes through the room as the President responds with a "Good Afternoo". The Vice President makes a move to help the First Lady with her chair, but the President waves him off and pulls the chair out for his wife. Several of his Cabinet members aren't happy with having the First Lady attend these crucial meetings, which had been brought to the President's attention by his VP. But the President can't do anything about it, because his wife didn't like the amount of time it took to get him help when he had his health scare, while in one of these meetings. But that's only because the President didn't want to leave the meeting after he was revived. She decided to attend some of the meetings because she feels she may be able to keep him calm if he begins to get heated. The President takes his seat then ask everyone to quickly take their seats. Alright., I'm sure by the expressions on your faces that you've read the report that was handed to you while you were waiting. He looks around the room and looks at the expression of disbelief on most of their faces as they talked amongst themselves. The Vice President taps an empty drinking glass with his pen to indicate to the Cabinet to quiet down in preparation for the President to speak. First of all, I want to remind each of you of the sensitive nature of what we are about to hear at this meeting. This is one of those times in our history that will define our administration and our nation. Now I am going to make this very brief, because in roughly 23 minutes, we are scheduled to speak to the first person or people responsible for launching their privately built spacecraft and achieving orbit around our planet.

The room erupts in questions by mostly the Office of Science and Technology. Ladies and gentlemen, the Vice President yells as he stands to his feet. Now the President and I would like you all to remember that this meeting, regardless of its' importance will be governed no different than our previous meetings. You will not whisper, shout or speak out of turn, "he says with a stern and forceful voice".

As a matter a fact, we need you to divide yourselves into your perspective departments and each department will have only two questions. So all of you that are not around the table, reposition yourselves amongst your departmental constituents and decide which two questions you will be asking. The scene now looks like a game of musical chairs as the majority of his cabinet shuffle themselves around the room. The VP then shouts to them to hurry up and take their seats. The President yells out, "you have five minutes to get organized and your asses back in your chairs"! As they finally start to show some sort of organization, the President, Vice President, and the first lady are talking amongst themselves. It bothers the VP that the only person in the room without a clearance is the First Lady, so he decides to grow a pair and looks directly at her and in a low tone asked, " with all due respect Mrs. Crawford, but don't you think it would be prudent for you to excuse yourself from this meeting, seeing that you don't have the proper security clearance to be a part of this highly classified discussion. Both the President and the First Lady stare at him in intense disbelief, because they have discussed her attending these meetings weeks ago and they thought they had this horse shoved in the can. Her facial expression and her posture changed in such a way that he knew automatically that he shouldn't have asked the question. With a reciprocal low tone, her response is sharp and unrestrained. "With all do respect Ben, my husband has cleared me to attend this meeting and I would appreciate it if this was the last time you would ask me to leave a meeting I've decided to attend. She continues to stare at him with a stern look on her face, which the President can well identify with. The Vice President shifts his attention to the President for a bit of support and a bit is all he gets. Now isn't the time to visit this old conversation, he says to both of them as he looks down the elongated conference table, then looks at his watch. "Alright people, we have only ten more minutes remaining"!

After each of your departments have come to a consensus on the two questions, please write your questions on the form that my assistant passed out prior to you coming in here. The Vice President can see that maybe five out of the seven departments have their two questions, but the other two are still bickering over which two questions they will submit. He gives his last bit of instructions to the room. One more thing, he says as everyone turns and looks at him. Make sure that your questions only pertain to your groups' area of responsibility. We don't need the science department asking questions regarding national security or vice versa.

Mean while the President is giving some last minute instructions to his wife. "Listen honey", he says under his breath as both of them lean toward each other. Oh no, she responds. You only call me "honey" for one reason, and just like in our bedroom, I can guest you want me to do something I normally wouldn't do. He lovingly reaches over and grabs her hand. I simply need you to listen closely during this meeting and not to ask any questions unless you absolutely have too. The First Lady is somewhat surprised that he would make that kind of request. Bill, I can understand this coming from Ben, but how can you expect me to just sit here and not participate in this meeting. As a former attorney and congresswoman, I would think my credentials would speak for themselves. I want you beside me as a mother to our children, so hopefully you can give me some insight on Mrs. Thomas' state of mind and her two girls. I need that insight of yours to tell me how she feels about her husband. That's what makes you such a good attorney and mother, he says as he smiles at her. She knows that if she wasn't his wife, she wouldn't be able to attend this historic meeting, so she agrees to be an observer for the most part. He sweetens the pot by telling her she can ask one or two questions, if she needs them. He stares sincerely into her eyes. She smiles at him and puts her other hand on top of his. "Alright", I'll only do it for you, because I see how important it is to you, but I won't promise you that I won't ask a question if I feel it's necessary.

She looks over at one of the Joint Chiefs sitting midway down the table and makes eye contact with Admiral Tolentino. Excuse me dear, but I want to go over and say hello to the Admiral and express my condolences to her on her mother's passing before the meeting begins. He looks at his watch. You'd better hurry, because we have less than five minutes. She hurriedly stands up and walks over to the Admiral. They have become close friends in the past year and speak to each other when they get a chance.

Most of the people in the room are talking amongst themselves and others are still looking over the contents of their binders that was provided to them a couple of days ago. It has been three minutes of everyone moving about the room and the Chief of Staff gathering the questions from each group. The Vice President motions for the meeting to begin and for everyone to take their seats and to please quiet down. The President feels that everyone should have had enough time to get their questions together. Whispers and the noise of chairs moving fills the room as small groups of people hurry back to their seats.

The First Lady and the Admiral abruptly end their brief conversation, the Admiral nod's her head in agreement to a lunch after the meeting. The Vice-President stands next to the President's desk and begins to issue last minutes to their staff on how the meeting will be conducted and some additional information. But within thirty seconds into the instructions, General Tabor begins to ask a question, but the President quickly cuts him off. "Just a moment General"! I understand how extraordinary this is, but we don't have a lot of time and I don't need you interrupting the VP to bombard him with questions. The General looks aggravated that he couldn't ask his question, but all he could do was to scribble the question on a pad in front of him, which he's hopeful he'll be able to ask during the meeting. Everyone else around him sits back in their chairs and gives the Vice President their full attention. The President looks up at his VP and gives him the nod to continue. Now from our latest data, we know that the people that are currently in orbit are an African American family from Jacksonville, Florida. From that statement, the room became so quiet you could hear a pin drop. The father's name is BK Thomas, his wife is Lorraine Thomas a stay-at-home mother, who ten years ago worked for the Federal Government as an Analyst out of Virginia. They have two daughters, LaChel and Kim, ages sixteen and twelve. As of yet, we can find nothing unusual about the parents or their children that would explain how they accomplished the development, construction and operation of the first privately owned orbiting spacecraft.

Now we do know that only four months ago the family was reported missing by the wife's mother, Sue Rambert. She stated that she believed her son-in-law may have abducted her daughter and grand daughters. She also visited the police department and wrote a three page statement explaining the mental instability of her son-in-law. Needless to say, she doesn't have a high opinion of him as a son-in-law or a human being. "Her words". She demanded that the FBI investigate her daughter and grandchildren's disappearance after local law enforcement filed the case as a missing person. But Mrs. Rambert was very persistent and after a month of badgering the Detectives that investigated the family's disappearance, they formally requested that the FBI investigate their case and provide a conclusion

Three weeks later, the FBI made the recommendation that the case should be changed from a missing person to an abduction and possible homicide. The information that the Vice President is now sharing with the Cabinet isn't in their handout. The President feels that now is the time for all of his staff to be on the same page.

He confirmed that Mr. Thomas was placed at an engineering firm located in Florida in order to developed state of the art weapons systems. Because of his extraordinary knowledge of Quantum Mechanics and Particle Physics, they thought it would be best to place him in the position of Chief Engineer of the Tampa Division. Mr. Thomas was also in the Naval Reserves with the rank of Lieutenant, but he was medically discharged after his car accident. After a year of recovery and a short employment with NASA, he was recruited by Sargeant Engineering and the Federal Government. What was the scope of the projects he would be developing", Admiral Tolentino asked? The Vice President hesitated for a moment before answering. There were several projects, but their main focus was the development of an orbiting set of

353

Quantum Plasma Canons", he said with a slight tremble in his voice. Once again, the room erupts in whispers as the staff talks amongst themselves. One of the scientists sitting in the chairs along the wall raises his hand to get the Vice President's attention. Yes, the Vice President says as he points to him. Sir, I do recall that particular project and I do remember that we had to put it on the shelf, because the project was riddled with all kinds of mechanical problems. Yes, your version of the project was and still is collecting dust, but we decided to transfer the complete development of the project over to Sargeant Engineering over a year ago.

The head of the Science and Development Department looks extremely surprised and annoyed, because he knew nothing about the transfer. He states that because of Mr. Thomas' leadership, his department solved most of the mechanical and programming problems and was forecast to complete the project within two months. Unfortunately, without Mr. Thomas' knowledge to resolve the few remaining problems, the project is once again in limbo. Sargeant Engineering is now close to bankruptcy because of the equipment, and money he stole. And thanks to him, hundreds of his fellow coworkers are about to be in the unemployment line. Do we have any idea if he's planning on selling this technology to the highest bidder, "asked the Secretary of Defense", who is sitting to the President's right, midway down the table? Before the VP could answer, the assistant assigned to the Situation Room signals to the VP that they have only two minutes left.

No, I'm afraid not, but we are about to find out in roughly sixty seconds". The tone in the VP's voice becomes menacing as he decides to reiterate what everyone in the room already knows. Last but not least, I would like to reiterate that this meeting his of the highest classification and if anyone in this room decides to leak any portion of what's about to be discussed or to have an aspiration to write a "Tell All" book; you'll be reading it and signing autographs from a prison cell. He then glares around the room to ensure that everyone can see the sincerity in his eyes. Everyone in the room knows he's serious, because he has destroyed his fellow constituents' careers for lesser offenses.

After he's certain his point has been made and getting the nod from the President, he signals to the Secretary of the Cabinet to turn on the cameras and to switch on the "On the Air" signs. This meeting will not be aired to the public, of course, but will be recorded for later analysis and for archival. This meeting is about to start so let's get our game faces on, the President says as he sternly looks around the conference room. The Vice President sits down and quickly writes down a few questions he wants to ask, if time allows. The room becomes quiet as the time slowly ticks away.

Aboard their ship, BK and his family are sitting in the main conference room preparing for their first conference with their Government, or anyone else for that matter. He wanted to ensure that they are taken seriously, so they are dressed in a formal dark blue jumper with the ship's insignia embroidered on the upper left-hand pocket.

All four look like NASA astronauts, which is what he intended. He has no doubt that this meeting will not go well. Their Government has probably already discovered everything he has done prior to the launch of his spacecraft. They will most likely use this information as leverage to get him to come back to earth, so they can incorporate his technology into their military capabilities and shelf the technology that would jeopardize the Conglomerate's authority.

He looks around at his family and gives a last bit of instructions. All right family, we have to show unity, confidence and above all else, a calm appearance in our resolve. If they get any hints of cracks in our unity, they will make every attempt to exploit it, which will justify any discussion they will make.

But Dad, how can you be sure that they are looking to take our ship from us, Kim asked. He's happy to hear that she uses the pronoun "our", rather than "your". We're potentially the greatest threat to our Government's hold on power over its' fellow superpowers. We're orbiting nine miles above the earth's surface, unsupervised. Our Government has a procedure for how they would acquire your services, whether you wanted to or not. First, they would approach you and ask to assist you by fully funding your project and will provide you with a workplace at their facility.

If you didn't like the terms of the agreement or you just didn't want to be associated with them; they would then just confiscate your technology in the interest of National Security. What do you expect them to do with us, LaChel asked? Nothing, Lorraine response. If they know what's good for them, she adds in a firm tone. Her family is in jeopardy and she doesn't like the idea of her Government potentially threatening them. BK puts his hand on Lorraine's hand and says, "just wait a minute".

MOM interrupts. BK, the President and his cabinet are now ready for our conference. Wait MOM! Don't connect us until I tell you, please. Yes BK, she responds. Family, you guys have information in your heads that can compromise our mission.

You must remain in control of your emotions. Try not to project a threatening or confrontational attitude. But your mom is right. They can't hurt us with any of their words or weapons, nevertheless we can't give them an idea that we are a threat to them by our words or attitudes. This mission is to usher in a new era of world peace and space exploration. But you know perfectly well what will happen if this technology falls into the wrong hands. Lorraine asked him a question she's been wanting to ask. We could be the reason for the starting of World War III! Have you really thought this whole thing out? He looks into each of their eyes. I have given a lot of thought to the actions we're about to take, but I come back to the same conclusion. Everything happens for a reason, therefore maybe my accident and subsequent spike of intelligence is something that was supposed to happen. Throughout human history, people like myself who have invented a tool or a device that we think will advance our society, but someone usually finds a way to twist that idea into a tool to destroy their fellow human beings. Just like Einstein, Carver and Newton, I truly believe I was born to do this. This is one of those discoveries that can propel humanity into the next stage of evolution. MOM decides to interrupt. I'm sorry BK for interrupting your pep talk, but we are now three minutes behind our scheduled conference call time, and I do not think it is a good idea to keep the leader of an entire continent waiting.

Alright family. "It's go time", he says with excitement in his voice. Wait a minute, Lorraine says as she looks at him. I need us to take hands and say a prayer. He isn't a very religious man, but if it helps his wife get through this meeting, that's what they'll do. Lorraine grabs BK's hand then reaches out to LaChel who grabs hers. BK then grabs Kim's hand and all close their eyes in prayer. Lorraine thinks for a second, then is about to say a prayer when BK surprisingly interrupts her with one of his own.

"Dear Lord, I know you and I haven't had many conversations, but I would humbly and greatly appreciate your protection of my family and grant us all wisdom to recognize and follow your will. May this technology that I'm about to bestow onto the world enable all who call the earth their home to make another step or two toward their destiny and place in the Universe. Amen".

Lorraine gives him a smile and a loving kiss on his cheek. The prayer was alittle too science and spacy for her, but she appreciated his gesture of love. Alright MOM, patch us through. The monitor switches from a picture of a tranquil ocean scene with gulls flying in formation above the small waves in the Caribbean somewhere. In a matter of seconds, the scene as well as the mood changes with the President sitting at a large conference room table fills the screen. He can't help but feel a little nervous as he realizes he's about to piss-off the one or more of the leaders of the free world. He couldn't even imagine what's going through his wife and daughters' minds at this moment. At first, no one says anything, but BK hears someone to the right of the President, asking if they could hear him clearly.

Yes, yes ... good afternoon Mr. President, BK shouts with nervous excitement. Lorraine puts her hand nearest him under the table and touches him on the leg to signal him to calm down. He doesn't acknowledge her, but she knows he got the message. The Vice President is the first to talk to BK. Good afternoon Mr. Thomas, it's an extreme pleasure and an honor to finally get the opportunity to talk with you and your family. The President can tell that his staff is already pointing at the large monitor and talking amongst themselves.

BK is about to introduce his family, but the President interrupts him. I apologize for interrupting you Mr. Thomas, but my staff as well as myself find it difficult to believe that you're in orbit above the planet at this moment. Why is that Mr. President, he asked with a smile. Because you're suppose to be in zero gravity, but you and your family are firmly in your chairs and we can't see any straps securing you. Maybe is this some sort of joke or maybe my staff has been deceived.

No, Mr. President you are not being deceived. I've just developed the technology to create artificial gravity. The scientists in the meeting can't contain themselves and start to talk louder, using words like fraud, liar, and a few other not so flattering adjectives.

The Vice President stands up for a moment and peers around the audience, as the room once again goes quiet. He then sits back down and gestures the floor back to the President. As you can tell Mr. Thomas, we and I do mean we, find that very difficult to believe. Our top scientist have been working on that type of technology for decades with very little success. The scientists in the audience once again softly whisper to each other as they nod their heads in agreement with the President. But you expect us to believe that you have done what teams of scientist and millions of dollars still can't do. Mr. President, I will answer that question and probably the other dozen you're not going to believe in due time. The President holds up his hand to interrupt him again. Mr. Thomas, before we continue, I would like to introduce you to the members of my staff, who will be asking most to the questions.

The camera pans back and now BK and his family can see a large number of people in the conference room. To my right is the Vice President, Benjamin Bentley. To his right is the Secretary of States, Sherry Thomson, beside her is the Secretary of Defense, Jon Martinez, beside him is CIA Director Dave Redner, and to his left of the Vice President is the Joint Chiefs of Staff: General Epps, Admiral Tolentino, General Tabor and General Downer. And of course, to my immediate left is the First Lady, Mrs. Lynda Crawford.

The rest of my staff are made up of noted Scientist and Analyst that are very eager to ask you a battery of questions regarding your ship. BK smiles. Yes, Mr. President, I bet they are, but first let me introduce my crew. The President smiles a curious smile because he called his family is crew, but then gestures to him to proceed.

The camera mounted within the monitor pans back as BK begins to introduce his family/crew. To my right is my lovely wife Lorraine, who is the Physician and Tactical Officer. Next to her is my youngest daughter, Kim, who is my Planetary Scientist and Communication Specialist.

And last but not least is my oldest daughter, LaChel, who serves as the ship's Navigation Officer, Science Officer and Ship's Engineer. And as for me, I am the Captain of this spacecraft and hold all other duties assigned. The President's camera tightens in on him and roughly five of his staff. While BK was introducing his family to him, the Vice President received a message from NASA and SETI confirming the location and approximate size of the object in orbit. He then relays the information in the caption function scrolling across the bottom of the television for everyone in the conference room to see. Well

Mr. Thomas, we would like to commend you on achieving a goal that countless governments' scientist and privately-owned industries have exhausted trillions of dollars, marks, pounds and yin to accomplish, but failed. Well done Mr. Thomas, well done. As the President stands and claps his hands; the camera pans back as far as it could, then the entire room stands and joins the President, which echoes throughout the room. BK smiles a bit and looks at his family in disbelief. He never thought that his Government would be giving him a standing ovation after what he's done.

Thank you Mr. President, he responds. We are honored that our Government is happy with our accomplishments and sacrifices. The President stops clapping and sits back down, which signals everyone else to do the same. The camera zooms back in on the President as he begins to speak again. Mr. Thomas, because of your great scientific accomplishments; I propose that within a time frame that you can schedule the re-entry of your spacecraft back to earth; we will honor you and your family with the largest parade ever held in Washington, DC. BK pauses for a moment, then thanks the President for his kind words of praise and the offer of a celebration for their accomplishments. The President is all smiles right now as he thinks this may be easier than he thought.

We are flattered and would like to thank you for your invitation to honor our accomplishments, and we would love to be your guest in D.C. once we have accomplished our mission. The President is still smiling when the Vice President ask, "what mission are you referring to"? BK gladly explains. We are up here orbiting the planet for one reason and one reason only. To jump-start humanity's exploration into space by sharing our technology with the world.

The President, Vice President, First Lady and all his staff for that matter, are speechless. I'm sorry Mr. Thomas, the President replies. What do you mean; you're going to share your technology with the world? This is something that has to be done, Mr. President. Humanity needs a push in the right direction and that direction is up into space. It's time for all humans that want to explore the cosmos to venture out and seek new challenges. "That shouldn't be your sole decision to make", Mr. Thomas, General Tabor exclaims. You have no idea what destruction you will unleash if you allow every nutcase, extremist or communist government to acquire that technology. Yes, I do General, he replies. I know what I plan on doing could enable Governments or individuals to develop powerful weapons, but I believe the mass majority of the people that acquire this technology will utilize it to advance humanity.

The President decides to try to reason with him. Mr. Thomas, please don't get me wrong - we are very impressed with the work you and your family have achieved. What you've accomplished will be invaluable to our nation and its people. But we feel that we can best look out for your best interest by providing you with a more structured and secure program to further develop your technology. See Mr. Thomas, many of our enemies are dangerously close to firing their warheads in our direction in response to your craft orbiting above their heads.

I know you don't have a clear understanding of these international issues and superpower politics, but nevertheless, you and your family are very much in play. You're not just jeopardizing your family's safety, but you are putting the entire nation and potentially the world on a collision course with World War III with your potential reckless actions. He understands the President's situation and under different circumstances he may have agreed with him, but he has risk too much to be persuaded at this point. He gives the President his full attention, but he's thinking there's no damn way his Government will get their hands on all of his technology. They would treat his ship like Grand Mother's Thanksgiving turkey. They would carve it up into various bite size meals and bury the remains they don't want to use at some landfill that they call a warehouse.

He's tuning out most of the lies the President is saying. I give you my word Mr. Thomas, you will have the best in manpower, facilities, a substantial budget and the freedom to continue making your groundbreaking advancement in space exploration. You will have full authority over the entire facility and manpower. We would just assist you with the security, development, and distribution procedures. BK adjust himself in his chair and attempts to interrupt the President, but the President persist in making his sales pitch. As your President, I feel an obligation to safeguard every American citizen and Mr. Thomas that still includes you and your family. He finally finds an empty spot in the President's speech to interrupt him.

Please, Mr. President, thank you and your cabinet for your gracious offer, but we don't have any immediate need for your protection or assistance. We are very safe orbiting hundreds of miles above our planet. And if you haven't realized it yet, we are more technologically advanced than NASA or any Government for that matter. You and the other governments of earth have nothing to offer us and frankly have no methods of forcing us to alter our plans. Even from LaChel's position at the table, she can see the level of tension in the Situation Room begins to show more and more.

The decorum of the meeting quickly breaks down. A voice sounds out on the other side of the Situation Room. Excuse me Mr. Thomas, and Mr. President; I am Dr. James Lutz, Director of the Science and Research Department. I'm sorry to speak out of turn, but I would like to ask a couple of questions, if I may, as the Doctor looks toward the President. He wasn't finished with his sales pitch, but gestures for the Doctor to proceed. First of all Mr. Thomas, on behalf of the scientific community; I would sincerely like to congratulate you and your family with this earth shattering achievement. We're still in a state of shock that you've single-handedly launched a spacecraft and achieved a stable orbit around the planet. Thank you Doctor, he politely responds. Mr. Thomas, my colleagues and I are wondering what type of propulsion technology powers your spacecraft. Well Dr. Lutz, I guess I can tell you since everyone will know in less than four hours. The ship's name is the "Pangea" and is powered by a Plasma Drive, which allows us to travel from here to Mars in roughly four to five days at full velocity. The conference room erupts in whispers and muffled comments of disbelief. The President is also unnerved, but he tries to remain calm for the sake of his Cabinet

Please, ladies and gentlemen, quiet down please. The President then gestures for the Doctor to continue. I'm sorry Mr. Thomas, but we find it hard to believe that you've solved all the problems of interstellar travel and the utilization of plasma to propel a spacecraft. BK understood this would be one of many technologically advancements that the scientist in this administration would find hard to believe.

Well Doctor, you have to admit that we're up here and you are down there, so you should come to the conclusion that I am telling you the truth". Well yes, you're correct, Mr. Thomas. You have certainly amazed all of us here. But how have you accomplished these scientific hurtles, when some of the greatest minds in the fields of Astrophysics, Mechanical Propulsion and Quantum Physics had such minimal success. BK his very happy to respond to his question. Well Dr. Lutz, I didn't have the complicated maze of bureaucracy looking over my shoulder and restricting what I can and cannot do. Current and past scientist are not only hamstringed by your lack of knowledge, but you're also restrained by the corporations that pulls the strings of the House and Executive branch of our Government and the Governments of our allies and adversaries.

As BK smiles at the Doctor, Lorraine looks over at him, because he could have left that last part out. But Doctor, in all honesty, I did have some help of some great minds, which helped me resolve some of the more complex problems. "Who would that be", Dr Lutz asked? Her name is MOM, he replies. He could hear muffled questions being asked throughout the President's conference room.

Are you trying to tell me that your mother help you develop some or all of your technology? No, MOM is the name of the artificial intelligence that I created, which assisted me in the development of my ship and most of my advancements. So, you've also successfully created some type of robot, the Vice President says in a shocking tone.

MOM was my second creation or maybe I should say my four, because I guess my daughters would be my first and second greatest creations, he says as he smiles at both of them. With help from my lovely wife of course as he looks at her and smiles. The Vice President interrupts him. Let's get this straight Mr. Thomas. You mean to tell us that in addition to building and launching an inter-planetary spacecraft; you've built a robot assistant that can solve complex problems? Yes, but don't call her a robot – she's far more sophisticated and complex than what you would call a robot. The President leans back in his chair and stares at the camera, which is normal for someone hearing something this shocking. Don't worry Mr. President. MOM's programming schematics and scientific documents will not be part of the download. Everyone else will get a watered-down version of MOM, because a spacecraft like this needs a sophisticated system to monitor and manage the ship's higher functions. Thank you, the President replies with a large amount of sarcasm. The Secretary of Defense breaks into the conversation. Mr. Thomas, can you at least consider exclusively sharing the blueprints to your robot. "Artificial Intelligence", not robot General, BK replies.

And no Sir! Mr. Thomas do you have any idea how many lives could be saved if the United States could build a small contingency of electronic soldiers that we can deploy in our hotspots around the world. We would no longer have to put our brave men and women in harm's way. We could remotely patrol the streets of hostile countries anywhere in the world and deploy them at a moment's notice, because they would be just stored in a military warehouse until needed.

He replies by asking the General how long would it take for the United States to misuse its' electronic soldiers or for someone to acquire the plans and sell them to the highest bidder. Now the world is consumed by superpowers continuously building soulless mechanical avatars and waging senseless wars. But just maybe, the same superpowers will build spacecrafts like mine to venture off the planet in order to find new challenges and resources. Another one of the President's Cabinet asks a question. Excuse me, Mr. Thomas.

I'm Dr. April Stokes of the National Oceanic and Atmospheric Administration and I understand what you're attempting to accomplish by sharing your technology with the world, but I agree with the President in regards to your methods of dissemination of your technology. You don't have to be a fortune teller to see the turmoil and possible destruction you will unleash once your technology is delivered to everyone's doorstep. I equate it to giving a chimpanzee a hammer, some wood and a couple box of nails and asking it to build a bookshelf. He's just going to wack everything with that hammer and destroy the room he's in and whomever is in the room with him. I can only see countries trying to use your gift to further their own agenda. You don't seem to realize that this project of yours is putting your nation and your fellow Americans at great risk. If your ship has any problems, which forces you to land – there is no guarantee that your ship and its technology would remain under your control. The President leans forward and raises his hand to interrupt her. That's the exact nightmare that continuously runs through my mind. Mr. Thomas, I just can't take that chance. That's why I am unfortunately going to have to order you and your family to land your spacecraft at Roswell Air Force Base in Arizona, immediately. The facilities there can accommodate the spacecraft and provide security for you and your family. But I give you my word as your President that you and your family will be rewarded and honored for your service and achievements to our nation. You'll have a team of noted scientists there to assist you with the development of any future ideas you may have. Even though he expected his government would take this course of action, his heart still sinks a little.

He didn't respond to the President for a couple of seconds. He signals to MOM to remotely pan the screen back, so he could see every person in the conference room as he makes his next statement, which he expects the President to snatch back the carrot and begin to use the stick. He looked squarely into the camera. Yes Mr. President. I do agree we are still and always will be American citizens, but we are foremost and always residence of this planet. We must do what is best for our fellow human beings. "Not just America"! I will not follow those orders and we will continue with our plans to share most of our technology with all Governments and citizens of the earth.

The Vice President face tightens, as he decides to give BK a little reality check. Just wait one minute, Mr. Thomas, he says in a stern tone. You developed that technology on American soil, using the money and equipment that you stole from Sargeant Engineering, who we had under contract. You've also committed bank fraud, two counts of reckless endangerment of a child and assault on a law enforcement officer, just to name a few of your felonies you committed before leaving the planet. And now you're turning your back on your country and potentially giving our enemies the ability to inflict tremendous damage on your fellow American Citizens. I think you are unaware of what some of these countries will do with that technology and how much you will be putting us into extreme peril. But if you comply with our order to land your craft and cooperate with the transfer of your technology to our custody, we may be able to reduce or totally dismiss those charges. The Joint Chief of the Army gets everyone's attention with his bellowing voice as he decided not to ask a question but to make a statement. With all due respect of your achievements Mr. Thomas and recognize that you are the most intelligent person on the planet, but I feel that you are somewhat naive and not sophisticated enough to grasp the complexity and the politics of dealing with various foreign adversaries. I refuse to hoist you up on our shoulders and tell you how great you are. The Vice President then begins to try to convince BK to change his mind by giving examples of great men and women that have develop technology solely for their country security. He rambled on for a minute or two before the Secretary of Defense, Edward Kerning chimes in to further emphasize the irreputable global damage his careless dumping of his technology would do to the global economy.

He continues by telling him that his Government has maintained the balance of power by always developing or acquiring the most advance technology to stay ahead of our adversaries. BK couldn't contain himself anymore, but before he would get a word out, LaChel interrupts the Secretary of Defense. Please don't talk down to us like we're idiots or one of your staff members, she says loudly. Those were different times back then. The government used so much propaganda on our grandparents and even our parents that anyone would see everyone other than an American as an enemy. He gives his oldest a look as to say, "tone it down and remember who you are talking too". LaChel has seen that look on her parent's face before when she has spoken out of turn or unknowingly raised her voice to an adult. So, she softens the tone of her voice.

Mr. President, I'm sorry for the hostile tone, but the United States' track record isn't that stellar either. The United States has done things that would make us look like the people or Governments that we label as evil. The Secretary of Defense decides to defend America's past and current actions. "See that's the problem"! People like you want to be safe and secure but don't want to pay the price for being able to sleep soundly in your beds.

She interrupts the General. I'm sorry General! I didn't catch your name? The General looks annoyed that he has to answer to a child that's younger than his grand daughter. He would have liked to have this debate with her father or mother, but he reluctantly response, "General Hunter", young lady! I take it your high school didn't take great importance in knowing the structure of your federal Government. LaChel gives the General a half smile. Only the important Government officials General Hunter, LaChel replies.

Now the General's facial expression and body language look more like he's trying to control his temper. It's obvious to everyone on both sides of the camera, that he is trying hard not to talk to LaChel like a new recruit. LaChel decides to smooth things over with an apology. General Hunter, I'm sorry. I shouldn't have said that. My parents have taught me to be respectful to my elders. LaChel once again smiles at the General and then at her mom and dad. The General looks at her and gives her a slight nod of his head, which indicates that he heard an accepts her apology. The President clears his throat, which catches the General's attention. He looks over at him and gives him a sign to maintain his composure. He acknowledges the President's gesture and begins to talk in a calmer and less demanding tone. I don't think you understand the point I'm trying to make, Ms. Thomas.

Oh, you can call me LaChel, General. The General pauses for only a couple of seconds, then continues. "Ms. Thomas", I was just trying to make a point about the United States history regarding the dissemination of information that the public should be aware of. This administration has always strived to be as honest and forth coming with the American public as our national security will allow. But I'm the first to admit that sometimes we are not at liberty to disclose all we know about some sensitive situations and materials. Lorraine decides to interject herself into the conversation. Mr. President, do we fall in that last category? The camera pans over to the President. What do you mean, Mrs. Thomas? Are we just some classified incident that the American people will never know of?

Yes, Mrs. Thomas. I'm afraid you are in that category, he replies in a matter of fact tone. But with time, the information and technology we learn from you will filter down through our society and everyone will benefit. But now the technology that your husband has in his possession poses one of the greatest threats that this free nation has encountered. Mr. President, my family and I don't agree with your assessment of this technology and the decision of our Government to secure it and lock it away. Mr. Thomas, I can see that we are at an impasse, but I would like to continue our conversation with you tomorrow around this time. I think it will be to both our benefits to have several of my economic professionals to speak with you regarding the impact of randomly disseminating your technology on the global economy.

Mr. President, with all due respect. I'm not changing my mind and tomorrow will be too late for any conversation on this subject. I plan to download this technology to the internet in roughly six hours. We're not asking for your permission. I just wanted you to understand what our plans are, and I knew it would be a long shot, but I was hoping you would be open to our decision. The President has a look of frustration in his eyes as he says, "I'm sorry Mr. Thomas, but we can't allow that to happen". BK scanned his family's faces, then looks back at the President. Well Mr. President, that sounds like a threat. Just how do you plan on stopping us? The President looks directly into the camera. "By any means at our disposal, Mr. Thomas"! You've put your family in extreme danger and I for one will have no problem with my decision. If you care about your life and unfortunately the lives of your family, please reconsider our generous offer, which will be a compromise that will benefit everyone. I'm not going to agree to exclusively sharing any defensive technology with you or any other Government, BK tells him. We are in agreement that the Governments of the world aren't ready for everything I have to offer. We are downloading passive technology. I'm only going to download technology that will enable private citizens and governments to explore space along side of us. There is nothing threatening or about this technology.

We will not allow the United States' sovereignty and security to be compromised, adds the Secretary of Defense with a bellowing tone. BK and Lorraine could tell by the President's demeanor that he was not moved by BK's statements. The President sits back in his chair. The Secretary of Defense clears his throat to get the President's attention. He President looks over at him and gives him a nod, indicating its OK to respond.

Mr. Thomas, we deal with government officials both friend and foe every day, but we don't have the luxury of putting our national security in their hands by just trusting them to do the right thing. If we did what you proposed, our enemies as well as a few of our allies would band together, which would shift the axis of power and would put our democracy in jeopardy. I'm afraid I for one would never endorse or recommend the President accept your proposal.

The Vice President interrupts the Secretary. Excuse me, Mr. Secretary, but I may have a solution to this problem that will satisfy both parties. Give us the opportunity to evaluate your technology at one of our facilities and I'm sure we can come to a compromise on the amount and method of dissemination of your data. Lorraine then chimes in. Mr. Vice President, I'm certain you're familiar with the term "Eminent Domain". The Vice President knows what she's alluding to but pauses for a moment to try to adequately answer her question. She proceeds to give him the definition. This term refers to the ability of the Federal or Local Government to seize and or acquire a private citizen's property without the citizen's agreement. The Government only has to pay the property own or inventor the local market rate for the property and in some cases, technology. He smiles at her as he tries to convince her why the term doesn't pertain to their situation, which was a lie. If he was a wooden boy, his nose would be halfway across the room. Lorraine allows him to ramble on for two or three minutes before finally interjecting her reasons for not believing his promises or their willingness to compromise. She asked him a second question. Have you heard of Seneca Village in New York? Lorraine can see that her question stumps him and reminds her of a question on the game show, "Who Wants to be a Millionaire", but no one in the room could call a friend. Cellphones were not allowed in the Situation

Room, so they couldn't google the question. Lorraine doesn't wait for an answer and continues on with her example. In around 1957, Seneca Village was a home for 250 people, which consisted of two thirds African Americans and one third Irish and Europeans. During that period of our history, New York was going through an economic boom and decided it needed a premier park in order to establish itself as a place to visit in the United States. Consequently, the Government of New York decided to use Eminent Domain to steal the property of those African Americans and Europeans and rename Seneca Village to what it's known today as "Central Park".

She ends her tour through revisionist history by telling them that this is only one of many examples of the Government's both current and past decisions based upon its' economic and financial concerns. She has no doubt that once they were on the ground, they will have no need or reason to compromise. She tells them, once you get our spacecraft and us into one of your military secure facilities, you'll have our technology in one hand and us in the other. "That's game over"! BK gives her the calm down signal again, but she waves him off with just one of her looks.

She continues. I think you fail to grasp the reality of the moment. My family and I are in orbit over 220 miles above your heads, speaking with you in an earth like environment, which you have acknowledged that you or anyone else on the planet for that matter hasn't achieved yet. My husband has accomplished one of the most significant and monumental technological achievements in man's brief time on our planet. But you fail to recognize or understand the gift he plans to give to you and the world. With your help and influence, we could assist humanity in the acclimation of their new reality, but all you can see is some technology you can exploit and how it can keep you in power and advance your selfish agendas. The President isn't use to hearing this type of dissension from his administration, let alone from one of his citizens that standing on her 220 mile soapbox. He doesn't want to lose his temper, so he takes a few moments in order to regain his composure. The First Lady can feel the tension in the air, so she decides to take this opportunity to intervene and take a different tactic. "Excuse me, Mrs. Thomas", she says politely! I'm a good judge of character, and you seem to be doting parents that are genuinely concerned with your girls' emotional and mental stability as well as their safety. May I ask your daughters how they feel about living conditions aboard the spacecraft and how do they feel about what you and your husband are planning to do? Lorraine looks over at BK and he gives her a look of approval. Lorraine looks at Kim and asked her if she wants to tell the First Lady how she feels about being aboard the ship? Kim feels nervous as she tries to get her thoughts together. It's just like when she's in her History class and her teacher wants her to standup and read her homework aloud.

"At least I don't have to standup", she thinks to herself. Well, if I'm being honest. I was pretty upset with my Dad for bringing us up here in the middle of nowhere and taking us away from everyone we know and love. But now that I understand the importance of what he's trying to do; I'm very proud of my Dad, she says as she looks over at him and gives him a big loving smile. The President then asked her a question. Now Kimberley, you mean to tell me.

Kim stops him in mid-sentence. From the teachers at her school and now the President that mispronounced her name, she hates being called "Kimberley". Excuse me Mr. President, but my name is Kim, not Kimberley. The President was surprised that she would interrupt him, but he disguises his irritation by giving her a smile before apologizing to her. I'm sorry "Kim", but one of my daughters' is named Kimberley, so I thought your name was short for Kimberley, he explains. She gives the President a little history regarding the origin of her name. I was named Kim after my mom's best friend, she says to reiterate her point of not being called Kimberley again.

"Alright Kim", the President says as he gets back to making his point. I just think you and your sister would be allot safer and happier if you were down here with your friends and grandmothers rather than floating in space, locked in an untested spaceship. BK knew that they would try to exploit their girls by preying on their emotional separation from their friends and family.

Lorraine and BK have explained to their girls the importance of not having any contact with friends and family right now. Of course, they were not happy with being so isolated, but with their parents help, they learned to tolerate their situation. BK assured them that they will be returning to earth once the information has been downloaded and the focus has been taken off them. He glances over at Lorraine, who looks as if she's having a difficult time containing herself too, so he discreetly rubs her knee under the table to put her at ease. She acknowledges it and reluctantly forces her mind and body to relax. The President continues his conversation with Kim. I read in one of my notes that you were a starter for your local soccer team and that it was a good chance that you and your team would have won the championship this year.

That struck a nerve with Kim, because she loved the game of soccer and loved playing with her teammates. Her parents did all they could to prepare her for this type of tactic, but it still makes her feel bad that she's not going to be able to help her team compete for the championship.

I would be lying if I told you that I wouldn't want to be with my friends running around the field right now, but what we're doing is bigger than a soccer game or even a plastic trophy, she says with conviction. My Dad just wants to make things better for everyone. I'm still getting use to this technical stuff, but what I do understand is pretty awesome. The President knew that BK and his wife have coached their daughters on what to say, so he's not surprised that he won't be able to use them to get their parents to land the spacecraft.

I'm very sorry Mr. Thomas, but it's my job to look at the big picture and I can foresee that what you propose to do will have horrific ramifications for our economy and consequently mankind. And as your President and the Commander and Chief, I have an obligation to not only consider your family's wellbeing, but the security of your fellow Americans. I can see that you have no intention of negotiating a reasonable compromise for returning your ship to earth, so again I'm giving you a direct order to land your spacecraft at MacDill Air Force Base. Then you and your family will disembark, and the United States Government will take the craft into protective custody. But you have the word of your President that you and your family will be treated with the utmost care and whatever legal problems you had prior to leaving earth will be resolved with no prison time or financial restitution.

BK doesn't say anything for a moment, which gives the President the impression that he's thinking about his offer and may make a counteroffer. So, you expect me to turn my ship and all its' technology over to you, so you can have your engineers and scientist take it apart? The President acknowledges that they shouldn't have to completely disassembled his ship, but they will have to remove components and parts in order to better understand how his technology works. The Presidents adds that he's confident, once we are all on the same team; we'll be able to build a more advance spacecraft. BK has no doubt of the President's sincerity, but he doesn't think that him or his cabinet has a firm grip on reality. I'm truly sorry that I can't follow that order, Mr. President. But, I think for good or bad, I truly believe this is the best method of ensuring man's survival and advancement. On that note, the Vice President slumps in his chair and the President's facial expression hardens while BK continues to explain why he's continuing his plans. We have been hostages to oil companies and Governments for too long. Sometimes change happens gradually and without anyone noticing, but some changes must come with an earth-shattering explosion of uncertainty and disbelief. And the explosion of data that I plan to disseminate will profoundly transform our world and move all humanity forward in our evolutionary journey.

"No Mr. Thomas", the Secretary of Defense shouts loudly! The camera pans over and focuses on the Secretary. Let's just be clear about what will happen once you disseminate your information throughout the world. The global economy will collapse and possibly hundreds of thousands of people around the world will die, because of you and your family's recklessness. The President looks over at him and signals with a look for him to restrain himself, but he's intentionally not looking in the President's direction. He has a point to make and he'll be damned if anyone's going to stop him or have him sugar coated.

Mr. Thomas, history will firmly place you in the category with all the other ignore genocidal killers, which you will so rightly deserve, because what you are so intent on doing will kill thousands. The Secretary then sits back in his chair and folds his arms but would not look over at the President. The President then takes over. I need you to understand that if you don't agree with our terms and continue with your reckless plans; I will have no choice but to revoke your citizenship. It was bad enough hearing her husband being called a potential mass murderer, but now the President is threatening to revoke their Citizenship or in layman's terms, kick us out of the United States

"Excuse me", Mr. President, Lorraine says trying to subdue her anger. Are you telling me, if we don't give you our ship and its technology, we will not be allowed to return to the United States, "our home", at any time? The President leans into the camera. Look! I have to do what I feel will benefit the nation. Your spacecraft and its technology are the most advance equipment developed, but if you don't follow the orders of your Government that's only looking out for your best interest and those of your fellow Americans. I don't have any choice but to consider you, your wife and daughters enemies of the state and will be dealt with as such. I'm very sorry Mr. and Mrs. Thomas, but you have a choice to make and I hope you make the right one. Lorraine looks angerly at the President, her eyes look like they could shoot fire. BK can see Lorraine's disappointment and anger in her eyes. He once again gestures to her to calm down. But she yells, "No, don't tell me to calm down"! Did you just hear what he said to us. Our government has the nerve to threaten us with being labeled enemies of the state if we don't do what they demand. Excuse me Mr. President, but you must be out of your damn mind, as she shouts at the monitor. BK isn't surprised and can understand her anger. Lorraine commences to graphically tell the President just what she thinks of his threats. I don't think you have the right to order us to do anything. We're not part of the military anymore. "My husband completed his 20 years"! We are now private citizens of the United States and if I remember you work for us, "Mr. President", she emphasized! The President is trying to get a word in, but She is relentless in her verbal attack. I want you to tell us what law we are breaking, she says with an abundance of attitude. She looks over at BK as he cuts his eyes at her. She understands exactly what he is thinking. She glances over at her girls who are stunned by everything that's going on. Of course, they've heard their mother go-off on their dad like that, but to loose it on the President of the United States was something they didn't expect. The President doesn't look too happy now, after getting lectured by who he considers to be a militant house wife, which he would never say out loud. Regardless of the anger and the confrontational attitude she just displayed, he is very proud of his wife, because she may now understand why he feels the way he does about their Government. The President then signals to the Admiral to read from the folder in front of her. BK sees the President pointing to someone and the camera panning over to the Secretary of the Navy. Admiral Tolentino to be exact.

She opens the folder and prepares to read from the first document. She clears her throat to get everyones attention. Mr. Thomas, I need you and your family to listen to what I'm about to read to you very closely. She begins to read in a very forceful and commanding voice. In accordance with Department of Defense, article 32, section 64, Byron K. Thomas has been re-inducted into the United States Navy at the rank of Commander, assigned to NAS Jacksonville, Florida, and must report on station no later than fourteen days after reading or being made aware of these orders. Failure to follow these orders will result in the immediate charges of Dereliction of Duty and Failure to follow orders of a Superior Officer, which will result in incarceration at a military prison for no less than five years. BK just smiles and shakes his head, because he didn't expect them to force him back into the Navy. "With all due respect, Admiral, but what the hell are you talking about"? "Commander"! I was only a Lieutenantwhen I retired from the Navy. "That's one hell of a jump, he says in amazement"? The camera pans back over to the President. Well, Mr. Thomas, in light of your vast knowledge and skills, we feel you should be promoted to a status that would reflect your astonishing accomplishments.

Dad, you're not going to let them do this too you? "Are you"! No, he says to her! Sorry Admiral. Why should I downgrade myself to Commander when I can stay up here and be a Captain, he says with a smile?

Thanks, but no thanks. I'm sorry you feel that way Mr. Thomas, but you have no choice. This is giving you a way out and allowing you to gain a bit a status in the process. I'm aware of your 15 years of service and that you receive a monthly pension for that service. But know the rules and regulations regarding receiving a pension from the military.

The Vice President shouts over the rest of the loud speaker. You're still part of the Government and part of the military, Commander Thomas! "You must comply with the lawful orders of your superior Officer and your Commander and Cheif"! Oh, I see now, Lorraine angrily and sarcastically responds. This is your plan "B". You're relying on my husband to blindly follow your orders by high jacking him back into the service.

I'm sorry Mr. President, but I've served my time and given all I could to the Navy. I won't let you take another day of my life from me and my family. I reject your attempt to entice me back into the military with a field promotion. In less than four hours this technology will be downloaded to every system that can process the information. Well Mr. Thomas, I'm afraid we are at an impasse. Both the President and BK just stare at each other intensely. Yes Mr. President, I guess that's the one thing we both can agree on. Mr. Stephen Hawking once said, *"Life on Earth is at the ever-increasing risk of being wiped out by a disaster, such as sudden global warming, nuclear war, or a genetically engineered pandemic. It's essential for humanity to spread out into space for the survival of the species"*. I really took what Dr. Hawkins wrote to heart and finally realized what I had to do. I came to the epiphany that my technology is too essential to humanity for one person or a single Government to control. This data has to be shared and developed by everyone capable of doing so. Both men were hoping the other would suggest some type of compromise that each could live with, but both feel they are right but the President doesn't truly realize that

BK has the advantage. The President finally breaks the silence. Mr. Thomas, I just want you to know that this is not an easy decision for me to make. I want you to know that I will be praying for you and your family. And I truly hope you will think about your fellow Americans and the hell you'll be putting them through. BK chooses his words very carefully. Mr. President, thank you for your time and your future prayers, but you would be better off praying for the entire world, because once this data has been disseminated – the world may be a little less separated. I have no doubt that what I give the world will be misused, but I think that's true of all innovative technology.

But for the most part, I think we all should be privileged to be a witness to the next technological advancements of mankind. I believe the humanity is about to make a huge evolutionary jump to the space age thanks to what my family and I are about to give them. The Secretary of Defense interrupts him by saying that's all well and good, but I hope you are prepared to have the blood of people around the world on your hands, because hundreds upon thousands of lives are about to be loss if you download this data to any nut or idiot on the street. "Now wait one damn minute", Lorraine shouts.

Lets take a trip down history's memory lane! Alfred Nobel invented dynamite, Richard Gatling invented the Gatling Gun, The Manhattan Project, which the United States used to annihilate two Japanese cities and kill 260,000 human beings. These great American patriots were mass murderers by your definition, or do they have special considerations. BK is impressed by his wife's knowledge of American history, but he knows her historical recollection has something to do with her time in stasis and his method of embedding information into her brain. The President addresses Lorraine's examples of Americans that have for good or bad, change the world. I understand what you're trying to allude to but those were different times and different situations. Please, lets just stay in the present day and time.

We must be responsible and consequently slowly feed this technology to your fellow citizens then to the world. I'm simply trying to make you understand that a steak is best enjoyed if you take small bites and not stuffing the entire steak and potatoes down your throat.

BK and Lorraine smile at the President's analogy of this serious situation. That's a good one, Mr. President, he responds. But using that same analogy; I'm just presenting an appetizing meal and leaving it to my fellow humans if it's something they want to try. It will be up to the government or the individual to decide if this technology is something they want to use. It's my opinion that humanity as a whole learns it's lessons by using the three "T's": Tragedy, Triumph and Time. Since I am taking "Time" out of the equation; I'm afraid we only have Tragedy and Triumph as factors. It will take a collective effort to ensure we learn through Triumph. But I'm not delusional, so I know there will be a certain amount of tragedy. That's my point Mr. Thomas. You can't foresee and we can't control what the people, let alone the various Governments will do with your reckless generosity. The United States and her allies have enemies that will use this technology to destroy us and themselves without a second thought. BK gives the President his full attention. Normally I wouldn't disclose this type of intel to someone without a clearance, but I have some documents regarding the activities of Iran, which I think will be a great benefit for you in making your decision to disseminate your technology to them. MOM interrupts them both by reminding BK of his schedule and that he has five minutes left. Alright MOM! The First Lady has a curious look on her face when she asked, is your mother up there with you too. BK and his family starts to laugh. No, Mrs. Crawford, BK response while him and his family continues to laugh. That's the ship reminding me of my schedule and that it's time to conclude the meeting. Phil Porter, who is the head of the Office of Science and Technology, yells from the back of the room. "You mean your ship can communicate with you". Of course, she can, but that is something you can read about in my download. I'm very sorry Mr. President but my crew and I have some work that has to be completed. Mr. Thomas, before you go. I hope I've made my position crystal clear and you understand why I can't let you put this country and our way of life in that kind of danger. Well Mr. President, since I can't make you understand why this has to happen, I feel you're going to do what you have to.

Thank you for this meeting Mr. President and I think you and your cabinet for listening to us. The President looks at him and his family in disbelief that it has come to this. "Why can't they see the logic in what we are saying", he thinks to himself. The President is coming to the realization that he will have to use deadly force to protect the rest of his citizens, and his position as Commander and Chief

"Mr. President", before we end this meeting, LaChel will read a couple of pages from the cover letter of the package we will be emailing. I'm hoping this will give you something to think about while you're making your final decision. LaChel clears her throat then adjust the paper in her hands then begins to read. *To the people and governments of earth. You may or may not know that currently there is a spacecraft orbiting our planet. You may think that this is some kind of joke or prank, but this is a very real situation. My name is LaChel Thomas and my father, mother and little sister are aboard the ship preparing to share with all of you the ability to build a craft similar to this one. My father designed and built this craft for the betterment of humanity and to share with all of our fellow human being.*

Of course, our Government and most likely your Government will not like you receiving and utilizing the information that will be disseminated to all operational computers throughout the world. As an attachment to this letter, I am including a package with various documents and technical illustrations explaining how you too can build a spacecraft similar to this one. Humanity is intentionally being held back and isn't advancing technologically fast enough and it's my hope that you as private citizens or companies will attempt to join us here in the great unknown. We know that like most history making achievements, some people will utilize the technology for the betterment of their finances and to even cast the demise of their fellow human beings. But we hope the majority of you that receive this technology will accept and use it with the spirit in which it was given. As she finishes the paper and places it down in front of her, she looks at her family for approval, which she gets with a returning smile from them. Of course, the President and his cabinet aren't moved by her brief speech and are certain that they will be the only ones that will hear it. BK knows that there's no reason to prolong this meeting and thanks the President and his Cabinet for listening to him and his family then tells the President, goodbye as he signals for MOM to stop the transmission.

Back in the Situation Room the transmission ends with a look of frustration on the President's face. The room then erupts in various conversations on everyones opinion on what has to be done and how they should do it. The Vice President thought the President was going to bring everyone to order so he could strategize what they should do next, but he just got up from his chair and headed toward the door. As he walks toward the door, he hears his VP asking him where he's going?

The President turns and tells him to close out the damn meeting. That means the Vice President will have to bring everyone to order, threaten them to secrecy and ensure everyone will be ready for the President's imminent orders. The First Lady is busy talking to the Secretary of Defense and doesn't notice her husband leaving the room. The President makes it to his office and flops in his chair like he had just finished working a ten hour shift delivering pizzas, which he wishes he was doing right now. Just when he thought he would have time to reflect on the meeting, a special line that hardly ever rings starts to fill the room with its' ominous ring tone. He doesn't answer right away, but just looks at the phone as if it was a venomous snake he didn't want to touch. He knows who it is and doesn't want to talk to the person on the other line, but he has no choice. He finally answers the phone with a shaky, "Hello Mr. Ortiz", which he doesn't think that's his real name, but that's what the voice on the other line asked him to call him when he first spoke to him three years ago. He's a member of the group of twelve called The Conglomerate and has been assigned to manage him and the United States Government. He has never met the enigmatic man, but he operates deeply in the shadows and his power has been proven to be vast and limitless.

For a second there, I thought you weren't going to answer the phone, the voice says with his deep voice and thick spanish accent. I was just busy talking over our plans to resolve the Thomas situation with a few members of my Cabinet, he says while loosening his tie and looking up at the ceiling. How can you do that when you're alone, Mr. President? The President sits up in his chair in surprise that he knows that there's no one in his office. He looks around the room and thinks that their must be cameras spying on him. "Who in the hell gave you permission to install surveillance equipment in my office", he yells as he looks around the room wildly. "You did Mr. President", the voice confidently replies.

I guess you didn't read the fine print when you accepted our millions of dollars these past three years. And I really need you to watch your volume and tone Mr. President, he says in a forbidding tone. He wonders how long he has been watched as he thinks back to some of the things he's done in the Oval Office, which he wouldn't want anyone to see. "Especially his wife". I understand how disconcerting it is to know that we have been recording everything that has gone on in this office, but this is one of the ways we know we will get our money's worth from our representatives.

"Representative" is a term that the member of The Conglomerate calls the leaders of the various economic powers. I need you to focus on those troublemakers orbiting above our heads and don't worry about how much amazingly disgusting dirt we have on you. The President is trying to keep his composure but he knows if they have half the recordings of what has been going on in this office, he might as well change his title from President of the United States to Puppet of the United States. And not the puppet that is controlled by strings but the one that has the puppet master's hand elbow deep up the puppet's ass. Just then, The Vice President, First Lady and Secretary of Defense burst into the Oval Office looking for an explanation to why he just left the meeting without addressing his resolution to the spacecraft problem with his Cabinet.

All three begin to ask him questions at the same time. He's about to put the phone down to his chest and answer them, but Mr. Ortiz instructs him to tell them to get the hell out of his office. He gestures to them to stop talking then tells them as sternly as he can to leave, because he's on an important call. The VP and Secretary reluctantly follows his instructions and leaves the office, but the First Lady doesn't think his blunt instructions refers to her, so she walks over to the couch, takes a seat and crosses her legs.

"Your wife has some great legs, but she has to leave too", Ortiz demands. The President glares at her as if she could read his mind, but she didn't or wouldn't take the hint. So he tells her she has to leave too and he'll see her later. She looks at him for a moment in disbelief that he's actually asking her to leave, then she stands and walks out of the Oval Office, with a bit of noticeable attitude.

Once the door closes, the President states that this is his office and he wants all the surveillance devices removed from his office, but he's cut off and told to just listen. This isn't your damn office, Ortiz blatantly responds. You are only leasing it for another eight months if you don't get me that ship. The President looks stunned by that bit of honesty. I'm going to do you a huge favor then I need you to do one for me, Ortiz says in a calm tone. "What favor are you doing for me", the President replies curiously. We were listening to the meeting and have unanimously agreed that Mr. Thomas and his family are hell bent on accomplishing their plan and nothing you say or do will deter them from this reckless endeavor. Mr. Ortiz, I think I can persuade him to come to his senses, but I think it will take the incarceration of his mother and his friends. I may have to call in a few favors in order to arrest them without cause, but I've done worst.

Give me an hour to have them in custody and I'm certain he will have a change of heart, he says with confidence. "No", Mr. Ortiz says sharply. There isn't anymore time for this back and forth crap, he yells. The President tries to convince him to give him some more time, but he yells at him to stop talking and listen, which the President immediately complies. I want you to understand the magnitude of this situation and what's at stake. There is no doubt that the ship has to be brought down, but the question is who's going to get the credit for doing it and who will get to the crash site first. If the Russians bring down the ship and claims the wreckage, the representative that manages the Russians will move up in status and I will most likely tumble down the ranks, because Mr. Thomas created this mess in the United States and on your watch, you and I are responsible, he says with a ominous tone. Consequently, my position and stature in the group will diminish substantially.

And needless to say, your status with me will also diminish. And if that happens, there is no doubt in my mind that I will be looking for another candidate for next years' Presidential Election. My VP is loyal to me and wouldn't accept the nomination or you backing him, the President fires back. "Oh no". I'm afraid you miss understood my threat. I truly believe in throwing the baby out with the bath water.

And I'm talking about the baby's tub, the baby's toys, and everything else that belongs to that damn baby. I have a number of senators that are chomping at the bit to lease this office and sit in your plush chair. That statement makes it clear to the President what's going to happen if he doesn't get that ship and its' technology. I'm doing you a favor by removing the burden of you making the decision to bring down that ship and possibly kill the Thomas Family. And what you're going to do for me is to get me that damn ship and its' technology once it hits the ground Mr. President, he says in a threatening tone.

The President doesn't want to take the chance of killing that family, but he doesn't have a choice now. All he can say is "I understand". "I hope you do", Mr. Ortiz says as he just hangs up the phone. The President slowly hangs up the phone and sits there in silence for about five minutes, while trying to convince himself that killing a family of four is justified and how he had no choice.

The morals that survived his climb to the Presidency continues to attempt to convince him not to kill the people he took a oath to protect, but his greed and fear of loosing his power and possibly his life beats his morality to a bloody pulp. He picks up his desk phone and asked his secretary to request the Secretary of Defense, the head of the CIA and the Attorney General to come into his office immediately. "Right away, Mr. President", she responds.

Back aboard the ship, BK tells Lorraine that he's going to need her help on the Bridge and to discuss their next move. He then turns to his daughters and instructs them to complete their lessons, work on your maintenance assignments, and of course clean your rooms, he says with a smile. "If you call those rooms", LaChel replies in a cynical tone. They stand to their feet and prepare to leave the conference room and go about completing their task, but LaChel is still a little concerned about the President's attitude and vailed threats.

She walks over and grabs her dad's hand. Dad, what do you think they're going to do about you releasing all of your data to everyone? He looks over at Lorraine, do you want to answer that question babe. The girls look over at their mother, and wait for her response.

Girls, don't worry about what the President was saying. He just wants us to comply with his demands and put all our technology under their control. Their weapons can't harm us or even reach this ship if we move to a higher orbit, but your dad can explain that better than I can. He tells them that it won't be necessary for the ship to move to a higher orbit. I have a point that needs to be proven to our government and I can't make that point at a higher orbit.

He doesn't want to say anything more about what he feels he as to do so he decides to change the subject. He pulls both of them into a comforting bearhug and tells them their mother is right and that they have nothing to worry about. The three stand there in a loving embrace, while Lorraine stands a few feet away smiling. It melts her heart to see how much her girls still love their father. He looks over at Lorraine and reaches out to her to join them. She slowly walks over to them and joins the love fest by squeezing the group tightly. This is the first time in months that he has felt the embrace of his family and he savors the moment for as long as he can. After basking in his family's love for a couple of minutes, he jokingly tells them to get off him and all four release their grips with smiles and laughter. If you girls have enough time after you've completed the things you have to do and you're still feeling apprehensive about our safety, just ask MOM to explain our defensive capabilities. I will be happy too, MOM responds. Does everyone know and understand what their assignments are today? "Yes", the girls respond in unison. Alright, lets get to it then. Everyone exits the conference room and heads to their assigned task. The girls walk down the passageway together talking about parts of the meeting.

"LaChel". I was a little scared before the conference, but now I'm even more scared knowing that they may try to shoot us down. He only implied that they may try to bring us down, but I just think he was trying to intimidate us. Kim gives LaChel a confusing look. What's the difference? Just don't worry about it, LaChel says with confidence! They are like ants trying to kill an anteater, she adds. Kim grabs her sister's hand and tells her she's still can't help but be a little scared. "Come on", LaChel says as she pulls her sister down the hall. "Let's go clean our rooms together and have Benny tell you some jokes", LaChel says as they both walk down the passageway hand in hand.

Meanwhile, BK and Lorraine are on the Bridge and Lorraine is sitting in his captain's chair and asking him why he needs all the gadgets connected to the chair. He tries to explain to her how he can control every aspect of the ship from that chair and how every starship captain has a chair similar to the one she's sitting in. She looks over the chair from left to right and up and down, but she still doesn't look impressed. "OK babe". Get out of my chair, he tells her. "Alright Captain Jerk", she says while getting out of the chair. MOM announces to the both of them that the United states has activated their satellite missile silo orbiting the planet and are preparing a firing sequence. Lorraine runs to her tactical station, which displays the location of the satellite in relation to the ship.

"The satellite is orbiting roughly two hundred and fourty miles from our current position", she says as she looks back at BK. He doesn't look too concern as he sits in his chair and activates the main view screen. BK asked MOM for the capability of the satellite and it's payload? The satellite has a four missile capacity with and each missile is equipped with a 1.2 ton warhead. Lorraine asked if they have a fix on our position? MOM tells her yes and that the targeting solution has already been uploaded into one of the missiles. "One of the missiles", Lorraine says curiously? I would think they would launch at least two missiles our way, she adds. "They want to bring us down without destroying the ship entirely", he says calmly. She walks down to him and stands besides him as he sits in his precious chair. We need to reposition the ship farther way from the satellite. BK hadn't told her his plans not to try to avoid the missile. He wants to prove to the Government and the Conglomerate that his technology is far superior to whatever weapons they have and they are powerless to stop him. Lorraine can read him like a Doctor Seuss book, and he doesn't have to tell her anything, because she can see what he's planning in his eyes and she's pissed.

The President and his Cabinet are now in Tactical Operations counting down the launch of the missile. "Have you made an accurate calculation of where the ship is most likely to come down", the President asked. The Joint Chief of the Air Force is standing around a table with about five Air Force Officers as they input numbers and angles into their tablets. "Well General", the President shouts impatiently from across the room. "Give me one mor minute, Mr. President", the General replies loudly while still going over the results of the targeting system's algorithum. The success of this operation is crucial to him remaining Commander and Chief and he isn't in the mood to wait for an answer to a question he felt should already have been calculated. "General", he yells!. Five seconds later, the General turns to him and states that the ship will be crashing within fifty square miles of the Kuril Islands. That's the area of operations for the 7th Fleet, Admiral Tolentino immediately responds.

But these calculations will only be viable if we launch the missile in the next ten minutes. After that timeframe, the ship may be crashing somewhere in North Korea's waters and they won't be too accommodating if we attempt to recover the ship and its' reckage. "General", you have my explicit permission to launch your missile and bring down that ship, the President says and then gives his authorization code.

"VP", the President yells to the Vice President to give his confirmation and code. "I concur", the Vice President replies, then gives his confirmation code. The Tactical Office gets the nod from the General, then he tells everyone in the room that the missile will be launch in two minutes and thirty-two seconds. He follows that statement with one word, "Mark". The Admiral of the 7th Fleet then sents out a classified message for two of his battle groups to randevu at the coordinates of the potential crash site and to take any and every possile action to recover and secure the spacecraft.

Lorraine gets close to her husband and tells him not to allow the missile to impact the ship. He hates that she can read him so well, so he admits that it is part of his plans to allow the missile to impact the ship to prove that the ship can take an explosion of that magnitude. "Babe, trust me"! "I know what I'm doing", he says while giving her a confident smile. "No", she yells as she grabs the sleeve of his jumper. Just because you are the smartest person on the planet, doesn't mean you can predict what's going to happen. MOM and I have calculated all aspects of the missiles impacting the ship and are one hundred percent certain that the shields and ship's outer membrane will absorb the entire missiles energy output, he tells her confidently.

Lorraine is astonished by his willingness to put his family in jeopardy just to prove a point to a building full of damn idiots. She decides to ask him about a variable that he or MOM hadn't added to their equation. "In your precise calculations, did you calculate the mouse factor this time", she says while angerly looking into his eyes. "The mouse factor", he repeats. "What does a mouse have to do with our calculations", he asked with a confusing look on his face. Just like you didn't see the mouse that almost cause us to abandon ship and possiblely kill your family; you can't forsee those types of variables that may unexpectively popup in your calculations.

While he is chewing on that tough piece of logic jerky, MOM announces that the missile will be launching within one minute and will impact the ship in three minutes and fifty-five seconds. Lorraine immediately orders MOM to instruct her daughters to report to the Bridge. "Yes Lorraine", MOM responds. LaChel and Kim are in the front room of their quarters being intertained by Benny. He is doing an impression of their dad, which is cracking them up, when his hand starts to malfunction.

"Damn it", Benny says without thinking. Kim laughs everytime Benny slips up and curses, because non of the other units aboard the ship has this ability. LaChel just looks at him with a shocked look on her face. "I'm sorry, I'm sorry, he says trying to stop his hand from flexing. Benny is complaining to the girls about how long his hand has been malfunctioning when MOM comes across the intercom system and tells Kim and LaChel to report to the Bridge right away. LaChel hadn't gotten close to completing cleaning her room and didn't want to start again. She tells her sister to come on as Kim asked MOM why they are going to the Bridge. Your mother and father are there and they want to speak with you. Benny yells, "Can I come".

MOM tells him that he knows the answer to that question. As the girls leave, Benny stops at the automatic door, which closes in his plastic face. He just hovers there with his malfunctioning hand as the fingers twitch uncontrollably. "Oh well", he says as he turns and heads toward the sofa. I guess I'll just go watch "The Real Housewives of Atlanta", he says as he grabs the remotes. At the Bridge, Lorraine tells BK that the mouse is just a metaphor for some small factor which can vastly affect the best laid plans.

He can understand what she's illuding to, but has confidence in his ship's ability and was about to rebut her mouse metaphor, when she grabs him by his collar while his still sitting his his captain. and tells him that this is not a damn debate. Of course, your vast intelligence will always convince you that you are right with all of your decisions, but you owe it to me to do what I want you to do this time, she says as she tries her best to shake him like a rag doll. The missile is fifty-two seconds out, MOM announces. He was about to open his mouth to say something, but Lorraine cuts him off by telling MOM to reposition the ship fifty miles away from it's present position then once the missile arrives at it's previous position, remotely detonate the missile.

And infiltrate Tactical Operation's computers and ensure that they are unaware of our new position, BK adds. Lorraine relaxes and lets go of his collar. Spock would have never did that to Kirk, he says as he straightens his jumper. "Who", Lorraine responds? Nevermind, he says with disappointment in his voice. She knew that he was referring to that Star Trek crap, but she just wanted to mess with him.

Just then Kim and LaChel walk into the Bridge and asked what's going on. MOM confirms that they are now fifty miles away from their previous position. She then starts to count down from twenty. BK tells the girls to take their stations, so the girls think that this is just another training exercise. Lorraine quickly walks to her station to track the approach of the missile, as MOM gets to eleven. This isn't what he wanted to happen, but he thinks his wife is right about him wanting to always prove that he's right and that could put them all at risk, because of his arigance. And she's also right, because at this moment he feels like Captain James T. Kirk. He turns on the main screen so they could witness the explosion. "Look at the screen", he tells his family. MOM continues the final countdown. Four, three, two, one. For a second, all they can see is the darkness and the dimness of the distance stars, but then there's a bright flash of white light, which illuminates about thirty-five miles of space for about fifteen seconds then slowly diminishes. The girls react in surprise and ask various questions about what just happened.Lorraine tells them that the Government just tried to force them down by damaging their ship with a missile.

But thanks to your mother, they failed and we're still up here, he says as he smiles at his wife. She smiles back at him, but she knows she has some work to do regarding his lone decision making behavior. MOM announces that the explosion's shockwave has been absorbed by the ship's shielding. "I knew it", BK yells as he smiles at Lorraine and the girls. But you were right babe, he tells his wife. She knows she has some work to do, but this is a good start, she thinks to herself. BK tells Kim to transmit the prerecorded message that she has been trained to do. She immediately starts pressing and swiping the screen on her console, which transmits the family's special message.

Back on the planet and at the White House's Tactical Operation Room, the President and Vice President think thay have been successful in bringing down the ship and are on pins and needles as they wait for the Air Force personnel to tell them what area the ship was heading on its' descent. The room is a buzz of activity as uniformed personnel are trying to make since of the data that is streaming into their systems and to locate the assumed descending ship's reckage.

The General is shifting from one station to another and asking questions and looking for himself at the small objects streaming down through the atmosphere. The President stands to his feet and crosses his arms in frustration while waiting for the General or someone to give him a status report.

The Secretary of Defense is tired of waiting and decides to head out of the gallery and down the few stairs to the Operation's floor to get some answers for the President and for himself. An officer at a station asked the General to come over and look at his screen and confirm what MOM is allowing him to see now.

The General and the Commander, who's in charge of the floor huddles around the junior officer and his screen. As they talk amongst themselves, the Secretary of Defense joints them as they debate about what they're looking at. "This is ridiculous", the President says aloud while still waiting for someone to tell him something. The group sitting and standing at the station are clear and agree on what has happened, but no one wants to tell the President what they see on the screen."General", the President yells!

He doesn't turn around for a few seconds, but the Secretary of Defense stares at the General intensely as if to say that, "he's calling you not me". The General turns around and slowly walks over where the President is still standing on the elevated platform. He looks up at the President as the President looks down at him. "Is the ship coming down in Seventh Fleet's area of operation", he asked?

"No Mr. President", the General answers reluctantly. "Where", the President angrily replies. The General clears his throat then tells him that the reckage that their tracking is the remains of the missile. We can only assume that the ship is still in orbit and possibly sustained little to no damage. They both stare at each other for what seems like an hour. The Vice President puts his hand over his face and the rest of his Cabinet that sitting beside and behind them are in stunned silence. The Presidents folded arms drop to his side as he walks back to his chair and flops down. But the bad news for them continues to rain down like a Florida hurricane.

All of the computers and tablets in the room start receiving a download of various documents. It's all the information about BK's ship and most of his technology. Even all the cellphones in the room, including the President's secure line, start buzzing, as a result of the compressed data packet BK is downloading to everyones cellphones. The President pulls his buzzing cellphone out of his jacket pocket and reads the email message. *"To all my fellow humans on earth that are reading this message. The information that has been downloaded to your phone and computer is a gift from me and I hope that you will use this technology to improve your life and the lives of your fellow humans".*

The Vice President and the Secretary of Defense are trying to talk to him, but he just looks at his phone for a moment then still sitting down, throws his phone across the room and into a workstation. Everyone in the room is silent as they stare at the now brooding President. He missed his chance and doesn't know what going to happen to him once he leaves the room.

Back aboard the ship, BK is now hugging and kissing his wife and daughters, because this is almost the completion of his plan. Now for the last phase. And that's getting his family safely back to earth without going to jail for the rest of his, and his family's life.

But for now, he's to happy to think about that right now. He gives his wife a big kiss on her lips then says "lets go have a nice family dinner and watch a movie". Lorraine tells hims that they first have to talk to his and her mother, so they know that we're alive.Kim and LaChel agrees with their mother. It's been too long for him not talking with his mother too and he agrees that it's time that their mothers know that they're alive.

We'll make the calls in the Media Room and you can call your mother first, because she's going to need a lot of convincing and she's going to do a ton of cursing, he says as he looks at Lorraine. I can guarantee that Grandma Betty will want to punch her son in the face too, once you tell her how you froze me and her grand kids like fish sticks.

BK thinks about that for a while then asked one of his girls if they want to tell his mother what he's done. His daughters gives him a solid no, which he expected. Lets get the hell out of here, Lorraine says with some excitement in her voice. BK grabs Lorraines hand and leads his family out the door and down the hallway, laughing and joking all the way to the Media Room.

To be continued

"Even though he has downloaded his technology to every computer on earth, The Conglomerate still wants BK and his ship.   He has cost them billions of dollars in revenue and the only restitution they will accept is his ship and his servitude.   Can BK get his family and spacecraft back on earth without the Government and most importantly The Conglomerate hunting them down.   In the next series, we will see."

Sequel Title
Smartest Ant on the Planet
The Colonization of the Moon

Made in the USA
Columbia, SC
11 February 2021